Born at Dawn

Born at Dawn

Nigeria Lockley

URBAN CHRISTIAN

www.urbanchristianonline.com

Urban Books, LLC
97 N18th Street
Wyandanch, NY 11798

ISBN 13: 978-1-60162-675-2
ISBN 10: 1-60162-675-4

First Trade Paperback Printing October 2014
Printed in the United States of America

10 9 8 7 6 5 4 3 2 1

Distributed by Kensington Corp.
Submit Wholesale Orders to:
Kensington Publishing Corp.
C/O Penguin Group (USA) Inc.
Attention: Order Processing
405 Murray Hill Parkway
East Rutherford, NJ 07073-2316
Phone: 1-800-526-0275
Fax: 1-800-227-9604

Born at Dawn

by

Nigeria Lockley

This book is dedicated to my eldest sister, Nicole Murphy.

During the summer of 1985 you gave me one of the
greatest gifts I ever received—you taught me to read and
now I give that gift back to you.

Can a woman forget her sucking child, that she should not have compassion on the son of her womb? Yea, they may forget, yet will I not forget thee.

—Isaiah 49:15 (KJV)

Acknowledgments

Thank you, Jesus, for all that you have done for me. Thank you for strengthening me through this process. Thank you, for blessing the work of my hands as you have promised. Thank you, Lord, for showing me that my God is very much alive.

To my husband, William Lockley, I am sure this was not what you signed up for, but thank you for remaining faithful through it all.

Aiyana and Arianna Lockley, thank you for sitting down quietly and watching TV while I was writing, thank you for tearing up the house while I was writing, thank you for asking me questions about the book while I was writing, and most of all thank you for being wonderful daughters while I was writing. Soon enough we will reap a great harvest.

The Lord blessed me with two mothers, one to bring me into this world and one to raise me. Thank you, Azziza Muhhamed, for being the vessel and thank you, Deborah Murphy, for being my caretaker. Mom, thank you for honoring my gift. Thank you for always giving me time to write, for reading my writing, and for attending all of my readings. I pray that you receive all that you have given me back one hundred fold.

Pastor Everton Dunkley, of King of King and Lord of Lords Church of God, thank you for being my spiritual Father. Thank you for instructing me in wisdom and righteousness. Thank you for showing me how to stretch

Acknowledgments

out on God. To my church family, thank you for sharing your prayers and your testimonies; they have blessed my soul.

Born at Dawn would not be possible without my sisters-in-Christ who saw this book in nearly every version that existed before it was fit to print. Thank you, Myriam Skye Holly, for your words of encouragement and inspiration. Sarah M. Adams, thank you for praying over me, with me, and for me.

Cassandra Allard Souter, thank you for participating in my informal readers group. I hope you are prepared to read the next book.

Tiffany L. Warren, thank you for creating the Faith and Fiction retreat. I am truly grateful for the many blessings that attending this retreat afforded me. It was there that I pitched this novel. Thank you, Pat Simmons, for making sure that I was pitch perfect—it worked. It was at the Faith and Fiction retreat that I met my great sister-friend-accountability partner, author Berta Reddick Coleman who encouraged and pushed me through this process. Michelle Lindo-Rice, thank you for sharing your testimony and knowledge.

Michelle Stimpson, thank you for sharing your faith through your pen from *Boaz Brown* to the conversations and messages we have exchanged. I have been blessed by you.

To my coworkers, Abena Sidibe, thank you for being a friend; Redell Armstrong, thank you for listening to my ranting and raving as I went through this process; Shirley Clarke, thank you for encouraging me with The Word; and, Edward Feuerstein, thank you for always rooting for me. At every job there are always people who go above and beyond and transcend their job descriptions and become more than colleagues. Shnique Clark, thank you for every nail biting moment you spent with me worrying about getting this manuscript together. Alyson Monghan Levy, thank you for always speaking a kind word into my life. To my students who have stayed on top of me and made sure I met my deadlines, thank you.

Finally, to my readers, thank you for taking time to pick up this book. I pray that you are not only entertained, but that you are blessed in the name of the Most High God, Jesus Christ.

Chapter 1

Marvin Barclay flicked on the light switch in the foyer and tossed his keys on the table next to the door. He crept into the living room, reached over the arm of the sofa, and planted a slippery wet kiss on his wife, Cynthia Barclay's, pouty lips. The smell of cigarettes and vodka leaped out of his pores.

Cynthia rose from the seat she'd occupied most of the night. "Where have you been, Marvin?" Cynthia inquired with her arms folded across her chest and the curve of her hip jutting out as far as it could.

"Are you for real? I came home looking for some loving, and this is what I have to deal with," he said, licking his lips and rubbing his work-worn hands along Cynthia's sides.

Cynthia contorted to get out of her husband's tight grip, backed up a few steps, and peered into Marvin's bloodshot, hollow brown eyes. "Where have you been?" she asked again.

"Don't start with me tonight," Marvin said, tossing his jacket onto the couch.

"Marvin, I'm not trying to start anything with you. I'd just like to know where you've been," Cynthia responded emphatically.

Marvin turned his back on Cynthia and walked up the hallway toward the bedroom.

"Marvin," Cynthia called to him marching behind him, "don't you dare walk away from me or—"

"Or else what?" he asked, stopping midstride, casting a side-eye stare full of malice in Cynthia's direction.

"Answer me. Where have you been?" Cynthia cried as Marvin turned the knob on the bedroom door.

In one quick step, Marvin was standing over Cynthia in the middle of the hallway. His warm breath scratched against her skin. "You don't want to know where I've been." His voice cracked. "Don't start this nonsense tonight. Where my boys at?" He began calling out his son's names. "Keith! James!"

"They're not here."

"Where are they, Cynthia?" he asked. His voice was marked with a slight hint of distress and his bulging eyes revealed his concern.

"They're at Sean's house waiting for you to pick them up." The kids often had play dates at their friend Sean Dillinger's house after their karate class on Saturdays. "Sean's mother called me more than two hours ago." She stated jumping back to the subject matter at hand. "Where have you been, Marvin?"

Marvin wrapped his thick, hard-knuckled hands around Cynthia's neck in response to her question. "Woman, you've been sitting here waiting to fight with me instead of picking up my sons?"

Marvin's grip tightened around Cynthia's neck. She clawed at his hand with her delicate fingers, trying to pry them from her neck as he lifted her from the ground. She flailed her legs in the air, sending one lancing kick to his kneecap. The kick pulled Marvin out of his blind rage. He looked at Cynthia dangling from the palm of his hand and released her. She hit the floor with a thud and shrank against the wall in the hallway lined with family photos that portrayed them the way she wished they were: happy, united, and at peace.

"Go and get my boys." Marvin tossed seven dollars at her.

"This is only enough for one fare." She shook her head in disbelief. "Maybe you forgot we live in New York City," she murmured gathering the sweaty, crumpled bills that had fallen around her.

Stooping down with his lips curled into a ferocious scowl he asked, "What did you say?"

"Nothing." Cynthia bowed her head waiting for Marvin to at least be an arm's distance from her face. That would give her a second or two to dart out of the way if he was going to punch her in the face.

"What do you want me to do, carry you to 118th and Lenox Avenue from here?" Marvin hiked up his pants leg, returned to an upright position, and kicked her in the knee. "Figure it out." He then walked away, leaving his wife in a positioned he'd left her in on more than one occasion.

"Thanks, Barbara, for letting Keith and James come over," Cynthia said as soon as Barbara Dillinger opened the front door of her brownstone. "Marvin got tied up at work." Lying, Cynthia fidgeted nervously on the stoop while waiting for the boys to come out.

"Looks like he's not the only one who got tied up," Barbara said, her hazel eyes filled with horror. She pointed at the welts Marvin's hands had left around Cynthia's neck. "Why don't you come in and relax for a moment?" Barbara opened the door wide enough for Cynthia to slide through. "The boys are upstairs playing, karate chopping and body slamming each other. A few more minutes of play isn't going to hurt them."

Barbara took Cynthia's black leather jacket from her and escorted her from the steps of her brownstone into the living room.

"I'm sorry it took me so long to get over here; I walked," Cynthia said, soaking up the place. In the two years that the boys had taken karate with Sean, Barbara's son, the two women had never actually been inside of each other's homes. Pickups and drop-offs were usually relegated to a switch at the doorstep of the parent supervising the play date or a meeting at the subway station.

"Please have a seat." Barbara swept her arm around the room inviting Cynthia to take a seat.

Cynthia looked to her left and then her right, trying to decide whether she wanted to take a seat on the mustard quilted leather sofa or the spoon-shaped zebra-print chair that faced the picture window.

"Would you like a cup of coffee or tea?" Barbara offered.

"Barbara, there's really no need in going through all of that trouble," Cynthia said settling herself into the spoon-shaped chair.

"And there's no need for you to go through all of that trouble either," Barbara chirped pointing at Cynthia's neck.

"Barbara, I'd rather not discuss this." Cynthia craned her neck toward the spiral staircase and called for her sons. "Keith, James," she shouted into the air.

"But I want to discuss it. Come here." Barbara grabbed Cynthia's hand and dragged her over to the full-length mirror that rested against an exposed brick wall near the window. "Look at yourself." Barbara gathered Cynthia's burgundy shoulder-length hair back as if she was about to put it into a ponytail. "This isn't right, Cynthia," she said, tracing the welts on Cynthia's neck with her French-manicured fingernails.

"Marvin is just going through something right now. He's trying to open his own business; he has me and the boys. It's a lot for him to handle." Cynthia fingered the welts herself wishing she'd tied a scarf around her neck.

"I don't think he's dealing with more than you are. You don't have to go home if you don't want to. You and the boys can stay here," Barbara offered, releasing Cynthia's hair.

Cynthia massaged her face with her hands. "We can't. I mean, I can't."

"You can't stay there either," Barbara interjected. "I know we don't know each other well, so this might seem strange or feel a wee bit uncomfortable, but if you won't stay here, at least let me take you to a shelter," Barbara begged Cynthia earnestly.

"And this might seem strange to you because we don't know each other well, but I took a vow, for better or worse. Now there's a reason those vows say for better or for worse; some days are going to be better and some days are going to worse. It just so happens that today was one of the worst." Recalling the days when Marvin was sweeter, gentler, romantic even, Cynthia massaged the welts around her throat. "Marvin isn't all bad, and I'm not all good, so it would be wrong of me to turn my back on my husband. I'm going to fight for this marriage until we get back to better days when we held hands and slow danced to Marvin's old records." Cynthia's high cheekbones rose as she smiled, lost in the memories of the days when the phrase "I love you" did not come after a bloody lip or bruised eye. "He wasn't always like this."

Cynthia touched the princess-cut diamond of her engagement ring, which rested over a simple gold band. She could still hear Marvin say in his rich baritone as he presented her the ring while they were seated by the waterfall in Harlem's historic Morningside Park, "A simple ring for the woman I simply want to spend my life with."

Cynthia held on to that memory as Barbara presented her with reality of her situation.

"So how long do you plan on suffering through this? What about you? What about Cynthia? What do you want for your life? Forget your marriage. I mean you. What do you want?" Barbara cocked her head to the side and stared at Cynthia's reflection in the mirror. Her hazel eyes felt like acid searing right through her skin. It seemed like she could see Cynthia's thoughts.

"Do you think all I have is all I want? Anyone who knows me will tell you I love to cook. That's the one moment of peace I get throughout the day. I wouldn't mind doing it professionally, but if I have no one to share my success with, what good would that do me? You know, when I first came to sign up at the dojo, Sensei Kelly told me it was full for the semester and there was a waitlist for the next semester, but I came at least twice a week to check if anyone had dropped out until one day Sensei just said, 'Mrs. Barclay, I have room for your boys.' If I didn't give up on a karate class, how can I give up on a marriage?"

"What good would being in a graveyard do you or your sons? What does your pastor have to say about this?" Barbara retorted without hesitation.

"My pastor?"

Barbara spun Cynthia around so that they were face to face. "You haven't told your pastor about what's going on?" Barbara said, wagging her finger. "That's a big no-no. You can't try to fight this battle on your own when you've got Satan right up in your house trying to kill you."

"Barbara, I don't have a pastor. I don't even go to church," Cynthia mumbled, her cheeks aglow from embarrassment.

"Huh?" Barbara inhaled and clutched her chest as if she was about to have a heart attack.

"No, I don't go to church. We can't all be the picture of perfection that you are," Cynthia sneered.

Barbara grabbed Cynthia by both wrists and pulled her to the nook in front of the picture window. Both women took a seat in the nook.

"'Except the Lord build the house they labour in vain that build it.' I am not perfect but I rely on the one who is to keep everything afloat for me. How is your marriage supposed to stand without the Lord's divine protection? Why don't you spend the night with the boys and come join me tomorrow at Cornerstone Baptist Church?"

"Thank you, Barbara, but no, thank you," Cynthia said, rising from her seat in the nook. "Marvin is expecting me back this evening. I could never stay out overnight, especially with you. He already thinks you're a bad influence with all your makeup and fancy clothes."

"There's a church on every other block in Harlem. Just promise me you'll find one to attend tomorrow." Barbara clutched Cynthia's hands and pleaded with her eyes.

"I'm not going to promise you anything, but I will think about it. Now could you please send my sons downstairs while I hail a cab?"

Cynthia let herself out. She took a deep breath of the evening cool, crisp autumn air that signaled the arrival of October in New York. With each breath Cynthia tried to purge her system of the words she'd heard.

A few minutes later, the boys bolted through the door and did their best imitation of a dog pile on Cynthia's back, breaking her train of thought.

"What took you so long, Ma? I thought you forgot about us," James said, wrapping his arms tightly around her waist. For a nine-year-old he had a strong grip thanks to all those karate lessons.

"Did you have a good time?"

"Yeah," James said smiling up at his mother.

"No," Keith said, stomping his foot. Cynthia already knew what was coming next: a complaint. Since turning twelve last month Keith wanted nothing to do with James. "This little punk was in the way all the time. Can I leave him at home next time?"

"Don't call your brother a punk. We'll see about that next time," Cynthia said, holding the cab door open for her two little men.

By the time Cynthia got the boys in the bed, her body felt like it had been run over by a street sweeper. She climbed into the king-size bed she shared with Marvin and rubbed her body against his to conjure up some warmth between the two of them. Marvin rolled over to face her and began to kiss her neck. He wrapped his hands around her slender waist and drew her into him.

"You know I love you, don't you?" he asked Cynthia, brushing her hair out of her face.

"I don't know. Do you really love me?" she whispered to him.

"Now why would you go and say a thing like that, baby? You're my number one." Marvin kissed her all over her face, stopping at her lips.

"Marvin, you don't treat me like you love me." She sighed.

Marvin narrowed his eyes. "Where are you coming from with all this, and where are you going with it? Who you been out there listening to?" Marvin drew the navy blue sheet back and sat up. "You been letting that bourgeois girl fill your head up with nonsense?" he said, mushing Cynthia in the head. "What did she tell you, to leave me? That you don't deserve this? Where is she at now, Cynthia? I'll tell you where; she's at home alone with no man and you're going to listen her?"

"It wasn't like that, Marv," Cynthia said, sitting up.

"You're dumber than I thought. You're actually gonna take advice from a lonely chick who just wants someone to join her. Ever heard the saying misery loves company? Did she tell you how it feels to sleep all alone at night?"

Cynthia shook her head.

"Well, you're going to find out tonight." Marvin twisted to the side slightly, drew his knee back and kicked Cynthia out of the bed. She bumped her head on the bedside table as she tumbled out. "Let's see if you're still talking that women's rights mess tomorrow morning," he said, throwing her pillow at her.

Cynthia collected her pillow and a light blanket from the trunk at the foot of their bed. She tiptoed down the hall and collapsed onto the couch, hoping her sorrow would get sucked up like a vacuum does loose change between the folds of the cushions. With her hands folded behind her head she stared up at the ceiling and asked herself over and over until she fell asleep, *is this marriage really all in vain?*

The next morning she woke up with a stiff neck and an even greater question looming in her mind: *what will I do if it is?*

Chapter 2

Cynthia took long strides across Amsterdam Avenue, dragging the boys across the street. Barbara's words had made a dent in her heart. Maybe all Cynthia needed was a dose of Jesus to relieve all the tension between her and Marvin. She peered up at the overcast sky and hoped the rain didn't begin falling before she reached the doors of Mount Carmel Community Church. They stopped abruptly at the entrance of Mount Carmel.

Her eyes fixed on the porthole window in the center of the polished dark mahogany doors of Mount Carmel. It was either Mount Carmel or Convent Avenue Baptist Church where her mother fellowshipped. Cynthia knew she didn't have the Baptist look down pat. Nor was she in the mood for her mother to parade her around the church. She simply needed to get in touch with heaven. That urgency led her Mount Carmel. Her nonexistent relationship with God and her husband's history with Pastor David weighed her down.

She took a deep breath. *You're too close not to go in.*

She bent over and straightened James's tie and wiped the corners of Keith's mouth with her thumb, dampened by the spit of her tongue.

"Listen, boys, when we go in here, I want you to sit down, sit still, and be quiet. It's different; just give it a chance, okay?"

The boys looked up at her and stared into her eyes, which were glowing and begging them to cooperate.

"Yes, Mom," they said in unison.

"But why are we here?" Keith asked.

"Because Mama needs to spend some time with Jesus, and so do you," Cynthia replied, pinching the tip of Keith's nose.

The floorboards creaked as Cynthia and the boys attempted to ease into the last pew. The boys fidgeted in their seats, tugging at the mustard suits they'd worn last year to their cousin Darlene's wedding. That was the only time they'd been in a church since they were christened. Cynthia's mother always begged her to come to her church.

"It's not right what you doin' to dem boys," Mildred had once said to her daughter as steam wafted up from her cup of tea. "It's not right. If you and Marvin want to live like heathens you can; you're grown and you got every right to. But dem boys shouldn't be denied the chance to get to know their savior. Jesus said, 'Let the little children come to me and do not hinder them, for the kingdom of glory belongs to such as these.' What do you think He's going to do to you if you keep raising dem like there's no God in heaven?"

"You're right, Mama. I'm going to take them soon," Cynthia would reassure Mildred every time she paused long enough for Cynthia to speak.

"You better be careful what you say, girl. He's listening too." Mildred had pointed her spindly finger at the ceiling. "You're making a vow to the Lord, and you can't go back on it."

Recalling that conversation, a tingling sensation ran up Cynthia's arm. She looked down at the pew bench on which she was seated. The twinge of pain Cynthia felt run up her arm snatched her out of her musings on the past and into the present. James was pulling at the cuffs of his shirt, trying to stretch them to his wrists. Keith tugged at the collar of his shirt. "Knock it off. Hold still," Cynthia leaned over and whispered to them as the choir began singing "Amazing Grace."

The sound of the organ behind the choir reminded Cynthia of the days when she sat beside her mother during Sunday service, sucking peppermint balls. It was easy for her to slip right back into place. By the second verse she was mouthing the song's words along with the soloist. Tears streamed down Cynthia's face, and she tilted her head back. She tapped her small feet as the tempo of the music picked up attempting to put the pain of the previous night behind her.

"Give God some praise," the devotional leader shouted into the microphone. "No matter what the devil has done to you, he couldn't kill you. My God said yes and here you are today. Stand up on your feet and give God some praise."

Hallelujahs rang out all around Cynthia. She looked around and tried to join in on the cries of joy, but the pain that filled her aching bones held her hostage. She mumbled a weak "Thank you, Jesus" in an attempt to be polite.

"God wants to heal you. The devil couldn't kill you, and God is waiting to heal you. But it starts with you," the preacher said, pointing at Cynthia. "He sent his son, Jesus, to reconcile men with God. And He is ready, willing, and able to reconcile all of your relationships. Some of you haven't spoken to your mother in years; some of you haven't spoken to your baby's daddy in months."

Amens mixed with chuckles escaped from the mostly female congregation.

"Some of you haven't spoken to your spouse in days. Let me ask you a question: how long has it been since you talked to Jesus? He can restore, and the work begins with you," Pastor David said, pointing at the congregation.

To Cynthia it appeared as though he had singled her out again and was pointing directly at her. Cynthia turned to the boys to check if she was just being paranoid. James's head hung, and drool was leaking on his jacket. Keith was thumbing through the hymnal. Since the boys could neither confirm nor deny what she was feeling, Cynthia tilted her head a bit to the right and tried to line her eyes up with the direction that Pastor David was pointing in, which led to her.

"We are always looking for God to work on the other person, and you know why the work isn't getting done? 'Cause Jesus is waiting for you to cry out 'Have mercy on me, thou son of David. Fix me, Lord. Save me, Lord. Give me clean hands and a pure heart, Lord.' When you start loving God right, you can start loving your neighbor right, you can start loving yo' mama right, you can start loving yourself right and realize if your baby daddy doesn't want to make you his wife, it's time to move on. You can start loving your husband right, with the meekness and submission that God requires of you women," Pastor David preached passionately.

Snickers and nods rippled through the crowd.

Cynthia wondered if the way in which she loved her husband was right or wrong. It must be wrong since she managed to wind up on the wrong side of his wrath so often, she concluded as fragments of last night flashed through her mind.

"I know it's a hard thing to do, ladies. I was raised by a black woman. The last thing y'all want to hear is submit to your husband, but we're doing it God's way, not our own way, and the man is the head of the woman. Check Ephesians 5:22–33 for that. If you have questions, bring them to Bible Study, ladies and gentlemen."

Cynthia had a question. *How do I get the man I love to stop beating me?*

"Now back to the Word," Pastor David said. "We first need to recognize what's wrong with us and let Jesus in to restore and redeem us."

Cynthia wasn't really sure whether she was to blame or Marvin was to blame for all that was wrong in their life. There was only one thing she was sure of: she didn't want to experience this agony and degradation anymore.

"Is there anyone here today who has not yet received Christ as their Savior? Is there anyone here today who is tired of the devil beating up on them and ready for a real victory? There's winning power in Christ! He has overcome death, hell, and the grave to be a living sacrifice for me and for you. Isn't it time to give Him a place in your life? Do you want joy? Do you want the peace that surpasses all understanding? Do you want the power to say, 'Storm, be still, because He that the winds obey lives in me'?"

Cynthia reviewed the questions in her mind. Tears plopped onto the back of her hand. She put her hand on the back of the pew in front of her to pull herself up. Her legs felt weak, and she felt the eyes of the congregation on her as she moved slowly down the aisle.

"Come," the pastor beckoned. "All of us are sinners. All of us have come short of the glory of God. Come. End it all here."

Cynthia, two other ladies, and a teenage boy stood in front of the altar. The pastor stepped down from the pulpit and came over to anoint each one with oil, starting at the young man. When he reached Cynthia, she looked up into his face.

"Praise the Lord!" the pastor shouted excitedly, throwing his hands into the air. "Where's your husband, sister?"

"I don't know, David . . . I mean, Pastor David," Cynthia murmured, looking at the floor.

"Pick your head up, sister." Pastor David gently cupped her chin, lifting her face so that his dark eyes met with her almond-shaped brown ones. "Jesus is the great equalizer. He died for all men. Church, this is a wonderful thing you are witnessing. This is the wife of one of my former best friends. Look how wonderful God is. I'm preaching a message on restoring relationships, and here is the wife of an old best friend. Isn't He a way maker? Hallelujah!"

That afternoon Cynthia accepted Christ as her personal Lord and Savior. When the service was over, Pastor David took her around to meet all of the members of the church. They welcomed her and the boys with open arms.

Brother Johnson, the choir director, hugged her, shook her hand, and hugged the boys. "Can you young brothers sing?" he asked, stooping over to look into their eyes. "I've been playing with the idea of starting an all-boys choir at the church, and you're welcome to join."

James and Keith just nodded and smiled as the next saint on the welcoming committee enjoined the circle that had grown around them. A bronze-colored hefty woman in a crooked and stiff two-toned wig stepped forward grinning from ear to ear.

"This is our lovely Sister Jeanette. She is our Sunday School teacher and the director of our women's ministry program," Pastor David said to Cynthia. "Jeanette, please give Cynthia a schedule. Cynthia, if you need anything, please, see me or Sister Jeanette, and we will help you as best we can."

Cynthia nodded as Sister Jeanette squeezed her hand before reaching into her purse and gave the boys some peppermint balls. "Cynthia, you know we have a yard out back; most of the other kids are playing out there. Is it all right if the boys go play?"

Cynthia nodded in agreement with Sister Jeanette. "Boys, go and meet the other children in the congregation. They're playing out back."

Sister Jeanette turned back to Cynthia and her brown button eyes radiated the warmth of a mother. "You've done a good thing today. You've done the right thing. The Lord will bless you and save your family if you allow Him to. Sister, you have to be open to Jesus, not just in your time of desperation and desolation. You have to commit your whole self to Him and His ways." She handed Cynthia a copy of the church program. "We offer babysitting on the nights we have classes, and we have counseling for domestic violence, too," Sister Jeanette pointed out while centering her wig and peering over her glasses at the poorly camouflaged welts on Cynthia's neck.

Cynthia didn't have a lie or defensive statement prepared that would get Sister Jeanette out of her face fast enough. She didn't expect to be found out on the first visit. Cynthia cleared her throat and straightened her back and said, "Thank you, Sister Jeanette, but I don't have much time to talk. I'll look at the schedule and come when I can."

Chapter 3

The transition from sinner to saint wasn't easy for Cynthia. The moment she walked in the door from her first trip to Mount Carmel, the devil was waiting to tempt her.

"Where you been all day?" Marvin huffed at her while she helped the boys out of their jackets.

"We went to church today, Daddy." At nine years old, James was the official family reporter. He was still struggling with learning the difference between what should be uttered and what should not be. "You should have come with us. A friend of yours was there."

Twelve-year-old Keith slapped James in the back of his head, trying to demonstrate his superiority. "He wasn't *there*. He's the pastor."

"The pastor?" Marvin asked with his eyebrows scrunched together. "Did you take the kids to that joke of a church, Mount . . . ?" Marvin snapped his fingers. "Mount . . ."

"Mount Carmel Community Church. It's not a joke. It's a lovely place, Marv," Cynthia said resolutely. "Are you hungry?" She quickly tried to stave off the inevitable—Marvin's monologue on the legitimacy of Pastor David's ministry.

According to Marvin, Pastor David could not be trusted since he'd abandoned his street life and friendship with Marvin to pursue the ministry. Every time they walked past Mount Carmel or anyone mentioned it, Marvin had to trudge through the past.

"Of course, I'm hungry. You left me here alone to fend for myself, and you know I can't go on without two things." Marvin wrapped his hands around her dime-sized waist, pulled her in close to his body, and stared in her eyes. "I can't go on without your loving." He brushed back a few loose strands of Cynthia's burgundy hair and planted a wet kiss on her lips. "And I certainly can't make it without your cooking, girl."

Cynthia could see through the act. She knew Marvin was trying to smooth whatever feathers his behavior had wrinkled the previous day, and it wasn't working. It took every atom of Cynthia's fragile being to cook Marvin's food without spitting in it. Cynthia called it a small victory every time she was able to inflict some pain on Marvin unbeknownst to him, like the time she put Ex-Lax in his cupcakes.

Small victories were no longer satisfying. She wanted more. Peace or blood. Cynthia envisioned Marvin's chiseled face bubbling upon contact with the olive oil that was now sizzling in the pan. "Peace, peace, think about peace. You just left church," she chided under her breath.

That kept her from acting on her impulses and the voices of vengeance echoing in her head.

"Marv, the food is ready," Cynthia announced.

"That was fast, babe."

In less than half an hour she'd whipped up grilled chicken breast sautéed in a mango paste with steamed broccoli. Rather than compliment her skills, he grabbed her wrist just as she placed his plate in front of him. "I don't want my kids around Dave," Marvin snapped.

"He's not the same anymore. He's changed."

With a raised eyebrow Marvin asked, "You sure about that?"

"I'm very sure, Marvin. He's a preacher for Christ's sake. How much more evidence do you need to believe that he's saved? Are you waiting for him to part the East River so you can walk through it on your way to work?"

"He ain't saved," Marvin scoffed. "He's what you call a hypocrite. How's he gonna preach don't drink and he was the first one drunk at a party? How's he gonna preach don't have sex before you get married and he used to have orgies? Where was his faith when he was right beside me robbing and stealing, huh?" Marvin stared at Cynthia hard.

"Marvin, I don't know about what happened then. All I know is he's living for God now," Cynthia replied smiling. She was completely convinced that Pastor David was a man of God. Based on the preaching Cynthia heard today there was nothing that Marvin could reveal about Pastor David's past that would hinder her. Everyone had a past.

"I was there. I know what he used to be, and he wasn't no man of God," Marvin said.

"Well—"

"What are you, some kind of cheerleader for him now? Get me a beer and be quiet," Marvin barked. "I don't want to hear any more about David and his funky ol' church."

With those words Cynthia swallowed her spit, beckoned the boys to come and eat dinner, and wondered when she would be able to share the news of her conversion with Marvin.

Keith walked out of the doors of the church complaining about having homework to do. James was crying about being cold and sleepy—the after effects of Tuesday night Bible Study.

Cynthia took a deep breath and hoisted James over her shoulder, exhaling once he was positioned properly. The frosty December air turned her breath into a vapor before her eyes. Cynthia was thankful that at nine the boy was still light enough to be carried.

"Little brother, replace that complaint with a petition," Pastor David commanded Keith. "Repeat after me: 'Father, I am striving to serve you. Please, Lord, renew my strength and increase my ability. In Jesus' name. Amen.'" He patted Keith on the shoulder after the boy obediently repeated his prayer. "You may hear otherwise, but there's nothing wrong with serving my God."

Cynthia craned her neck over James's limp body to say, "Thank you, Pastor David."

"Sister, where's your joy?" Pastor David asked. "You're not supposed to leave church looking sad. You can't leave your joy inside the church, especially when I'm getting ready to lock the gate." He laughed. "Didn't you learn anything tonight? Come on, be honest. Maybe it's time for me to change my approach."

"Pastor, it's not you. Your teachings are fine. It's just . . . just . . ." Cynthia searched for the right words. She'd been in the ring for twelve rounds with Marvin and had lost every round. She searched her heart for the words that would convey the extreme frustration she felt without her having to repent after uttering them. She'd come to the church seeking refuge. A little over a two months later she still felt like she was getting whipped by the winds in the rainstorm.

"There are some things going on in my life right now that I'm having trouble dealing with."

"Are you headed down the hill?" Pastor David asked, pointing toward the neighborhood below.

Cynthia nodded yes. Her demeanor must have indicated that this conversation might take a minute.

"I'll walk you down." They began to tread down the hill. Pastor David continued counseling Cynthia. "You're having trouble in your life because you're trying to deal with it, and Jesus is the one who deals with it all. Actually, He's dealt with it already. On the cross, He said 'it is finished.' Through the shedding of His blood, any- and everything that tries to come against us has already been defeated. The resolution to some problems will manifest itself sooner than others, but all to the glory and honor of Jesus. Sometimes you have to wait—"

"Cynthia! Cynthia! I thought I said I didn't want you around this joker!" Marvin flew up the hill toward them, stopping them in their tracks with his ranting.

"Praise the Lord, brother!" Pastor David exclaimed, extending his hand to Marvin who swatted it away as if an inconsequential fly stood before him buzzing.

"I'm not your brother," he said to Pastor David and then turned his attention toward his wife. "Cynthia, what are you doing out here with him?" Marvin asked prying James out of her arms. Keith shrank behind his mother before Marvin could snatch him up too.

"Marvin, it's nothing for you get upset about. It's all my fault really. Bible Study went overtime, which is why I'm walking Sister Cynthia and the boys down the hill."

Marvin looked Pastor David up and down quizzically, trying to understand why Pastor David insisted on speaking to him.

"I'm not interested in nothin' you got to say, Dave. Can a man converse with his own wife?"

"Pastor," was Pastor David's only response to Marvin's ire-laden question.

"You ain't a pastor, and you're certainly not my pastor."

"Marvin, please show Pastor David some respect," Cynthia begged, gently tugging Marvin's sleeve.

"Without Jesus, it's hard for a man to respect himself, let alone another human being. You can't expect him to not act like the devil when he's full of the devil," Pastor David said to Cynthia without flinching under Marvin's solemn stare.

Marvin scraped his finger across his neck. He took one huge step, inserting himself in the space between Pastor David and Cynthia. Pastor David had the same light shining in his hazel eyes Marvin had seen in him when they first met in middle school and earned the moniker the Drop Boys because either one of them was willing to drop anyone where they stood.

"Don't have any cross conversations with my wife. When I see a man, I'll give him his props, but I don't see one. Only a snake turns his back on his friends to save his own useless skin," Marvin spat.

"You're right. My skin is useless, but I never went anywhere that you couldn't, Marvin."

"Is that right?" Marvin snickered. "Listen, David." Marvin poked him in his chest. "I told her once and she didn't listen, so now I'm telling you. Stay away from my wife and my kids. They don't want any of your poison."

In the fifteen years they'd been together, Marvin could not recall Cynthia setting foot in a church; at least, not of her own volition. They'd attended the customary Christmas services, had the kids christened, but nothing more than that. The last thing Marvin wanted was some woman thumping the Bible at him.

"Marvin, be careful not to hurt yourself," Pastor David said, unmoved by Marvin's rant. "She is a child of God, and He isn't going to tolerate you keeping her from Him. She has dedicated her life to God, and you can't get in the way of that."

Marvin switched his murderous gaze from Pastor David to his wife. *Slap her now or later, now or later, now or later*. Marvin weighed his options. Even though Pastor David was some type of do-gooder now, Marvin was sure he'd rise to the occasion if Marvin did anything too rash. Pastor David was no welterweight boxer, but he certainly knew how to throw and land a couple of effective punches.

Even though it's been years since Pastor David had thrown a punch Marvin knew he would definitely try to defend the honor of one of his 'sistas.'

It was best that he deal with Cynthia when they got into the building. The middle of 145th Street was too public. If Pastor David interfered and Marvin beat him down he'd always be seen as a menace for beating up on a member of the clergy, and if Pastor David got the drop on him, his rep was out the window.

"Let's go, Mrs. Barclay." Marvin cupped Cynthia's elbow as he led her and Keith down the hill.

"Sister, 'wait I say on the Lord and be of good cheer.' There's no need for you to live in fear. Everyone in the church will support you."

"Yes, Pastor," Cynthia said without looking back.

Upon entering the apartment, it seemed as though Marvin had returned from the dark place his mind often took him. A subdued silence occupied the space: the calm before the storm. Cynthia carted both boys off to bed and kissed them on their foreheads before exiting the room.

She walked to the master bedroom and right into Marvin's wrath. "Who's in charge here? Didn't I tell you not to go to that church anymore?"

Before Cynthia could utter a response, Marvin used his fist to jog her memory. "I do not want to hear anything else about David, that church, or the Bible."

"What are you going to do, beat the Holy Spirit out of me?" Cynthia spat blood with each word. Marvin lunged at her. "Help me, Jesus! Help me, Jesus! You said you would deliver me." Before Marvin could reach her, he stumbled on his own boots, fell to the ground, and busted his lip on his own teeth.

Inside Cynthia did cartwheels then reprimanded herself for wanting to see him hurt. Not every fight ended like this one, with Marvin on the floor. Cynthia tried to apply the biblical principles laid out at Wednesday afternoon women's ministry meetings. Most recently the group was focused on 1 Peter 2. Cynthia was struggling with verse twenty-three especially. That verse was a jagged pill to swallow. "He was reviled and reviled not again." Holding her tongue was something she struggled with daily.

Physically, at five feet and three inches, she was no match for Marvin, but every now and then she could whip him with her words—another small victory. Sometimes her tongue lashings led to more bleeding and bruising.

Cynthia crept out of the room to dress her wounds. She applied as much pressure as she could to stop the bleeding and used ice to bring the swelling down as she conversed with her Father to heal her heart.

Chapter 4

"Are you telling me this is my fault?" Cynthia tightened her shoulders and pointed at the dark blue ring below her left eye. Her twisted mouth and aggravated tone expressed her frustration. After three weeks of attending spiritual counseling, her patience was wearing thin.

"Sister, calm down," Pastor David said stretching his hand toward Cynthia. "You misinterpreted what I said. Nagging doesn't help the situation. It only antagonizes him, frustrates him, and you know him. He's the 'hit first, take names later' kind of guy. The Bible says it's not with all your words that you will win your husband over, but with a meek and quiet spirit."

"A meek and quiet spirit? What does that mean, Pastor?" She rested her elbows on the oval-shaped conference table in the Upper Room, which served as the location for First Sunday fellowship dinners, the adults' Sunday School class, and Pastor David's counseling sessions.

"You already know what it means to be quiet, but meek means to be patient, to be humble and long-suffering just as Jesus was. It's that kind of behavior that will help you get through this storm." Pastor David leaned back into his chair and stroked his goatee. It seemed as though he was patiently awaiting the protest brewing in Cynthia's dark brown almond-shaped eyes.

"Pastor David . . ." Cynthia paused and stared at a portrait of Jesus hanging on the cross surrounded by darkness. "I'm not Jesus. I can't carry the cross and take the beatings. Isn't that why He went through what He went through, so I wouldn't have to?"

"Must he bear the cross alone? Sister, may I speak freely?" he asked.

"I thought you already were."

Pastor David sat upright in his seat and blurted out, "You made a judgment call. You chose the wrong man, and now you're calling on God to clean it up like He's some maintenance man. That's not what it's about, sister. If you want to see this thing turn around, then you must acknowledge your role in it and worship God in spirit and in truth."

He's a man of the cloth. Watch what you say to him. "Pastor, you better put the kid gloves back on. Remember, I'm a baby Christian still struggling to climb up that mountain. I've only been saved since October and it's, what, January now." Cynthia paused to count the months on her fingers. "That's just three months. I can't take too much more of you reprimanding me."

"A man's word is his own burden. If what I've said to you is wrong, God will deal with me, but you have to believe you are a child of God and trust that He will fight for you. The same rules that apply here apply at home. Your pride causes you to react to everything Marvin says."

Cynthia rolled her eyes and tried to imagine the clean-shaven, statuesque Pastor David as Marvin had described him—running around wielding a knife beside her husband just to steal some pocket change—to take her mind off the fact that he was the man of God over her. Seeing him as a regular human being made this spiritual whipping a little bit more bearable.

Pastor David rose, placed his hands on his hips, and tried to mimic a woman's voice as he continued to counsel Cynthia. "'How dare he talk to me like that? Who does he think he is?' How many times have you had those thoughts before going off on him or joining him in a heated argument? Do you see how your behavior contributes to the situation?"

Cynthia just stared past him with her eyes fixed on the woman hanging her laundry on her fire escape across the street from the church.

"But woe unto a man who thinketh he is something when really he is nothing," he said, clearing his throat and returning his voice to his normal pitch. "It is the Lord who raised you and will save you, but He can't help you if you insist on doing it your way."

"So, what am I supposed to do, just grin and bear it? You know this doesn't even make sense." Cynthia pushed her chair back from the conference table and stood. "This will be my last session, Pastor. I thank you for your help." She put her head down and focused diligently on removing her wallet from her tote bag. She'd had enough of the charade and hearing the same advice: just wait on the Lord. *I'm not getting any younger.*

"Why?"

"May I speak freely?"

He nodded.

"Since you have never been married, you may not realize this, but marriage is a partnership that takes two people." She held two fingers in the air. "Two not one. Why should I be here alone?"

Pastor walked around the table, taking wide, hurried steps to reach Cynthia before she broke for the door. "You should be here because you are the Christian. You are the saved one, the woman standing in the gap for your family. When your hands are like this"—Pastor David took her tote bag and let it fall to the floor. He tossed her wallet on the table and pressed her palms together as if she was praying—"they are more powerful than any punch Marvin can throw.

"And when your head is lifted like this," he said, tilting her chin toward the ceiling, "and the only words you are uttering are prayers to God, your words hold more weight than anything he has to say. If you give up, what will happen to this marriage? God can fix this. You know that, right?"

She nodded in agreement with him. Truthfully, she wasn't really sure that God could fix it. "Thank you, Pastor David, for your time," Cynthia said, bowing in front of him with her hands still folded like she was praying. "Here is my offering for your counseling ministry." She grabbed her wallet from the table and pulled out a folded twenty dollar bill.

"Cynthia, I don't want your money and neither does God."

"Then what does He want from me, Pastor?" she asked completely exasperated.

"Submission."

Cynthia waved the money at Pastor David. "Please, just take my offering and let me go." The word 'submission' sounded like an obscenity to Cynthia. She'd been submissive for their whole marriage. Where was God and his warring angels that would do battle on her behalf? There had to be another way to resolve this issue that didn't involve submission and Cynthia planned on finding it with or without Pastor David's approval.

Chapter 5

Based on how Marvin's eyes bulged and the way he slurred his words, Cynthia could tell he'd been to Tropics Bar and spent some time receiving counsel from his favorite spiritual advisor, Jose Cuervo. It was the same thing every time he came home like this. He moaned about the burden of raising two kids in the city, the stack of bills on the counter that were turning into its own entity, and how Cynthia and the kids were draining him. They also prevented him from saving up enough money to open the garage he had always wanted. Cynthia had no desire to engage in this conversation after a draining session with Pastor David.

"Fix me some food," Marvin demanded, pushing the bedroom door open.

"You know where the refrigerator is."

"I said fix me some food, Cynthia."

She refused by paying him no mind as she lay in the bed flipping through a magazine.

"Fix me some food." Marvin pounded on the bedroom door. "Now, now, now," he growled through clenched teeth.

"Marvin, I am so tired of you," Cynthia replied calmly, not even glancing up from the pages of *Essence* magazine. The article she was reading stated that a woman needed to voice her opinion in order for a relationship to work. Cynthia felt she'd been silent for too long. The article only confirmed her belief and the notion that submission was not the answer.

"That's not very Christian of you. You think being married to you is a picnic? Look at this house." He walked to the bed and pulled Cynthia out of it by her hair. When she rose, he dragged her through the apartment, squeezing her arm. "What is this?" he screamed, pointing at their living room.

The coffee table was covered with video game cases and beauty magazines, and the boys had left their bikes lying on the floor near the door.

"I almost killed myself coming in here," Marvin complained.

Silently she wished he had.

"If you had come in here at a decent hour, maybe the lights would have been on and you wouldn't have such a hard time navigating through the apartment," she said, snatching her arm away from him. Cynthia rubbed her arm before the soreness could settle in.

"Navigating . . . Spell it. This ain't the ocean. I shouldn't need a compass to get around my house. Aren't you supposed to be submitting to me and honoring me, not talking back? What are they teaching you at that church? You stay home all day long, and this is all you can get done?"

She touched her eye—the ring around it was a marker of her last beating—then she considered her arm. To appease him, Cynthia went into the kitchen and got started on the dishes left over from this evening's round of tacos. But even that was not enough to stop tonight's rant.

"You're holding me back, Cynthia. My garage could have really taken off by now. I see what you're doing," he said, shaking his finger at her. "Telephone bill, Con Ed, cell phone. School lunch? Why am I paying for school lunch if they take lunch with them to school?" Every question he asked was laced with disdain.

"They don't take lunch with them every day, Marvin."

"Stop being lazy," Marvin shouted at her, bunching up the bills in his hand. "Make them boys lunch every morning."

"I do make them lunch every day, Marvin," she said, spinning around to face him, shaking the soap-covered spatula she held at him, "but they like to eat the chicken nuggets and pizza at school."

"So put some frozen pizzas in their lunchbox. All these bills are holding me back."

"From what?"

"From opening the garage. I told you the bank said I need twenty percent of the startup cost."

"Marvin." Cynthia pointed at herself. "That doesn't have anything to do with me. It's not my fault you have bad credit," she declared. Cynthia directed her gaze back to the sink full of suds and turned the water up to full blast, the steady stream drowning out the sound of Marvin's voice.

"Yeah, well it is your fault; it's your fault I can't save money. All you do is spend, spend, spend. You got me paying for school lunch, karate, afterschool programs. Why do I have to pay for afterschool and you're here all day hanging out?"

"I stay home all day hanging out?" Cynthia blurted out. "Filing medical claims is not hanging out. I am the best medical biller Dr. Chang has ever hired. When I'm at home I'm working."

After she had James, Dr. Chang allowed her to work from home, enabling her to extend her maternity leave. Even after James began preschool, he continued to allow her to telecommute. At first, he'd required her to come in to the office once a week, then once a month. Since the claims she filed were rarely rejected, she began to come in only when he needed the books looked at or a new biller had been hired. Dr. Chang also served as the boys' pediatrician free of charge and his wife was Marvin and Cynthia's physician.

"What kind of work do you do, polish your nails?" Marvin asked.

"When I'm home, I'm on the clock. I can't have the boys running around here while I'm working, and I'm not a maid. Maybe you should be here helping out, not hanging out with your friends and your whores," Cynthia cracked back.

"At least they keep a clean house," he barked, walking away from her.

Cynthia could hear the scripture ringing on the inside: *be angry and sin not. Be angry and sin not.* They had just finished reading James 3:8 in Bible Study.

But the tongue can no man tame; it is an unruly evil, full of deadly poison.

She watched him, trying to hold back the obscenities that popped into her head. "I'm working and doing the best I can. Besides, it's only three days a week. Dr. Chang has been kind enough to support our family as it grows by allowing me to telecommute and still function as office manager, and you want to question what I do. Are you serious? Why don't you get another job? You can tow trucks at Milton's garage and do security at night or something," she suggested.

"There you go trying to tell me how to be a man," Marvin said, hovering over her. "Aren't you supposed to revere me or something?" Particles of spit flew out of his mouth and landed on her cheek as he went into a rabid rage. "I don't need another job. You need to make some cutbacks."

"Just shut up, Marvin," Cynthia retorted, walking away from him. "I am not even going to entertain you tonight. The devil is a liar. Why don't you go take a shower and lie down?"

"Entertain me? The devil? Did you just call me the devil? Did you just call me a liar? You know, I'm not even sure why I married your raggedy behind. How's that for some truth?" he asked as he walked past her on his way to the bedroom.

Raggedy.

The word stuck in her mind, and the devil used it as leverage to push her into a battle she certainly couldn't win.

Marvin eased down the hall, so smug and unapologetic.

Cynthia followed, spewing ugly words of wrath and desolation and hurling curses she'd learned from him at his back like darts.

"Is this more of the fine teachings you're getting from your dearly beloved pastor?" Marvin asked. "You're gonna be sorry for this come morning." Marvin looked at her over his broad shoulder and grinned before retreating to the bedroom.

Cynthia felt good watching him walk away. She had stood up to him, and it did not end with her cowering in a corner massaging a bruised arm or in the bathroom in front of the mirror playing artist trying to find the right mix of concealer and foundation to camouflage a black eye. As his final words resounded in her ears, she realized he had still beaten her that night.

The tears came slowly. Her shouting match was a small victory that still somehow equaled a loss. She choked back the snot that gathered in her nostrils, stared out the dining room window at the curve of the moon, and tried to recall what it was Pastor David kept telling her about words and a burden. She couldn't quite figure out how she and Marvin went from canoodling in the park after dark to hating the sight of each other.

Before heading to bed, Cynthia propped open the door to the boys' room. Usually after a fight, James could be found sitting in the middle of his bed with his legs folded. He sat up listening to the arguments to see how far they would go. If it didn't sound too volatile, James just sat up until she walked in, her face flush and ashen from the ceremony of crying and rinsing her face with cold water. Only once did he bother to wake up his older brother to break up the commotion. When they ran out of the room, Marvin had Cynthia pinned against the bathroom door with his hands wrapped around her arms so tightly Cynthia's flesh was bursting through the spaces between his fingers.

Tonight he was in his usual position. His smile was bright enough for Cynthia to recognize in the dim light cast by his Spider-Man nightlight. She plopped on his bed with a heavy and pronounced sigh and asked, "What's up, partner?"

"Nothin', Mom. Are you all right?" James asked.

"Of course I'm all right," she said while smoothing out the waves of his hair. "I am pretty tired. I should be in bed and so should you. Tell me, what can I do to get you back to sleep?"

"I always sleep better after I eat some ice cream," James said smiling at Cynthia.

"James, I was thinking of something more like reading a book or tucking you in tightly."

"Mom, I'm getting too big for you to read to me at night. How about I hold your hand and you escort me to the kitchen?"

"Come on, kid."

Together hand in hand, they marched into the kitchen. Cynthia scooped vanilla bean ice cream into small plastic bowls, then they leaned on the counter, racing to see who could finish their ice cream first, then James went back to bed.

Cynthia shuffled into the dining room and flung herself into a chair. Her shoulders shuddered as she tried to subdue her cries.

This wasn't the life she had imagined for herself and apparently she wasn't a part of Marvin's vision for himself either.

Chapter 6

Every morning Keith woke up at six, but he would lie in the bed pretending to be asleep, waiting for his mother to sashay through his door and wake him with wet kisses on his face. This morning he heard nothing. He enjoyed listening to his mother's slippers graze the parquet floor as she sang old love songs he didn't quite understand. Recently, she'd switched to singing hymns he didn't quite understand either. That didn't matter. The soft hum of her voice put Keith's mind at ease.

By the time his digital clock read 6:15, Keith sat up. He sniffed the dry air, and all he smelled was the stale odor of last night's fried chicken. He waited a few more minutes before he rolled back the covers and got out of bed. He didn't want his mother to know he was capable of waking up and getting out of the bed on his own, but he knew if she wasn't up yet, they would be late for school. He crept down the hall and cracked his parents' bedroom door. He peered in and only saw his father in the bed. Keith shut the door and walked down the hall to check the kitchen. She wasn't in there either. Keith walked through the apartment checking the living room and the bathroom. When he couldn't find her, he ran to his bedroom to check the clock—6:30. He only had forty minutes to wake up James and get him ready before the school bus arrived. Keith considered waking up his father, but he was afraid Marvin would wind up beating him for his mother's unexplained absence.

He walked back into the hallway and stood in front of a picture of Cynthia holding him when he was a baby that hung on the wall. He had no idea what to do. He just stared at his mother in the picture.

Wake up your brother. Be quiet. Try not to wake up your father, but hurry up; the bus will be here soon, he could hear a voice on the inside of him say.

Dread filled his heart at the thought of being responsible for this task. James was difficult to wake up, even for their mother. Keith walked into the room with a sense of determination and tore the covers off his brother and shook his bed, calling out his name in a hushed tone. James didn't stir. Instead, he continued snoring. Keith scurried to the bathroom and ran the cold water over a rag. He ran back to the room and wiped James's face. James bolted up out of the bed.

"Keith," he whined, blinking repeatedly while wiping the corners of his eyes.

"Keep your voice down before you wake Daddy. We're going to be late for the bus. Hurry up and get dressed so we can eat breakfast."

As Keith watched James climb out of bed, he realized he was still in his undershirt and boxers. He walked to the window at the foot of his bed and stared out the window for a while, hoping to see his mother walking up the block from the corner store. Some mornings if she was missing some ingredient or if she wanted to read the paper with her coffee, she would run to the store as the boys dressed. Keith would wave to her as she glided down the street. He looked out for her burnished burgundy bob. All he saw was the lady who talked to herself underneath the tree across the street from their building.

"Where's Mommy?" he heard his little brother ask.

"She's not here, James."

"What did she make for breakfast?"

"Nothing."

"Is she at the store?"

"Shut up with all the questions and just get dressed," Keith snapped at his little brother. "We're going to have some cereal."

With that, James walked out and headed to the bathroom to brush his teeth as Keith stared out of the window while putting on his school uniform shirt. He fought back the tears he wanted to cry. He knew that wouldn't bring his mom back. When he searched the house for her, he noticed the things she cherished like the red pumps she kept at the foot of her bed in case of fashion emergencies or last-minute meetings were gone. Slowly, he buttoned up his blue collared shirt and pulled his gray sweater vest over his head. James burst through the door screaming, "Where's my mommy?"

"Be quiet. She's gone and she's never coming back," Keith replied, poking his head through his shirt. He walked to the door, pushing James out the way and leading him to the kitchen. "Come on, let's eat."

He pulled out a blue glass bowl. He recalled seeing his mother use it when preparing breakfast. Yanking it out of the dish rack, pots, pans, and plates crashed to the floor.

"Be careful," James shrieked at his older brother. "You don't want to wake Daddy up. You know what will happen if we do."

Keith shot him a glance that meant "shut up." Keith scampered into the dining room and dragged a chair into the kitchen, using it as stool to reach the cereal cabinet above the counter. He pulled out a box of Kix.

"I don't want any cereal."

Keith showed him a box of Lucky Charms.

"I don't want any cereal," James said shaking his head from side to side.

"I don't care if you want cereal or not. You're going to eat." Keith hopped down from the chair, still clutching the box of Lucky Charms. "We're going to be late for school."

"How come you got more cereal than me?" James complained after Keith filled their bowls.

"'Cause I'm older than you," Keith replied.

When Marvin appeared, the boys quickly shut their mouths, realizing they had exceeded the noise level their mother often warned them about. He walked into the kitchen and turned around several times, looking from the spilled milk to the boys, looking at the cereal and scuff marks on the floor and then looking back to the boys.

"Cynthia. Cynthia," Marvin yelled anger etched on his face.

"She's not going to answer you," Keith said, looking into his cereal.

"Cynthia, please stop playing around. You may be angry with me, but this is childish," Marvin shouted down the hall. "Come on out of that bathroom."

"Daddy, Mommy's not here. She left, and Keith said she's never coming back," James whined.

"What nonsense did you tell this boy, Keith?" Marvin demanded.

Keith looked up at his father and back down at his cereal. There were only a few marshmallows floating in the bowl. Slowly, he scooped up each marshmallow, stalling for time before he had to look up at his father again. He really didn't want to explain to Marvin that his mother was gone. Besides her missing pumps, Keith discovered her laptop was missing as well. He'd searched high and low for the laptop; his English homework was saved on there. Nor did he want to be the one who explained she wouldn't be returning. Cynthia had never left home without telling them where she was going and the few things that she valued were nowhere to be found. Keith knew things would never be the same in their home.

"Keith, do you hear me talking to you, boy? I'm only going to ask you one more time. What did you tell him?"

"She's gone. She's gone. You drove her crazy, and she ran away." Keith jumped up screaming, "I hate you. I hate you!" Keith tore away from the table and ran to the door. Much to his surprise, his mother had taken the time to place their coats and backpacks by the door. He grabbed his coat and bag while running out the door.

"Wait for your brother, Keith."

Keith sat on the edge of the steps in front of their apartment building. When his father came through the burgundy doors, Keith fled from the steps and took a seat on the curb.

This is all your fault, he thought, glaring at Marvin. Keith had the same cinnamon-colored skin as his mother, and the slight trace of red emanating from his cheeks meant he was furious with him. Keith glanced over his shoulder at his father. He'd thrown on a pair of black and red mesh gym shorts he normally reserved for the house and a pair of blue sneakers. Keith figured he was probably freezing, and he deserved it. Marvin stared back at his son.

The school bus pulled up directly in front of Keith. Marvin walked up behind him before the driver opened the door. He placed his heavy hands on his son's frail shoulders and told him, "She'll be back. Don't worry."

Chapter 7

Cynthia was awakened by her mother's pounding on her bedroom door. She had hoped her mother wouldn't notice her presence right away; she wasn't ready to explain what she was doing there. She wasn't even sure what she was doing there yet. She used the spare key that Mildred had given her in case of emergency. At the minimum Cynthia thought she'd be able to get a good night's sleep and find some clarity in the confines of her mother's home.

"Open the door, Cynthia! Quick! Get on the fire escape. Marvin is on his way upstairs."

Cynthia hustled to her bedroom door, which still harbored posters of rappers Lil' Kim, Biggie, and Mase in their heyday.

"Get on the fire escape. Close the window behind you. You know how crazy your husband is. He's not going to take my word that you're not here and he's going to want to look around."

"Please don't open the door, Ma," Cynthia pleaded.

"I'd rather let him sniff around than fuss with him at my door this early in the morning. Here," Mildred said, chucking Cynthia's duffel bag and sneakers across the room after tripping over them. She drew the iron gate behind her daughter, locked the window, and smoothed the curtains. She then she tucked the edges of the aged striped fitted sheet under the mattress of Cynthia's daybed before she exited the room.

"Open up, Mildred!" Marvin screamed as he banged on her front door.

For the first time in thirty years, Mildred was glad she lived on the sixth floor of her walkup building. From up there she had a clear view of everyone as they entered and exited her building. It also gave her time to get things together. By the time Marvin reached her apartment, Mildred was seated at her dinette set eating breakfast. Mildred opened the door and found Marvin slumped against the doorway with one hand clutching his chest.

"Is everything all right, Marvin?" Mildred asked, folding the lapels of her purple terrycloth robe closed.

Marvin stood upright and clenched the frame of the door.

Mildred looked up at him. He glared back at her through bloodshot eyes. She'd never seen him like this and hoped he didn't do anything crazy. She slid her hand into the pocket of her robe, fishing for the pocket knife she'd purchased a few weeks ago after a serial rapist began attacking women in her neighborhood. "Marvin, what is it?"

"You know I didn't come here for a cup of coffee. Where's your daughter?"

"What are you talking about?" Mildred asked gingerly hoping that Marvin wouldn't call her bluff.

Marvin bulldozed his way past Mildred and entered the apartment and began surveying the place, leaving Mildred with no chance to deny him entrance. His eyes darted from the plate of bacon, cheese grits, and pancakes on the table to the small kitchen. He walked into the kitchen and peered around.

"Marvin," Mildred said placing her hands on her hips, "can I help you? You're certainly not going to find Cynthia in my kitchen."

"Those stairs left me winded. I just want to grab a glass of water." He flashed a smile at Mildred. It did nothing to ease the tension. The madman look in his eyes only demonstrated how phony that smile was to Mildred and made her increasingly uncomfortable.

Mildred brushed past him, bumping him with her shoulder on her way to the sink. She grabbed a mel-on-colored plastic cup from the dish rack and filled it to the brim with tap water. "Here, boy." She handed him the cup of water. "Now, what nonsense you got going on? What do you mean you can't find your wife? If your wife is missing, you should have gone down to the police station, not here."

"Your daughter isn't missing." Marvin took a sip of his water. "She's here, and you're hiding her." He slammed his cup on the counter and walked out of the kitchen to resume his canvass of the apartment. Mildred returned to her seat at the table and plucked up a few scoops of grits.

"She ain't here, Marv." *God, please forgive me for lying.* "I know it's been a long time since you've been here, but there's nowhere for her to hide."

Leaving no corner unexamined Marvin walked around Mildred's matchbox apartment. He pulled open the doors of her linen closet, only to find shelves of neatly folded towels, laundry detergent, and plastic gloves from the hospital where she worked. Next he popped open the door to Cynthia's bedroom. He stepped inside, looking down at the pink wall-to-wall carpeting. He glanced at her daybed, looking for a wrinkled or turned-back sheet. He opened her closet door searching for signs of Cynthia's presence, but all he found were remnants of her high school days. His search turned up nothing. He exited Cynthia's room, turned to his left, and stared at Mildred's closed door.

"Your search ends right here. You're not going in my room looking through my intimates." Mildred seized the opportunity to reclaim control of her home. Fastening the belt on her robe, Mildred walked to her front door and propped it open. "Listen, Marv, why don't you just calm down? I doubt this is anything serious. If she comes by here, I'll tell her to give you a call, okay? Now, why don't you run along and get to work. Give my boys a kiss."

Marvin inched his way to the door still scanning the apartment for evidence of Cynthia's presence.

"Come on now, boy. I've got to get to work too," Mildred said waving her hands up and down to shoo Marvin out of the door.

"Y'all better not be playing with me," he said in a menacing tone; then he walked out the door.

Mildred peered out her living room window, which faced busy Eighth Avenue, and watched Marvin weave through the herds of people and disappear around the corner. She ran to Cynthia's bedroom, flung the window open, and slid the gate open.

"Hurry up. He's gone, but he had that crazy mad-dog look in his eye. He might walk to the alley to check if you're out here. Come on. Move it, girl. Move it."

Quickly, Cynthia stepped off the fire escape and out of the cold. Mildred hurriedly shut the gate, scraping the heel of Cynthia's foot. Cynthia collapsed on her daybed with her eyes closed.

Stroking the stray strands of gray hair that had escaped from her bun, Mildred said, "Just relax. He will keep you in perfect peace if you keep your mind on him."

"Not now, Ma." Cynthia sighed.

"It's always the right time for Jesus, chile. Don't start talking foolishness," Mildred snapped in a warning tone.

Cynthia sat up in her bed and placed her hands on her hips. "Ma, I don't mean to be disrespectful, but you're not there with me when I'm going through, and I'm beginning to doubt that Jesus is either."

"That's true. I'm not there with you, so that's not disrespectful. That's just stating the facts, but Jesus is with you always, unless you leave Him out," Mildred preached pointing at Cynthia. "Listen, next time you want to crash here just call instead of creeping up in here. You almost got you head busted open in Jesus' name.

"While you're here, maybe you should consider letting Him back in. Try to relax. Stay away from the windows, and whatever you do, don't open the door. I made breakfast. If you're hungry, there's a plate in the microwave."

"Oh God." Cynthia sighed. "Only a few hours have passed and things are already getting crazy. Maybe I'd better go back home. What will the boys eat for dinner? Dinner; I don't know if they've eaten breakfast."

Taking slow, deliberate strides over to Cynthia, Mildred bent down and kissed her forehead. To Mildred it seemed like it was too little too late for Cynthia to begin pondering her actions. Now was a time to pray for Jesus to stretch forth His hand and touch this situation.

"Whatever is going on, I pray Jesus delivers you and strengthens you during this storm. I'm a little nervous about leaving you here alone, but I can't take any more days off. There is one person I know who can help you in this situation."

The precarious mention of a storm was enough to set off a bomb inside of Cynthia. She didn't understand why everyone chose to refer to the nightmare she was living as just a storm. Why did everyone refer to this nightmare as a storm? This wasn't torrential rains just passing through. She'd been dealing with this for a long time now, and her deliverance was long overdue.

***

Marvin plodded down the marble steps of Mildred's building after an unsuccessful attempt at playing detective. Mildred's was his first stop because it was rare for Cynthia to venture outside without first discussing it with him. She didn't even go into the office without letting him know in advance. Marvin laughed to himself. Cynthia had nowhere to go. Most of the friends she had he chased away a long time ago and the few who were left ran away when she started thumping the Bible at them.

Shortly after they got married, Cynthia attempted to make new friends, but Marvin found fault with each and every one of them. If they were single, he complained they might influence Cynthia to cheat. If they didn't have a job, he complained they were just trying to sponge off Cynthia. Marvin was a middle-of-the-road kind of guy. He never gave more than what was asked of him, and he didn't want anyone around whose opinion might bear any weight on their relationship.

Marvin looked at his watch. It was already 8:30. Surely he would be late for work as he had to be there at nine. He whipped his cell phone out of his back pocket to call dispatch and let them know he would be coming in late because of a family emergency. His pace was slow and steady as the January wind grazed his skin. He pulled his hood over his head and zipped up his North Face as the rest of Harlem zoomed past him. One thought after another flooded his mind as he walked to the subway. What if she didn't come back? *Of course she'll be back,* he thought as he hopped down the steps past a man helping his girlfriend with one of those oversized metal European strollers. *Of course she'll be back. What's a woman without her man?*

Chapter 8

The garage's banner flew proudly in the air announcing
NEED A TOW, MILTON'S WILL GET WHERE YOU NEED TO GO.
Marvin cringed at the sight of the sign or anything related
to the garage. The only thing that would make him happy
was seeing his own name on the banner. This morning he
had another cause for cringing.

As Marvin approached Milton's garage, he saw Jade,
the evening dispatch operator, sitting outside on a milk
crate with her slender legs crossed. He could see her
luminous smile from the corner. He was shocked to
see her there but relieved. He hadn't seen her since he
switched to the day shift, which was nearly three months
ago. When Marvin used to work the late shift, he'd spend
most of it on the radio talking to Jade. She'd call out a
location and then she'd page his truck. They went back
and forth all night. Before he could reach the entrance,
Jade was already standing up waving at him.

"How you doing, buddy?" She grinned.

"Hey, Jade. What are you doing here?" As soon as he
looked into her honey-colored eyes, some of the anxiety
he was experiencing over Cynthia's disappearance melted
away.

"Antoinette came in late this morning, so I stayed a
couple of extra hours to cover for her. When I checked the
roster and saw your name, I decided to stick around and
wait for you," she said, punctuating her sentence with a
wink.

Jade's warm greeting relieved Marvin, but in between each word she uttered, his thoughts darted back to Cynthia. As excited as he was to see Jade, as much as he would have enjoyed engaging in some risqué conversation with her that morning, especially after a night of fighting with his wife, he wanted to run inside and check the desk for any messages from Cynthia. Surely, she'd gone to Dr. Chang's office and had forgotten to tell him she was going to work for a meeting or to settle a claim. He'd looked for her laptop before leaving the house and couldn't find it. After all these years of working from home, every now and then she went into Dr. Chang's office to check the paperwork, organize the office, order supplies, or do anything else Dr. Chang asked her to do. She had become an informal office manager. Marvin thought she was crazy at first for doing all of that extra work, but Cynthia reminded him Dr. Chang had been good to them.

Months had passed since Cynthia had been summoned to the office for an emergency audit or to handle a rejected claim that required her attention. However, right now he needed for her to be at Dr. Chang's filing a claim.

Jade must have noticed the pensive look on Marvin's face. "Are you okay?" she entreated, rubbing his arm to coax a response out of him.

Marvin took a deep breath, sucking in the vanilla scent Jade was wearing. Normally he would have said something fresh, but he simply replied, "I've just got some things on my mind, Jade."

"What happened, Marv?" Jade asked in a singsong voice. "Your wife finally up and leave you?" Jade chuckled.

Marvin stared directly into her eyes. He cracked a sparse smile. He didn't want Jade to know how true that statement was. "We had a big fight last night." He leaned into her, brushing the hair out of her face so he could see her eyes better. "All I need right now is someone to tell me I'm a good man."

"You're a good man."

"Good and late," Marvin's supervisor, Rodney, shouted. "Are you going to tow some cars or what?" He stared at the pair and opened his flabby jaw wide, which usually marked the commencement of a speech about responsibility and the duties of a husband to his wife.

"Well, Marvin?" Rodney cleared his throat.

"See you around, Jade," Marvin said, dipping his head under the gate to enter into the garage, barely glancing in Rodney's direction. He darted to the operator's desk upon entering and began combing through the message book.

"You got one message from Milton," Rodney shouted in his standing position under the gate. "Rig fourteen is broken. I think it might be the carburetor. You're going to have to take five unless you come in early and work on fourteen before your shift starts; it's too late for that now, isn't it? Why didn't you call in sooner, man?"

Despite rig fourteen being Marvin's favorite tow truck, he didn't have it in him at the moment to focus on fiddling around with the insides of a truck when the insides of his own personal life were discombobulated. "I'll take five out for a run. If Milton calls, just tell him I didn't want to get all greasy and dirty before my shift starts, but I'll work on it after my shift is done."

About three hours into his shift, Marvin radioed the garage to check if Cynthia had called but she still hadn't. He called her cell phone nine times, and it kept going to her voicemail. He called their cell phone carrier and asked them to locate her, but the GPS application on her phone wasn't active. They would only be able to track her if they had a court order from the police. He argued with the customer service representative for ten minutes.

"I'm her husband," he pleaded over and over.

"I'm sorry, sir, but those are the rules. Besides, if you're her husband, you would know where she was. Thank you for calling TRS Connect and have a good day, Mr. Barclay," the customer service representative said curtly before hanging up on him.

By the time Marvin returned to the garage, he'd given up searching for Cynthia. He'd spent his shift listening to Jeffery Jordan, an average Joe turned love doctor/preacher, on the radio declaring to all his followers if you love someone sometimes you really have to let them go, and if it's truly meant to be, the person would somehow make it back into your life.

That was enough to calm down the beast inside of Marvin. He accepted the fact Cynthia might still be angry about the fight they had last night. After parking his truck at the end of his shift, Marvin used the phone in the office to reach out to his wife.

"Cyn, I didn't mean those things I said last night," he started with his message after going straight to voicemail yet again. "You know I love you. I don't know why I said those things. You know I need you. The boys need you. Just come home and we can work it out. I've almost got enough money to open my own garage. Everything is going to be okay. Please, believe me. It will get better for us . . . between us," Marvin whispered to her voicemail.

He hung up the phone and walked to the back of the garage with his head down so low his chin touched his chest. He ran his hand across the hood of number fourteen. The cool metal made the hairs that had been standing up on his arms all day lay down. He popped the hood. Rodney had mentioned something about the carburetor. While he was tinkering around under the hood, Antoinette came running to him with her jiggly arm outstretched waving the cordless phone at him.

"Is it my wife?" Marvin asked eagerly.

"No, Marv. It's your son, Keith, and he says it's an emergency."

Marvin snatched the phone from Antoinette's plump hand. "What is it, Keith?"

"Are you going to be home soon, Dad? We're hungry."

"Where's your mother?"

"She's not home. I know we're not supposed to bother you at work, but Mommy said to never touch the stove without adult supervision. We each had a sandwich when we came in."

"Keith, I'll be there soon. I'm going to leave right now." Marvin handed the phone back to Antoinette. "I've got to go. Tell Milton I'll explain later," Marvin said, flying out of the garage. *What if she never comes back? Of course she'll be back. Get a hold of yourself,* Marvin thought, checking himself. Cynthia may have wanted to leave his sorry behind, but she would never leave James and Keith. Her world revolved around them.

A solitary tear streaked his face. They'd been together for nearly fifteen years now. Marvin couldn't even begin to imagine a life without his wife. The tears continued falling. He sat down on a bench at the bus stop. He knew the boys were waiting, but he couldn't get on the train crying like this. He rode the bus downtown and transferred to the one that went across the bridge. As it crept along, Marvin stared out the window, his face ashen from the flood of tears. His eyes fixed on the green waves of the East River while his mind conjured up a plan to build a bridge that would bring Cynthia back.

Chapter 9

An hour had passed since Keith called Marvin at the garage. The boys sat at the dining room table staring at each other in silence. Keith had given James some soda and some ham and cheese to pass the time, but he could tell James was still hungry. He couldn't hold still. His eyes were fixed on a red spot made by some Kool-Aid he spilled a week ago their mother couldn't get out of the tablecloth. He wrapped a loose thread hanging from the tablecloth around his finger until he lost the feeling.

Normally, Keith would be wearing his Spider-Man mask and tearing through the apartment swinging from imaginary webs. Instead he was watching the clock that hung on the wall behind the table.

Eight o'clock. He pounded the table, causing it and James to jump. He wondered why his mother had left them with Marvin. James leaped from his chair and ran to his book bag. He sat on the floor with his legs folded like a W, pulling out papers, stickers, empty candy wrappers, Pokemon cards, his science textbook, and a brown paper bag that contained semi-crushed Devil Dogs. He held the bag in the air, waving it at his older brother. He ran back to the table and snatched two napkins from the silver holder. He opened the plastic wrapper with his teeth and put one on each napkin. James slid one toward Keith and bit into his. Keith eyed the Devil Dog suspiciously.

"How long was this in your bag?"

"Like . . ." He took a massive bite of his Devil Dog, nearly swallowing the whole thing. "Like, two days," he replied, licking the sweet white cream filling from the corners of his mouth.

Keith inspected the Devil Dog, looking for signs of age. Satisfied with the result, he took a bite. By the time he took his second bite James was licking the chocolate from his fingertips.

"Go take a shower, James."

"Uh-uhh," James refused.

"Go now," Keith said forcefully.

"No. I'm waiting for Daddy. Maybe he's going to bring us something to eat. What if it's messy like spaghetti and I have to take another shower?"

"It's almost time for bed, and Daddy isn't going to bring us anything, so just stop wasting time," Keith insisted.

"Yes, he is." James nodded.

"No, he's not!" Keith shouted at James. "Just go and take a shower."

James rose from the table. "When is Mommy coming home?" he asked as tears lined the rims of his eyes.

Keith sighed. "She's never coming back."

"She is coming back. Remember the last time she was really mad at Daddy and we went and stayed at Grandma's?"

"She's not coming back."

"How do you know?"

"'Cause I know. This ain't like the last time. Just go." Keith pointed toward the bathroom. "And take a shower so you can go to bed."

James dragged himself down the hall to their room. Keith didn't want James to be up when their father strolled in drunk and empty-handed.

It was 10:30 p.m. when Marvin came home. Keith sat at the table rubbing his eyes as he watched his father stumble through the front door. He kicked Keith's school bag out the way then wobbled over to the dining room table and used his knuckles to prop himself up.

"Did your mother come home yet?" Marvin asked.

"Did you bring us something to eat?" Keith countered questioning his father.

Keith stared at Marvin as he stood there empty-handed. His eyes flickered in the light, begging Marvin to do more, be better. *I need you to be better.* The words rumbled around inside of Keith, but at twelve he didn't know how to say them. Marvin reached into his back pocket and pulled out his wallet. He took out a couple of dollars and extended his arm to Keith.

"Go to the chicken spot and get something to eat for you and your brother. I know you're upset about your mother taking off like that, but until she comes home I'm all you got."

Keith studied his father. His irises were completely red. Sweat dripped from his brow as he shifted his weight from side to side to maintain his balance. Maybe Marvin meant it as a peace offering, a request for forgiveness, and a promise to do better. Keith didn't need it. He focused all his energy on holding back his tears. His stomach rumbled, urging him to take the money. He also heard his mother's voice saying, "Children shouldn't be in the street after dark." He couldn't fight it anymore. A tear slid out of his eye. To Keith it seemed as though the room had begun to spin as his chest heaved. All he wanted to do was scream for his mother to come and save him because he knew Marvin was only a few seconds away from flying into a rage. Marvin would definitely strike him if he cried for Cynthia.

Swallowing the knot that had formed, he grunted to clear his throat, and began walking to his room.

"Who do you think you are? Don't you ever turn your back on me." Marvin pounced on him, snatching him up by the collar of his shirt, and slamming him against the wall. Keith yelped as Marvin pressed his elbow against his chest.

"You're gonna respect me. You may hate me, but you're gonna respect me." Keith stared up at his father, with tears running down his cheeks. "Do you hear me, boy? You're going to respect me."

Keith coughed as Marvin shook him. A new knot had formed in his throat and was choking him. Keith remained silent as Marvin eased off him slightly.

"Do you understand me?" Marvin asked.

"What are you doing, Daddy?" James asked as he emerged from the boys' bedroom.

Marvin glanced at James then at Keith still pinned to the wall. He loosened his grip and slid his fingers down Keith's shirt, straightening the wrinkles.

"Uhh, I was just talking to your brother. You boys better get in the bed. It's getting very late and y'all got school tomorrow." Marvin crouched down to pick up the money he'd dropped then he stuffed it into Keith's hand. "Use it for some afterschool snacks or for lunch. What time does your mother usually wake you boys up?"

"At six-fifteen or six-thirty," Keith answered dryly, walking into the bedroom. He turned the light off and left the door open for James.

"Good night, Dad," James said, running back into the room.

The following morning Keith arose at six. He kneeled at the foot of his bed and began to pray. "Father God, umm . . . I don't know what to say or how this thing is supposed to work, but if you're out there—I mean up there—please send my mother back to me. I really need her. We really need her. I'm sorry for not listening. I'm sorry for all the bad things I've done, but I promise if you send her back, I'll be good. Amen."

Keith rose from the floor, hunched over from the hunger pains attacking him. He held his breath as he turned the doorknob waiting to see his prayer answered. He hoped to find his mother lying in bed. He wouldn't ask any questions about her absence, just jump in the bed and snuggle up next to her. To his surprise, Marvin wasn't even lying in the king-size bed. Keith walked into the room and stared at his mother's nightstand. None of her jewelry was gone. Maybe she would come back. He walked to the window, raised the blinds, and flung the window open.

His mother always said fresh air made you feel better. Keith stood in front of the window with his arms outstretched waiting for the wind to carry him away. An early morning zephyr danced with the trash in the gutter while a cool spring breeze too light to carry Keith's burden floated past the window. Keith ran his fingers across the top of her armoire. The smooth cool cherry wood reminded him of touching his mother's skin. He leaned over the armoire and took a deep breath, sucking up the scent of jasmine from one of her perfumes. He picked up the small bottle and held it close to his chest, deciding to take it with him as he headed out the room. He needed some semblance of her to make it through the day.

He trudged down the hall planning breakfast. James had wanted toast yesterday, but there was no time and he didn't want to make any. Their mother had often reminded Keith that as the big brother it was his job to take care of James. She would say, "Don't be like Cain. Love your brother with a godly love. Protect him and take care of him."

Keith felt like he'd already failed and only one day had passed. Today would be different. Keith decided he'd buy lunch and dinner with the money Marvin gave him the night before.

Marvin's snoring met Keith as he approached the kitchen. He continued into the kitchen after deciding it would be best to let Marvin rest considering how badly last night went. After washing the dishes and cleaning the counter, Keith went to go wake up James who lay in the bed snoring like their father, with one leg hanging over the side of his fire engine bed. Keith kicked his foot several times until James sat up rubbing his eyelids.

"Did Mommy come home?"

"Well, good morning to you, too." Keith placed his hand on James's shoulder. "I know this is hard for you to understand, but she may not be coming back. The sooner you accept it, the easier this will be for all of us. Come on and brush your teeth."

They went into the bathroom and stared at their reflection in the mirror as they brushed their teeth side by side like any other morning. Keith hummed "Sometimes I Feel Like a Motherless Child" as he gargled. Every time he'd heard his father play the record he couldn't grasp the concept: a child without a mother. Now the song would be his theme song. Keith went back into the bedroom to find some clothes for James.

"Your clothes are on your bed," he stated as he headed into the kitchen. He put the end pieces of the bread he'd hid in the produce box of the fridge for today's breakfast in the toaster and divided the remainder of the Lucky Charms into two bowls. He sat down on the stool that Cynthia used for reaching the cabinets. Before he could enjoy a spoonful, the bread popped out of the toaster. As he buttered the toast he could feel something looming behind him. It was Marvin standing in the arc of the doorway.

"Good morning, son," he said and then repeated the same to James as he passed him in the hallway.

James hurried to the kitchen to join his brother for breakfast.

"Cereal again?" James looked over at Keith.

"This is all we have and you're lucky I saved this last night. You don't like it then don't eat."

They sat in silence. Keith was dreaming of French toast, eggs, and bacon and James was probably imagining a platter of waffles and Canadian bacon.

"Get your book bag on. It's seven."

Keith's command woke James from his fantasy.

Keith went to his parents' bedroom door and knocked.

"Come in," Marvin called out from the other side.

Keith pushed back the door. Marvin was sprawled out across the bed still in his uniform.

"It's almost time for us to get on the bus," Keith said, not even bothering to cross the threshold.

Keith didn't wait for Marvin to respond. He walked off and grabbed his book bag from his room. James sat on the floor gathering all of the junk he'd left on the living room floor the night before. He quickly stuffed everything into the bag then scurried to the door.

"Listen, boys," Marvin said, placing his hand on Keith's shoulder, "I know yesterday was rough, but today will be better. Don't worry about your mother. I'm gonna go to the police station today, and they're gonna help us find her."

"Okay, Dad," James said, smiling.

Keith opened the door for his brother and remained stoic. His father's promise of a better day could not bring him to smile. From what he understood about the police they weren't that great at solving crimes and Marvin wasn't that great at following through. Keith highly doubted that this day would give him much to look forward to.

Chapter 10

Marvin stripped out of his uniform, took a long, hot shower and shaved. He couldn't go to the police station to report Cynthia missing looking like a fugitive and smelling like booze. He looked in the mirror. His eyes were still bloodshot. They burned from fatigue and the strain of holding back tears. He didn't want to cry in front of the boys, but he was so lost. Cynthia did almost everything for all three of them, and now he was alone. Marvin threw on a pair of navy blue track pants, a white T-shirt, and the matching fleece jacket.

As he walked the seven blocks to the police station, he called the garage to let Milton know he was having a personal crisis. After trying to get Milton to let him have the day off, Marvin was flustered, weary, and in no mood to play when he reached the glass doors of the 30th Precinct. He yanked the door open and walked up to the female desk sergeant who was in the middle of calming a woman.

"Excuse me," Marvin said calmly, staring into her eye. "I'm in need of some help."

Marvin used the power of his commanding dark brown eyes to gain the attention of the desk sergeant. The moment she looked away from the frantic mother and over at Marvin's brick brown skin and clean-shaven face and excused herself to slink over to him, he knew he was going to be taken care of right away.

"Good morning, sir. Can I help you?" she asked, smoothing down the hairs at the nape of her neck.

"Hey, lady, I was here first," cried a guy.

"That's Sergeant to you," she said, tapping her finger on her badge. "Pipe down over there or you'll be the last one here." She turned her attention back to Marvin. "Now, how can I help you, sir?"

Marvin noticed the desk sergeant's eyes roving up and down the rough terrain of his body as he hiked up the sleeves of his fleece jacket and unzipped it to the middle of his chest. The scar on his forearm looked like he'd participated in his share of knife fights and gang turf wars. The pressure of her ominous eyes made Marvin regret making this trip. One thing he had learned from his various run-ins with the law was they weren't very helpful.

"Sergeant, I would like to report a missing person."

"Okay, sir. Can you explain the circumstances under which this person went missing? Do you believe this person may have been abducted? What is your relationship to the missing person?"

"It's my wife."

"Your wife?" The desk sergeant pointed to the bench that lined the wall facing the desk. "Have a seat over there. Someone will be with you as soon as possible." Her rich and melodic voice tapered off as she walked away.

"Isn't there some paperwork I should be filling out?"

"Have a seat, sir," she commanded without looking up. Marvin tapped the heel of his Nike Foamposites on the beige laminate flooring while he waited for someone to ask him what was going on. He tried to signal for the desk sergeant's attention several times, and she shut him down every time with her favorite eight word phrase: "Someone will be with you in a moment."

After an hour, a woman in a navy blue pantsuit approached the bench, which was now occupied by five other people squeezed on top of one another. "I heard there's someone here to report a missing person." She scanned the bench and polled the group with one finger.

Marvin hopped to his feet. "That would be me, Officer."

"Detective Grayson," she said, extending her hand to shake Marvin's. "And you are?"

"I'm Marvin Barclay, and I would like to file a missing persons report for my wife, Cynthia Barclay."

"Mr. Barclay, please follow me." Detective Grayson led Marvin through a swinging door and to her desk. "Have a seat, Mr. Barclay." Detective Grayson pointed to metal folding chair adjacent to her desk.

Marvin squirmed around in the small seat trying to get comfortable while Detective Grayson asked him questions. "Sir, how long has your wife been gone, and what led you to believe she's missing?"

"She's been gone since Monday, and I believe she's missing because she's gone."

"Mr. Barclay, my next question may be a difficult one. How are things at home?"

"Why? Do you know a marriage counselor we should visit? Shouldn't you be asking me to sit down with a sketch artist? Get out of here with that nonsense." Marvin dismissed her with a flip of his hand. "I need to speak to someone else. Is there another detective here who can handle my case?"

"Mr. Barclay, please quiet down."

A few detectives looked up from their desks.

"Yo, can I get another detective over here?" Marvin asked, looking around.

Jumping from behind his cheap, banged-up desk, one officer ran up to them and positioned himself right between Marvin and Detective Grayson. "How can I help you? I'm Detective Laurel, Detective Grayson's partner."

Marvin stood still and tried to assess whether Detective Laurel had added himself to the equation to help his partner or to help him. His American-pie smile, erect posture, and mouse brown eyes conveyed a sincere look of concern and worry.

"Listen, buddy," he said, placing his hand on Marvin's right shoulder. Marvin tilted his head and looked down at Detective Laurel's hand. "I'm going to need you to take it down a notch. Why don't you come with us to an interview room and tell us your story there?"

Marvin followed the detectives to a dimly lit gray interview room.

"You want some coffee or something?" Detective Laurel asked Marvin.

"Yeah. Black. Three sugars."

"Detective Grayson, could you handle that for me while I chop it up with . . ."

"Marvin Barclay, but Marvin is just fine." Marvin simmered down and warmed up to Detective Laurel. He knew a man would understand the situation better than any woman.

"Here's the deal, Detective Laurel. My wife went missing sometime early Monday morning. She wasn't home when I woke up, and she hasn't returned since. She's about five three, her hair is just off her shoulders and dyed a reddish burgundy color." Noticing the detective wasn't taking notes or anything he asked, "Uh, shouldn't you be writing this down?"

"My fault." Detective Laurel reached inside his black blazer and pulled out a little spiral notebook. "What's her name?"

"Cynthia Ann Barclay."

"Does it appear as though there was a struggle? Do you think this is a possible abduction?" Detective Laurel asked poised to take notes.

"I don't know how it happened or when it happened, but she's gone."

Detective Grayson returned with Marvin's coffee in a large white Styrofoam cup.

"Maybe you can explain what your marriage was like to my partner and me."

"We had our good days and our bad days, you know what I mean, man," Marvin said, plucking Detective Laurel's solid gold wedding band.

Detective Laurel nodded and smiled in agreement with Marvin.

Marvin slurped up some coffee and asked, "What happens next? Do I sit down with a sketch artist, or do we create a timeline of what she did on Sunday like they do on *Without a Trace?*"

"Mr. Barclay, you've watched one too many episodes of *Without a Trace*. We don't need a sketch artist; a photo of the missing person is usually sufficient," Detective Grayson stated very matter-of-factly. "In this case our next step is not to take any steps, Mr. Barclay."

"What?" Marvin's grip tightened around his cup.

"Mr. Barclay, this may be hard for you to grasp, but there is no hard and fast rule that says an adult must remain in their home." Detective Grayson stuffed her hands into the pockets of her trousers and continued, "Just because your wife isn't there doesn't mean she's missing."

"What is she saying, that y'all are not going to look for my wife?" Marvin asked, looking at Detective Laurel.

"With no evidence of foul play, we have no reason to believe your wife has been abducted but it is possible that she just left you, Mr. Barclay."

Marvin squeezed the coffee cup so tight the hot black liquid came spilling out of the cup. It ran down his hand over his arm and dripped off the table, forming a small puddle. Both detectives winced at the sight of the scalding hot coffee. The sting of it felt like a splash of water to Marvin in comparison to how his anger burned inside of him.

"We've been together for fifteen years. Cynthia has never gone anywhere without telling me. She has slept in the bed with me every night since we got married, and the only time she wasn't there she was at her mother's. I've already been to her mother's house, and she ain't there." Marvin slid out of his seat. "One thing I know is somebody better find my wife or some heads are going to be rolling." He pointed at Detective Grayson.

"Are you threatening me?" Detective Grayson leaned over the table and flexed her shoulders.

"I don't recommend we continue this line of conversation. Mr. Barclay, let's remember Detective Grayson is a woman and an officer of the law," Detective Laurel said in a stringent tone.

"I can't tell," Marvin said, looking at her flat chest, sharp hips, and plain, pasty face. "That's my wife out there on the streets. My wife." He slapped his chest. "And my tax dollars are in your pocket, so somebody in here better get to investigating before I have Help Me Howard from channel eleven in here investigating why no one wants to find a black woman who's missing. Now who's going to start printing the missing person fliers?"

"Mr. Barclay, I'm sorry, but until there's some evidence of foul play, we will not be investigating your wife's disappearance. I recommend that you check with your friends and family for some answers," Detective Laurel said in response to Marvin's threat.

"Detective Laurel, I'm sorry, but I'm not leaving until you begin investigating my wife's sudden disappearance," Marvin said calmly.

He reclined in the hard gray plastic chair and whipped out his cell phone. Marvin fiddled around with the phone and avoided making eye contact with the detectives until he heard the other line ringing. He pressed speaker and placed the phone on the top of the metal table.

"Channel eleven community news desk."

Marvin looked up at the detectives, and they both looked at each other.

"Do you have a newsworthy story that needs to be covered?"

"Yes, I do."

"What is the nature of this story?"

"My wife went missing yesterday and the officers at my local precinct are refusing to investigate."

Detective Grayson folded her arms across her chest while Detective Laurel signaled to Marvin to hang up the phone.

"Did you say your wife is missing, sir?"

"Yes, and no one wants to look for her. I think it's because we're black, and I don't know how to explain this to my sons. I promised them I'd do something, so I came to my local precinct, met with some detectives, and they've done nothing. What am I going to tell my boys?" Marvin asked, adding a little hiccup at the end for sympathy.

"Sir, what's your name?"

"Marvin Barclay, and my wife's name is Cynthia Barclay."

"Mr. Barclay, my name is Shana, and we are going to help you get to the bottom of this. I'm going to transfer you to one of our investigative journalists. I just need some more information. Which precinct did you go to, and what are the names of the detectives you spoke to?"

Marvin looked up at Detective Laurel and mouthed the words, "you're going down."

"I'm at the 30th Precinct in Harlem, and the detectives I met with are Gr—" Detective Laurel pressed the end button before Marvin could get out all the syllables in his partner's name.

"All right, Mr. Barclay, you've got our attention. We'll look into your wife's disappearance," Detective Laurel said.

Chapter 11

Mildred was seated at the front desk at Harlem Women's Services when Detectives Laurel and Grayson walked in looking for her. Her head was buried in her pocket-sized New Testament.

"Good afternoon. I'm Detective Grayson and this is my partner Detective Laurel." Detective Grayson pointed to her left at Detective Laurel. "We're detectives from the 30th Precinct and we're looking for a Ms. Hathaway."

Mildred peered at them over her red-rimmed spectacles. "Is this about Cynthia?"

"Are you Ms. Hathaway?" Detective Grayson asked.

"Of course I am. Did my crazy son-in-law contact you?"

"Yes, ma'am. It seems your daughter hasn't been home in two days. He said this isn't like her. Mr. Barclay seems to think there's a possibility she may have been abducted early yesterday morning on her way to the supermarket."

A tumultuous laugh escaped from Mildred's throat, causing the guy from housekeeping to pause in front of the desk mid-sweep. "Kidnapped?" She continued to chuckle, covering the wrinkled corners of her mouth. "Detective . . . uh . . ."

"I'm Detective Grayson and this is Detective Laurel," she said, pointing at her partner again.

"Well, Detective Grayson and Detective Laurel, I'm sorry my son-in-law wasted your time. My daughter has not been kidnapped. She has been staying at my place."

"Do you know why, ma'am?" Detective Laurel asked, scribbling in his little notepad.

"Excuse me." Mildred stood at the desk and turned to the pudgy girl seated behind her. "Esther, please cover the desk while I talk to these detectives. If there's an emergency, page me. Otherwise just register the patients." Mildred turned back around to face the detectives and tapped on the counter to get their attention. "Detectives, follow me," she said.

Mildred led them down the sparkling white corridor to an empty examination room. She sat down on the bed, her short, stout brown legs hitting the metal footrest. "I'm not sure what happened, Detectives. She barely spoke to me yesterday, then he showed up at my house looking like the devil escaped from hell. I told him she wasn't there. If we can keep it that way, it would be greatly appreciated."

"Ma'am, this is official police business. We can't just conceal our findings."

"That's fine, Detectives. I'm not asking you to conceal any evidence or anything like that. I'm just asking you not to tell Marvin she's at my house. Tell him you don't have any leads yet or something official sounding."

"Is he violent?" Detective Grayson inquired.

"Has Aretha Franklin gotten fat?"

Detective Laurel laughed. Detective Grayson shot him a stern look. Detective Laurel straightened his polka-dot tie and cleared his throat. "Ma'am, we can help if this is a domestic violence situation."

"Listen, I don't want to get anyone in trouble. Just give me a chance to try to get her back home before you tell him you located her."

"Ms. Hathaway, maybe we should try to talk to her," Detective Grayson proposed.

"What kind of detective are you, Grayson? Can't you recognize a clue when it's handed to you? She doesn't want to talk to the police. If she did, don't you think she would have called you a long time ago? Just leave me your card and I'll have her call you or something." Mildred held her hand out.

Detective Laurel pulled out his card from his pocket. "Ma'am, this is our number at the station on the top and my cell phone number at the bottom."

"What are you doing?" Detective Grayson asked, nudging her partner.

"Haven't you heard the expression 'Mother knows best'? She knows her daughter, and she knows the situation. Mr. Barclay never mentioned any turmoil. We know where she is, and we know she's safe. Let's give it some time. Besides, we've got a ton of paperwork sitting on our desks and a couple of leads to follow up on."

Mildred's eyes met with Detective Laurel's pensive brown ones. "My daughter's safety is the only thing on my mind right now. If there's anything to tell, you'll be the first to know. Now please excuse me. I have to get back to work."

"Thank you, ma'am, for your time," Detective Laurel said.

I gotta get that girl back home.

"When are you going back home?" The only sound that followed Mildred's question was the clink of the spatula against the pan and the crackle of the fire underneath it.

Mildred tried to take it easy on Cynthia. It had been three days since her daughter had crept into her apartment. When she'd gotten home from work the day before, Cynthia was still refusing to eat. All she asked was that Mildred didn't open the door if it was Marvin. Mildred didn't think it would be wise to mention the police had shown up at the hospital. So, she kept that to herself.

This morning things seemed a little different. Cynthia emerged from the bedroom with a slight smile. Her eyes were still swollen and cloudy from crying.

"When are you going back home?" Mildred repeated her question while flipping the eggs. The only response she received was a hiss from the sizzling eggs in the pan.

"Tia." Mildred called Cynthia by her nickname to get her attention and create a sense of safety for her. "Did you hear what I said?" Mildred stomped her foot on the wine-colored linoleum in her kitchen.

"I heard you, Ma."

"Well, then answer," Mildred demanded, snapping her head around to look at Cynthia.

"It's complicated. You see—"

"I don't need to know what happened." Mildred plated their omelets and bounced across the kitchen carrying them over to the table. "I don't want to get involved in your business. I was just wondering when you plan on going home. Have you checked on the boys since you've been here?"

Cynthia poured herself a glass of orange juice and took small swigs. The two women ate in silence.

"No, Ma, I haven't called them."

"They're all right. Keith called me the other night asking for dinner. I dropped off some Popeye's. Everything seemed fine. Now for my other question, when are you going back home?"

"I don't know when I'm going back."

"What do you mean you don't when you're going back?" Mildred pointed her finger at her daughter. "Jesus, restore this child's mind. You have two kids who need you, girl."

"They have a father. He can take care of them."

"Look here, you know Marvin isn't fit to take care of a Baby Alive doll." Cynthia chuckled a little. "Listen, this is the perfect time for you to see God move. Why don't you let Him be your defense and try to work things out with Marvin?"

"I just couldn't take it anymore. Neither one of us is fit to raise children," Cynthia replied.

"Oh hush with that foolish talking," Mildred said waving her hand at Cynthia. "If you couldn't raise them, God wouldn't have given you them boys."

"He didn't give Keith and James to me for them to see me like this." Cynthia raised her shirt to reveal the bruises she had, bruises she'd managed to hide for years. "I feel like . . . like I just can't do it anymore."

Mildred sucked in as much air as she could as her eyes roved the rough terrain that Marvin's beatings had turned her daughter's body into. Mildred had an idea what was going on. She had no idea it had gotten this bad. Suddenly Cynthia's unannounced trip to her house made sense. "Oh Lord, you're having a nervous breakdown. Repeat after me: 'God hath not given me a spirit of fear, but of love, power, and a sound mind.' Cynthia, you have a mightier spirit within you."

Cynthia groaned. "Ma, listen to me."

"No, you listen to me. I got some money stashed away. Why don't you bring the kids here and go have a spa day all by yourself. Let Marvin go off and hang out with his hoodlum friends while you just kick back and relax. You do whatever you have to in order to get it together."

Cynthia dropped her fork. "I don't need a spa day. I need to break away," she said. "Ma, don't you ever think about your life? Like, what it would be like if you had never had me? Don't you want something more?"

Mildred bit a piece of bacon and the crumbs bounced off her copious lips. She slid the platter of bacon toward her daughter. "Help yourself," she uttered as she rose from the table. Mildred went into her bedroom and returned with a large purple Bible tucked under her arm.

"You think this is all I ever wanted? Hmmph. You don't even know the half." She pulled her chair up next to Cynthia and crossed her legs. "How old are you, Tia?"

"Ma, you know I'm thirty-three," she said, shaking her head.

"Well, that's how long I've been wrestling with what would have, could have, and should have been. You think I've always wanted to just be a nurse?" A hearty laugh snuck out, and Mildred covered her mouth. "The Lord blessed me with that job. I was able to provide for you with it, but what I wanted to do all my life is dance and sing."

Mildred pulled out a faded orange-hued photograph with bent and frayed edges. Cynthia ran her finger over the face of the barefoot girl in a gold sequined body suit with her feet in first position and her hair in a tight bun. Large doe eyes and a wide grin stared back at her.

"That's how I met your father. I met him that very night. I was performing at The Sugar Shack. I came on stage in a tear-away tuxedo. I was gorgeous. Do you think I spent my whole life in this robe?" Mildred hopped up and let her robe fall to the floor. She pranced around in her peach chemise and matching shorts.

"Girl, I was fine. I shimmied, I twirled, and I pranced up and down the stage singing. After my set some of the other performers said if I really wanted to jam, I had to hit the Blue Note, and that's where I found your father, backstage. He was playing the piano with a band called Alma that night. It was something I'd never seen or heard before—a Latin jazz band. I was enamored. Women always warn you, 'Watch out for the dude with the sax.' 'Stay away from the guy on the bass.' No one warned me about the guy on the keys. No one told me to stay clear of Kirk." Mildred looked down. "F and F. I should have known." Mildred rose, gathering the plates and scraps. "You want some coffee?"

"Sure. What's F and F?"

"F and F? Fast fingers and fast feet. We kissed. I closed my eyes, my clothes were off, and by the time I opened them he was gone. He stuck around until you were three years old then he took off. He sent me postcards from his tours and money for a while. Once that stopped reality set in. I went back to school. Of course, I wanted something else. That's why I hosted those house parties, but I also wanted something different, and that's what I got; I had you. Of course, I think about what life would be like if I never had you; every mother has. Maybe I'd still be with Kirk. Maybe I'd be famous with my own band on the road every day or maybe I'd be singing at the Jazzmobile with Jan Parker. But when you have children, you learn that your life is not your own."

Mildred brought two cups of steaming coffee to the table. She sat back down at her end and put her feet up in the empty seat between her and Cynthia. The steam wafted up and danced in front of Cynthia's face. Those words did not seem to pacify the burgeoning war inside her.

"Ma, it feels like the walls closing in on me." Cynthia wiped the tears from her eyes before they fell. "I don't want to become some kind of prude, like you shuttling back and forth between trustee meetings and Bible Study all the while masking a black and blue eye."

"Why don't you take a nap, watch some soaps, and go home tomorrow?"

Cynthia nodded with the corners of her mouth turned down in displeasure.

Completely ignoring Cynthia's increasingly despondent attitude Mildred continued speaking. "You know them boys miss you. You better get it together and go see about my grandsons. If you don't I'm going to keep telling you my war stories, *Mildred's Melodies*. That was going to be the name of my first album. Maybe now I could do a gospel album, *To God Be the Glory.*" She waved her arms as if she was painting a large canvas. "All is not lost once you realize Jesus paid the cost."

From the corner of her eye Mildred noted the time: 9:30. Today she was working the twelve to eight shift. She had plenty of time before it started, but she wanted to get a head start so she'd have some time to call the detectives and tell them Cynthia would be returning home the next day.

Mildred walked to her bedroom, humming, "No Turning Back."

"Where are you going, Ma?"

"I have some errands to run before my shift starts. I'd ask you to come, but you're in hiding. I'll see you later," Mildred said doubling back to kiss Cynthia on the head before disappearing into her room to get dressed.

Ten minutes later Mildred emerged from her room in her scrubs. She collected her purse from the coffee table, a lime green shawl from the arm of her sofa, and some change for the bus from a crystal jar on the end table. Cynthia sat at the table, winding a loose thread hanging from the tablecloth around her middle finger and her ring finger, contemplating her next move.

"Ma, I'm not hiding. I'm waiting," Cynthia said to Mildred's back as she walked out the door.

Chapter 12

Cynthia punched in the number to Dr. Chang's office. It was a few minutes after four, and she suspected she'd catch him between patients. It was the fourth day she'd been at her mother's and her mind was not equipped to focus on filing claims about broken arms and mild coughs.

The last thing she wanted to do was bail out on Dr. Chang, but if she didn't take a step back to figure out what was going on, someone would be filing a claim for her medical expenses soon. There were two other billers who worked in the office: Rita, a full-time biller who complained all the time about Cynthia working from home; and Jenna, a forty-something mom trying to make the return to the workforce since her two sons had started college. They weren't as thorough as Cynthia, but the two of them should be capable of handling the claims in her absence, she hoped.

"Chang," the doctor said in his thick Chinese accent screaming into the receiver.

"Hi, Dr. Chang. It's me, Cynthia."

"Hi, Cynthia. How are you? Is something wrong with one of the claims?"

"No. I've got a real serious problem," Cynthia announced. "I need to take the week off due to a family emergency. You've got enough money in this month's budget for Jenna to work extra hours this week if you want to stay ahead. I'm not at home right now. If you need to reach me for anything, I have my laptop. Just shoot me an e-mail and I'll respond either via e-mail or telephone."

"Can I help you in any way? Are the kids all right?" Dr. Chang asked his voice full of concern.

Cynthia laughed at her boss. Dr. Chang was good like that. Maybe it was because he was a doctor. He was aware of his employees' humanity and their frailty. As long as you communicated with him and gave him enough time to find someone to cover a shift, he didn't mind if his staff took time off. "Only you, Dr. Chang. Other bosses would lose it, but you want to help me."

"If you're no good to yourself then you're no good to me, that's my philosophy. Take all the time you need."

After checking in with Dr. Chang, Cynthia figured it was time to check in on her home. First she dialed star-six-seven to block Mildred's number before dialing the number to her home.

"Barclay residence." The squeak and formalities were definitely Keith.

She held her breath. She wanted to knock him down with her usual barrage of questions: How was school? Did he have a lot of homework? Did James get into any trouble?

Before she could release the words, Keith spoke to her.

"I know it's you. I knew you wouldn't desert me. I know you had to go. We ate breakfast this morning. I gave James Lucky Charms and I ate Lucky Charms with toast. We had school lunch today. I don't know what's for dinner 'cause Daddy's not home yet. He thinks you're going to come home. I know you won't. I was afraid this day would come. I always thought you would take me with you or at least James. You'll come back for me, won't you? I'm sure of it. I'm almost done with my homework, and James is working on his handwriting. Don't worry about dinner. Daddy will be home soon."

"Who are you talking to?" James chirped in the background.

"Call me back tomorrow, Mom," Keith whispered before hanging up the phone.

A smile spread across Cynthia's face as she returned the cordless phone to its base. Keith was taking charge and taking care of everything like a little general. She marveled at how he knew what concerned her: if they ate breakfast, homework, and he even mentioned his father. He was only twelve years old, and his relationship with his father was as shaky as a loose tooth while chewing on an apple.

It was her fault. She allowed Keith to witness their constant bickering. He'd been exposed to the intimate details of his parents' relationship, from their financial worries to his father's inability to commit to his mother. Cynthia knew it was inappropriate for Keith to hear those things, especially as he was growing older. Since she'd started attending Bible Study, she had begun to control her response to Marvin's attacks and redirect the children while these battles were being hashed out. Yet it seemed like the more she backed down and declared peace when Marvin was in one of his moods, the more antagonizing he became.

"Don't turn your back on me," he would scream if she tried to ignore him.

If she said, "This isn't the appropriate time to discuss this," he would cut her down like a tree at a sawmill.

"You only have two children in this household. You better mind them and not me," Marvin would bark at her.

The boys sat seething and breathing in these toxic fumes. Their fights, like carbon monoxide, were odorless, colorless, and seemingly tasteless but poison none-theless. The chronic exposure to their fights led to the same symptoms: depression, confusion, headaches, and poisoning of the heart. Cynthia's greatest fear was the boys would eventually grow to disrespect her and any other women with whom they had a relationship.

The disjuncture between Marvin and Keith disturbed Cynthia. Rarely did they speak to each other except during the typical male communal moments like a bad call during a football game. The longing to close the gulf was apparent in Keith's actions. All of his favorite teams— the Jets and the Knicks—were the same as Marvin's, regardless of their records and various setbacks. Cynthia blamed herself for getting between the two of them. A man should be able to talk to his son, but Keith often opted out of conversing with his father by sticking to one-word answers rather than launching into the monologues about his day he shared with his mother.

Cynthia cracked the window open and inhaled the afternoon air. Her missing status made her a prisoner of 116th Street. It also allowed her to relinquish her responsibility to her home and focus on her. Cynthia was able to get her best thinking done when she was cooking or cleaning.

After she called Keith she spent the two hours straightening up Mildred's apartment and thought it was time for a break. Marvin, however, did not agree as he used Mildred's answering machine to bust up her break time. Cynthia was in the middle of lounging on her mother's white Italian leather sofa with her feet resting on the glass coffee table when the phone rang.

Marvin's voice sounded like gravel as he pleaded for her to return home over the answering machine while the boys fought in the background for the remote control. Keith was saying something about homework and James was crying for *The Simpsons*. Marvin's sorry almost sounded sincere.

"Mildred, if Cynthia is there, please play this for her. I'm sorry for everything. We need you. I'm lost without you. I don't even know what to make them for dinner."

Just as she leaned toward the end table where her mother's telephone sat, contemplating picking it up, the answering machine cut him off. He called back citing more domestic duties that only Cynthia could take care of.

"Keith has soccer practice on Friday. I have no idea where his uniform is and James has a science project due on Friday that he hasn't started yet, and I don't have any more clean overalls." Before the machine had a chance to cut him off again, he cried out, "Mildred, if she's there, please, *please* tell her we need her."

Cynthia stood and headed to her mother's bedroom. She felt like diving into her mother's bed and hiding behind the mosquito nets. She took a seat in a wicker chair with the rounded back near her mother's oak dresser. She marveled at Mildred's exquisite taste and sense of design. Tonight Cynthia needed a place to hide, and she knew she would not be found in the jungle.

Years—three to be exact—had passed since she'd last sought the comfort of this room. She hid in the folds of her mother's comforter and drowned all her sorrows in Mildred's chocolate stash.

She rummaged through her mother's lingerie drawers in search of some chocolate to nibble on. Although the décor had changed one thing had not; Mildred still used her lingerie drawer to stash her snacks. Cynthia ripped open a bag of peanut M&Ms with her teeth.

Marvin had left those same messages on Mildred's answering machine when Cynthia had fled their happy home after catching Marvin with another woman when he was supposed to be working.

The irony of that day had never struck her until now. She was supposed to be at home working also, but a patient who had no insurance came into Dr. Chang's office to discuss his bill. Since Cynthia was the head biller, she had to come in to meet with him and create some sort of payment arrangement. When she finally took a break, she stepped out the office to catch her breath and grab a bite to eat. Strolling eastward across East Eighty-sixth to Gray's Papaya, she spotted Marvin on the corner of East Eighty-sixth Street and Lexington Avenue. There he stood holding hands with an extremely shapely, tall woman. He had moved a stray strand of her jet-black hair that disrupted her linear blunt-cut bangs. She leaned in, kissed him on the neck with one hand resting on his chest, and he cradled her.

Gentle. He was gentle with her. He held her like a bird with a broken wing.

When she got home, instead of preparing an afternoon snack, she'd packed bags for herself, Keith, and James and left a sticky note on the door:

> *Marvin, I saw you on the corner today. Don't worry, you can keep her. I'm taking the boys so the two of you can have plenty of room to roll around.*

Cynthia met the boys on the sidewalk like she normally did and took them to her mother's house.

Every day after work Marvin came to her mother's house begging for her return, for a week. He even slept in the doorway of Mildred's apartment.

How did we wind up here? How did I wind up here? Cynthia found herself staring at a shattered version of herself in the mirror over Mildred's bureau. Cynthia bit the right corner of her mouth. She could taste the words of encouragement she'd been fed. Today they felt like a belch. The sweetness was long gone.

Jesus, I just don't want to fight anymore.

Chapter 13

The rich scent of garlic greeted Mildred as she stood outside her door. The table was set, and Cynthia was hovering over a pot of pesto sauce, licking the spoon, a change from the dark corner of the couch she'd been planted in for the past three days.

"Don't you put that spoon back in the pot," Mildred scolded.

Cynthia shot her mother a glance coupled with a side smile. The muscles in her face had finally given up their protest. Mildred walked into the kitchen, keys in hand, and scanned the area. Her counter was decorated with basil leaves and black pepper, and the sink was full of dishes.

"What is all of this?" she asked.

"Dinner. You've taken care of me all week. You helped me to see this should be our last night together. We're having broiled tilapia, linguine in pesto sauce, and French-cut string beans sautéed in a garlic almond butter sauce."

Relief swelled in her at the thought that Cynthia had heeded her advice and was headed back home to her family.

"Girl, you don't know anything about cooking," she joked, leaning against her daughter's shoulder. They both laughed. Why on earth a black woman would want to cook Italian food was beyond Mildred, but every time Cynthia got in front of stove she was transformed into a world-class chef mixed with a dash of sunshine.

"Go change your clothes, Ma. The food is pretty much done. Prepare yourself for a feast."

Behind the closed door of her bedroom, Mildred rummaged through her purse in search of the detective's card. She'd decided against calling him the other day since Cynthia still seemed to be in a funk. Her head seemed to be on straight now.

"Come on, Ma, it's getting cold," Cynthia shouted from beyond the door.

Steadying her cell phone in one hand and the card in the other, Mildred replied, "Give me a minute." She punched in the number and was relieved when the phone was answered on the second ring. "Detective Laurel, please."

"This is Detective Laurel."

"Good evening, Detective Laurel. This is Ms. Hathaway, Cynthia Barclay's mother."

"Good evening, ma'am. I'm so glad you called. My partner was ready to knock on your door this evening. Is Cynthia still at your house?"

"Yes, but she just announced that she is ready to go. She'll probably be gone as early as tomorrow morning."

"Thank you so much for your help, Ms. Hathaway. I wish all of our missing persons cases ended like this."

Mildred waved her hand in the air as if the detective stood right in front of her. "No problem, Detective. I also want to thank you. Have a good night."

"There's just one more thing that I need from you, Ms. Hathaway."

"Anything. Do you need me to come down to the station and fill out some kind of report or something?"

"No, ma'am. Don't worry about that. We take care of all the paperwork. Ma'am, I want you to hold onto my card. You expressed Mr. Barclay has some violent tendencies. I want you to keep my card in case he doesn't welcome her home so easily or any problems arise between them later on. Please, please don't hesitate to give me or my partner a call."

Cynthia rapped softly on the door. "Your food is getting cold."

"I'm coming. Thank you, Detective. I've got to go. Good night," she replied without even acknowledging his concern. She placed the phone and the business card on top of her bureau.

Donning a soft blue floral house dress, Mildred stood in front of the mirror and considered her daughter's plight. Sympathy ate at her heart. She understood the difficulty of maintaining a relationship, maintaining your sanity with a man who was completely unstable, and raising children. The relationship Mildred shared with Kirk, Cynthia's father, was beleaguered by some of the same demons that plagued Cynthia and Marvin's: alcohol and rage tempered with unbridled lust. Last she heard Kirk had made it big in the UK. For Kirk, big was a gig that lasted more than a week and offered him a plethora of women for him to choose from.

Praise be to God He delivered me.

The rich aroma of Cynthia's garlic butter sauce called her back to reality. With her eyes lifted to the ceiling, Mildred whispered, "Even to a thousand generations, please, Lord, guard the fruit of my womb," before walking out the room.

Mildred took her place at the table. Mildred and Cynthia sat across from each other, their eyes casting reflections of each woman's pain.

"I know you don't want to talk about what happened, but I'm glad to see you're feeling better," Mildred said between forkfuls of linguine. Cynthia's gourmet meal was a sure sign all was well.

"I'm not really feeling better, but after talking to you this morning I know what I have to do now," Cynthia said firmly.

"Praise the Lord!" Mildred exclaimed. "God is good, isn't He? He can turn any gray sky blue."

"Why don't you tell me some more of your stories from the Blue Note or sing one of your songs from your unreleased album," Cynthia said, chuckling.

A guttural laugh escaped from Mildred. "You serious, girl?"

Cynthia nodded.

Mildred stood, using her knuckles to push off the glass dinette table, tapping her foot on the floor. "'He don't love me no more. He don't love me no more, so I'm headed for the door before I don't love me no more,'" she sang in a throaty alto unaware of her prophetic lyrics.

Chapter 14

The ten o'clock nightly news had just begun, and Mildred was already snoring on the couch. Cynthia watched her for a moment then kissed her lightly on the forehead and placed her left arm on her chest. She pulled her pink hood over her head, creeping across the threshold of Mildred's apartment and out the door. Tiny droplets of rain kissed her shoulders on her way to the subway.

Cynthia jumped on the A train headed downtown to the Port Authority. Clutching her duffel bag, she gazed at an ad inviting New Yorkers on a one-day getaway and transposed herself into it. A grin surfaced as she imagined herself a head chef at a gourmet restaurant exhausted from bending over pots tasting sauces, yelling over the hustle and bustle of her busy kitchen, far from the angry shouts and stinging slaps of Marvin.

When she reached the Port Authority she had no real destination in mind. All she wanted was to get on the first bus leaving with an available seat. The slick hair of the girl behind the counter sent the dull light bouncing off her head. The combination of her gum cracking and the clacking of her acrylic nails on her keyboard put Cynthia into a daze.

"Cash or credit? Mizz, you paying cash or credit?"

Cynthia dug into her pocket and pulled out crumpled bills. She straightened them out on the countertop before handing them to the girl behind the counter. She snatched her ticket and ran through the beige and orange terminal to catch the eleven o'clock bus to Richmond, Virginia.

There was a small line at the gate: a young girl clutching a baby wrapped in a yellow blanket, an old man and woman standing arm and arm, and a middle-aged man. None of them seemed to notice Cynthia as she eased into the line. She stood behind the lady with the baby.

Father, please forgive me. I'm not waiting for anyone to tell me how to live my life. Her legs shook. *Please take care of my babies. I don't know what I'm doing, Lord, but I need to get out of this. I have to get away from here. Just make a way for me and watch over my boys for me until I can come back for them.*

Tears rolled down her cheeks in unison with her silent prayer. The guilt of leaving behind her sons was heavy on her shoulders. The confusion in her spirit and her inability to provide for them at this very moment outweighed her guilt and urged to get on that bus. Marvin wasn't in the running for father of the year; however, right now he could offer the boys some stability and provide for them.

The ticket agent opened the door, and the line began to move. The wind was stiff and bone chilling. She hesitated before stepping out the door to head to the bus, the wind in the terminal garage pushing her out. She chucked her bag under the bus and took a seat near the driver.

She closed her eyes as Midtown rolled past her. Sleep seized her, taking her to her sons. They stood in the middle of their bedroom floor clutching each other. Marvin stood in the living room screaming her name. She shook in her chair squeezing the armrest until her palms were sore.

The smell of grease, the crunch of fried chicken, and the piercing cry of a suckling baby asking for his mother's milk woke her. Through one eye she watched as the bus turned the corner into the parking lot of the Main Street bus station. She stood and stretched, staring at the rising sun pushing back the navy blue blanket that veiled the Richmond sky and exposed its soft periwinkle sun.

She stumbled off the bus, her legs weak from sitting so long. The light breeze caused her to shiver and the hairs on her arms to stand up. She inhaled, the taste of dawn tickling her tongue. She looked over her shoulder at the baby smiling at her, his eyes twinkling in the sunlight. They exchanged smiles. She knew the feeling that his bright expression conveyed—her life awaited her. She scooped her bag from beneath the bus and bounced into the depot.

Every person she passed on the way to the information booth greeted her. She was still a bit too groggy to deliver anything more than a grimace. She acknowledged them with a simple hello and a nod. A young man with jade green eyes sat at the information desk drumming on the counter.

"Good morning, ma'am. What can I do for you?" the young man asked.

"I just arrived, and I'm looking for a place to stay," Cynthia said humbly.

"Well, there's a Holiday Inn just around the corner."

"Actually, I was hoping for something a little smaller, a bit more intimate. Like a bed and breakfast."

"A bed and breakfast? Those can be pretty pricey," he said, looking Cynthia up and down. "I do know of a quiet boardinghouse that aspires to be a bed and breakfast. Would that work for you?"

Cynthia nodded at him, and squinted at his name tag. "That will do, Jared."

"It's a real nice place over there in Church Hill. You ought to take a cab there. Just tell him you want to go to Miss Ruthie's place and he'll know where to go. I don't think she's opened her doors just yet, but you're welcome to try."

"Thank you."

"No problem, ma'am," he said, winking at her. He handed her a tourist map of the city.

Cynthia took a seat on an orange plastic bench and studied the map of the city, searching for the residential and shopping areas. She needed to figure out what she was really doing there, buy some clothes, and find a more permanent place to rest her head before the money on her prepaid card ran out. Her prepaid MasterCard was the one secret she'd kept from Marvin. Cynthia didn't know that much about finances; neither did Marvin. After having Con Edison turn their lights off one too many times Cynthia started loading money on to a prepaid card. Her own diligence shocked her when within four years of opening the card she'd managed to put away $6,000.

Returning her attention to the map she laughed out loud when she realized why Jared had winked at her; in the course of their short exchange he'd circled his home on the map and wrote his phone number.

It was 6:45 in the morning and the day awaited her. Cynthia rose, ambled to the bathroom and washed her face. She slapped herself for not purchasing a toothbrush or toothpaste at a rest stop. Her stomach roared. She placed her hand over her belly, attempting to silence it. She rushed out of the bus station and hailed a cab that was idling on the corner. Her stomach shouted at her again, and she jumped in, slamming the door.

"Miss Ruthie's please. The guy in the depot said you'd know where to go."

"I sure do, ma'am," the cabdriver said, tipping the brim of a ratty old burgundy and white snapback cap. He rolled down the windows.

The early morning breeze whispered, "Hello," welcoming her to Richmond.

Cynthia sucked in the air, the scent of the crisp, fresh-cut grass and the morning dew filling her nostrils. "So this is what freedom smells like," she said, yawning.

The cab zipped past rows of houses and some familiar sights like McDonald's and Taco Bell. American flags hung from porches and were erected in the center of the lawns of Church Hill. The homes were traditional colonial models juxtaposed against cemented sidewalks and a couple of morning joggers.

A hand-painted sign in the middle of the yard of green grass greeted Cynthia, announcing she'd reached her destination: MISS RUTHIE'S FOR TRAVELERS, REGULARS, AND EVERYONE IN BETWEEN. Cynthia swallowed in the home with its long wooden porch and two red doors at each end. From what she could tell, the two-story home probably lodged about five to ten people at a time. The grass was trimmed low and crunched under her feet. The steps creaked as she approached the open door. She rapped lightly on the screen.

An old woman with big tortoise-rimmed frames resting on top of a neat French braid opened the door.

"Welcome, when you're at Ruthie's you're at home," she said, opening the screen door and beckoning Cynthia to come in. "You're right on time for the early bird breakfast special."

"Good morning. I'm looking for Miss Ruthie."

"Excuse me, where are my manners? Good morning. Follow me right this way to the dining room."

"No, thank you, ma'am. All I'd like to do is see someone about checking into a room."

The old woman smiled and cuffed her arm around Cynthia's, leading her to the dining room. "You from New York? Must be 'cause you city folk are always in a rush. Now lissen here, girl, we don't conduct business on an empty stomach. You might as well sit down and have some grits and coffee. Shoot, we even got cappuccino, and you know you city folks love some cappuccino. Come on now. You know the mind don't function right when your belly ain't full."

The old woman's smile and gentle urgings reminded Cynthia of her mother. All she needed to do was add a Bible verse or hum a hymn and Cynthia would really be feeling at home.

"What if—"

"Don't worry yourself, girl," the old woman cooed "Tomorrow has enough evil in it; let's deal with the here and now. Even if we don't get you into a room, you can still break bread with us on the house. How does that sound?" asked the old woman with her hand resting on gold doorknobs.

Cynthia could hear the clanging of the silverware and the oohs and ahhs of the boarders on the other side of the door. She smelled the fresh-baked biscuits and skillet-fried bacon. Her stomach began to holler at her. Before Cynthia could mouth the word yes, the door slid open, unveiling a delightful smorgasbord of breakfast: cheese grits, flaky biscuits, scrambled eggs, eggs Benedict, tarts draped in jam, and bacon and sausage links huddled together on a silver tray, living in harmony before being devoured. A pitcher of fresh-squeezed orange juice and apple juice sat in the center of everything, and a pot of coffee circulated among the people seated at the table. A man with a strong gray moustache, a young couple with their baby, one woman with a her cheeks full of blush that resembled crushed raspberries, and two gentlemen who were arguing about last night's game of Texas hold 'em that went awry rounded out the early bird breakfast crew.

"Ay, Walter, do me a favor and take this here young lady's bag and put it by the checkout for me, honey," the old woman said to the man with the gray moustache.

"Give me a minute, Ruthie."

"Walter!" Miss Ruthie exclaimed.

Walter jumped up, smoothing his moustache. Cynthia looked at Miss Ruthie and laughed.

"I feel so foolish. You're Miss Ruthie. Why didn't you stop me sooner?"

"'Cause you city folks are so persistent, you would have insisted I give you a room straight away," Miss Ruthie replied. "We would have had an argument and started off on the wrong foot 'cause I don't take no mess in this here house. Besides, it ain't wise to do business on an empty stomach. Ain't no need in feeling foolish. It would be foolish for you to miss this breakfast. Sit down and help yourself. Whatever demon you running from can resume chasing you 'round about noon."

Cynthia took the empty seat next to the gentlemen arguing about poker. She hoped her wounds weren't as visible to other guests as they had been to Miss Ruthie. Cynthia loaded up on bacon, eggs, and the homemade biscuits.

After breakfast Miss Ruthie checked Cynthia in and escorted her to her room on the second floor.

"It's pretty small," Miss Ruthie stated as she opened the door to the room.

The sunlight cast a shadow on the wooden floor, the breeze ushering the carnation-colored curtains into the room.

"But it will do. Miss Ruthie, do you know where I should go if I'm looking for a more permanent place to live?" Cynthia inquired.

"You thinking about moving down here?"

Cynthia sat on the foot of the bed and wound the loose thread from the cover around her fingertip. "Yes."

"Do you have any children?" Both of their eyes fastened on the gold band and diamond ring on her left hand.

"Well, do you? I can see that you're married. You got any kids?"

"I'm going to get them when I get everything settled," Cynthia said lowering her head to hide her shame.

"We have a phone downstairs if you want to call them. I'll ask around, see if anyone knows where you can find an apartment. Actually, there's a young fellow at the bus depot."

"Jared?"

"You city girls sure are fast." Miss Ruthie laughed.

Blushing, Cynthia replied to Miss Ruthie's insinuation, "I met him this morning."

"Yes, he knows his way around Richmond quite well and could probably help you out. He's into real estate. He's planning on becoming some kinda tycoon. Why don't you take a nap, and I'll call the bus depot for you? You want him to come by tomorrow?"

She sucked the inside of her cheek as she thought of her boys swallowing spit, hungry, afraid, and alone because she'd left them. A pool of tears filled her eyes. "I'd rather not waste any time."

Ruthie planted her wrinkled hand on Cynthia's drooping shoulder. "I don't know what you're running from, I don't know who you're running to, but I do know that He," she said, pointing to the ceiling, "wouldn't give you more than you can bear."

"Miss Ruthie, at this point, I'm not even sure if He cares. Would you just phone the bus depot for me? Please excuse me. I need to rest."

Cynthia glared at Miss Ruthie's back as she walked out. *You don't know me. You don't know what I can bear.*

Chapter 15

Though it was only seven a.m., the precinct was full of commotion. Some hookers were handcuffed to a bench. One of them called out to Marvin. "Aye, daddy, why don't you get me outta here and I'll take care of you," she said, licking her lips. She had on pink lipstick that made her lips look like fluffy cotton candy. She crossed and uncrossed her legs several times, inviting Marvin to sample her wares. Marvin tried to fight the temptation, but she was smack in the middle of his line of vision. She wasn't half bad for a hooker, he thought, staring at her fishnet stockings and plastic platform pumps. He missed the feel of a woman, the scent of a woman. He missed his woman.

"Hey, buddy, can I help you?" the desk sergeant shouted at Marvin over the raucous voices of a young couple shouting obscenities at the officers bringing them in.

"Good morning. I'm here to see Detective Laurel."

"Concerning what?"

"My wife has been missing for five days now, and I'd like to know if anyone is actually looking for her. I've got two little boys, and I have no idea what I'm supposed to do for them. Neither of them will speak to me. I forgot to make them lunch to take to school this morning, and—"

Before Marvin completely broke down, the desk sergeant cut him off. "Sir, let me page Detective Laurel. You can have a seat on that bench right there." The sergeant pointed to a bench that formed a triangle around a column in the middle of the floor. The only empty space was directly across from where the hookers sat. The one in the fishnet stockings blew kisses to Marvin while he waited. As he stared at her puckered lips, all he could see was Cynthia's face.

"Good morning, Mr. Barclay," Detective Laurel said a few minutes later, smiling at Marvin.

"Are you smiling at me because you have some information on my wife or because you're happy to see me?"

"No, I'm surprised to see you. What can I do for you, Mr. Barclay?"

Marvin stood and looked Detective Laurel square in the eye. "You can find my wife instead of walking around smiling like you're a contestant in a beauty pageant. She's been gone for five days now, and I haven't heard anything on the news about her, I don't see any flyers attached to the streetlights, I didn't read anything in the newspaper this morning." Marvin stepped closer to Detective Laurel. "What's going on?"

"Mr. Barclay, I'm going to have to ask you to calm down." Detective Laurel held his hand up to Marvin's chest. "I may be wearing a suit, but I'm still an officer of the law." Marvin took two steps back. "Your wife's case has been closed."

"Closed? Is this because she's black? If she was some blond chick from Long Island the feds would be looking for her. Can you guys actually close the case after five days? I can't believe this. I'm going to call channel eleven back," he said, digging in his back pocket for his cell phone.

"As we speak, your wife should be on her way home, if she's not there already."

"You found her?" Marvin asked standing on the tips of his toes. He had to restrain himself from jumping up and down.

"I spoke to her mother last night, and she assured me Mrs. Barclay would be returning home," Detective Laurel said.

"Her mother? She's been staying at her mother's all of this time?"

"Mr. Barclay, I cannot disclose any information we discovered during the course of the investigation. What I can tell you is that she is safe and on her way home."

Marvin balled his hands into fists and clenched his teeth. "Wait 'til I get a hold of her. Thank you, Detective," he said abruptly and headed toward the exit.

"Mr. Barclay." Detective Laurel grabbed Marvin by the arm. "I recommend you keep your cool and welcome her home with open arms."

Marvin waved his hands in the air, brushing off Detective Laurel's last statement. He was as mad as the devil. He stormed out of the police station, bumping into people on the street as he rushed to the corner. He knocked over a woman pushing a toddler in a lime green umbrella stroller as he hustled to Eighth Avenue to flag down a cab. It took five minutes for a cab to stop for Marvin.

"One-sixteenth and Eighth," Marvin ordered. He threw his seven dollars through the partition to indicate he was not in the talking mood. He stared out the window and drummed his fingers on the leather seat while the cab zoomed through Harlem. Everything looked like a blur to Marvin. A soft breeze snuck in the cab. The leaves on the trees shook, but the only thing Marvin could see clearly were his hands wrapped around Cynthia's tender neck. His thumb pressed against her jugular as her eyes bulged out of her head while she clawed at his hands trying to pry them from her neck.

He was just two blocks away from Mildred's when a traffic jam arose. Con Edison trucks were blocking one lane of traffic. Marvin sprang from the back seat of the cab, leaving the door open behind him. He leaped up the stairs two at a time and leaned on Mildred's door, pounding on it.

"Open the door, Mildred. I know she's in there. Open the door."

"I'm Going Up Yonder" blared from the stereo, drowning out his continuous pounding.

He kicked the door. "Open the door!" He kicked again. "Open the door!"

One of Mildred's neighbors cracked her door open. Her diaper-clad toddler slipped through the crack. His bare feet slapped the linoleum floor. She ran after him cooing, "Come back here, li'l man. Come back here."

"You better watch that baby instead of me," Marvin instructed the young mother when he noticed her staring at him. Then he returned to kicking on Mildred's door.

Mildred unlocked the door but kept the chain on. Through the crack she peeked out. Drops of sweat the size of grains of rice ran down both sides of Marvin's face and lined his forehead. His mouth hung agape as he panted to catch his breath.

"Marvin, you must have lost your mind, banging on my door like that. Are you trying to get me put out?"

"Mildred, the two of y'all better stop playing with me. Where's Cynthia?"

"She's not here."

Marvin leaned on the door to put some pressure on Mildred to confess. "You're lying. I spoke to the detective, and I know she's been staying here. Cynthia! Cynthia!" Marvin stood on his tippy toes, bobbing his head, making every effort he could to peer into the apartment over Mildred's head.

"Marvin, she's not here. She left yesterday," Mildred insisted in a panic.

Marvin smiled at Mildred then laughed. He took a few steps back and charged into Mildred's door. It shook in her hand and the chain tightened.

"Marvin." He stepped back preparing to charge her door again. "What are you doing?" Marvin dropped his right shoulder low, tucked his hand in and rammed his body into the door for a second time. "Stop this in the name of Jesus."

"Stop! I'm not going to stop until your door falls off the hinges, then I'm going to drag her out by the hair. If she wants to come and stay with you that's fine, but she's going to come and get these kids and take care of her responsibilities," he hollered.

"You will stop in the name of Jesus. I already told you she's gone. She left last night."

"You're lying."

Another one of Mildred's neighbors opened his door. "Sister Mildred, are you all right in there?" he called out, twisting his neck to get a glimpse of her through the crack in her door.

"I'm fine, Richard. Don't worry about me," Mildred said calmly.

"Are you sure? Do you want me to call the police?"

"Beat it, church boy. Mind your business. This is a family matter," Marvin interrupted.

Backing up, Marvin prepared his body once more for another collision bucking up like a ram prepared to battle an enemy. Mildred rapidly took the chain off. Marvin came barreling through and crashed right into her dinette set, shattering the glass table top and knocking over her chairs.

Marvin looked up at Mildred as he leaned on one of the legs of the table. He pushed himself up to a standing position.

"You lucky I didn't call the cops on you." Mildred wagged her finger at Marvin. "Cynthia left yesterday."

"Cynthia. Cynthia." Marvin shouted her name looking around in disbelief.

"Marvin, quit with all that racket. She's not here!"

"Yeah, right," he said, walking past her to the living room. "When I came here on Tuesday she wasn't here, and now you're telling me she was here but she left yesterday. What does the Good Book say about telling lies? If she wants to extend her vacation, she can. It can be forever. I'm ready for a divorce. Divorce!" he shouted again, turning toward the bedroom.

Mildred jumped in front of him and put her hand up. "You're not rifling through this place again. I already told you she's not here."

"Well, she certainly didn't come home yesterday, and I'm not leaving until she comes out." Marvin walked to the dinette set, snatched one of Mildred's black chairs, and collapsed into it. Mildred walked to her room and came out with her purse and cell phone. Marvin was seated with his legs cocked open, with his left hand cradling his right hand which was balled into a fist. The broken glass crunched under his feet as his leg shook.

"Get up, Marvin. Come on. Let's go."

"Are you finally going to get my wife?" Marvin asked breathing in and out deeply. This whole situation was pushing him beyond his limits. He needed to destroy something or drink something.

"No. We're going to the police station," Mildred charged. "She's really missing. She told me she was ready to leave and when I woke up this morning she was gone. She must've left here last night."

Marvin shrank back in the chair and then stood up.

"Come on," she said, grabbing her faux fur coat from the closet near the door.

Marvin walked down the steps slowly with Mildred and ran off when they reached the street.

The choir was rehearsing when Marvin stormed through the doors of Mount Carmel Community Church. With each step, the floor shook. "I need to see the pastor." His voice couldn't penetrate the soloist's rendition of "His Eye Is On the Sparrow" or the drone of the organ. He shouted until he reached the pulpit and tapped the choir director on his shoulder. "Is the pastor in?"

"Yes, he is. Is there something I could help you with, sir?" the choir director asked.

"Yeah, you can help me by letting me see the pastor," Marvin demanded, his bloodshot eyes bulging out of his head.

"He's in his office." The choir director nodded toward a flight of steps to the right of the pulpit. "Brother, umm?"

"I'm not your brotha." Marvin brushed past him, heading to the steps.

The choir director ran after him, grabbing Marvin by the sleeve. "You can't go down there."

Marvin responded with wild swings. Pastor David emerged from the staircase in the midst of the organist struggling to pull Marvin off the choir director. "Brother Johnson, Brother Terry that will be enough. Our battle is not with flesh and blood, is it?"

Marvin stopped swinging at the sound of Pastor David's voice. His whole body heaved as he stood over the choir director.

"Let this be a lesson learned to all of you. Give no place to the devil. How could one man walk in here and stop an entire rehearsal?" Pastor David asked holding up one finger.

"But, Pastor, I was trying to protect you," cried the choir director.

"My Heavenly Father will protect me. I have on my helmet of salvation, my loins are girt with the truth that is the gospel of Jesus Christ, the breastplate of righteousness, my feet shod with the preparation of the gospel of peace, and I have my shield of faith to quench the fiery darts of the wicked."

"But, Pastor—" Brother Terry cried, coming to his feet.

"And where is your sword?" Pastor David asked, patting the Bible he held tucked under his arm. "How could you even think about going into a battle without the Word of God? When the devil tempted Jesus, every word Jesus used to answer him came from the Word of God. Let this be a lesson to all of you."

Pastor David turned to face the choir and continued his impromptu sermon. "You can't beat the devil if you're using your own weaponry. Everything we do must be done the Lord's way or we will fail.

"My office is downstairs," he said to Marvin. Pastor David turned and headed to the staircase that led to his office. Marvin followed close on his heels.

As soon as Marvin began walking, a woman in the choir cried out, "Bless him, Lord. Bless him, Lord."

They walked down the steps in silence, ducking their heads as they crossed the threshold that led directly from the staircase straight into Pastor David's office. Marvin inspected the room. Nothing in there looked like the old Lawrence David he knew. Bible scriptures written in calligraphy hung on the wall, photos from the pastor's anniversary dinner decorated the bookshelves. Two plush beige chairs were in front of the desk. Marvin dragged his fingers across the oak desk and rubbed the placard that read PASTOR LAWRENCE DAVID.

"If you're the real deal, why you ain't got a door?" Marvin wondered aloud.

"Jesus is the door, and I have entered in. There was nothing that stood in front of Jesus and his disciples. He did not have a door, stanchions, or barricades to keep people away. He was and still is accessible to anyone. If I am His minister leading people to Him then there shouldn't be anything standing in their way. Have a seat," Pastor David said.

"I didn't come here to be ministered to. I came here for my wife. Where is she?"

"I don't know." Pastor David stated very matter-of-factly.

"Don't give me that crap. She's been here every day since she came to this church, and now you want to tell me you don't know. You've been seeing her more than I have."

"Then maybe you ought to come too, if you want to spend time with her. A family that prays together stays together."

The ceiling vibrated as the choir began rehearsing again. Marvin could hear "Oh, Search Me, Lord."

"Look." Marvin sighed. "I'm going to be honest with you, cuz. We go way back. I'm scared. She's left before, but she's never been gone this long. What if she doesn't come back?"

"The Lord knows what we desire. Maybe He's given you what you desired most. He's taken her and removed her."

"You don't know what I desire," Marvin growled.

"You're right. I don't know," Pastor David said folding his hands. "I can only go by what I see, and based on the way you treat her, I see a man who doesn't want a wife. Thus, she's been removed."

"If you know where she is, you better tell me, man." Marvin reached across the desk and grabbed Pastor David by his shirt.

"Touch not my anointed and do my prophet no harm," Pastor David said.

Marvin clutched his shirt tighter. Grinding his teeth as he stared in Pastor David's eyes in search of the fear that his wild rampages would usually elicit, nothing but determination radiated from Pastor David's eyes.

"'He that toucheth him hath touched the apple of mine eye.'"

Marvin was moved by the words of the scripture, although he didn't know where they could be found. He released Pastor David and plopped into one of the chairs in front of his desk. Pastor David sat down in his leather recliner, and they both stared at each other.

Pastor David's eyes became large saucers as he stared at Marvin who sat up at attention as Pastor David began to speak again.

"Marvin, you may have come here for Cynthia, but what you need to find is salvation. Choose life and not death, brother, or else everything you have will be taken. I see you in a dry and thirsty land, and what you need is a sip of living water."

Marvin rose. "If you're not going to tell me where she is, then say that instead of wasting my time with all of this Jesus crap."

"I haven't wasted your time. You have wasted your time"—Pastor David pointed at Marvin—"with the devil, Marvin. Harden not your heart. The Lord is trying to tell you something. Right now." Pastor David tapped on the top of his desk. "The Lord showed me a vision of you in a desert canyon wrapped in layers of soft black bandages that blew in the wind. You were surrounded by Cynthia and the boys, but with every step that you took toward the edge of the canyon, one of them disappeared; first Cynthia, then Keith, then James. By the time you reached the edge, you stood there alone, but on the other side of the canyon, Marvin, you and your family were full of life, vibrant, seated on the desert floor as I preached to them."

"Well, I don't want to hear about your visions." Marvin exhaled hard. "The only thing I want to hear about is where my wife is. Can you tell me that?"

Pastor David humbly shook his head no.

"Then I'm out," Marvin announced, turning his back on Pastor David as swiftly as possible.

"Marvin."

Marvin looked over his should midstride.

"You're going to lose everything if you continue living this way."

Chapter 16

There was a sense of peace that radiated from her face, and she spoke in a soft whisper, but the shaking of her hands gave away her heart. Mildred prayed in her heart standing before the desk sergeant.

Detective Grayson was the first to greet her. "Hello, Ms. Hathaway. What can I do for you?"

"Please find my baby. I'll tell you anything you want to know. I know I wasn't very cooperative before, but I'll tell you anything," Mildred said desperately.

"Follow me." Detective Grayson led Mildred to an interview room in the back of the precinct. "Ms. Hathaway, please have a seat. I'm going to get Detective Laurel. Do you want some coffee?"

"Please," she begged, grabbing Detective Grayson's arm, "forgive my folly. I was proud and boastful, but I don't know anything more than you. I'll speak to anyone, including you. Please, just help me find out what happened to my baby." Mildred stuffed a small photograph with wrinkled edges into the palm of Detective Grayson's hand.

The faded sienna photograph was of a slim woman with jet-black hair in two plaits draped over her shoulders, a young Mildred, holding an infant swaddled in blankets—Cynthia.

For a moment, Mildred fought back tears. She didn't want to cry, especially in front of Detective Grayson, recalling how she'd snubbed her the first time the detective had shown up at her job insisting on speaking with her daughter. Now Mildred wished she had let Detective Grayson in. Now she wished more than ever that she'd done a better job protecting her baby.

Detective Grayson clenched her teeth and made a weak attempt to sound enthused about helping Mildred. "Ms. Hathaway, I want to help you, but it's my understanding you told my partner you convinced Cynthia to return home, so we closed the case."

"I thought she was going home. She said she was going home last night, but this morning Marvin showed up at my house pounding on my door." Tears fell from her face with every word. "He said she never came home."

"Ma'am, are you sure she said she was going back home?"

"Yes."

"I want you to think about this very carefully," Detective Grayson said slowly. "What were her exact words to you? Did she say she was going home, ma'am? We see this sometimes with women in abusive relationships. They can't take the abuse, so they leave. They're unable to get a divorce so they break away."

Mildred followed Detective Grayson to her leg that was shaking like a jackhammer. Mildred placed her hand on her leg to stop it from shaking. "She didn't run away," Mildred began defending her daughter. There was no way Cynthia would do what Detective Grayson was accusing her of. "She wouldn't leave those boys. She couldn't leave those boys. She loved them. She was learning to persevere through her trials not run away from them."

"Where was she learning this?"

"At her church, Mount Carmel."

"Is it possible she went there after leaving your house?"

"Anything is possible, but I think something happened to her." Mildred paused to wipe the sweat from her brow with the back of her hand then continued. "When Marvin came to my house, he knew she had been there. I didn't tell him that. You told him that. You led him to her."

"Where is your son-in-law now?"

"I don't know."

"Why didn't he come here with you, Ms. Hathaway?"

"I don't know. He took off running when I said let's go to the police station." Her face wrinkled as a terrible cry escaped from her mouth. "I . . . I think he done something to her. He's crazy, Detective Grayson, he's crazy. He came in screaming and banging on my door this morning. When I told him she was gone, he just ran off." She stood shaking her finger at Detective Grayson.

Mildred straightened her cotton-candy pink button blouse and smoothed her collar. She rubbed her sweaty palms on her pants leg and gripped her handbag tightly in an attempt to compose herself. She mumbled a verse from Ecclesiastes under her breath, "'Do not let your mouth cause your flesh to sin,'" before raising her eyes to face Detective Grayson.

"I did not come here to cast blame on anyone or point fingers. That's the devil's job. Nor did I come here to waste time, which is what we're doing," Mildred said, glancing at her gold-plated watch. "My daughter is missing. I would like for you to reinvestigate the case, and I believe your prime suspect is trolling the streets of Harlem as we speak."

Mildred did not want to believe Cynthia had walked out on her family, even though it certainly appeared that way. She called her job and told them she was taking the night off. She walked home from the precinct looking for clues her daughter might have left behind on the sidewalk: a piece of paper, anything that said Cynthia was here.

When she reached the inside of her apartment, her purse fell to the floor and she fell to her knees.

Chapter 17

Jared's aptitude for real estate was definitely greater than his fashion sense. He came to pick up Cynthia that afternoon in plaid shorts and a mustard-colored polo shirt that was a bit too snug. Cynthia doubted she should trust his judgment based on his appearance, but when she considered how far her own flawed judgment had gotten her—emotionally and physically abused for the last ten years of her marriage—it was time to listen to someone else's advice. The temperature had risen to a comfortable seventy-one degrees, so Cynthia ditched her sweatshirt for a crisp white T-shirt and a pair of boot-cut light blue jeans.

"I know a great building on Riverside Drive that you'll love. You're going to think you're back in the city."

Cynthia looked at Jared with one raised eyebrow. It was impossible for her to hide her distrust.

"Listen, I'm not that interested in you. Miss Ruthie told me you're married, so don't worry. I'm not going to pull any funny business. Hop in"—Jared opened the passenger side door for Cynthia—"so we can hurry up. It's quite a ways from here. You're going to need a car, too. You do know that, right?"

"I need a lot of things," Cynthia said stepping into the car. "Jared, can we just focus on one issue at a time? What makes this place so special?"

"You'll see."

Jared was right; 2020 Riverside Drive was where she wanted to be. Miss Ruthie was right; Jared would be a tycoon of some sort soon enough. He used his connection with the building manager to get Cynthia in the building with no background check. She did have to put up three months' rent in advance. Between the swimming pool, wall-to-wall carpet, and deck, it only took a moment for the money and keys to change hands. Now Cynthia stood in front of her new apartment door. She stroked the smooth beige metal door, thrust her key into the lock, but hesitated before turning the key.

Suddenly it struck her: she'd never lived alone in her life.

Before shacking up with Marvin, she very briefly shared an apartment with two of her friends from high school who were attending the same college. She spent most of the time locked in her bedroom. Although her high school chums were supposed to be pre-med, it seemed like they were studying pharmacology, and they spent a lot of time sampling the drugs. They threw wild parties that rivaled Mardi Gras, which Cynthia enjoyed for the most part, but when they lasted more than a day, it left Cynthia repulsed by the smell of stale sweat, liquor, and the lingering aroma of whatever narcotics had fueled their bacchanal.

When she'd had enough she packed her things and trekked back to her mother's apartment in Harlem. She brushed aside the memory of those wild and hazy days. Now she was taking the plunge into a realm she'd never been in before. Cynthia turned the lock and pushed the heavy door open. A drab and dingy olive green rug welcomed her to her new pad. Cynthia made a mental note to change that rug, reasoning she could not look at it forever. Cynthia walked straight ahead to the patio doors. With her face and fingers pressed against the glass, she watched the James River roll. Cynthia slid the door open a tiny bit and slinked through the crack.

She planted herself in the plastic chair the former tenants left behind. Cynthia rested her feet squarely in the center of the round glass table with black legs, another throwback from the prior tenants. The quiet calmed her.

January in Richmond seemed much more luscious. She sucked in the sweet Richmond air. Cynthia had never felt this kind of peace.

She wrestled with her mind to keep it focused on her future hope. Again the voice of Pastor David and the Word confronted her: "Your hope should be built on nothing less than Jesus Christ and His righteousness."

Shaking her head at the sky, she proceeded to pick a fight with God. "Jesus, I was depending on you to bring me out, but it seemed like you weren't thinking about me. That may be contrary to everything that everyone says you are, but you're going to have to show me a little something more."

Cynthia waited for God's judgment to fall on her. She waited for the river to flood or a random object hidden in the huge, soft tufts of clouds that streamed past her to drop out of the sky. Nothing happened, furthering the notion in her mind that she was the last person on the Lord's to-do list.

The sun setting over the river morphed the blue sky into a wondrous fusion of magenta and turquoise. It seemed as if the cotton-candy sky was smiling at her, so she smiled back. Cynthia inched her way from the table to the banister captivated by the river. The light swirl of the water sounded like the river was serenading her. She leaned over the banister to hear the cryptic message clearer; then she realized it wasn't the river she heard whispering to her. It was water running in her bathroom. The sound escaped from the cracked bathroom window adjacent to the balcony.

Cynthia left her bags on the deck and whispered a prayer on her way to the bathroom: "Jesus, forget all that nonsense I was just talking out there. Please don't let there be some crazy person who refuses to vacate the premises in the bathroom with a gun getting ready to commit suicide. That's the last thing I need right now."

A crazy renter with a gun wasn't inside the bathroom; a bare-chested man brushing his teeth over the sink giving her the side-eye mid-brush was waiting on the other side of the door. Cynthia closed the door then opened it again. He smiled at her in the mirror, spit in the sink, and turned to face her.

"Hi, I'm Cheo. I knew this apartment came with a lot of amenities; however, Mr. Clarke never mentioned a beautiful woman would be here to greet me."

His Sugar Daddy complexion, lean body, taut torso, and kind words warmed her skin enough to cause her to blush. "I'm sorry," she said, clearing her throat, "there must be some kind of mix-up. I thought this was apartment sixty-three."

"It is, ma'am."

"Hi, I'm Cynthia . . . Cynthia Hathaway," she said, extending her hand to shake his. "Mr. Clarke told me I could move in today. I'm sooo sorry, I guess he figured you would have been out by now."

"Gone? Whatchu talking about, Willis?" Cheo said, scrunching up his thick black eyebrows. "I just arrived. I moved in this morning."

"What? I'm supposed to move in here today." Cynthia pirouetted and went off stomping down the hall. "That idiot."

"Hey, calm down." Cheo placed his warm palm on her bare shoulder. "Let me go grab a shirt, and we'll head down to the office together to straighten it out."

Cynthia paused, staring at his smooth golden brown skin. He made her want to fling open every window in the apartment and scream; she'd never felt drawn to a man besides Marvin like this before.

"Okay?" he asked, looking down at her using his doe-shaped eyes to question her. "Or we can take care of this New York style, Cynthia?"

"No, we could try it your way, and if that doesn't work, I'm going to go Harlem on Mr. Clarke."

Cheo's short sprint to the bedroom was like an anatomy class for Cynthia. She spent the duration of his departure analyzing his back. It was covered in big red letters with a black outline that read: R.I.P. MADRE, MI ALMA Y MI CORAZÓN. Cynthia wanted to use her fingertips to trace the outline of his tattoo, to trace the curve of his spine, and every other sculpted line on him. She didn't know what those words meant, yet she could feel the power of them.

"Come on." He walked ahead to open the door for her. Seeing him fully dressed did not extinguish the fire burning in her belly. His navy V-neck T-shirt and sand-colored shorts only seemed to enhance his picturesque beauty. She followed the scent of sandalwood and berries that he left in the air to the elevator.

They stood in front of the elevator bank, each striving to ignore the kinetic energy in the air. Cynthia shifted her weight from side to side. She could feel him watching. The hairs on her arm rose. With her eyes fixed on the elevator display, Cynthia devoted herself to a silent invocation for the elevator to arrive. Her hope was that it wasn't full of people. She needed to avoid being close to him. Cheo seemed like everything she had ever wanted in a man. Despite the magnitude of his beauty, he was certainly the last thing she needed at this juncture in the road.

The metal doors whined as if it hurt them to open. The elevator was empty. *Thank you, Jesus,* she thought. In unison, Cynthia and Cheo entered. Cynthia pressed herself against the wall, trying to blend in with the wooden panels. Cheo flashed his award-winning smile to break up the awkwardness filling in the elevator.

Neither one uttered a word as they walked up the long stretch of hallway on the ground floor. The click-clack of Cynthia's shoes against the white tiles let everyone know she meant business. She took note of the location of each amenity promised: the gym; the business center fully equipped with a fax machine, copier, computers and Internet access; and state-of-the-art Laundromat.

Mr. Clarke opened his door before they had the opportunity to knock. "Mr. Clarke, there seems to be small problem," Cheo said.

"A huge problem," Cynthia added, placing her hands on her hips.

Cheo shot her a quick glance. "Remember we're going to do this my way," he whispered to her.

"What seems to be the problem, Cheo?" Mr. Clarke asked, skirting around his desk with his eyes fixed on Cynthia. He stood in the center of them with his arms at his side like a soldier waiting to receive a command.

"Apparently, you rented apartment sixty-three to both of us," Cheo said pointing at himself and then Cynthia.

"No, I gave you sixty-eight, and I put her in sixty-three."

Completely armed to fight this battle, Cheo withdrew his copy of his lease from the pocket of his cargo shorts with a chuckle, and Cynthia muscled up a slight grin. "No, you put us both in sixty-three." Cheo pointed at the apartment number printed on his rental agreement. "Now, I don't mind rooming with her, but she's not convinced that type of living arrangement would work out."

"God ain't make no mistakes when he made me, and I don't make mistakes when I do business. Where's your lease, young lady?" Mr. Clarke implored with his palm extended in Cynthia's direction.

Cynthia flung her mouth open ready to share a word with Mr. Clarke, and none of it was from the Good Book. Cheo moved closer to her and squeezed her wrist to silence her. "You gave us both sixty-three, Mr. Clarke. She has the key and you escorted me up, r'ember?" Cheo asked. His question perturbed Mr. Clarke and left him scratching his head. "Don't worry, it's no problem now. If I belong in sixty-eight then that's where I'll go. Just toss me them keys." Cheo extended his palm for the proper set of keys. Mr. Clarke opened the lock box on his desk and tossed a set of keys at Cheo. "Thank you, Mr. Clarke. We can deal with the paperwork some other time."

Cynthia was so glad she'd agreed to let Cheo handle the whole situation. Cynthia was in awe at how quickly Cheo waved good-bye to Mr. Clarke with his right hand and used his left hand to usher Cynthia out. He'd managed to clean everything up without a cuss word and remain poised under pressure. Cynthia liked that but recognized she shouldn't.

"Thank you," she whispered, avoiding eye contact with Cheo. "I've been wondering something though."

"What?"

"How did you know I was from New York?"

Shoulder to shoulder they marched through the parted doors of the elevator; the wall Cynthia erected between them was slowly decaying.

"Hmmm. Your lack of patience, your no-nonsense, 'I get what I want when I want it and I want it in a New York minute' attitude, and your beauty."

Being around Cheo took her breath away. For the second time, Cynthia cleared her throat, trying to gracefully request a break from Cheo's oppressive stare. When the elevator doors opened on the sixth floor, Cynthia sped down the hall ahead of Cheo.

"I kind of started unpacking, so give me a minute to get it together," Cheo said.

Cynthia didn't reply; she just stared up at his fleshy peach lips.

"Okay?" he prodded.

"Yes, that's fine. I'll be on the deck if you need me," she said, crossing the threshold of the apartment they'd shared momentarily.

"And I'll be in the bedroom should you need me," Cheo said smiling.

Cynthia stepped onto the deck and spread her feet shoulder-width apart, observing her new territory. Day had turned into night. Her mental evaluation of her present situation was interrupted by visions of Cheo's thick black curls and high cheekbones. Cynthia stared up at the night sky. The stars entreated her; their glimmer put her into a trance so deep she didn't hear Cheo knocking on the glass door before he stepped onto the deck.

"Would you like to touch them?" he whispered. His rich voice boomed in her ear, startling her. Cynthia turned around to face Cheo, hiding her smile with the palms of her hands.

"We don't have stars in New York."

"None at all?"

"Okay, so I'm exaggerating a bit. We have stars. You can't see them as clearly as you can here." Cynthia blushed grinning at Cheo.

"I know what you meant. I'm just giving you a hard time. I'm all packed, so I guess I have to go to my apartment now. It was fun sharing a place with you. Hopefully I'll see you soon."

"You know where I live."

"Yes, yes, I do. Don't forget you can find me in sixty-eight."

"I won't," she said, gently leaning into him, clinging to the banister with one hand in an attempt to restrain herself. She hadn't flirted with anyone in so long, she was afraid of coming off as desperate.

Cheo adjusted the straps on his backpack, slung a duffel bag over his shoulder, and grabbed his rolling suitcase. Cynthia walked him to the door and opened it.

"Okay, it's all yours. Good night," he said as he walked out.

"Good night," Cynthia said, closing the door simultaneously hoping the next time she opened it Cheo would be on the other side.

Chapter 18

"Senorita, senorita, please open the door. Please, I am desperate. I need your help," Cheo shouted between each bang on the metal door.

In three days, Cynthia hadn't gotten an ounce of sleep. She didn't unpack nor had she left her new apartment. The center of the olive green rug became her permanent station. Incomprehensible mutterings and accusations laden with guilt dribbled out of her mouth. The word "monster" filled the air.

Riverside reminded Cynthia of the lofty buildings on Central Park West that overlooked the park. In her fantasy world, her work as a personal chef to celebrities like Beyoncé had earned her enough revenue for a place like this in New York. Riverside was too close to the river. The combination of the constant chirp of crickets, the dizzying buzz of fireflies, the golden glow of the moon bouncing off the walls, and visions of Keith's sunken cheeks and James's thick-lipped smile every time she closed her eyes made it impossible for her to sleep.

Wrapped in a hug from her own arms, Cynthia rocked back and forth as the walls of the apartment closed in on her. She would have succumbed to the guilt that was eating her alive if Cheo hadn't come knocking on her door.

Cynthia hoisted herself up from the carpet and cracked the door. Her eyes were glazed over from lack of sleep. Cheo's jaw fell open, his chin touched his chest; the look in his eyes told her she looked like an extra from Michael

Jackson's "Thriller" video. Cynthia licked her lips and wiped the corners of her mouth in an attempt to compose herself. "Yes?"

"Ummm . . . I . . . uh . . ."

"Yes?" Cynthia implored with raised eyebrows, trying to exude an air of importance and give Cheo the impression she was busy.

"Uh, my furniture is supposed to be delivered this afternoon, and my boss wants me to come down to the office right away. I was, ah, wondering if you could hang out in my apartment until I got back."

"Until you come back? Where do you work?"

"By day or night?"

Cynthia responded to Cheo's joke by folding her arms, jutting her hip, and cocking her head in b-girl stance that said "come on now, stop playing."

"I work at the *Richmond Sun* when I'm not working on my travel books."

"When I said where, I meant like the address, like how far away will you be and how long will it take you to get back?"

"Oh, I don't know." Cheo shrugged his shoulders. "An hour or two."

"Are you sure you want me to stay in your apartment? I mean, you don't even know me."

"But I want to know you," Cheo said, placing his hand on the top of hers, which gripped the door. "Besides, if you take anything, I know where you live. Listen, I promise to be back as soon as possible. *Tienes hambre?*"

"What?"Cynthia asked with an upturned lip.

"Are you hungry? If you wait for my furniture, I'll bring you back something to eat and we could get to know each other."

The idea ping-ponged around in her head. Cynthia didn't want to be holed up in his apartment any more than she wanted to stay in hers, but the rumbling of her stomach reminded her that besides not sleeping in three days, she had not consumed much food either.

"Okay?" Cheo asked.

"Yes, I'll do it."

Cheo reached into the back pocket of his black cargo shorts for his keys. He gently placed them in her palm. "*Muchas gracias,* senorita. You really are as sweet as you look. *Ciao,*" he said over his shoulder, bounding down the hall.

Cynthia plowed to her bathroom. Dark circles the size of Saturn's rings engulfed her face. Wild strands of her hair hung limply around her face. She turned on the cold water, parted the glass shower doors, and thrust herself into the cascading current of cold water. The frigid temperature sent a shock to her system large enough to wake her up for a little while anyway. She emerged from the shower with a sense of purpose.

Cynthia was apprehensive about going to Cheo's place. For fifteen years Marvin saw to it that Cynthia didn't get within ten feet of a man without him. The only time he couldn't regulate her choice of company was when she was in church. Now she was about to enter a man's apartment under the guise of friendship. The sweat on her palms and the beat of her heart suggested something more was in the works.

With the twist of the key, Cynthia contemplated the likelihood of the friendship budding between her and Cheo becoming more than a platonic relationship.

In three days Cheo had managed to take advantage of the space. He already slathered some pasty pumpkin hue on the walls. Two large treelike plants now resided on his deck and one in the corner of his living room. Cynthia treaded across his oyster-colored rug to the kitchen, wondering how she got stuck with olive green. She was looking for anything that she could use as an excuse to deter the potential romance. Cigarettes, pornography, a Cheese Whiz obsession. Anything.

The cupboards were bare except for a lone box of crackers, peanut butter, and a jar of olives. She popped open the refrigerator. It adequately reflected his bachelor lifestyle. Two six-packs of beer, three limes, and a box of Domino's pizza with one slice of pepperoni decorated his refrigerator. She strolled down the hallway straight to his bedroom.

A chocolate comforter formed a makeshift sleeping bag for Cheo in the left corner of the room. His duffel bags occupied the space beneath his windowsill. Cynthia peered out of his window. He had a boring view of the traffic on Riverside Drive.

The blaring toot of the intercom snapped her out of her hypnotic daze. Hanging on to the wall for support, Cynthia shuffled to the intercom. "Yes?"

"Delivery for Mr. Cheo Rivera."

"Send them up." Cynthia opened the apartment door and left it cracked so the movers could enter easily, and she could exit right behind them. She could hear their booming voices as they tried to figure out which way to go. A few moments later they came barreling through the door.

One of them looked like a grizzly bear from the back, and before he crossed the threshold, he shouted over his shoulder, "Where do you want this, miss?" It was a high-back champagne-colored couch; gold swirls decorated the upholstery. The grizzly bear used his right shoulder to sweep the sweat from the side of his face.

Cynthia looked around the living room. "Uh, I don't know."

"Could you hurry up and make a decision?" the guy holding the other end of the couch pleaded. "This thing is pretty heavy."

Embarrassed, Cynthia giggled. "I'm sorry. This isn't my apartment, so I don't know where anything goes."

"Coming through," chimed another couple of movers carrying a chaise longue that matched the couch, forcing Bear and his partner to bring the sofa all the way into the apartment.

They walked past Cynthia and placed it against the back wall of the living room. "Put that over there, Larry," said Bear, pointing at an empty space opposite the deck. "With the front facing the deck. We'll be back, ma'am."

They trotted in and out, toting more champagne and gold furniture, two end tables, and a peculiar-looking coffee table with a square opening in the middle for storage. Cynthia stood in the middle of the living room observing them as they transformed the living room into a showroom at Bob's Discount Furniture. The telephone rang, interrupting the choreography of Bear's moving day dance.

"Aren't you going to answer that, ma'am?"

"This isn't my place."

"You know it could be the guy who does live here calling to check on things," the other mover suggested.

Cynthia stood next to the phone, feeling a bit trepidatious about answering the phone. She let it ring two more times before picking up the receiver.

"Hello."

"Cynthia, it's me, Cheo. What are you doing answering my telephone?"

Cynthia let out a squeal. "Cheo, oh my God. I am sorry."

"Relax; I was just kidding. I was just calling to make sure everything was okay over there."

"I'm sorry. I don't know you well enough yet to tell the difference."

"Yet? That means I have a chance," Cheo squeaked into the phone. He cleared his throat and continued in a slow and seductive tone. "Believe me, *mamí*, I plan to teach you everything there is to know about me."

The rhythm of Cheo's words sent shockwaves rippling through Cynthia's body. With a shake of her shoulders Cynthia reminded herself that she was not in Richmond for romance. "Everything is fine. The movers are here right now," Cynthia said after reclaiming control of her thoughts. "Is that all?" She rejected Cheo's offer by not acknowledging it.

"*Ay Dios mio*. Do you think you could do me one more favor?"

"Cheo, you're asking for a bit much now, don't you think?'

"Please, Cynthia, *por favor*. It's really very simple. I forgot to leave them a tip. Would you—"

"Cheo, I really don't know you well enough to feel comfortable lending you any money."

Cheo chuckled at Cynthia's assumption and speedy rejection. "No, *mi amor,* I was just going to ask you to go into my closet to get the money. There's a shoebox located on the bottom right hand corner full of papers, and at the very bottom is a pink envelope with money in it. Could you give them each fifty bucks?"

"Each?"

"There's only four of them, right?"

"Yes."

"Okay then give them fifty bucks apiece. They've been really good to me. They've handled the furniture with love and care, as if they knew my mother before she passed. One more thing. Do you want light or dark—"

"I don't drink," Cynthia said firmly cutting Cheo off.

"Besides a few beers, I don't either. Do you want a light soda like Sprite or something dark like a Pepsi?"

"A Pepsi would do just fine."

Cynthia hung up the phone, excused herself, and eased into the bedroom.

She kneeled down in front of the closet, which was adjacent to the bedroom door. Most of the papers in the box were requests for Cheo to pay his student loan bills. The one exception was a picture of him with a chestnut-colored girl. Cynthia wondered where his beauty queen girlfriend was at right now to help him with all this.

Brushing the picture aside, she proceeded to pull out the pink envelope. Cynthia removed the $200, and in the process she also unearthed a card with hearts on the front of it. She figured it was a love note from the chestnut girl. Upon opening it, she immediately recognized some of the words from the tattoo on Cheo's shoulder blades.

Te quiero, mi amor. Tu es mi corazon y mi alma.
—Tu madre

As she read the rest of the card she felt like an idiot as she recounted the grumbling that was going on in her head: *Cheo, I know you can barely read in Spanish so I want this to be clear, I love you. You are my heart and soul. —Mamí.* The card came from his dead mother. Cynthia stopped snooping and trotted back to the living room.

When she entered the living room, the movers were dragging in a tall bookcase. "In the old house, this was in the bedroom," Bear said, looking at Cynthia.

Cynthia pointed straight down the hallway and took a seat on the hard high-back sofa. The other pair of movers brought in Cheo's platform loft bed.

"You got anything to drink, ma'am?" asked the scrawny mover. "I forgot my Gatorade at the last house we worked in."

"This—" Cynthia began.

"Isn't your place," they all said in unison.

"Well, how about at your place. You got something to drink over there?" the scrawny one continued.

"Actually, I just moved in as well, and I really don't have anything either, but here." Cynthia doled out the tips. Each man snatched their cut. "Why don't you guys take a break and go get yourselves something to drink?"

"Woohoo!" the scrawny one exclaimed in a singsong voice.

"That won't be necessary, ma'am. We're almost done," Bear said, jabbing the scrawny one in the ribs hard enough to put him in check.

"Awww, just go ahead." Cynthia winked at the scrawny one. "A short break won't hurt. Consider it a morale booster."

"Thanks, ma'am. You want us to bring you anything back?" Bear asked.

"Yeah, you look like you're the one who's been doing the moving," another one chimed in.

"Thanks, ah . . ."

"Harold, Harold Johnson," Bear said, extending his paw for a handshake. "This wise guy over here is my cousin, Larry Johnson, and this here"—he planted his hand on the shoulder of the scrawny one—"is Mike Johnson, my nephew, and the quiet one is my son, Derek Johnson. How about you, ma'am. What's your name?"

"Cynthia, Cynthia Hathaway." Cynthia was shocked at how easily her maiden name rolled right off her tongue after only using it a couple of times. "Harold, I would really appreciate it if you brought me back a hot dog and Slurpee from the 7-Eleven."

The door slammed behind the Johnsons. Cynthia lay down on the chaise longue, tracing the swirls the gold made with her fingers. She liked the chaise longue, but she found the rest of the set to be a little bit gaudy and tacky, from the faux ivory-topped coffee table to the gold embellishment on everything. It looked as though Midas used the furniture as a canvas for finger painting.

The furniture didn't seem to coincide with the man she'd met. The impression she gathered from Cheo's rugged clothing and his loft bed was that he delighted in the simple things and would never go for this champagne and gold spread. The fact that Bear had mentioned the furniture came from his old home totally escaped her. She continued tracing the gold pattern until she fell asleep.

The blend of the men pounding on the door and screaming, "Open the door, lady," jolted her right out of sleep. She woke with a stiff neck and her eyes bulging out of their sockets from fear. The last time she heard pounding like that, it was Marvin at her mother's door. She leaped out of the chaise longue to open the door. "Sorry, fellas," she said, wiping the drool from the side of her mouth with the back of her hand.

"It's quite all right, ma'am," said Bear. He scooped up two white lamps with gold lampshades. The others were on his heels carrying a small wooden and metal computer stand, which they took in the bedroom.

"Here you go, ma'am." One of the movers handed Cynthia a bag.

"Thank you." Cynthia put the bag on the counter and began removing its contents.

"You can get back to your nap now. We're done," Bear informed her.

Cynthia spun around, smiling. She wiped her hands on her pants, which had become wet from holding the Slurpee, and offered one to shake Bear's hand.

"Thank you, Bear . . . I mean, Harold. Cheo was right. You guys are really good."

"Thanks, ma'am. Remember to call the Johnsons for all your moving needs. Have a good day," Bear said, bowing and backing out of the door.

After the men left, Cynthia hopped onto the counter, taking a massive bite out of her hot dog, and whispered a thank you into the air. They'd gotten her not one but two hot dogs. She swallowed the first one and just as she was about to take a bite out of her second, there was a knock at the door.

"Mr. Rivera, it's Meridian Moving and Storage."

Cynthia slid off the counter and opened the door.

"Hi, Mrs. Rivera?"

"No, but you can bring the boxes right on in." The men in black overalls wheeled in boxes that conveniently compartmentalized Cheo's life: living room, kitchen, bedroom, *Mamí,* and travel.

"Where do you want them?"

"Just dump them in the living room." She polished off her second hot dog while they dumped the boxes in neat piles around the living room and walked out. Cynthia slurped her Slurpee and noticed the tape peeling slightly on a box that was labeled LIVING ROOM. Gently, she smoothed the tape back, and it rolled back up.

Cynthia battled with the bad tape and her own desire to know more about Cheo. Her inquisitive spirit got the best of her. After three solid attempts at smoothing the tape back into its proper position, she decided this was clearly the universe's way of giving her access into a world she desired to enter.

She peeled the tape back, opened the box and wrangled out a small black rectangular picture frame that housed the photo of a gypsy-eyed woman with long waves of black hair that stopped at her elbows. Her bronze skin

glowed beneath a turquoise frock that clung to her broad
hips. White and gold rosary beads hung from her neck.
The backdrop of the photo was magnificent. She stood
sandwiched between two palm trees barefoot in emerald
green grass, and her twinkling, smoldering eyes and
dainty mouth captivated Cynthia.

"*Mi madre,*" Cheo said. His voice startled Cynthia. The
picture frame crashed to the floor as it slipped out of her
hands.

"Oh my God." Cynthia said quickly bending down and
scooping up the picture frame. "I'm sorry." She placed the
picture on top of the box.

"It's okay," Cheo said, heading to the kitchen. He
placed the bags he was carrying onto the counter.

Cynthia followed him. "No, it's not okay. I shouldn't be
going through your things, and I would hope if I left you
alone in my apartment . . . not that I would ever leave you
alone in my apartment," she said, pointing her finger at
him, "but if I did, I wouldn't want you rifling through my
things."

"Chicken parm or lasagna?"

"Chicken parmesan."

Cheo took out the chicken parmesan, a plastic fork,
and some napkins. "Here." He handed her meal to her.
"Listen, it's really okay. I'm sure on the rare occasion you
would leave me in your apartment, you wouldn't leave me
alone with just my wits to entertain me."

He walked past her into the living room and picked up
the photo. "Besides, I can understand your enchantment;
es mi foto de favorita de mi madre."

"What, man?"

"I'm sorry. I keep on speaking to you in *Español.* I
only do that when I feel comfortable, which means you
make me feel comfortable. That's my favorite picture
of my mother. That was when she was beautiful and

carefree. That picture was taken on her last day in Puerto Rico in the yard of her best friend, Luz." Cheo recounted his mother's journey to America from her early days in Spanish Harlem to Virginia.

Cynthia watched Cheo draw his fork to his mouth. His lips formed words, but she couldn't hear a thing he was saying. The perfect curve his mouth made and the blush pink color of his lips held her mind captive. She rested her cheek in the palm of her hand in order to resist the urge to lick the sauce from the corner of his mouth.

"Spanish Harlem, *tu sabe?*"

"Huh?" she asked, climbing out of the fog.

"Do you know Spanish Harlem?"

She nodded. "Yes, I know Spanish Harlem. I used to live in Harlem. Do you know Harlem?" she asked, biting into her chicken parmesan.

"Yes, I've seen it. It's very beautiful: the architecture, Convent Avenue, Sugar Hill, 125th Street. *Sí*, I know Harlem."

"You're a man about town." She laughed.

"I'm glad you're feeling better. You looked ghastly before."

"Why thank you for noticing. Actually I haven't slept since I moved in, and then I sat down on that"—she pointed at the chaise longue—"and it was all over. The next thing I knew it was dark, quiet, and I was dreaming. You know how you can repay me for babysitting your apartment?"

"No, but I'd love to know how. Does it involve kisses at all?"

"Uh, no." She rolled her eyes playfully. "You can repay me by taking me to get some furniture like this."

Cheo laughed, his throat warbling as he responded to Cynthia's request. "I'm sorry, but I won't be able to do that. All of this furniture was purchased in New York, and in case you can't tell, it's *muy viejo*."

She was relieved. Truly she didn't want anything that looked remotely similar to Cheo's furniture, except for the chaise longue. "Well, do you know anywhere I can get furniture here?"

His pink lips stretched across his face into a smile. "It would be my pleasure to take you around. In the meantime, why don't you phone home? The sound of something or someone familiar will put your mind at ease."

"Thanks, Cheo. If you don't mind I'm going to excuse myself right now. I don't want to keep you up too late on a Tuesday night, and I'd really like to go make that call."

Cynthia walked out the door leaving Cheo no chance to suck down the huge chunk of lasagna lodged in his mouth to properly say good-bye.

Chapter 19

Cynthia was sorry she left, and Keith was even sorrier she was gone.

It amazed Cynthia that Keith could tell it was her. The same way a mother knew her child, Keith recognized his mother in every measured breath. He knew it wasn't a prankster or one of his father's shorties pleading for attention, although the person who anonymously called never said a thing. He also knew better than to tell his father about her calls or to tell his mother what was really going on while she was gone.

"I miss you. We all miss you, even Dad. He's been trying to get it together. It's hard. When you come back, things will be better. You are coming back, right? James has been getting in trouble. You know how he is."

Cynthia smirked at the receiver.

"Grandma is coming to get us this weekend. She's taking us to church. She said in a time like this we need a savior. When I get there, I'm going to pray for you, Mom."

His words broke something inside of her. No boy should be praying for his mother in that capacity. Cynthia kissed her index finger then touched the base of the receiver with it. She hung up the phone. She squatted to the ground right there in the gas station and cried. It was time for her to hurry up and get in the position she needed to be in to provide for her sons.

Cynthia knew what she had to do next: get a job. She didn't think that would be difficult at all. In her mind considering how sweet Dr. Chang was all she'd have to do was call him and tell him what's going on and he'd allow Cynthia to work from here. Dusting the seat of her pants off, Cynthia stood and positioned her fingers on the dial pad of the phone. She froze. There was still one problem if Cynthia continued to work for Dr. Chang; there was the possibility that Marvin might still be able to locate her. That cautionary thought caused her to pause in the middle of dialing the area code and return to her new residence.

Cheo was correct. A call home was all she needed to fall asleep. It took some time for her to get Keith's words out of her head and adjust to not having a bed. Without so much as a warning sign, sleep crept up on her and robbed her of her time to wallow in self-pity and guilt.

Cynthia waited for her Saturday shopping trip to enlist Cheo's help in finding a job. He picked her up around 11:00 a.m. to have brunch before they went shopping. They shared a humongous platter of chicken and waffles in a diner on Hull Street.

"I know this isn't the kind of brunch you're used to in New York. Welcome to the dirty, dirty." They both cracked up at Cheo's impression of a thug.

"Just stick to your Rico Suave routine."

Cheo dropped his fork on the table. "You think this is some kind of act?"

With hunched shoulders and a tilted head, Cynthia asked, "Well, isn't it?"

"*Mira, mamí,* look around, there aren't too many guys around here who look like this." Cheo waved his hands up and down. "I have a job and don't have any kids, so you're fooling yourself if you think I'm doing any of this to get some sex."

Those curt words shocked Cynthia. She'd heard much worse from Marvin. Still she wasn't expecting anything like that from Cheo.

"This is a serious conversation that should be held over dinner, or at the very least lunch, not brunch. Please don't mistake my advances for an act. I just want to be there for you, and I hope you will let me." He took another bite of a wing and wrapped his free hand around hers.

"My savings are going to be gone soon. I need a job." Cynthia covered her mouth in shock that she had just blurted that out.

"A job, no problema." Cheo leaned back in his chair and whipped out his cell phone, crossed his legs, and began yammering away. "Hey, Mitch. How are things going? Good, I'm glad to hear Tricia and the boys are doing okay. Listen, I've got a friend over here who needs some work. You think you can do something for her?" Cheo flashed Cynthia the thumbs-up signal. "She'll be down there bright and early." He put his phone away and leaned in closely to Cynthia. "On Monday morning go down to Office Staff 911 on Main Street, ask for Mitch, and he'll hook you up."

"Cheo, what are you saying?"

"I'm saying if you can read, write, and type, then you've got yourself a job. That was Mitchell Montgomery, the CEO of Office Staff 911, the largest temp agency in Richmond, and he's agreed to hook you up. I accept kisses as a form of payment." Cheo pointed at his cheek.

"How did you do that?" she asked nonchalantly trying pretend she was not extremely impressed.

"Being a photojournalist for the *Richmond Sun* has its perks. No one wants me to catch them on their bad side, so everyone does what they have to do to remain on my good side." Cheo licked his lips and proceeded to chow down on the remainder of his chicken wing.

Cynthia entertained the idea of giving Cheo a kiss, but a voice inside her head reminded her of her commitment to Marvin.

"Cynthia, I don't know what happened to you. I don't know what he did to you. What I do know is those things won't happen to you again, not with me." Cheo arched his eyebrow and leaned in a bit closer to her.

"Cheo, I'm messy."

Placing one hand over hers, he scooped it up and kissed the back of her hand. "Please, let me help you put everything back on the shelf."

Chapter 20

The constant ringing of the telephone didn't prompt Marvin to move from his spot on the couch. He raised his index finger pointing in the direction of the ringing and mumbled, "Keith," from under his blanket.

"Hello?" Keith said into the telephone receiver. "Yes, he's here, hold on. Daaad," Keith shouted. "Dad, the phone."

Marvin pulled the purple crochet blanket from over his head and let it fall to floor. Cynthia knitted it when she was pregnant with James. She was hoping for a girl the second time around. Muddy Waters' "Come Back Baby" bounced from the walls. Marvin snatched the phone from Keith and returned to the couch. "Yeah," he grumbled into the receiver.

"Are you okay, Marvin? I saw Cynthia's picture on the news. Why didn't you tell me?"

"I just thought this was going to go away quickly and then she just never came home. Now the police are trying to make up for lost time quickly. They're hoping some media coverage will get her home soon."

"You should have said something to someone at the garage," Jade said reprimanding Marvin.

"Jade, umm, it's kind of a personal thing," he said in a slow drawl.

"I know, but it's also something you shouldn't be going through alone. You and the boys need some kind of support."

"Well, uh, we been doing all right," he said languidly. It was the early evening, the shades were drawn shut, something red and sticky covered the living room floor, Keith's car collection was parked randomly throughout the house, and dust was mounting on the furniture.

"Well, until things are settled, is it fine by you if I come by and check on you from time to time?"

"I'd like that." Marvin smiled at the thought of seeing Jade's honey-colored eyes and bright smile. That was exactly what he needed, he thought, a break from the haze that had settled over his life this past week.

"Would you like me to come over tonight," she moaned into the receiver.

"Yes, I would like that very much. You know I live in Harlem."

"I'll pull your address from your file and get one the guys to drop me off nearby," she said.

"See you then," Marvin said hanging up the phone.

Marvin opened the door the first time she knocked without asking who it was. After several visits from the police and Mildred, since she had convinced them he may have done something to Cynthia, he'd stopped asking who it was and had begun hoping one of these days when the bell rang, it would be Cynthia saying she'd lost her keys.

He'd rehearsed it several times. She would stand at the doorway brushing down the hair at the nape of her neck, twitching nervously. "Marvin, I couldn't find my keys. I knew you would be upset, that's why I didn't come home. I've just been searching everywhere for them." And then all of this would be over like a dream.

When he opened the door, it was Jade standing in the doorway in a burgundy belted trench coat that hugged her petite waist. Her hair was slicked back, drawing attention to the fire brewing in her honey-colored eyes.

"Marvin, are you going to let me in?"

He stepped aside so Jade could cross the threshold. Jade's eyes widened as she looked at the dilapidated apartment.

"Jade, I'm sorry about the mess. I wasn't expecting you so soon."

"Marvin," she said, slowly unbuttoning her coat, "I could tell by the sound of your voice that you needed someone." Jade took a few steps farther into the apartment. "Where are the boys?" she asked resting her coat on the arm of the sofa.

"In their room playing video games," Marvin whispered, "and it's best we don't disturb them."

Marvin studied Jade as she walked through the apartment as if she'd been there before. She grabbed a blue tumbler from the cabinet and poured Marvin a little gin and juice that she'd brought along with her.

Marvin sat down at the dining room table, staring in amazement at how quickly she'd adapted to her new surroundings.

"There's nothing like a wet palate to relieve the stress of the day," she noted as she placed the tumbler in front of Marvin.

Marvin took leisurely sips of his gin and juice while Jade immersed herself in the mess Cynthia's absence had created. She dived into the disaster like an Olympic swimmer.

Starting with the kitchen, her bun began to unravel with each stroke she put in while scrubbing a pot with rice stuck to it. Marvin watched her as she tossed stale food in the garbage. She spent, stretched, and pulled in one fluid motion. Her slender body looked like melting wax. After the kitchen she began working on the mess in the dining room.

"Do you want any of these?" she asked, her hands filled with a bunch of business cards and store circulars.

Marvin traced the cards' edges imagining they were her collarbone. He plucked Detective Laurel's out of the bunch. "You can chuck the rest."

She worked on the living room, stacking up his record collection. Marvin's eyes followed her as she bent down to pick up the crochet blanket. When she rose, she found herself eye to eye with Cynthia. It was a portrait of Cynthia in front of city hall on their wedding day, holding a small bouquet of flowers. Her admonishing gaze transcended time and filled this moment. He wondered what Jade would do now that she'd been confronted with the reality of the situation: she was just filling in.

He'd known for a long time she had been waiting for this very moment.

She'd been waiting for him since the very day he strutted into the garage like a peacock, with his broad shoulders spread and his goatee trying to hide the dimple in his chin.

"Excuse me, miss. Where is the office?" He'd leaned over the desk and asked in a slight hum rather than shout over the clanging and banging of the trucks and the grating of the gate used to transport trucks in and out of the garage. He preferred to get up close and personal; it was part of his charm.

He laughed a little, recalling the dazzling smile Jade had flashed in an attempt to extract more than a name. Yet he remained reserved throughout her performance. She'd tilted her head, batted her eyes, and propped her breasts on the counter while pointing him in the direction of the office. He'd remained focused on his goal: secure a job to feed his family. There would be time for the women later. Marvin made sure to let her know there was a small opening for her in his world by the way he held her hand as he thanked her for helping him: his heavy hand resting on hers, his fingers lodged between hers, squeezing tightly with each syllable.

That was so long ago. But her presence and the craving in her eyes revealed she had not forgotten their first meeting either.

Marvin's eye darted back and forth from the full moon to Jade's confrontation with a photo of him and Cynthia. He knew he wasn't the same man in the photo or the one she'd met in the garage. He was a little bent, a crooked version of himself, but there was enough left over for Jade to grab on to. He cocked his head to the side and raised his top lip a bit, signaling this was the opening she had been waiting to slither into.

She glided into the dining room and embraced him as he sat on the plush chocolate seat. "I'm going to go home now. Marvin, call me if you need anything." She leaned closer to him. Her breasts grazed his back; her breath set his skin aflame with every syllable she cooed hitting his neck.

"Anything, Marvin. Anything."

"Jade, it's too late for you to go home alone." Marvin stood.

"You can't leave the boys alone. Don't worry about me," she said, resting her hand against his chest. "I'll be just fine. As a matter of fact, I'll call you when I get home, Marv." She smiled. "Okay?"

He scooped up her delicate hand and cradled it in his palm. "Thank you, Jade. I hope you'll come back. Soon."

"Take it easy, Marv. I'll see you soon."

As soon as the lock turned and Jade was out the door Marvin found himself alone again with Muddy Waters. It was just him and his records. When he inherited them from his father, he was the same age as Keith. The records weren't the only thing passed down. Marvin inherited his philandering ways from his father who had a second family in Brooklyn. Marvin never knew his father all that well; he didn't get the chance to. The moment Marvin's mother, Arlene, found out about his other family, she put Marvin's father out. He still came around every now and then for a drink, for a smoke, and for a kiss.

The only difference between Marvin and his father now was that Marvin didn't have to leave his home to get a drink, a smoke, or a kiss.

Two days later, Jade returned on her day off with bags from McDonald's for the boys and drinks for Marvin.

This became Jade's regular routine and Marvin liked it. She came over two or three times a week instead of trying to set up shop. Somehow Jade had managed to get on to the day shift making her visits to Marvin's easier. She usually came over after her shift while the boys were sleeping. She'd tidy up and then, no questions asked, she'd take Marvin by the hand and guide him to the bedroom or they'd lie on the couch wrapped in each other's legs, smoking cheap cigars, listening to Charlie Parker.

The evenings he spent with Jade were enough to keep him until his wife came back home.

Chapter 21

"Here you go, Cynthia. I wanted to personally deliver this to you." Mitchell Montgomery said smiling from ear to ear. "Luckily you started before the payroll closed."

Cynthia smiled back at Mitchell. "Thank you, Mr. Montgomery, for everything."

"Call me Mitch. Any friend of Cheo's is a friend of mine. Please let me thank you for two weeks of excellent service. The bank called to tell me what an excellent job you've been doing as a teller and to open a permanent account with us for all their staffing needs. What have you and Cheo got planned for Valentine's Day?"

Cynthia was dumbfounded by Mitchell's question. Not only were she and Cheo not as close as she'd like to be; she hadn't even realized that it was Valentine's Day. All of her time in Richmond had blurred together and January had somehow turned into February.

"Ummm, we don't really have that type of relationship, Mitch."

An awkward silence filled the reception area of Office Staff 911.

Quietly she said, "Thank you," while keeping her eyes glued to the floor to avoid the stares of every other temp in the office awaiting their check.

"Don't spend it all in one place," Mitchell said. He slid Cynthia her check and handed her the clipboard to sign for it.

"I won't. Have a good day, Mitch," Cynthia said before walking out of the smoky glass doors of Office Staff 911.

Cynthia paced in front of the doors of 7-Eleven acting out her conversation with Barbara, her only buddy back in the city. It was either call Barbara or call her mother. Cynthia already knew where Mildred stood far as Cynthia's wifely duties were concerned. Barbara was the closest thing Cynthia had to a friend. Their sons' karate class and play dates was no longer the only things that united them. After delivering the inspirational speech that compelled Cynthia to acknowledge how dysfunctional her relationship with Marvin was, Barbara had a new space in Cynthia's heart. Cynthia stuck her hand in her back pocket to make sure her first paycheck was still tucked away safely.

"Collect call from Cynthia Barclay. Do you accept the charges?" the operator asked.

"Yes, I accept the charges." Barbara waited until she heard the click of the operator disconnecting from the phone before she began to speak. "Cynthia, are you all right? Where are you?"

"That's not important right now."

"Are you kidding me? Where you are is so important that you've been on the six o'clock news. This is getting serious now."

"Are you able to talk right now, Barbara?"

"Let me just go into another room. Sean is in here sprawled out across the floor playing checkers with his cousin."

Cynthia hummed the *Jeopardy!* music in her head as she waited for Barbara to change locations.

"All clear. Go ahead, girl."

"I'm sorry I had to call you collect, but I need a favor from you, and I can't risk anyone knowing where I am right now. I can't believe he went to the news with this.

I don't know if I can trust you, but I guess I'll find out, Barbara. You're the closest thing I have to a friend."

"Whatever it is, Cynthia, I've got your back."

Cynthia exhaled, relieved Barbara was willing to help her out. "If I send you some money for the boys, would you be willing to give it to Marvin until I can get on my feet? You absolutely can't tell him you got the money from me."

"Cynthia, I don't know about this. This sounds kind of dangerous. I mean, what am I supposed to say when he asks me where I got the money from? I don't want to tell any lies."

"That's none of his business. No, you're right, Barbara. Forget about it. I'll have to figure something else out."

"Isn't there someone else who can do this?"

"Barbara, I don't have many friends. No one knows where I am right now, and I want to keep it that way. If I contact my mom she's going to try to convince me to behave like a good Christian woman and just pray until Jesus makes a way. It's not like I can call Marvin and offer to send the boys some money and I just can't have my boys doing without."

"Oh, girl, what have you gotten yourself into?"

"I listened to you and started thinking it was time for me to change this situation. Just forget about it. Forget I ever called you," Cynthia said her voice wavering.

"No, please, Cynthia. I said it before and I meant it. I really want to help you. What did you have in mind?"

"I just started working, so I was thinking I could send you some money for the boys each time I got paid until I'm able to come back for them."

"Okay, but there's one problem," Barbara said in a singsong voice.

"What?"

"Your crazy husband. He really doesn't seem that fond of me. Why would he take a handout from me?"

"Barbara, you have a way with words. You're a lawyer," Cynthia said trying to shore up Barbara's ego. "Use some of that courtroom magic to convince him to take the money. That shouldn't be hard since you can convince people to give you money." They both laughed into the telephone.

Barbara jumped aboard Cynthia's runaway train. "You're right; I can think of something. Maybe I'll ambush him at karate. Hopefully he's not with that woman."

"A woman? What woman?"

"I didn't catch her name. I overheard him say to the girl at the desk she was a friend from work, but they looked very comfortable for friends."

Cynthia relaxed into the phone bank at the side of the gas station, racking her brain to figure out whether Antoinette or Jade had stepped up to the plate that quickly. Antoinette was not a viable option for Marvin, he was never into big girls, but if he was as desperate as Keith said, then he could easily take her on. Jade, on the other hand, was more his speed: nice eyes and thick thighs. She never met a man she ever said no to, Cynthia figured, based on all the cleavage she had exposed every time Cynthia visited the garage.

"You know what, right now Marvin can't be my issue," Cynthia stated after coming to the realization that if her disappearance hadn't caused him to change worrying about him wouldn't either. "I'll call you back with all of the Western Union details, and I'll include the fee for the collect calls. Thank you so much, Barbara."

"Don't hesitate to call me. Whatever it is, I've got your back," Barbara said definitively before hanging up.

Cynthia hung up the phone and leaned against it for support. Her knees still felt weak when she thought about her babies alone without her.

After talking to Barbara, Cynthia returned to her apartment to celebrate what remained of Valentine's Day. She clipped the stems of a bouquet of flowers she'd purchased from the flower shop on her ride home. She danced slowly around the apartment to what had once been her and Marvin's song, "Lovin' You" by Minnie Riperton. She wondered who he was loving on right now. A soft rap on her front door interrupted her musings.

"Who is it?"

"Cheo."

In no mood for company Cynthia contorted her mouth into a scowl before opening the door. The sight of Cheo's warm skin juxtaposed against the stark white button-down shirt was enough to melt that scowl away. She indulged in every detail from the deep curl of his black hair to the three open buttons on his shirt that revealed a bit of his chiseled chest down to the pressed beige cargos slightly draped over a pair of white and burgundy Adidas Samoas.

"Happy Valentine's Day." He causally leaned on the frame of her apartment door and drew a bouquet of blue roses and orange Asiatic lilies from behind his back. "Would you be mine?"

Blushing, Cynthia covered her mouth. "Cheo, I don't know what to say."

"Say you'll come out with me. Let's have dinner."

Cynthia bit down on her lip and contemplated her options: an evening alone with Minnie Riperton and memories of the good old days with Marvin or chow down with Cheo.

"Well?" he implored.

"Can I go dressed like this?" She waved up and down her body. He looked pretty casual, but she had no idea whether her peach tee and mint jeans would work out.

"I don't see why not."

"Come inside while I change my shoes and slip on a jacket."

Within a few minutes, Cynthia emerged from her bedroom in nude pumps, and white peplum-cut leather jacket. She could hear Cheo let out a low moan. She hoped that indicated she was the right blend a casual and sexy.

"I'm ready," she announced.

"Yes, you are," Cheo said, grabbing her hand tightly.

He led her by the hand to his sedan, creating a sense of safety and security Cynthia didn't realize she'd missed or longed for.

The fifteen-minute ride to the restaurant was mostly silent with brief interludes of small talk. Cynthia didn't want her confusion to turn this event into something sour.

When they pulled up in front of the Avalon Restaurant and Bar, Cynthia watched the couples walking in hand in hand and arm in arm snuggled against each other. She wasn't sure what Cheo was expecting to get out of this date, nor had she figured out how far she was comfortable going. As if he could read her mind, Cheo cupped her hand in his.

"It's just a dinner between friends," he stated in a reassuring tone.

Her palms were sweating and her heart was swelling. Cynthia doubted that she was supposed to be this excited about having dinner with a friend.

Like a true gentleman, Cheo opened the door for her and lead her through the white-trim doors of Avalon. He waved at the manager who was in the middle of a dispute with a customer about the bill as the hostess led them to a booth in the back of the restaurant.

"Mr. Rivera, your server will be with you momentarily."

"Thank you."

Once the hostess reached her post, Cynthia lit into him. "Mr. Rivera, do you entertain your friends here often?"

"I most certainly do," he said innocently. "The hostess works the day shift in the mailroom of the *Sun* and gives me a discount whenever I come around. What do you think of the place? They have a great menu. Order whatever you'd like."

Cynthia scanned the place; the brown mahogany booths and the incandescent lighting were perfectly suited for the warm atmosphere. If this were her own place, she'd paint the walls a coral pink to offset the brown and add a little ambiance.

"It's nice. I guess." She shrugged.

Their server placed two glasses of water with a lemon in front of each of them.

"Give us a few more minutes." Cheo dismissed the waiter. "I know the restaurants are much fancier than this in New York."

"It really doesn't matter how fancy the restaurant is. It's all about who you're with," she replied before taking a sip of her water.

"Am I good company?" he asked then raised his hand.

"Don't answer that. Let's enjoy the evening." Cheo signaled for the waiter to return. "Do you know what you want?"

Cynthia shrugged. Nothing really stood out to her except for the glow of Cheo's eyes.

"Let's have the fried Brussels sprouts with butter roasted pine nuts, the barbecue shrimp, and the truffled skirt steak," he said to the waiter. "How does that sound to you?" he asked Cynthia.

"I trust you, Cheo."

With the glowing stamp of approval on their order the waiter scooted off to the kitchen.

"Do you really trust me? It seems like you're holding back." He leaned in closer to the table. "Cynthia, I can't pretend I'm not attracted to you. I don't want to just be your friend."

Her mouth fell open at his confession. She'd noticed what she thought was longing in his eyes and felt the temperature of her body rise every time she laid eyes on him but this was more than she was prepared to handle.

"I want to. There aren't words to describe what I want to be for you," he whispered before he reached over the table and kissed her.

The touch of his lips was enough to set off every alarm in her body. She exhaled and took a sip of her water. What was the likelihood that Prince Charming would show up while she was still married?

"I haven't been with a woman in a year."

Cynthia raised her eyebrow at Cheo in disbelief.

"Seriously, Cynthia, I haven't met a woman I felt this energy with, and I don't believe in casually sleeping around. I mean it when I tell you I haven't been with a woman in a year." Cheo placed his hands on top of hers. Nothing but warmth radiated from his hands.

"Cheo, I'm not what you need," Cynthia said empathically easing her hands from under his grip.

"But you're what I want."

Chapter 22

Cynthia dangled her leg over the side of the plastic lounge chair by the pool watching Cheo swim laps. It was the eve of Cheo's departure to Bermuda to take photos of the Bermuda Jazz festival for his latest release, *One Love,* a musical travel guide of the Caribbean. This would be the first time that they would be separated in the two months since their first date on Valentine's Day.

Cynthia saw Cheo's head bob to the surface of the water then his sculpted body popped out of the pool. According to Cheo they just had to take advantage of the unusually high eighty-six degree temperature this spring. She adjusted the chair beside her so he could lay his head in her lap and lounge in the chair as well. They watched the sun go down, the moon rise, and stars come alive.

Slowly, Cheo was able to get the walls of Jericho that surrounded her heart to come down.

Seemingly from out of nowhere Cheo asked, "You know what I miss most about my mother?"

"What?"

"Her *gandules.*"

Cynthia looked down into Cheo's eyes quizzically.

"Beans. But not just her beans. I miss her cooking period. Even after the cancer got bad, she would still make my favorite meal, *pastelles y arroz con gandules* whenever I came over. That's no easy meal to prepare when you're well. *Ah, la amor de un madre, tu sabe.*"

"No *sabe.* I have no clue what you are talking about."

"If you want to say I don't know it's *Yo no sé not no sabe,*" Cheo said, enunciating every word. "*La amor de un madre* means the love of a mother," he said making extravagant hand gestures. "There's nothing like it, especially for her son. I'm sure a mother loves her children whether it's a girl or a boy, but there is something special about the love shared between a mother and a son. I've never discussed my mother with any woman I've been with, but you're the first woman to fill her *chanclas* so to speak without stomping around in my life and damaging her memory."

Cynthia lifted her head toward the sky in an effort to suppress the tears forming. His words hit her where she was weak. The tears leaped out of her eyes like a runner jumping over hurdles and landed right on Cheo's face.

"*Mi amor,* are you all right?"

Cynthia cradled his face and envisioned her own sons alone staring at the Harlem sky wondering where their mother was.

"Cheo," she said, sniffing, "I'm fine. Your words touched my heart. You're right, there's nothing like the love of a mother." Cynthia kissed Cheo on the cheek and motioned for him to rise. "I'll miss you. Have a safe flight."

"You're leaving me already?"

"You know I have to work in the morning. Mitch hasn't given me a break since you asked him to hire me. If he keeps this up, I may have to ask you to tell him to fire me." She laughed, slapping Cheo on the shoulder. She pulled her peach cover-up over her bathing suit before walking away.

As she sauntered away Cheo called out, "I can't wait until the day when you don't have to leave me."

Cynthia had to get away from Cheo before she broke down and spilled all the beans. She highly doubted he would be as enamored as he was if he knew she was on the run from an abusive husband and had two kids. It was too late to call Keith, but she had to know if everything was all right. Cynthia dried off and changed into a smoky gray velour suit and walked to the 7-Eleven down the road to call Barbara.

"Yes, I'll accept the charges," Barbara moaned. "Cynthia, do you know what time it is?"

"I'm sorry, Barbara. Cheo was talking to me about his mother, then I started to miss the boys, and you're the only way I can have access to them."

"Who's this Cheo character? I've never heard you mention him before."

"He's just my neighbor," Cynthia said, smiling playfully. "He's a good guy."

"Don't get sidetracked by this guy. Remember why you're there. You're not there to frolic with the foreign exchange student who lives down the hall from you. You're supposed to be establishing a safe home for you and your sons," Barbara said sternly.

"I know, which is why I was calling, just to check if you've seen them or anything."

"I've only seen them in passing at the dojo. I've been using the money you send to pay for their classes because Marvin won't take a thing from me. He won't even allow the boys to come over and play with Sean, and I'm sorry, Cynthia, but I can't send Sean over there to the devil's lair and you're not there."

"I understand. I'm sorry I woke you."

"Don't be. Anytime you need me, I'm here. When do you plan on getting a cell phone?"

"I'm trying to stay off the grid. I don't want Marvin tracking me down until he gets out of my system," Cynthia said scoping out her surroundings. The mere thought of Marvin catching her had her sweating like a crackhead going through withdrawal.

"Why don't you try a prepaid cell from MetroPCS or something like that? The police can't even track those." She paused momentarily. "I hope you don't mind me asking, but how did he get into your system in the first place?"

Cynthia rolled her eyes as she recalled the first time she met Marvin at a party her college roommates were throwing. She inhaled and could still smell his cologne, Fahrenheit.

"Cynthia, are you there? If it's too much to go into you don't have to."

"No, it's not too much. I met Marvin at a party while I was in college. He hounded me all night for a dance. I rejected him each time until one of my roommates put in a good word for him. His arms wrapped perfectly around my waist. My mother warned me about him. She said he was good for nothing, but the way I felt in his arms, I just knew she had to be wrong. On our first date, he took me to an African restaurant, and we walked through Mount Morris Park hand in hand. We danced under a thick of trees to a soloist in the park playing the saxophone. 'Please don't let me go. In your arms I feel like a man,' he whispered into my ear."

The corners of Cynthia's eyes became wet. Marvin's square jaw, brown almost black eyes, and thick frame began to manifest.

"He promised me that every day we would dance. For the first time ever in my life, I felt like a woman. He aroused something in me and every time we were apart, something inside of me cried out for him. Things were fine until he lost his job and his mother in the same month. We'd just moved in together. My mother temporarily disowned me and we were all we had. I just wasn't enough."

"Nothing can heal a broken heart but Jesus," Barbara interjected.

"Then the drinking started, and then the fighting started. And I . . . I . . . I promised him I wouldn't turn my back on him." Cynthia wailed into the phone.

"Hey, hey, Cynthia, get a hold of yourself," Barbara shouted. "He beat you. You did not turn your back on him. You finally got the courage to save yourself. Self-preservation is the only thing that keeps a species going."

"I should have been more supportive," Cynthia said chastising herself.

"Right now you need to think about how you can be supportive to Keith and James who witnessed him demoralize, demean, and disfigure you. How much longer do you think it will be before you're ready to get the boys?"

"I don't know. I'm still just temping."

"Come on, Cynthia. You've got to get yourself together. No judge is going to award you custody without a full-time job, and time is a major factor. You've been gone for four months and the more time that elapses without you being accounted for, it weakens your case."

Cynthia drummed her fingers on the top of the pay phone. "I know, I know. I'm going to get it together soon. Good night, Barbara."

"Good night, Cynthia. God bless you. I'm praying for you."

Cynthia hung up the phone and let her hand linger on the receiver. She felt the tears coming. Cynthia wondered if prayer could reach her. *I don't even think you can still see me, Lord.* Cynthia put her hands together to form a cup and covered her face to prevent the tears from breaking through. The five-block walk back to her building seemed like miles. All she wanted now was for someone to hold her, and Cheo wasn't going to be home until Monday evening.

Chapter 23

Hard work became Keith's best friend. Every morning he rose and got breakfast started. After the first month without his mother he chucked her rule about touching the stove. It was time he figured out how to work it without burning down the house.

He wanted to create a sense of normalcy for James who was growing stranger by the day. His words had become fewer and fewer with each day that Cynthia was gone. Every day at school some teacher or counselor tried to get one of them to talk about what life was like at home. James remained tight lipped to keep himself out of trouble. Keith kept quiet out of a warped sense of allegiance to his father who was now playing the victim and because he'd developed an attitude of contempt toward the authorities in the school.

He'd heard the whispers when he walked by the teachers' lounge. "The man must be a monster if she left the kids behind."

"A woman does not just up and leave her kids. Something else is going on."

Marvin told the boys the buzz would die down quickly; however, it just never went away. Keith knew the concern they expressed was just a cover-up to satisfy their longing for information.

With thoughts of James' struggles on his mind and his own desire for his mother to return Keith kneeled down to start his day with a prayer. Before he could recede into the comforts of talking to the Father the telephone interrupted Keith's daily morning prayer for peace, video games, and his mother, not always in that order.

"Hello." The only response Keith got was some honking in the background and the repetition of shallow breaths.

"He's not speaking anymore, James. He doesn't talk. Ever since you left, he's stopped talking. I think he's trying to save all of his words for you. I told him he needs to practice speaking so he won't forget by the time you get here. Grandma says he's got a mute spirit. She's been fasting. Mama, when are you coming home? It's not getting easier around here. Daddy's hanging in there. He doesn't hit us or nothing like that, except for this one time, but we worked that out. Why can't y'all work it out? I'm sorry, I know I'm not supposed to be in grown folks' business, but . . . but I think this is my business too. Why can't y'all just work it out?" he pleaded.

The dial tone told Keith they couldn't, at least not today; but her call was clearly a sign God could hear his prayers. He decided he would add his parents getting back together to his list. The past four months had turned him into a man-child. He prayed, cooked, washed clothes, and sometimes played.

Keith looked around at the mess waiting for him that Saturday morning while Marvin snored away another hangover on the couch. He tugged at his white T-shirt and looked up to the ceiling. *In the meantime, Lord, could you send another one of Daddy's girlfriends this way? I can't handle this mess today.*

Cheo stepped off the elevator and followed the scent of Adobo to apartment sixty-three. He knocked on Cynthia's door before even going to his; he had to be sure that aroma of heaven was escaping from her place.

She greeted Cheo with a warm smile. Her hair sat on top of her head in a messy bun held together by a purple sash. "Cheo, I was just getting ready to ring your bell."

"You were? For what?"

"I wanted to find out whether you'd gotten in from the airport, and if so I was going to ask you to join me for dinner." She stuck her neck out and asked, "Well, do you want to join me?"

"I just came—"

"I'm having Spanish food," she sang, daring him to say no.

"*Por supuesto,*" Cheo said, parting his lips to reveal his choirboy smile.

Cynthia laughed. "I may be from New York, and we may have known each other four months now, but I just managed to figure out that *viejo* means old. Come again, *por* what?"

"I'm going to buy Rosetta Stone for Christmas." Cheo chuckled. "*Por supuesto* means of course I will join you, *mamí.*"

"The food is almost ready. Leave your bags by the door. Have a seat on the deck."

Cheo took a seat on the deck in the forest green chairs that had been there when they moved in. Cynthia trotted out carrying a bottle of sparkling apple cider, candles, and two champagne glasses. Cheo stared at the sky, sucking in deep breaths of the crisp air laced with the smell of yellow rice.

He tried to figure out what Spanish restaurant Cynthia ordered the food from. In the two years that had passed since his mother died he was unable to find a Spanish restaurant in Richmond whose food filled the air with an aroma that spoke directly to his belly, crying out "come and get me" like his mother's food did.

"*Ay, mi madre.*" He sighed up to the sky.

Cynthia used her foot to ease open the sliding door of the deck. In her right hand she held a platter of yellow rice and beans that she plated to look like a volcano erupting. The rice rose into the shape of a mountain in the center of the plate and the red kidney beans oozed out the top and down the side of the mountain like lava. In her left hand she held a plate of rectangles covered in brown paper bags sealed with white and red string. Cheo began to salivate at the sight of the small bricks of meat. He rubbed his hands together as he watched the steam rise. He couldn't wait to pluck the strings off the *pastelles* and devour them.

Cynthia placed a plate in front of him, and he noticed her orange-stained fingertips. At that moment Cheo realized this food did not come from some restaurant but from her kitchen and her heart.

"Don't start without me," she ordered him, licking her lips and adjusting the strap of her white camisole. She trotted back into the apartment to let her hair down and grab some matches for the candles. Cheo couldn't resist the temptation before him. He scooped up a spoonful of rice and funneled it into his mouth. The rice rolled around on his tongue. He eked out a partial smile because his mouth was full as she stepped through the door with her burgundy hair sweeping her shoulders. Like her, the food was full of flavor and love.

Cooking became a game between the two. It was an acceptable form of intimacy that didn't push Cynthia across the borderline into adultery. The more time they spent together, the larger her desire for Cheo became. He was everything she had never had: doting, daring, an artsy intellectual who didn't have to use force to assert his masculinity, and he was *fine*. Thoughts of Marvin sat on the backburner of her mind. Cheo was everything she wanted Marvin to be.

Chapter 24

"You know what I could really go for right now," Cheo shouted to Cynthia from the living room.

"What?" Cynthia stuck her head out of the kitchen door. Her eyebrows arched into a furrow. "Whatever it is, I hope it doesn't involve us lying on the floor to eat."

Cheo folded his hands behind his head and relaxed into the olive carpet. He focused on the blades of the ceiling fan as he formulated his answer: "Jerk chicken."

In the past year Cheo had flown all over the Caribbean, and jerk chicken was the first of Cheo's exotic requests when he returned from a trip to Jamaica. Their meals started out as simple classic Puerto Rican dinners like *pernil* with rice and beans or fried beef steak. Cynthia surprised him each and every time with lavish lime-infused *chuletas, carne guisado* with artichoke hearts, and even fresh flan. Cheo amped up his requests after she mastered most of the Puerto Rican dishes he requested.

"Jerk chicken?"

"Oh yeah. It's this spicy smoked chicken they—"

"I know what jerk chicken is," Cynthia said, emerging from the kitchen, a knife in one hand and a shallot in the other.

"Have you ever tasted it? It is delicious, especially from the side of the road. After a week of being home, I can still taste it."

"Well, I can't possibly make that for lunch."

"Huh?" Cheo gasped for breath.

"What is it?"

"I can't make lunch either." Cheo jumped up from the floor and dusted off his pants. "I have to turn my story in to the paper."

"Are they finally letting you write?"

"Yes, I finally convinced Bradley if I can write a book and take the photos for it, I can take photos and write newspaper articles as well. If I don't get it on his desk by five, I'll never get a shot like this again." Cheo planted a kiss on her cheek. "*Cena?*"

"Dinner?" she asked. Cheo gave her a thumbs-up. "Yes."

As soon as Cheo walked out of the door, Cynthia was on her laptop searching for a recipe for jerk chicken and where she could go to get the ingredients. She had to travel to four different stores and buy a small tabletop grill she could use on her deck to make Cheo's request. Cynthia delighted in the pursuit, preparation, and the product. All of the running, sweating, trimming, and stuffing stirred up feelings and memories of her youth.

Tears fell from her eyes as she chopped the small yellow Jamaican peppers for the jerk rub. Cynthia thought of the lavish dinner parties her mother used to throw.

Of course, that was before Mildred met Jesus and Cynthia met Marvin. In the middle of her nostalgic reverie, Cynthia paused to ask the Lord a question that had been troubling her for so long. *Lord, if you could deliver my mama from cigarettes and partying, why couldn't you deliver me from Marvin?* Cynthia waited for a response from Him and as usual she got the same reply: silence. Immediately she returned to her jerk rub.

Preparing meals for Cheo roused mostly positive feelings in Cynthia. It even elicited some creativity that Cynthia never even knew she possessed. The creative control she had over each meal and the atmosphere was a relief from the ennui that had taken over her life since she began temping. Typing e-mails and transferring calls was typically how she spent her day.

She sifted through departmental mail, fought off flirtatious bosses who tried to use permanent positions as bait for a date, and pretended to be amused during customary lunch with the other temps on the job. Lunch consisted of tales about their languid baby daddies or trifling ex-husbands who had snuffed out their dreams of the white picket fences by leaving them for the other woman. Cynthia adjourned each lunch psych session by saying, "At least he never beat you."

Thinking about past memories and regrets always ate up the time. Before Cynthia knew it Cheo was standing outside her door knocking on it and tapping his toes to the rhythm of Bob Marley's "Three Little Birds."

"Come in, mon," Cynthia shouted over the music.

Cheo entered the apartment. Cynthia had transformed it into another world. Not only had she managed to make jerk chicken with fried plantains, and rice and black beans, she'd also adorned the walls with paper palm trees, a path of rocks led to the deck, and Bob Marley's rich voice filled the air. Cynthia wasn't sure what drove her to such great lengths when it came to preparing meals for Cheo. What began as a small gesture of appreciation had turned into elaborate feasts. She blamed it on his thick eyebrows, the curl of his long, tender eyelashes, and the furtive glances he shot at her across the table during the meals.

Cynthia smiled on the inside as Cheo began to salivate at the sight the plate of mango and avocado salad topped with crushed coconuts in the middle of two plates of rice and beans, jerk chicken, and plantains garnished with cabbage leaves she carried in her hand.

"De food is ready, mon. Go sit down." Cynthia raised her chin in the direction of the deck.

Cheo stared at her as she walked toward him carrying two coconuts. She'd tried her best to make herself up like an island princess. Cynthia planted a purple orchid in her hair, gold dust shimmered on her shoulders, and her lips were covered in a peachy gloss.

Her hope was that her talent and dedication captivated him. She'd taken him up on his challenge and not only proved her skills in the kitchen, but she demonstrated an understanding of presentation.

"Tek a seat," she urged him in her faux accent. "Dis is de wickedest jerk chicken you go find in dis parish." She handed him a coconut filled to the brim with coconut water.

Cheo smiled, sliding the door to the deck open. He followed her onto the deck. They sat down and ate, drank, and laughed in the glow of dusk that settled around them.

"This wouldn't be a real Jamaican experience without some dubbing on the dance floor." Cheo stood with his hand extended, waiting for Cynthia to grab on when the beat to another Bob Marley classic, "Turn Your Lights Down Low," dropped. With mixed emotions, Cynthia eased out of her chair and into his arms. She embraced him with her whole body.

Her heart raced and her head pounded as she considered how quickly and tragically this would end if Cheo knew about Marvin and boys. Tonight definitely had to be their last rendezvous she reckoned before things got complicated. Although Cynthia didn't think she was entirely responsible for her attraction to Cheo. After all it was the Lord who'd made Cheo so majestic.

Cheo squeezed her tightly in his arms. Reminding her that no man not even her father had cared enough to embrace her like that.

"I've waited so long for this," Cheo whispered into her ear.

"Me too," she replied as Cheo leaned into her. They swayed in time to the music with their lips locked.

Resting her head on Cheo's chest after separating, Cynthia wondered how much longer he could wait for her.

Chapter 25

Cynthia still needed fresh air to start her day, even on this warm, sticky morning. She opened her teakwood blinds and opened the door to the deck. There was a knock on the door. Instinctively she knew it was Cheo. Without asking who it was or looking through the peep-hole, she let him in.

Her evening with Cheo had revived her. Cynthia felt like a honeysuckle whose petals had just been sprinkled with morning dew. Humming "No Woman, No Cry," she trod across the rug into the kitchen. Cynthia put on a pot of coffee and washed the remainder of the dishes from last night's dinner. The aroma of Bustelo and Cynthia's soft purr drew Cheo into the kitchen. He stood behind her, placing his thick hands on her hips, bending down to kiss her on the top of her head. He sniffed the orchid that was still planted in her hair, a remnant of last night's bashment.

"Good morning, *mamí*." Cheo snatched an apple out of the fruit basket on the counter. When he bit into it, Cynthia's lips curled up in disgust with a little grunt.

"*Que?*" He shrugged. "I drank the water in Mexico, and I've been eating your cooking. I believe I will survive." Cynthia splashed the soapy water at him.

"I'm joking. I love your food, as a matter of fact, *yo tengo hambre.*"

Cynthia glanced at him. "Just keep it local." It may have taken a few months but she knew that phrase meant he was hungry. "Toast, eggs, oatmeal, *tu sabe?*"

"Okay, babe. I'll be out on the deck."

Cynthia met him on the deck with a platter of toast, egg whites, bacon, and a cup of Bustelo with the steam rising from it.

"*Gracias, mi amor.*" Cynthia bowed her head and headed back into the apartment.

"Cynthia," he called to her like she'd gone far away, "aren't you going to eat breakfast with me?"

"Yes. I just need to go get the blender. I made an apple, mango, banana smoothie."

"That can wait. Have a seat." He patted his leg for her to sit on his lap. "Puhlease. I want to talk to you about something, something serious."

She trembled as he uttered those words, "I want to talk to you." She wasn't prepared for this moment, not yet.

"Cheo, I want to talk to you about something too. I need to tell you something that has been on my mind for a while."

Cheo stood and placed a single finger over her lips. "May I go first?"

Cynthia nodded.

"Have you ever considered going to a culinary arts school?"

"*Que?*"

"Have you ever thought about going to a culinary arts school; you know, to learn how to become a chef?"

Cynthia laughed hard and loud. "Culinary school . . ." She'd given up on the idea of using school as a means to fulfill her dreams. She'd gotten a bachelor's degree in psychology because she thought it was the easiest way to satisfy her mother's dream of raising a doctor without having to work on a cadaver. The idea of dealing with blood and any type of human secretions mortified her. The thought of letting her mother down was even scarier, so she clawed her way through college only to discover

she still had several years to go before she was even close
to hearing someone refer to her as "Dr. Hathaway." She
never followed up because Marvin was supposed to have
her living in the lap of luxury after he opened his string of
custom detailing garages.

"I'm too old to go back to school."

"You consider thirty-four to be too old? Are you kidding? You're never too old. Don't you want to become a
chef? You light up like Tokyo at night when you're in that
kitchen, and the food you cook is so delicious." Cheo put
his fingers to his lips and blew a kiss. "I mean you put a
lot into the preparation and presentation of these meals.'

"So?" She shrugged.

"So, you mean to tell me you've never considered it?
The thought never crossed your mind?"

"Yeah, I considered it. Yeah, it crossed my mind, and
like a stray cat crossing my path, I let it keep on walking.
At thirty-four, the one thing I do think about often is
time, and I don't have much of it to waste. Cooking school
costs money that I don't have."

"*Mamí,* I know somebody at the Culinary Arts Institute, and I told him about your gifts. He can get you into
the school, or at least a job."

"A job? I have a job already."

"You're a temp," Cheo said, shaking his head. "That's
not a job."

"You know what? I know it's not as glamorous as being
a photojournalist for the *Richmond Sun,* but it pays the
bills, and it certainly keeps your belly full, Mr. Rivera."
She hissed slapping him in the midsection.

Cynthia walked away from Cheo to her bedroom. She
wished the apartment wasn't covered in wall-to-wall carpeting so she could stomp down the hall. Cheo's criticism
of her life hurt her to her core. Cynthia didn't really enjoy
temping, especially at the rate Mitch contracted her.

Cheo's offer managed to disgruntle her simply because he was trying to tell her what to do. "Take a deep breath. Don't get all crazy; just cut your losses now," Cynthia told herself before walking out of her bedroom.

When she opened the door, Cheo was leaning against the wall near the bathroom with his hands stuffed into his faded blue denim jeans with his bottom lip turned down, looking like he had just lost his puppy. Cynthia brushed past him into the kitchen and poured herself a glass of water. He walked up behind her, his shadow encapsulating her.

He gently placed his hands on her shoulders. "Listen, Cynthia."

She spun around and shouted, "No, you listen, Cheo. I don't need you coming in here telling me who I should be and what I need to do. I already lived that life, and I'm not going back to it." She folded her arms across her chest and dared him to say another word.

"Cynthia, *calmate.* Bring it down a notch," Cheo said subtly. "You're blowing this whole thing out of the water. I'm not trying to tell you what to do. I just thought—"

"Cheo, I don't need you to think for me," she screamed, pointing a finger in Cheo's face.

"This discussion could go on forever, back and forth. My friend's name is James Sullivan, and he's the owner of Sullivan's Eatery. I'm going to leave his card on the table. Call him, don't call him, it's your choice. I was just trying to be helpful and cut you a break."

"I don't need you to cut me a break," Cynthia snapped at him, sucking her teeth. "Who do you think you are, God or something?" She gave him a full neck roll.

Cheo waved his hands in the air. "Ya, ya. That's it. *Salgo porqué tu estas loca.*" Cheo twirled his fingers at the sides of her head, making the international sign for crazy. Cheo turned his back to her and walked to the door. "*Cuando tu siente major, lláme.*"

"*Lla* what? You better not be talking about my mama."

He cracked the door and poked his head in and translated for her. "I said, when you feel better, give me call."

With that final word, the door slammed behind him. Hot tears streaked her chocolate skin. This wasn't supposed to end like this. Cynthia dragged herself down the hall and entered the bathroom. She avoided looking at herself in the mirror while removing her clothes. She stepped into the shower, turned on the water, and closed her eyes as the water fell on her head. She didn't plan on their discussion going around that corner.

Cynthia wanted to throw Cheo out, not have him walk out on her. Marvin used to walk out on her in the middle of their fights when he had enough of her shrieking. Every single time she planned on keeping her cool, being the bigger person, and walking out of the room, Marvin always managed to push her to her breaking point then walk away.

After traveling 335 miles, desperately trying to free herself from Marvin's grip on her pulse, here he was interrupting her life. It didn't help that Cheo's "let's talk" discussion was about the quality of her life rather than the discussion she'd imagined in her head about fidelity and the seriousness of their budding romance. Cynthia envisioned Cheo whispering the words "I love you" in her ear as she sat in his lap. Although she had every intention of rejecting his advances for the sake of her kids and not wanting to be confined by another man, it hurt her heart to know that after all she had done for him, all he could think about was putting her to work.

Still she had to admit his idea sounded like a good one; however, she wouldn't be making that confession today.

Chapter 26

Her bath, which was really a masquerade ball to hide her tears in, left her feeling cleansed and rejuvenated. Crying was the last activity she wanted to engage in, especially over a man. She was trying to put that all behind her. Cynthia threw on a pair of gray and pink sweatpants and a pink tank top and started cleaning house. She cleared the dishes from the table, scraped the food in the garbage, all the while sucking her teeth at Cheo's voice in her head: *estas loca*.

Maybe she was crazy. What else would cause a woman to abandon her home, her hope, and her children and then get involved with another man? The answer to the question didn't come; only more questions came, like maybe it was reverse. Maybe she'd been crazy to stay with Marvin so long. Maybe what she was doing with Cheo wasn't right, but men did this kind of thing all the time, right?

After the household chores were done, Cynthia sat at the dining room table with her legs folded and a cup of coffee, thankful that her present assignment at the Credit Union of Virginia had ended early. It would have been impossible for her to serve anyone with a smile today. The bank had contracted her for a month. After she'd flat out rejected the bank manager's request for her to stay late and take care of the evening deposits, Mitch called her up to let her know the bank would be fine without her services.

She picked up the card for Chef Sullivan and flipped it over and over in her hand. With every flip she attempted to coax herself into placing the call. There was nothing wrong with accepting help from a man especially since this involved cooking. There was potential nestled in the numbers printed on the card. A steady job had to be better than temping for dogs disguised as businessmen. A smile spread across her face as she imagined herself on the Food Network hosting her own show. Cynthia cradled the card in the palm of her hand until sweat caused its edges to wrinkle.

"I am not doing this for him. I'm doing this for me and for my boys." She pulled out her Android and phoned the restaurant. The first time she called no one answered. She paced the floor a few times then dialed the number once more.

"Ummm, Sullivan Eatery, tickling the taste buds of Richmond for twenty-five years. How may I help you?"

"Hello?"

"Yes, hello," a gruff voice barked into the receiver.

"May I please speak to Mr. John Sullivan?"

"He only answers to Chef Sullivan," the voice on the other end informed her.

"I'm sorry," Cynthia said adding a little sugar to her tone. "Please excuse me. May I please speak with Chef Sullivan?"

"If you wish to make a reservation, ma'am, please call the restaurant's main line. Do you need it?"

"I'm sorry; I'm not calling for reservations. I'm calling about the culinary arts school."

"Then I recommend you call the school. Have a good day."

And just like just her career as a chef was over before it got started. Cynthia drew back the blinds—she'd had enough of the light—sat down on the couch, hiked her knees up to her chin, and wrapped her arms around her legs. Cheo's words hung over head: "He could get you in the school, or at least get you a job."

She rocked back and forth on the couch trying to dodge Cheo's words while her mother's words of encouragement swam in and out of her ears. "If you knew better, you would do better. That's why you got to learn to wait on the Lord, wait I say on the Lord."

Either her imagination or her pride took over her senses as a vision of herself began to materialize. The scent of parsley filled her nostrils. She could feel the steam from the pots and pans on her skin and hear the faint sound of applause when she stepped onto the dining room floor of her restaurant. Cynthia entered into a dangerous conversation with herself.

I saw myself free from Marvin's abuse and I freed myself. I can see myself in that kitchen, and I'm going to get what I want. I'm not waiting on God, as slow as He is.

Cynthia licked her lips, which had become dry in her brief moment of hysterics. She picked up the phone and pressed the talk button. No one was going to stand in the way of her second chance at life.

"Sullivan Eatery, tickling—"

"Chef Sullivan, please," Cynthia said sharply, cutting off the gruff voice that attempted to deter her earlier.

"He's extremely busy right now. May I take a message?"

"Well, this call is extremely important. Please put me through, sir, or I will continue to call until you do."

"This is Chef Sullivan." He cleared his throat. "What can I do for you?"

"John Sullivan?"

"Yes, and I am in the middle of several catastrophes that are poised to ruin my career. My food orders for a major dinner party were mixed up, my secretary is out sick, and I'm on the verge of a nervous breakdown. This call better be of the utmost importance."

"My name is Cynthia Hathaway, and I am a friend of Cheo's. Cheo Rivera."

"Ahh, yes, he did mention he knew a little firecracker who liked to cook. Unfortunately, at this time all of my classes at the institute are full."

"I could work with you . . . I mean, for you. I don't know if he told you this, but I'm in my thirties already. School is the last thing that I'm interested in. I love to cook, but I've never done so in a professional setting. I just need a chance, a stepping stone, a diving board, a—"

"Enough with the metaphors. I get your point, young lady. Cheo said you're good. Let's see just how good you are. Help me salvage tonight's dinner and we'll go from there," Chef Sullivan said.

Fifteen minutes after getting off the phone with Chef Sullivan, Cynthia pulled in to the parking lot at Sullivan Eatery in the used Camry that Cheo had convinced her to buy a few weeks ago. The restaurant was alluring in a nostalgic kind of way. A red carpet and gold stanchions led to the front door. Cynthia knocked on one of the glass panes in the door. Slowly it creaked open. A young pimpled-faced, awkward redheaded girl opened the door.

"Daaad," she hollered through the restaurant. "Daaad!"

Cynthia fixed her eyes on the big bronze P in the PLEASE WAIT TO BE SEATED sign in order to avoid the eyes of Chef Sullivan's awkward teenage daughter. Her pensive gaze and her oafish stance reminded Cynthia of her own awkward teenage days. Cynthia feared looking into her icy blue eyes to discover she hadn't gotten far from those days. Luckily, as the girl began her inspection of Cynthia's skin for a single blemish, Chef Sullivan burst through the heavy black velvet curtain that concealed the dining area. The curtain hung open a bit, dangling from Chef Sullivan's broad shoulders.

Cynthia managed to get a glimpse of the gold ceiling and three-tiered chandelier in the center of the room. "Susan, use the telephone to call me next time. That incessant howling is causing the chandeliers to shake." He paused, directing his Mad Hatter glare to Cynthia. "So, you're the firecracker," he said, petting his goatee while looking down at Cynthia.

"Hello, Chef Sullivan, I'm—"

Chef Sullivan placed his finger in front of his lips, silencing her. "There's no time for formalities or cordialities." He turned his back on her and disappeared behind the velvet curtain. Cynthia pranced behind him.

As he walked and talked to her, his hands swung back and forth as he elaborated on his problem. "There was an accident on the interstate. My delivery of halibut won't be here until five o'clock, which is absolutely unacceptable since the guests are scheduled to begin arriving at that time."

"Serve something else."

"Something else? What else? Every dish on the menu is centered around the halibut. Mrs. Tailor specifically requested a seafood dinner for her and the mayor's twenty-fifth anniversary, and I don't have anything else in stock in large enough quantities to serve the whole party. I am ruined," Chef Sullivan moaned. "Ruined!"

Cynthia looked at the rounds of tables already set with place markers for the Richmond elite, from members of congress to Cheo's boss. The gold-trimmed white plates glistened on top of the burgundy and gold tablecloths. She rubbed the tables with her fingertips to feel the starch and grazed the centerpiece filled with lilies. Cynthia snapped her fingers. "Let's start with a coconut shrimp mango salad medley and a grilled shrimp lying on a bed of cellophane noodles propped up on a pillow of sugar snap peas and baby corn covered in oyster sauce," she said, using her fingers to illustrate her vision.

"Tilapia. I know where we can get some fresh tilapia."
She clasped her hands together and held them near
her chest. "Tilapia sautéed in a rich velvety cream of
mushroom sauce accompanied by asparagus almondine
and artichoke hearts stuffed with crab meat. Bread and
roses! Fill the dining room floor with rose petals; stuff the
baskets with warm bread. They'll have sea scallops and
pineapples on skewers for appetizers."

As she walked in a circle around the table rattling off
seafood dishes they could prepare in a moment's time,
Cynthia noticed that Chef Sullivan was tracking her with
his glacier blue eyes. Smoothing the hair at her temples,
she assured him everything would be fine.

"I know we just met but in case Cheo didn't inform
you, this is what I do." His eyes widened and he latched
on to every word she spoke. Cynthia could tell that his
impression of her was changing.

"I don't know how comfortable I am with these ideas.
I can't just give you free course in my restaurant, dear,"
Chef Sullivan said nervously.

Ignoring Chef Sullivan's worries Cynthia continued,
"Ah-ha! Flounder or sea bass. That's it."

"Bass."

"Yes, bass. Citrus-grilled sea bass garnished with
rosemary swimming in watercress and splashes of red
and purple onions."

"Cheo was right, you know your stuff, but where are
you going to get all of this from on such short notice?"

"I'm sure that a few of your regular vendors would be
willing to help us out in a jam. If you have a computer
with Internet access that I can jump on, we can take care
of this in a minute."

"In the office," he said, pointing to the ceiling. "It's
upstairs. Susan can show you where it is."

Cynthia shuffled through the velvet curtain. Susan was leaning over the hostess podium with her arms dangling over the top snapping her fingers to "Love in the Club." Cynthia grabbed her arm, jerking her headphones out of her ears.

"I need your help. I've got to use the computer in your dad's office."

Susan perked up and flashed a dry smile. She led Cynthia to a door to the far left of the main entrance and up the steps.

"Downstairs is for storage, freezers, and champagne. You need a key if you want to go down there; my dad has the key." Susan shot Cynthia a raised eyebrow stare.

Either Susan was trying to feel her out or squash any thoughts Cynthia might have about taking advantage of Susan's eagerness to help and her father's gullibility. Cynthia wasn't mad at the girl.

Chef Sullivan's office was a stark contrast to the pristine and elegant dining room he presented to his patrons. Heaps of paper covered his desk; crumpled receipts littered the ground like rice grains after a wedding. The right side of the office wall was covered by a bookcase that resembled the Leaning Tower of Pisa and housed a collection of cookbooks from Ellie Krieger to Gordon Ramsay.

There were books on meals from Japan to Timbuktu. The fourth shelf down was home to multiple copies of the same book, *Southern Cuisine,* by Chef Sullivan. Cynthia took a copy off the shelf and stroked the glossy embossed smiling face of Chef Sullivan in a quaint country-style kitchen with the windows open and black-and-white tiled floor. He held a pan of honey-glazed ham over a counter of fresh vegetables.

"That's Dad's book. As you can see by the many copies he still has, it didn't do so well. I told him no one wants a white man teaching them how to cook Southern dishes. He should have cashed in on the diet craze. Everyone in America is obsessed with weight loss; just write a cookbook about healthy eating or diet foods and we'll be featured on *Extra*. Noo, he couldn't do that. He's a real chef." Susan plopped into her father's high-back chocolate leather swivel chair. "What do you need me to help you with?"

Cynthia picked up a receiving paper from the floor and pulled a pen from her silver hobo bag. She jotted down a couple of ingredients. "Okay, Susan, go to goodtimegrocers.com and order these things. I order stuff from them when I'm cooking at home. They're fast and efficient. Be sure to select in-store pickup for today." Cynthia leaned over the desk to toss her list to Susan and then she darted down the steps.

Chef Sullivan met her at the foot of the stairs. Every vein in his neck was popping out.

"Chef, don't worry; everything is going to work." Cynthia stroked his arm gently. "Do you have some petty cash or something for me to get this fish?"

Chef Sullivan reached into his apron and pulled out his expense card. He stuffed it into the pocket of her jeans. "This is not a black card. Don't think about running off with my card or there will be serious repercussions," he explained. "We're expecting two hundred guests. Can you handle that?"

"It's handled." Cynthia saluted Chef Sullivan, ran out the restaurant, and into her car.

She peeled out the parking lot headed to the Broad Street Fish Market where she got the tilapia and bass. Once she secured the fish, she phoned the restaurant.

"Chef Sullivan, begin the appetizers. I'll be there shortly with our main course options and the roses."

"Where are you?"

"Gotta go. I'll be there in a second. There's a cop car behind me," Cynthia said, tossing her phone into the passenger seat. She cruised at the speed limit until the police cruiser sped by her and turned right. Once the cop car was out of sight, Cynthia did some driving that rivaled the Indy 500's highest ranked female driver Danica Patrick. She zigzagged through traffic, merely slowing down at stop signs rather than actually stopping at them. Sweat ran down her sides as she hurried to get back to Sullivan's Eatery.

It suddenly became clear to her this was the moment she had been waiting for. This was her opportunity to be more than Marvin's wife and more than a victim; this was her chance to live. Cynthia had been experimenting with food and recipes since she was teen. Mildred spent a lot of time at work leaving Cynthia with two options: play with food or boys. Food seemed to be the safest. With the life she wanted so close to her reach, Cynthia came down hard on the accelerator until she reached the restaurant's parking lot.

The glass door rattled under Cynthia's pounding. Chef Sullivan opened the door, a film of sweat covering his brow. His wild gray hair stood straight up, and his eyes bulged out of his head; his whites had turned red.

"Where have you been?"

"Chef, there's no time to converse. Get someone to pluck these rose petals. I don't know why I didn't think of this before. We need caviar and some peaches. You've got some of that on hand, right?" Chef Sullivan rolled his eyes as if he were taking inventory in his mind before nodding.

"We've got three hours to turn this thing around now," Chef Sullivan pointed out.

She brushed past him, her arms filled with parcels. The folds of the curtain latched on to her foot, causing her to stumble. Chef Sullivan stretched his long arms over her head to pull back the curtain just enough for Cynthia to slither through. She briskly cut across the dining room with the chef on her heels.

"I'm going to need help arranging the tables. Can you get someone to help me?" she asked over her shoulder.

Cynthia used her back to push open the kitchen doors. She walked in on a sous-chef steaming crab legs and the line chef doing prep work for what looked like a stew. She dropped her bags on the counter and began emptying the contents onto the steel countertop.

A hush settled in the kitchen. All that could be heard was the purr of Diana Ross singing the "Theme from Mahogany""

"I'm Cynthia. Who's getting the caviar and the peaches?"

No one answered her. They all returned to their jobs.

"So, no one can hear me?"

Chef Sullivan stood behind Cynthia with his hands on his hips. He cleared his throat and placed one hand firmly on her shoulder. "Everyone, this is my little firecracker Cynthia—"

"Hathaway," she interjected.

"Yes, Cynthia Hathaway, and she is a guest chef tonight. I want you to follow her directions as you would me and assist her in achieving her vision. Maurice, pit the peaches then fill them with caviar. Jules, there's a bundle of roses I left on the table out there. I need you to pluck the petals and cover the floor with them."

"I didn't join your team to become a florist," Jules said rolling his eyes.

"Our survival depends on this night. Be a team player now or be prepared to become a florist. Carnie, follow Cynthia out to the dining room so she can show you how to position the tables." Chef Sullivan paused and stared at his staff as if he was inviting them to jump ship if they wanted to.

Cynthia sucked up as much air as she could and closed her mouth. She could smell the contempt brewing.

"Let's move now. We've got less than three hours to turn this thing around," Chef Sullivan said clapping his hands rapidly.

Although Cynthia didn't care for imperious mannerisms, she adopted them right away, snapping, clapping, and pointing her fingers as she navigated through the stations of the kitchen to check on everyone's progress. In one fell swoop she'd found herself a home in Chef Sullivan's kitchen.

She stopped at the chopping station, leaning over Maurice's gaunt shoulders to make sure he carved the peaches perfectly. She even checked on the bass Chef Sullivan was rubbing down as she grabbed snatches of crab meat and stuffed them into the artichoke hearts. She'd found it, the "it" everyone searched for, among the clanging pots, rising steam, and parsley.

Chapter 27

Cynthia could feel Chef Sullivan's eyes on her. She looked up long enough to catch the look of amazement plastered on his face. Cynthia hadn't stopped moving since she'd burst through the restaurant doors that afternoon. At the moment she was busy hunched over a table scraping leftover food into a gray basin that the busboys were only allowed to bring out at the end of the night.

While there were customers, they bussed and cleared the tables using the same round, sparkling trays that servers used when bringing the meals out. Chef Sullivan cringed at the sight of those basins. To him it seemed as though they screamed, "Someone named Alice works here," and he didn't want diners to have that image in their head while munching on his butternut squash soufflé.

"Here, I saved this for you." Chef Sullivan handed her a small platter containing a caviar-filled peach with bits of shredded coconut and a glass of champagne. Cynthia smiled at the plate. In all the melee surrounding the evening, she'd only performed the standard taste test. She didn't have the opportunity to nosh on anything on the menu except for a few pieces of shrimp that she popped in her mouth when no one was looking.

Yet she knew the night was a success because of the many toasts and the numerous trips she had to take from the kitchen to the dining room for Chef Sullivan to introduce his new apprentice chef. Someone from the

Richmond Sun had even taken her picture. She wished Cheo could have seen her. Her first bite into the peach sent her eyes popping out of her head as the caviar and the luscious peach crashed into each other on her tongue.

"Amazing, isn't it?" Chef Sullivan raised his eyebrows. "Now take a dollop of this," he said, pointing to the coconut and ginger sauce that garnished the plate. Her eyes rolled back as she sucked the tangy sauce off her fingertips.

Chef Sullivan clapped. "Now please try to imagine these tables filled with people doing the very same thing." Cynthia smiled at him.

"It was magnificent, and you, my little firecracker," he said, shaking his crooked pointer finger at her, "are a gift and a curse. None of these dishes are on my menu. What shall I do when the mayor's guests return requesting citrus-grilled bass, caviar-filled peaches, and rose petals on the ground?"

Using a small piece of leftover peach rind, Cynthia scooped the remaining sauce off the plate. Between smacks and sips of champagne, she replied, "Tell them those items are not on the menu. The entire menu was prepared in honor of the mayor's twenty-fifth wedding anniversary, and should they elect to have Sullivan Eatery cater an event a similar menu can be prepared for them."

"Oh yes, I love it! Personalized menus; where did you come from?"

Laughing at Chef Sullivan's compliments, Cynthia rose from the table and placed her dishes in her basin and began collecting the silverware.

"What are you doing? Put that stuff down, girl. When you cook for Cheo you may have to clean up, but in this restaurant, the chef does not cook and clear the dishes. Don't get used to it though. As an apprentice chef, you will be cleaning the kitchen and doing whatever I tell you to."

Relieved of dish duty, Cynthia asked, "Chef Sullivan, do you think I could take off now since my services are no longer needed?" She curtsied.

"But we haven't even discussed how I'm going to accommodate you or your schedule."

"My mama always told me that it isn't good to make a business decision without sleeping on it. Chef Sullivan, if you wake up hungry, call me and we'll chew the fat so to speak. I'm terribly exhausted. May I please go home?" Cynthia cupped her hands in front of her chest and batted her eyelashes enough times to wear him out.

Chef Sullivan stood directly in front of her, placed his hands on her shoulders, and began spouting off his wisdom. "Cooking is about love. It's about follow-through and dealing with disasters. You are the first apprentice chef who has demonstrated that understanding. I'm going to excuse you this evening. Tomorrow, it's full speed ahead. I want you to be forewarned: only the food we cook has the luxury of being exhausted."

An orchestra of crickets singing in the ribgrass greeted Cynthia when she arrived at home. Usually the crickets made her cringe, and the sight of the people in gym at midnight would make her heart ache for New York, but nothing could bring her down right now. For good measure she charged up the steps.

The stairwell opened up directly in front of Cheo's apartment door. She raised her fist to knock then changed her mind. Planning her peace treaty breakfast, she strutted down the hallway to the beat of the salsa music erupting from Cheo's apartment. A bright pink Post-it was waiting for her at her door. Again Cheo had beaten her to the punch.

Lo siento mi amor.
Cheo

She repeated the words *lo siento* over and over trying to conjure up the meaning. She played back the times she'd heard him using it, when he bumped into the old lady in the elevator and every time he was late: *Lo siento, lo siento. I am sorry, I am sorry.*

Cynthia entered her dimly lit apartment wondering if sorry and a Post-it could fix everything she had done wrong.

Chapter 28

"What a vision," Chef Sullivan said as he exited his Acura MDX after parking it in his reserved spot.

Cynthia was leaning on the side of her maroon Camry wearing a lilac Peter Pan–collared blouse and a pair of art deco–printed pants. The side-eye stare that Susan gave Cynthia made her feel uncomfortable. Cynthia managed to eke out a shaky smile to hide her concern. She couldn't figure out whether what she spotted in Susan's eyes was a dislike or distrust.

"Darling, you shouldn't have wasted this outfit on me." Chef Sullivan double kissed Cynthia. "Besides, this isn't just a meeting." He locked arms with her, and led her in slow stroll through the parking lot to the restaurant. "It's a follow-up interview of sorts. Tonight you are going to be helping me cater a dinner party for Terrence Hadley. He's a visual artist on the rise, and after he heard about the mayor's dinner, he called me last night and begged, pleaded, and canceled his catering order at Chez Josephine, which is nonrefundable at this point."

"I have a change of clothes and flat shoes in my gym bag. I'm ready to chef it up," Cynthia retorted, bobbing from side to side like a boxer preparing to spar in front of the door.

The locks on the door clinked with the twist of Chef Sullivan's key. Susan and Cynthia entered shoulder to shoulder and stood at attention in front of Chef Sullivan.

"Susan, take her to the office. Cynthia, you can use my bathroom to change," Chef Sullivan directed before disappearing behind the curtain.

While they walked upstairs to the office, Cynthia tried to think of what she could say to win Susan over. She'd already deduced she'd made a number of enemies in the kitchen on her first night at the restaurant and Cynthia was sure that tonight would be no different. She felt she needed as many people as she could get on her side if she was going to survive, and the boss' daughter was certainly a good ally to have.

When they reached the office, Susan twisted the gold handle on the door and allowed Cynthia to enter first. "I know what you're up to, and he's not going to buy it," she said slamming the door shut behind them.

Midstride Cynthia turned back and asked, "What?"

"You're not the first and you certainly won't be the last. I've seen a lot of women come in here trying to pass sex off as skills so that my father would back them. You're definitely different. You've got guts, you've got style, you've got what my dad calls 'pizzazz,'" Susan said, making quotations in the air, "but it won't work here, and unfortunately for you, you can't even go down to the Culinary Arts Institute and weasel your way into a class since you didn't do things the proper way."

Cynthia wanted nothing more than to slap the child upside her head, but she let her continue. Now was not the time to give way to her emotions when everything was riding on this one opportunity. This could be the break she needed to get her boys back.

Susan shrugged at Cynthia. "I guess you're just going to have to go back where you came from."

"Well, Susan, you best believe I've got skills. Don't you worry about your precious daddy, sugar, because I didn't come here looking for a man. I came here looking for myself, and I'm sorry if I happened to rain on your parade because I found myself here. Now if you'll excuse me, I need to change my clothes." Without Susan's permission, Cynthia entered Chef Sullivan's private bathroom. She undid the buttons on her blouse and slipped into a classic white T-shirt and a pair of khaki capris that hugged her waistline.

With a smile slathered across her face Cynthia waved at Susan when she exited the bathroom. "Sue, let's go take care of business," she said still smiling.

"My name is not Sue. It's Susan."

"I'm sorry, sugar," Cynthia said, walking ahead of Susan down the steps.

For the rest of the week, Cynthia's made a point to end all her sentences to Susan with "sugar" and a smile. Unlike every other apprentice chef who spent hours practicing the pilot for their cooking show during their down time, Cynthia helped with every aspect of the restaurant. Everywhere that Cynthia turned she ran into Susan. First she stumbled upon her when she was stacking the meat freezer. Next she found her while she was bussing tables with the busboys when Chef wasn't looking. After closing, Cynthia could be found either bussing tables or sweeping the floor.

During Cynthia's initial days at the restaurant, Susan's feelings for her seemed to waver like a weathervane during a storm. But by closing on Saturday night, Cynthia was able to break the ice. She pulled the ear buds out of Susan's ears and asked her to join her in the main dining area.

"Come on. I'm going crazy in there talking to the broom."

"He only responds when you sing to him," Susan said.

"Now, see I didn't know that. Would you be a dear and show me? What's his favorite song?"

Susan strong-armed the broom out of Cynthia's hand and belted out, "'I'll give up anything, anything and everything, just to see you smile,'" into the the broom handle like it was a microphone on the *X Factor* set.

Cynthia basked in Susan's smile. It had been a year since she'd made a child smile. Although it wasn't one of her own, it was enough.

Chapter 29

Rolling out of bed, Cynthia cracked her neck, stood up, and stretched. She rolled her eyes at her reflection upon spotting the bags beginning to form beneath them. Another night of sleep had escaped her. The meteoric rise to the top of the food chain at Sullivan's Eatery didn't come cheap. She'd been clocking fourteen-hour days for the last six months and getting two to three hours of sleep when she wasn't being haunted by the life she'd left behind or tormented by the huge hole not speaking to Cheo had created in her life.

It was a silly fight that resulted in nothing but her feeling embarrassed, confused, and frustrated by her own doing. She'd decided that Barbara was right; she didn't have time for frolicking with the "foreign exchange student down the hall." Of course, now she regretted that decision and wished she had just accepted his Post-it apology. At least she wouldn't feel so alone.

A small voice inside of Cynthia suggested she return home.

"Can I?" she asked her reflection. "Should I?" She imagined the greeting she'd receive from Marvin: some choice words that could be spelled with four letters and a few jabs.

What about the boys? the voice inside of her countered.

Every day she promised herself she'd go back for them, but with each passing day, she established another reason why she couldn't, and today was no different. She, along with the rest of the staff, had been summoned to Chef Sullivan's home in Chesterfield for an early morning meeting.

Chef Sullivan usually held a staff meeting the first of every month to set goals, celebrate birthdays, and plan future menus. For whatever reason he'd decided that the November meeting would take place at his home.

Cynthia put on a coral-colored fitted tee and slouchy leatherette sweatpants and hopped into her car. She used the time in standstill traffic on the highway to put on her makeup. Based on Chef Sullivan's reaction when she stepped out of her car, the makeup application skills she'd acquired while covering up Marvin's handiwork had begun to wane.

"Did you sleep with the devil?" Chef Sullivan asked, making circles in the air near her eyes as they stood in the driveway of his five-bedroom gray and white brick home. Chef Sullivan was way too observant for it to be Sunday morning.

Spreading his arms open wide to embrace her, he asked, "What's going on, honey?"

"I can't even begin to explain it to you." Cynthia feigned a smile in an attempt to dodge the barrage of questions she could see forming in Chef Sullivan's eyes. Cynthia was excited to see the home Chef Sullivan. She'd developed a close affinity with him after working side by side with him for six months. The liberties he'd given her in the kitchen made her feel welcome and capable of anything. Nevertheless, her lack of sleep wouldn't allow her to enjoy the moment.

"An early morning mimosa will get rid of whatever is ailing you."

"Chef. It's eight a.m." Cynthia balked.

"Didn't I say early morning? Come, come, hurry up and get inside before one of my neighbors sees us." Chef

Sullivan wrapped his arm around Cynthia's and began walking. "They're always trying to get in here. Susan says I'm paranoid. I don't buy any of that 'we just want to welcome you to the neighborhood' stuff. I think they're nosy and want to scope the place out."

Cynthia wobbled up Chef Sullivan's cobblestone walkway in her wedges using the chef as a crutch to keep from falling down. When they reached the steps, Susan pulled the door open and shouted, "Good morning. I love that dress, Cyn. Turn around."

Smiling at the compliment, Cynthia spun around in slow motion. She'd also gotten quite close to Susan in the past six months.

"That dress is gorgeous. Cheo is going to die when he sees you in that." Chef Sullivan picked up the porcelain tray that was resting on the table near the door. "Mimosa, hors d'oeuvres, mademoiselle?" He bowed slightly while offering her some fruit kabobs.

"You didn't tell me Cheo was coming. I can't stay. I have to go," Cynthia cried fanning herself. She didn't know whether she should be happy or nervous about seeing Cheo again after so long. Panic was the first emotion to set in when she thought of being in such close quarters with Cheo. She hadn't planned what she was going to say to him. She'd done so well at avoiding him.

"Don't be silly. You have to stay. We're having a meeting and I'm not even sure I understand why you're not speaking to him."

"You wouldn't understand," Cynthia barked back.

"Please take a sip." Chef Sullivan shoved a mimosa into Cynthia's hand. "Susie, go to the kitchen and finish plating the fruit kebabs please." Once Susan turned the corner, Chef Sullivan continued, "Cynthia, are you all right? You've been snapping at people a lot in the restaurant lately. I can't tell if you're coming or going."

"It's . . ." Cynthia hesitated. "No, I'm not all right. I haven't been sleeping because I'm a monster."

It occurred to her that she could reveal her secret now and be freed from her burden, but she didn't want to let Chef Sullivan down.

"Whatever it is we can work through it." He held her free hand tightly. His eyes were full of sympathy.

"I just haven't been able to sleep lately," she said between sips of her mimosa. "I've got a lot on my mind."

"Listen, I know an excellent doctor who can help you with your insomnia, and there will be plenty of people here to keep you and Cheo separated."

Chef Sullivan led Cynthia to the living room. The sunlight cast a resplendent glow through the floor-to-ceiling windows. The contrast of the white crown molding set against the azure blue of the walls made it seem as if they were outdoors.

"Anything you want is at your fingertips." He pointed at the large banquet table set against the wall.

The scent of sage and bacon dragged Cynthia over to the table. Freshly baked banana bread, seared scallops flanked by bits of bacon, sage, and almond fritters, and a pot of peach-coconut and pistachio quinoa porridge greeted her. "Chef." She gasped, looking back at him.

"Susan said I went overboard, but I wanted you to feel at home. I want everyone else to be inspired. I was thinking we could go bigger than our usual give-a-gift donations to charity for Christmas this year. You already know how much I love giving to charity, so I thought we could try something new for Thanksgiving: Adopt-a-Family." Chef Sullivan smiled warmly as he revealed his plan to Cynthia. "We'll all invite a family who's struggling, or someone that we know who might be spending dinner alone this year and I'll invite the families from the Home Again family shelter to celebrate Thanksgiving."

"That sounds great."

"It gets better. We're all going to work together to plan the menu, which will feature dishes made by every chef or cook in honor of one of the families or people we've invited. My hope is that today we'll be able to start brainstorming together."

Cynthia groaned, pained by the thought of having to collaborate with her peers who had been less than welcoming since the first day she stormed into the kitchen of Sullivan's Eatery.

"This meeting will be fine, I promise you," he said, squeezing Cynthia's hand. "Since the whole staff will be here, I'll make sure everyone is in check."

The doorbell chimed, announcing the arrival of two line cooks and three waiters. Each of them had a mimosa in their hand, their eyes fixed on Cynthia, and their mouths curved like the spout of a teapot prepared to shoot off some steam before Susan could escort them to the living room.

Cynthia ducked out of the room through the dining room and into the kitchen. She helped Susan plate the honey coconut couscous and sundried tomatoes and basil toast. She garnished the platter with rosemary and a drizzle of balsamic vinegar.

"Where's the back door, Susan?"

A tidal wave of laughter took over Susan.

"I'm serious," Cynthia whispered, looking over her shoulder for the chef. "I'm not going to make it through this meeting. By the time it's over your father will fire me."

"What are you talking about? He loves you like you're his own," Susan replied.

Cynthia brushed her side bang out of her face. "This meeting is going to be awkward as it is with the other cooks and me in the same room, and then add . . ." Cynthia's voice trailed off.

All of the breath in her body left when she caught a glimpse of the seasonal blond wait staff handing Cheo a fruit kebab and mimosa. His skin glowed against his charcoal gray linen button down. His smile was warm enough to illuminate the room and melt her heart. Her gaze followed him as he walked arm in arm with the waitress into the living room.

"What's going to happen with the other cooks around?" Chef Sullivan asked creeping up beside Cynthia.?"

The sound of Chef Sullivan's voice caused Cynthia to jump. She hoped Chef Sullivan had only caught the remark about the other chefs and not a whiff of her longing for Cheo.

"I was saying I can't stay. Between Cheo and the other chefs, I'm not going to make it. What is he doing here anyway?"

"I want Cheo to take photographs of the event. I think it would make great publicity for the restaurant. As for the other chefs, would it make you feel more comfortable if I have a talk with everyone?" Chef Sullivan offered, stroking Cynthia's shoulder.

"It won't change their mind about me, and it certainly won't change mine. I don't belong here in more ways than one," she said, picking at her cuticles.

"You're right, Cynthia. With your skill level and passion, you belong in your own kitchen, but until that happens for you, Sullivan's Eatery is your home. Anyone who disagrees with that is going to be on their own." Chef Sullivan pierced the carving board with a knife, punctuating his sentence.

Chef Sullivan grabbed her hand and dragged her back out into the living room. A few staff members were seated on the ombre green sectional, some at the banquet table, and others stood marveling at the view the floor-to-ceiling windows provided.

Clanging his fork lightly against a champagne glass, Chef Sullivan signaled for everyone's attention.

"Good morning, everyone. I called this meeting to discuss our plans for our Thanksgiving program and menu. First I must address an issue that has been troubling me for quite a while now, and I cannot take it any longer. I like to have a certain atmosphere when I'm working as I'm sure you all do, but the conditions under which some of us have to work right now are totally unfair."

"Tell me about it," someone said from the banquet table.

Cynthia rolled her eyes at the jeer, which she knew was intended for her. "See what I mean?" she whispered into the chef's ear.

Still clutching Cynthia's hand, Chef Sullivan walked over to the banquet table and delivered the rest of his chastisement from there. "It has been brought to my attention that some of you do not wish to work with Cynthia and have been making her feel unwelcome in my kitchen. Well, let me remind everyone that this is my kitchen and whoever does not approve of my hiring decisions can find another restaurant to work in because my money is on this little firecracker right here." Cheo and Susan began to clap and cheer from the back of the room. Chef Sullivan waved at them to knock it off, wrapped his arm around Cynthia's shoulder, and pulled her in close to him like a proud daddy at an awards ceremony. "If you want to oust her then you better out chef her because she is not going anywhere."

The scent of anise and curry powder emanating from Cynthia's door and the sound of her singing dragged Cheo to her apartment. He stood there poised to knock, listening to her belt out "Superwoman." Singing was as much a part of her cooking process as chopping an onion. Cheo lowered his arm at the thought she could be working on something special for Chef Sullivan. His head hung so low his chin touched his chest. Paciencia. *Be patient.* His bones longed for her, and this morning was no different.

He heard through Chef Sullivan that she was thriving at the restaurant. According to Chef Sullivan, she'd brought in new flavors and used her office manager skills to whip things into shape at Sullivan's Eatery. Yet she had nothing to say to Cheo in the six months and two days that passed since he walked out on her. He had walked past her apartment door the next day so he knew she'd received his Post-it apology, but she had not responded yet. *Maybe she didn't think it was as cute as I did.*

He marched back to his apartment, plopped down on his chaise longue, and called his old buddy Chef Sullivan for some advice and another little update since he didn't have the heart to intrude on her.

"Cheo, what's going on, man? Why don't you come down here and sample some of tonight's menu? You know your girl created it," Chef Sullivan said.

"That's why I called you. I wanted to ask you a question."

"Is this off the record, Mr. Rivera? You reporters are always trying to get the scoop."

"I'm no reporter. They only let me write one article. Seriously, it's a personal question. How long do I have to wait for her?"

"Until she's ready. You can't rush a woman into anything she doesn't want to do or you won't want to do it either. How serious is it?" Chef Sullivan inquired.

"I think I have a heart condition,'" Cheo sighed, "and I only began showing signs once she was out of my life."

"What I recommend is you come by. Let's talk about this thing in person because I can't sit down and talk to you on the phone. I'm in the middle of World War III ever since I brought her in here. Every chef in here hates her guts right down to the line cooks. That speech I gave during the meeting didn't go over well either. Now I have to keep an eye on everyone and everything because they'd do anything to sabotage her."

"Chef Sullivan, I'll be down there in a few."

"Cynthia won't be in until the restaurant is open, which gives you plenty of time to get in and out if you hurry. Don't worry; we're going to get you two back together."

Chapter 30

Every morning Cheo's Post-it saluted her. Cynthia stuck it to the refrigerator, and it became a haunting reminder of the night she turned into a banshee, screaming and whipping her head around, protesting Cheo's help.

She fingered the upturned edge of the Post-it and smoothed down the top right-hand corner that threatened to stop sticking to the refrigerator. She missed his lips, the curve of them and the feel of them. That morning when she woke up, she played with the thought of apologizing with a cup of *café con leche* and a knock on the door. Everything would go back to the way it was. On the other hand, she shuddered at the thought of having to admit she was wrong. Cynthia redirected her attention to the task at hand: curry waffles. They were a hit on *Iron Chef,* and she was determined to create her own version to share with Chef Sullivan that afternoon in preparation for the Thanksgiving charity event the restaurant was hosting.

The competition between apprentice chefs from the Culinary Arts Institute class and the sous-chef Chef Sullivan employed at the restaurant was heating up, and every one of them had one goal in mind: sink her battleship. Those who had been under his tutelage for years resented all the perks Cynthia received after just walking in off the street. She was creating menus instead of spending hours carving peppers and learning how to garnish plates. Her rapid ascension to apprentice chef without so much as taking a class threatened to dismantle the hierarchy of kitchens everywhere, and not one of them was willing to see that happen.

She reached up in the cabinets and began plucking spices from the shelf. She dumped coriander and curry powder in a wooden bowl and began pounding on it ferociously in an attempt to silence the thunder that was cracking in her head. Besides neglecting Cheo, she had not called Keith in the six months that she had been working at Sullivan's Eatery to check on him and James. It didn't seem like a phone call would be enough to rescind the damage she'd done by being away. She felt guilty for not being there. She felt guilty for enjoying not being there. Part of her felt like it was too late to salvage her relationship with her sons.

After a year away from them it still felt unnatural for her to be away from them. Cynthia managed to keep the boys from haunting her at night through a combination of sounds from the Amazon, a lavender-scented aroma-therapy eye mask, and the occasional Ambien that the doctor Chef Sullivan had recommended prescribed to her so she could fall asleep.

She had yet to find a way to deter the boys from invading her daytime thoughts, and every now and then her maternal instinct kicked in and she found herself in dire need of taking care of someone.

Besides her calling, Cynthia found someone to mother at Chef Sullivan's. Susan, the chef's redhead daughter, had become her temporary solution. When Susan was around, Cynthia directed all of her maternal affection toward her.

Cynthia greeted Susan every afternoon with crepes and fruit skewers or a batch of crème brûlée. Once Susan finished her afternoon snack, she joined Cynthia in the kitchen. Everyone would watch Cynthia mince onions and dice peppers for one of her creations while Susan sat on a stool with her raggedy red Converses perched on the stainless steel countertop. Cynthia would swat them down while Susan cut up slices of sweet buttery Havarti cheese and stuffed them in her mouth between syllables as she expounded on the intricacies of life in middle school.

Thinking about how much her relationship with Susan had blossomed seemed to calm some of the rumbling inside of her. Her day went by so much smoother and faster when she spent it sharing tips on how to minimize pores and which boy to avoid with Susan. As thoughts of her sons surfaced between each twist of the mallet and mortar, Cynthia thought it would be great to go in early and surprise both Chef Sullivan and Susan with her curry waffles.

November in Richmond was often filled with sunny skies and sixty-degree temperatures, but the overcast sky and subtle breeze made it cool enough for Cynthia to don a bold tangerine tailored blazer over a white scoop-neck top, slim dark-rinse boot-cut jeans, and brown flats. She walked carefully to the door of Sullivan's. Balancing the platter of curry waffles in one hand she tried to push the door open with the other.

She flicked her wrist to see the time. It was ten a.m.: too early for the doors to be open but late enough for someone to be working. A gust of wind blew right through her, compelling her to get off the street before the downpour began. She pounded on the glass with her free hand, wishing she had an umbrella as she felt small droplets of water hit her head.

She gave a sigh of relief as the doors of Sullivan Eatery opened. "What took you so long?" she asked, expecting Susan to open the door for her. Instead she looked up into Cheo's dark eyes.

There was a subtle beauty to the brokenness in his eyes that completely captivated her.

"I'm sorry."

"For what?" she asked, pursing her lips together. "It's not your job to get the door."

"Is this how you want to play it?"

"Let's not do this now," she said shaking her head.

"Don't you miss me at all?" he asked with sad eyes.

"Cheo, please, let's not do this now, especially not here." She softly laid her hand on his chest. The fervency of his heartbeat shook it. Cynthia hoped he'd allow her to end things peacefully before either one of their hearts got broken.

"When can we do it then?" he implored.

"Soon. We will talk soon," she stated flatly.

For Cynthia soon meant never. She hoped Cheo picked that up from her tone of voice.

"Well, at least let me help you inside with this." His hand grazed her forearm as he lifted the platter from her arm. The slight touch shook her like a small pebble does when it's thrown into a pond.

On second thought I hope he didn't pick that up.

Chapter 31

Cynthia rubbed her eyes to make sure she wasn't seeing things. The hexagon clock that hung on the wall in front of her bed read 7:30. *This is not possible,* she thought. *Who could be ringing my bell at this time in the morning on my only day off?*

Cynthia was double booked daily. She'd been stretching herself tissue paper thin by doing some freelance catering on top of working for Chef Sullivan, and she'd finally begun taking classes at the Culinary Arts Institute.

The lack of sleep was frying her brain. She deemed it a worthy cause though. With the money she saved from the catering gigs, she planned on opening her very own restaurant and getting her boys back. Chef Sullivan's pep talk about her capabilities during their monthly meeting back in November had inspired her to seriously pursue getting her own restaurant, and she had not slowed down. It was now February, and in the three months since that meeting she'd sat down with a bank loan officer at Virginia Credit Union. Now that all her dominoes were lined up perfectly, she was prepared to make reparations.

But first she had to answer the door.

Cynthia flung on a robe and snatched her door open, prepared to give the person on the other side a piece of her mind.

"Good morning, senorita."

Cynthia shrank back and clutched the neckline of her robe. She took a deep breath before saying his name.

"Cheo, what are you doing here?" She studied him. The sight of him made her quiver. This morning there was something irresistible about him.

"I want to make peace with you, *nena*." Cheo reached for her hand. "I miss you. I miss your laughter and your smile. I miss your voice. I miss the bounce of your hair and the sparkle of your eyes." He delicately stroked the side of her face with his knuckles and kissed her. She collapsed into him like a building hit by a wrecking ball.

"*Lo siento, mi amor, lo siento.* Do you understand that?" Staring deeply into her eyes, he translated, "I'm sorry, my love. I'm sorry," then drew her in for a long, passionate kiss.

Cynthia placed her hands on her lips after separating from Cheo. Never had she been kissed like that. She appreciated his honesty and willingness to take the fall for the rift she'd caused. Cynthia inhaled, filling her lungs with his John Varvatos cologne before speaking. "Would you like to come in? I haven't prepared anything yet, but I can whip you up something in a moment."

"Actually, I wanted to take you out. I was thinking we could get some brunch and go to church," he said gently tapping her nose.

"Church?" she shrieked like a mouse caught on a glue trap.

"Church. You know the big building, pews, hymn books, clapping, and some precious child singing. Don't tell me you're one of those atheists."

"Cheo, why do want to go to church?" she asked, ignoring his statement.

"Why don't you want to go to church?" he shot back.

Cynthia massaged her temples. She was sure she would have to confess her sins to Cheo, and she was not prepared in any shape, form, or fashion to do so.

"Seriously, Cheo, why do you suddenly want to take me to church? You haven't arranged for me to marry one of your cousins for a green card, have you?" she joked.

"*Mi madre* always told me, '*Hijo, cuando Jesús bendice usted debe dar gracias.*' When Jesus blesses, you should give thanks." He took her hand into his and kissed the back of it. "Cynthia, He has blessed me with you. No one has made me feel this good since my mother died, and I know that He blessed you. Your photo is in the *Richmond Sun* like every weekend. You're cooking for celebrities and politicians. You're really blowing up. *Que razón* do you have not to go to church?"

Cynthia withdrew her hand from his grasp and scratched her shoulder. "Cheo, we should probably discuss this inside. It's a long story."

"Just put on your Sunday best, Cynthia. There's one thing I've learned in all my travels; no matter how far you go, the good Lord is always ready to welcome you home. *Vete,* go, go," he said, waving his hands at her.

Cynthia retreated to her bedroom and probed her closet for a business suit that could double as a church outfit. She settled for a belted A-line red dress and paired it with a black cardigan for a cover up. She pulled most of her hair up and created a side bang for a little extra flair.

"You do realize we're going to church?" Cheo asked when he saw the way her dress hugged her svelte frame and the lift that her black pumps gave her.

"Cheo, don't tell me you went and got all born again on me."

"I don't know if I would go as far as to say I'm completely saved. I'm trying to live the best life I can possibly live, and I've learned that only happens when you're obedient to God."

"Is that why you've been taking it so slow with me?" Cynthia placed both hands around his waist squeezing him tightly.

"I've been taking it slow with you because . . . because I love you. I know how Jacob felt when he saw Rachel because that's how I felt the moment I saw you."

Cynthia shook her head no.

"I used a lot of the time that we spent apart attending church. Just give it a chance. I'm trying to do things a little different, but I want you to be a part of my life."

"I'm not promising you that I'm going to get all sanctified and fire baptized, but I'll go see what all the fuss is about," Cynthia said finally giving in.

"Dayspring Church of Divine Healing and Prophecy." Cynthia mouthed the words skeptically as she read the church awning when they pulled up in front of it.

Cynthia's heart sank in her chest at the thought this could be the moment she was outed. She buried her face in the palms of her hands as she pictured the pastor of Dayspring Church of Divine Healing and Prophecy walking up to her calling her out of the pew for a little prayer, a little deliverance, and a little healing. Meanwhile, he'd do some major revealing after the Spirit dropped a little word in his heart.

Cheo squeezed one of her hands. "Babe, I promise it won't be that bad. You're going to like it. Trust me."

They were forty-five minutes late, which only left them with the option to sit separately near the front or squeeze into one of the middle rows. They squeezed into one of the middle rows. Some of the members of the congregation insisted they hurry up and sit down while the man of God was on the pulpit.

"When you're out of the will of God that is the most dangerous place you can be. It's a scary and dark place that Satan tries to decorate with your heart's desire just to keep you content, just to keep you bound," Pastor

Wyatt informed his church. Cynthia recognized him from his picture, which was neatly placed in the corner of the church's awning.

Cynthia clawed at a spot on her neck that suddenly began itching. She tried to focus on the array of colored hats and the few crying babies rather than the words that convicted her heart. Pastor Wyatt was on fire, speaking the truth, and filling the parishioners with the good news, which was bad news for Cynthia.

With only one year left on her apprenticeship and a little more than a quarter of the $75,000 a bank loan officer told her she'd have to come up with before they'd grant her a $300,000 loan and Cheo seated beside her, she knew today's Word was written for her.

Cynthia watched Cheo lap up the Word. She indulged in Cheo's profile: his defined nose, his cheekbones.

"Stop making excuses for why you can't get out of sin, why you can't give it up, and get over it. Jesus died to give you the power to free yourself from everything that seeks to destroy you and your relationship with Him," Pastor Wyatt declared.

"Preach!" someone shouted from the back row.

Cynthia's legs shook with each word the pastor spoke. "God knows what He wants to do for you. He has plans for you to prosper and bring you to an expected end, but you keep getting in the way. Your way isn't going to work. Only what you do for Christ will last. Stop living in the past, and focus on the future Jesus has prepared for you."

Cynthia squirmed in her seat like a worm on a hook. She could not hold still for one minute of the two-hour service, and every time she looked at Cheo, he just nodded and smiled at her as if everything was copasetic.

After the service Cheo and Cynthia drove to a nearby café for brunch. They sat in the booth in silence. Cheo dived into his platter of banana and walnut-covered

French toast seemingly unaware of Cynthia's discomfort, and Cynthia focused on her buttered toast, which was all her stomach could handle after the service.

"Is everything okay? You haven't said a word since we got out of service. I am so glad to see the Lord stirring something up inside of you. Maybe now you'll be able to put your demons from the past to rest and settle into this new life and receive everything the Lord has in store for you, including me."

"Demons?" Cynthia dropped her toast onto the platter.

"Don't be ashamed. We're all battling something. Maybe now we can face this thing together head-on."

"Cheo, you know all of that stuff the pastor was preaching about being out of the will of God? Is that us? Is it wrong for us to start seeing each other again?"

Cheo sipped his coffee. "Love isn't wrong, Cynthia. We just have to do it God's way; you know, no hanky-panky. Hopefully we can still smoochie smoochie. I'm going to have to ask Pastor Wyatt about that."

"Cheo, stop saying you love me."

"*No entiendo.*"

Cynthia wiped her hands with her napkin. "Cheo, just stop it," she snapped.

"How can I just stop loving you?"

"You can't love me, Cheo. You don't even know me," Cynthia said so loudly the other customers in the restaurant looked back at their booth.

"Then let me get to know you. If you think your huffing and puffing is going to sway me that easily this time, you're wrong. Let's not do this here, Cynthia," he pleaded, reaching for her hand. She snatched it away from him.

Cheo leaned in closer and seized the other hand. "Let's not do this at all today. Let's just enjoy each other."

"Well, I'm done." Cynthia threw her napkin on top of her half-eaten toast. "I'll be outside."

Cynthia hurried outside, trying to block out Pastor Wyatt's distinctive deep voice. Snippets of his sermon kept replaying in her ear and her boys' faces kept circling in her head. She crossed the street, pulled her cell phone out of her purse, and dialed the number of someone she knew really loved her.

"Hello," Marvin grunted. "Hello, you better say something or I'm going to hang up this phone."

Cynthia flirted with saying something. As she stretched her lips to say, "Marvin, it's me," her tongue felt like she'd licked the back of an alley cat: bristly. The phone shook in her hand making it hard for her to tap the end button. While she struggled to drop the call she could hear Keith trying to get the phone from his father.

"I got it, Dad. It's probably one of my friends and you scared them," Cynthia heard Keith say.

"Hello. Hello," Keith repeated. "We can talk now."

Cynthia inhaled deeply.

"Ma, I went to church today. I hope you did too. I had a breakthrough today; at least that's what Grandma said. My heart isn't hurting so much anymore. The police stopped looking for you but I know that you're coming back. They say you ran away and they can't prove Pops had anything to do with it. I know it has to be on your own terms now. When you're ready, I'll be waiting for you. Until then, I have to go. Pops is calling me. I started calling him Pops. I think it sounds cooler. Ma, could you try to be ready soon?"

Chapter 32

Everything in him yearned for Cynthia. Marvin never thought he would miss Cynthia this much, and the yearning demanded to be satisfied. That was why he accepted all of Bridget Johnson's, his current girlfriend's, advances in the produce aisle of Finefare. She helped him clear up his confusion between regular strawberries and organic strawberries. She definitely wasn't as sweet as Cynthia or nearly as easy on the eyes. She was willing to cook, clean, and give him what he needed. She was like a live-in nanny with perks.

After crashing at his place for two of the six months since they'd met, Marvin finally broke down and gave Bridget a key. She could not stand being relegated to operating on the same schedule as the boys and Marvin in order to get in and out of the apartment. If she was not free to come and go as she pleased, she told Marvin, she was going back to her place.

It shocked Marvin that after nearly two years without Cynthia, he was still struggling with her absence, juggling trying to find a replacement, deal with the boys, and advance in his business efforts. Prayer didn't seem to be working out for any of them. Every Sunday Mildred picked the boys up and hauled them off to that hole in the wall, Mount Carmel. Marvin didn't agree with her decision to take them there, and he could barely understand why she would trek all the way up there to go church when there was one near her house. She said it was for normalcy. He figured it was to piss him off.

Either way, at this point, Marvin didn't care because God was obviously too busy or not listening to their petition for Cynthia's safe return. And it provided him the opportunity to do what he did best. While the boys were out, Marvin entertained his lady friends. He had a steady stream of them on rotation after Jade who lasted three months.

He didn't manhandle any of the others after Jade since the police were still sniffing around from time to time. With no body and no clues, Cynthia had Marvin looking like the black Scott Peterson who was convicted of murdering his wife back in 2002.

None of Marvin's women, until Bridget Johnson, could really handle his erratic behavior, the drinking, and the boys. Keith was too grown and James was silent and weird. She was the next runner up in Marvin's Be My Wife pageant.

Marvin never really thought twice about the new dynamics of his family until he returned from work at about seven o'clock one Friday evening. He stopped in the kitchen to wash his hands in the sink and get a beer. When the top of the beer can snapped, Keith called out to his father from his bedroom followed by Bridget from their bedroom. Marvin determined from the desperation in each voice that both of them had been waiting for Marvin to come home, hoping for the coveted opportunity to be the first person to report what had transpired between them that day.

Marvin hustled into his son's room. The door squeaked as Marvin pushed it open and glanced at James's empty bed. "Where's your brother?"

"He's at Grandma's. Pops, I need to talk to you about something," Keith said in a deep voice that marked his passage from child to his teen.

Marvin cringed every time Keith called him Pops. He never complained though. Marvin didn't think a fourteen-year-old almost as tall as him should be calling him Daddy anymore.

"Shoot. You want a beer?" Marvin asked, toppling over with laughter. Keith's stoic look told Marvin that this was no laughing matter. "Sorry, I was just joking."

"Can you close the door?"

Marvin closed the door and took a seat on the bed beside his son. "What's up, man?"

"Why do you keep telling these chicks that our mother is dead?'

"Huh? You lost me at chicks. What chicks?"

"Women. Why do you tell these women that our mother is dead?"

"Keith, if you met a girl and she told you her old man left her, wouldn't you want to know what happened?"

"I guess so." Keith shrugged his shoulders then asked, "What does that have to do with Ma?"

"What do you think happens when I meet a woman and have to tell her my wife left me and my two sons?" Marvin rose from Keith's bed and stepped in the center of the room. "Well, what do you think happens?"

"I'm sorry, Pops. I didn't think you wanted me to actually answer that."

"Knock it off. Just tell the truth. You don't know what happens." Marvin paused, giving Keith a moment to think about what that conversation actually sounded like. "I'll tell you what happens, most women don't ask. Either she's the kind of woman who thinks she's a love doctor and can repair my broken heart or one who's scared to be hurt so they run like I've got a disease or something because no woman runs off and leaves her kids behind unless the husband is some kind of a whack job."

"When they do ask, you don't have to tell them that she's dead," Keith said softly.

"I never told anyone that she's dead," Marvin said, clearly confused about where his son was getting his info from.

"We heard Bridget on the phone this morning saying Ma is dead. Jimmy lost it. He broke down crying, threw his plate on the floor, and spit on Bridget. I had hold her down and try to keep Jimmy off of her at the same time. Now if you didn't tell her that, where did she get that from?"

"You know it ain't none of your business what I tell her, but since I'm so glad you're speaking to me, I'll humor you. I didn't tell her she was dead. I told her she's gone. She assumed I meant she died, and I never corrected her. Is that all?"

Keith lowered his eyes to the ground and nodded. Marvin took a few steps toward the door then abruptly stopped.

"Wherever she is, she's never coming back, so what's the difference?" he asked looking back at his son.

"Pops, on Sunday Pastor David said Christians have the power to speak things into existence. I don't know if that works for people like you, but if Pastor David is right, then I'm right my mama isn't dead. She's alive, and she's going to come back for me."

Marvin pulled the door shut tightly behind him. He looked up and gazed into Cynthia's eyes. He drifted past each photo of her holding the boys in her lap. He smiled at Cynthia in the photo, thanking her for them.

"What happened?" he asked the photo, rubbing her face. "We could have gotten through it like we always did." He stared into her almond eyes. "I'm sorry."

"Mar-vin," Bridget hollered from the bedroom in her haughty voice. "Mar-vin."

"I'm coming," he answered, then resumed his conversation with the photo of his wife. "Cyn, I'm sorry, but it's time for me to let go." He put his beer can on the floor and proceeded to lift each picture frame from its mount on the wall. For a moment, he stood in the hall with his hands full of frames and pondered whether he should chuck them.

Bridget continued to scream his name, interrupting his decision-making process. Marvin really wasn't sure whether taking down the pictures would help. On more than one occasion he'd caught the boys in the hallway staring at her photo as if they were trying to memorize what she looked like. He on the other hand didn't want or need a visual reminder of what was missing from his life. Finally, he decided to leave them on the table for the boys to sort through. They could keep them if they wanted or burn them. Marvin turned off the light and shuffled down the hall.

He opened the bedroom door and found Bridget splayed across the bed in a bejeweled royal blue satin nightgown that hugged her body like a glove. The scent of cinnamon filled the room, and the tea light candles placed on the windowsill added ambience. Marvin did an about face.

"What is it, Marv?"

"I forgot my beer."

"I got something better, baby." She jumped out of the bed and opened the top drawer of Cynthia's armoire, pulling out two glasses and a bottle of brandy. She filled each glass to the brim. Bridget sashayed over to Marvin at the door and placed his glass in his hand and shut the door behind him. She kissed his neck.

"Bridge, I know the boys ain't easy, but cut them some slack," he instructed as she kissed his neck. "Don't talk about their mother in front of them."

"Mar-vin," she cried, sucking her teeth, "do you know what Keith did to me? He put his hands on me and James spit on me."

Marvin stepped back until he was near the door to create a little separation between them, "I don't care." He walked over to the bed, took a seat on the end, and began to remove his work clothes. "I don't care what they did or what they said. You were talking about his mother right in front of them. What did you expect to happen?" Marvin pulled the covers over him. "Put those candles out before you start a fire."

Chapter 33

The walls of Mount Carmel rocked with rejoicing when the men's choir commandeered control of the pulpit from Pastor David. Every person in the congregation rose to their feet with their arms lifted as they began to sing "He That Believeth."

"Aren't you glad about everlasting life? It's not only in the future that we have access to these promises. In this world, also we will be blessed by God. He's ready and waiting to fulfill our heart's desire if we are willing to fulfill His Word."

Pastor David stared at Keith and James in their long black and royal blue choir robes. They'd become faithful members of the congregation in the two years that had passed since Cynthia left. Sister Mildred served as a good steward over the master's sheep by helping get them there, and once they were there, it was all business.

The boys focused on the sermon, sat still, and soaked up whatever they could from the message. A dark cloud hung over their heads, especially James, who seemed to be there in the physical but not in spirit; he didn't even open his mouth to sing while he was on the pulpit with the choir.

Pastor David could see the oppression of the enemy trying to surround them. At the end of every service, Pastor David tried to greet every parishioner, and his spirit urged him to be sure to catch the boys before they walked out the door.

"Church, we've got to get it together and remember who the blesser is and how He works. God is moved by faith. Your faith that Jesus Christ is the son of God, Lord over heaven and the earth, compels God the Father to make a move on your behalf. Hebrews 11:6 tells us we must first believe He is and that He rewards those who diligently seek Him. Do you believe that He is?"

The amens came rolling out. One sister with a red hat that sat on top of her head like a fan threw her hat on the floor and broke out into a chorus of hallelujahs!

"If you know that He is then, seek Him. Look high and low for Him, and He will bring the things that you want if they be in His will for you to have." A hush fell over the crowd. "Oh, Mount Carmel, what's the matter now? You didn't hear the words you wanted? Well, He's not going to give you something out of His will and you shouldn't want anything out of His will. You should want His fullness. Wake up early to meet Him, and go to sleep late expecting His coming, and He will bless you, church. Amen."

Pastor David turned the pulpit over to the evangelist to run the altar call and administer the benediction before dismissing the congregation. He wanted to be free and ready to greet the boys as soon as the service ended. James was the first he approached. Pastor David fixed the collar on James's navy blue suit. "You're looking mighty sharp there, young brother. God is blessing you, I see." James nodded at him. "You're not even going to give my God some praise?"

"Please excuse him, Pastor," Mildred said rising to her feet in James's defense. "He doesn't speak to anyone. I think a mute spirit done took a hold of his tongue. When you have a moment, Pastor, please pray for my little grandson."

Pastor David motioned to one of his deacons to bring him anointing oil, then let the oil drip onto James's head and tapped his chin for him to open his mouth.

"Stop!" Keith exclaimed. "He doesn't need that. He stopped speaking when she left. Can't anyone see that? His voice went out the door with her." Keith's nostrils flared, he swallowed hard, and he held his eyelids open to imprison the tears building up. "I don't know where she went, but she took his voice with her. Why won't God make her bring it back? Why won't He make her bring back his voice?"

Keith's pain jumped out of his throat and slapped his grandmother in the face, backing her into a seat on the first pew. Tears streamed down her face like the rapids of a river. Pastor David wrapped his arms around Keith and pulled him close to him.

"I know she's coming back. She's coming back for me, but she's been gone so long with his voice. How long can James wait? Pastor, why won't God make her bring back his voice?"

"You have to understand something about God, Keith." Pastor David bent down and stared into his eyes. They weren't the eyes of a fourteen-year-old. They were the haunting eyes of an old, tortured soul. "God loves us very much, so He doesn't make us do things. God will not make your mother come back. If she returns, it—"

"When she returns," Keith interjected. "When she returns."

"All right, brother. You got it. Last month's sermon, the power of the tongue; let's speak this thing into existence. When she returns, it's going to be on her own, and when she's ready. What you have to do, son, is be steadfast. Love God with all of your heart, stay away from all evil, pray for her, and thank God for her."

"How long?"

Pastor David paused and questioned Keith with his eyes. He didn't like this question. This was a dangerous one, the sort that gets you tangled up with the devil because you can't wait for God to work things out.

"How long am I supposed to wait?" he asked again.

"Until it's done, but have faith and praise Him knowing that it is so," Pastor David said with full assurance.

"My father says she's not coming back."

"Keith, what do you believe?"

"She's coming back, Pastor. I believe she's coming back."

Chapter 34

"What did you say your name was again?" Marvin asked, shrugging his shoulders to shake himself out of Bridget's grip. She was using her fingers and lips to explore the rugged terrain of Marvin's body, making it hard for Marvin to focus on something as simple as a name.

"Yes, this is Marvin Barclay, but who is this?"

"Mr. Barclay, this is Ms. Reid, the social worker at Leadership Academy," she said, carefully pronouncing each word. "I am sorry that you have to begin your Monday this way, Mr. Barclay. Keith's promotion is in doubt and James's teachers would like to know if he has been receiving any sort of speech therapy or counseling."

"Promotion in doubt? Counseling? For what? There's nothing wrong with him. He's just not that talkative," Marvin said, attempting to deny the crisis that had besieged the family two years ago.

"Mr. Barclay, do you know what PTSD is?"

"Yeah, it's a nice way for y'all to call soldiers crazy. My boys ain't crazy," Marvin declared slightly on the defensive.

"No one is saying they are crazy. Keith has become more aggressive and less focused on his coursework, and it is my understanding James has not spoken since your wife left. I think it's time you sought some professional help for your family."

Marvin cleared his throat, readying himself to deflate her ideas. "Listen, miss, my boys are doing just fine. The next time you're looking for someone's business to mind, make sure it ain't mine."

Bridget pumped her fist beside Marvin's and nodded in agreement.

"Mr. Barclay, this is a courtesy and my suggestion isn't really optional. Many teachers have voiced their concerns about both Keith and James to me, and if they don't begin attending some sort of counseling program then I will be getting child services involved."

"Are you threatening me?"

"No, I'm just doing my job, Mr. Barclay, and it's time for you to begin doing yours. I know that mental health issues are touchy, especially in the African American community, but this is not a time to let pride or stigma get in your way. You must find someone to counsel the boys. When you come in to sign the papers stating you are aware that Keith may be held back, you can let us know who is providing your sons counseling, or we can assist you in finding a good match. The guidance counselor is available to meet with you any day this week. For which day of the week should I schedule the appointment?"

"I'll get back to you." Marvin pressed the talk button on the house phone and slammed the receiver down onto the table. Reclining in the chair with his arms folded and his foot rapidly tapping the ground he conjured up as many excuses as he could to invalidate what the social worker suggested.

His excuses turned into wishes. He wished he could get some guidance from his own father right now, but even if he were alive, his advice probably would not have been beneficial.

The more Marvin thought about his own father, he realized when it came to the maintenance of his household he had become an absentee landlord just like him. His father was diligent in taking care of all the surface matters. Marvin and his mother always had food, a roof over their heads, and a little pocket change; however, when it came to the interior, his father was nowhere to be found. The most Marvin could recall getting out of him by way of conversation was, "Take care of your mom when I'm not around, kid."

Interrupting his musings, Bridget gently gripped his thigh and asked, "What happened, Marv?"

Bridget was perched beside him on the edge of the couch staring intensely at him. This was what he wanted, someone with whom to share his pain, but he wasn't satisfied with her presence. His wish was that Cynthia was there, then he wouldn't be facing this alone. Teenagers are bound to get into something, and whatever the boys got themselves into, it would have been easier to handle with her by his side.

"Marvin, talk to me. What is it?" Bridget asked with her lips poked out to form a little pout.

"The school says I have to take the boys to counseling."

Bridget turned up her lip. "Counseling? Do you want those people all up in our business?"

The world seemed to be closing in on him again. Johnnie Walker Black could take care of this, or he could actually take care of this, but how? Rising from his spot on the couch, Marvin began pacing.

"Marvin—"

"Shush," he said, cutting Bridget off. "This is way too much for Monday morning. I just need to figure out how I'm going to do this. That low-rate health insurance Milton offers doesn't cover counseling, and you're right, I don't want them all in my business."

All the muscles in Marvin's back tightened as the thought of displaying his dirty laundry to a stranger entered his head. There was no way he was going to sit in front of someone and boohoo about his problems and have his sons sitting up there crying about how hard life was.

Bridget slithered up behind him. The satin of her nightgown brushed against his skin as she began rubbing his back. "Don't get all worked up."

"That's easy for you to say." Marvin wriggled out of her grasp. "You're not going to have social services investigating you or trying to take your kids away."

"Don't get short with me. This ain't my fault," Bridget insisted.

"You're right, Bridge. Come here." She scurried into his extended arms. Marvin kissed her forehead lightly. "I just need to figure out how to deal with this now," he stated, squeezing her tightly.

Marvin's ascent up the hill from St. Nicholas Avenue to Amsterdam was painful. With each step he took toward Mount Carmel a small fraction of his pride died. He didn't want to ask Pastor David for anything that even resembled assistance, but Pastor David knew his sons well and could advise him or direct Marvin to the place where he could go to get the help that was necessary for him to keep what was left of his family together.

He'd purposefully waited until noon to visit the church in order to avoid running into any of Pastor David's fake bodyguards or anyone else he knew. He had to maintain his bad boy rep in the streets.

When he reached the church, he could see some lights bursting through the windows, breaking up the dense fog that covered the city. With a bowed head Marvin walked through the doors and up the aisle of the sanctuary. His eyes roamed the perimeter of the church in search of a member of the congregation or one warm body. Being alone in the church really made Marvin nervous. By the time he reached the altar, he found four warm bodies bent in supplication; one of those bodies belonged to the person he was in search of.

"David."

Pastor David immediately raised his head and peered over his shoulder. Although at least two decades had passed since they'd spent time together, Marvin could still read Pastor David; the twitching in his left eye meant he was pissed. The only thing Marvin didn't know was what the cause was. Did him interrupting prayer bother him, or was it the fact that Marvin wouldn't call him Pastor David? He wasn't sure why. Something in him would not allow him to call a man he knew had once robbed people—a man who he'd seen nearly beat several people to death all on separate occasions—Pastor. And he certainly was not going to show any reverence to someone who abandoned him.

"How can I help you, Brother Marvin?" Pastor David gripped the altar, using it as a crutch to pull him up.

Marvin took his time answering Pastor David, pausing to frame his response in such a way that it didn't seem as though he needed the pastor or his God. "Can we talk some place private, man?"

Pastor David whispered some words to the three people on the floor praying then held up two fingers indicating Marvin should follow him. Pastor David led Marvin down to his office.

"What is it?" Pastor David demanded as soon as he crossed the threshold.

"The social worker at the boys' school called me today and said that they need to attend counseling or else they're going to sic child services on me," Marvin said quickly divulging what he considered to be a very personal matter.

"Do you want me to pray for you?"

Marvin shook his head and stuffed his fists into his pockets to help reduce the risk of him hauling off and punching the scriptures out of David. "Do you think this is some kind of joke?"

"No, brother, that's what I do when I think something is serious; I pray and that's what I instruct the members of my church to do, which is why I was upstairs praying with that family when you walked in." Pastor David walked to his desk, flipped through some papers then looked at Marvin again. "If you don't want prayer, Marvin, what do you want?"

"I wanted . . . I mean I thought you would know where I could send the boys to get some counseling. I don't want to lose them." Pastor David's eyes widened as Marvin began to expose his sensitive side. "I know you don't believe me. I wouldn't expect you to understand. I love my boys."

"I don't doubt that you love them, but your brand of love is not real. If you love them, you'd consider getting yourself some counseling as well," Pastor David suggested.

"Me." Marvin rolled his eyes and chuckled. "Me, Marvin Barclay, attend counseling like some little—"

"How are you going to have that kind of attitude and send your sons to counseling? Discussing what bothers you is not a demonstration of your weakness. Being able to articulate your feelings without being ashamed of them is a demonstration of your power as a man. Why don't you model that for them? I'll even counsel you."

Marvin broke out into laughter. "You can't be serious. Now you want to be my friend after deserting me? Are you serious?" Marvin hawked and spit into the garbage can to get rid of the sour taste that filled his mouth when he thought of David's transformation from thug to pastor and what that meant for a then-sixteen-year-old Marvin. It meant he'd lost the only person in the world he called friend. He lost the only person he knew would give his life for him. Pastor David had taken on multiple knife-wielding gang members to save Marvin.

"If you're serious then I am," Pastor David said, intruding on Marvin's stroll down memory lane. "Jesus never asked us to do anything He wouldn't, and as a good father you shouldn't either. Model this process for them."

"You want me to share my pain with you?" Marvin pointed at Pastor David. "This was a waste of my time. Why are you Christians always telling people what Jesus did? He did that stuff because He could."

"And so can you, Marvin."

Chapter 35

After receiving two more follow-up phone calls from the social worker at Leadership Academy and some encouraging words from Bridget, Wednesday morning Marvin found himself rocking back and forth in one of the comfy chairs in the room that Pastor David referred to as the Upper Room.

It just looked like a conference room with pictures of various scenes from the Bible. One picture struck a chord within Marvin: Jesus on the cross surrounded by darkness. Marvin did not want to equate himself with God. He wasn't that crazy or arrogant, yet he felt like he was carrying the world on his shoulders. While he meditated on the black that surrounded him, without Marvin's permission tears streamed down his face. He didn't realize he was crying until Pastor David handed him a small box of tissues.

Blotting his tears, Marvin initiated the session. "So, how does this thing work, David?"

"Well, first we establish boundaries. We figure out what's off-limits and what's allowed. For instance, calling me David is off-limits. If this is going to work, we both have to take each other seriously," Pastor David stated matter-of-factly before unbuttoning his navy blue blazer and taking a seat across from Marvin at the conference table.

Marvin scoffed at the idea of creating boundaries when the two of them once had no boundaries. They were joined together like sneakers and shoelaces and now he wanted to set up some regulations.

"Nah, man." Marvin shook his head and drew a line across his neck. "That's a no-go. You're not going to tell me what I can and can't say. That's not going to work for me."

"Listen," Pastor David said, sitting upright with his hands neatly folded on the table, "drawing boundaries goes both ways. You can tell me which areas in your life are off-limits and I won't bring them up; at least, not right away. My only request is that you refer to me as Pastor David. Respect me as I have respected you. Now, if you can agree to this let's open in prayer."

"Do I have to hold your hand?"

"Not if you don't want to, Marvin."

"Go ahead and pray . . . Pastor."

Marvin closed his eyes and latched on to the words. He recognized strength, faith, man, humble, forgive, sins. Although he couldn't follow or grasp the scriptures Pastor David recited as he prayed, Marvin could feel something stirring inside of him. He refused to attribute it to the Holy Ghost or the tinge of jealousy he felt toward Pastor David's relationship with God or the peace and tranquility that radiated from his face when Marvin was all twisted into a knot around himself.

Please just say . . .

"Amen." They exhaled together.

Scratching his goatee, Marvin began, "Well, you already know why I'm here. I need some help. There, I said it. I need help."

A smile broke out across Pastor David's face.

"Now don't go getting all excited over there, Pastor. I'm not saying I'm getting baptized tomorrow. I'm just saying that I've made a mess of things and I need to know how to fix it," Marvin said rubbing his head.

"Follow Jesus."

"Is Jesus your answer for everything?"

"Yes."

"Well, if Jesus has all the answers, could you get heaven on the line and ask Him why He couldn't make my wife stay? I mean she was a member of your great congregation and all." Marvin stretched his arms out wide and waited to see Pastor David wince after that potshot.

"Have you asked yourself what you did to make her go?"

Marvin winced. "That's below the belt. I know I haven't been the best husband, but I can only be the man I know how to be. My pops wasn't around."

Pastor David raised an eyebrow. Marvin tried to explain why being raised by a single mother was more than a sob story. "Hear me out, Pastor; don't judge me. You know he wasn't around, and when he did show up, regardless of what condition he was in or what he did, my mother doted on him. I . . . I . . . I just wanted a small piece of the glimmer of love I'd seen so often in my mother's eyes when she looked at my father."

"Even if it required you to use a little muscle to get it?"

Using one hand, Marvin massaged his temples. Apparently Pastor David wasn't holding anything back.

"Another low blow," Marvin cited.

"You used to box if my memory serves me correctly." Pastor David bobbed from side to side in his chair like he was shadowboxing. "How do you recover from a low blow?"

"A punk takes the five minutes to recover and a fighter thugs it out."

"Then the question is which one are you and what is it that you are willing to fight for."

"If you're asking me did I hit Cynthia, then the answer is yes, I did. Does that give her right to walk out and leave me with these boys? After all my father did to my mother, she didn't up and disappear. How many women you know do that kind of thing? She promised she would be here."

"Our time is almost up, Marvin, so I can't answer all your questions. There is one who can and will, whether it's in this life or the one to come. I want you to consider this until our next session: what did you promise her? Is there a way for you to keep that promise even now? Do you want to close us out in prayer?"

"Do I have a choice?" Marvin inquired.

"Yes, that's why I asked." Pastor David chuckled. "You don't have to if you don't want to."

"I'll do it. You Christians take too long when you're praying. Give me your hands." Marvin paused shocked by his own words. Pastor David extended his arms across the table and placed his palms into Marvin's hands. "Lord, we thank you for the birds and the bees, the flowers and the trees, and we pray that someday you meet our needs. Amen."

"Birds and bees?"

"Shut up," Marvin said waving his hand at Pastor David. "My mama taught me that prayer." Marvin and Pastor David fell over the table laughing hysterically.

"When you were a child, you spake as a child. Now you're a man. It's time to put away those childish things, Marv. Read 1 Corinthians 13 this week. It's all about love. You need love. That's the only thing that will keep this family together."

Marvin closed his eyes and spoke to the Lord in his heart. Love was a strong word that he'd had no use for until now. If Marvin was going to learn to love, the Lord was going to have to show him how personally.

***

A week later the boys joined Marvin in the Upper Room at Mount Carmel for the next session.

"What are we doing here, Pops? I thought you didn't like Pastor David," Keith inquired while they waited for Pastor David to join them.

"There are some things we need to work on, boys, and we have to do them together."

"Yes, unity," Pastor David chimed in on the conversation as he entered the room.

Marvin observed his friend's attire. There was nothing too flamboyant about his appearance: freshly ironed khakis and a plaid button shirt.

"It takes unity to make a family work," Pastor David continued, "and the only way you're going to be unified is if you use the love of Christ to hold you together."

Clearing his throat, Marvin looked at Pastor David. "We're not here to get saved, Pastor. Let's just run a regular session." Marvin unzipped his beige track jacket. "Let's deal with the issues at hand. My fourteen-year-old son is going to be repeating eighth grade." Marvin slapped Keith across the back of the head. "And this one over here"—Marvin pointed at eleven-year-old James, who was seated to the left of him with his thumb in his mouth—"thinks he's a mime. I read that chapter you told me to read, and I don't see where the Lord mentioned anything about that."

"I see you're prepared to dive in head first, Marvin. Let me take my seat." Pastor David hustled around the conference table to his seat. "You want to open us up in prayer, Marvin?"

"I'm good. Do your thing, preacher man," Marvin said nodding at Pastor David.

Pastor David opened the session with a great prayer that invoked the God of Abraham and Jacob. Marvin watched Pastor David through one eye, wondering if this prayer was really going to be powerful enough to touch his situation.

The boys shot up like bamboo reeds. Every time Marvin blinked, James's legs had gotten longer and his silence greater. Meanwhile, Keith's mouth had gotten smarter and his heart colder. Marvin had very few moments of clarity, and there were very few days that he recalled being sober besides these two counseling session since Cynthia left. Something was definitely working, yet Marvin still didn't buy into this whole "Jesus can fix it" motto or the idea of counseling.

"Marvin, since we've met privately already, I'm going to open the floor up to Keith and James. This is a safe place, and you guys are free to discuss what you want, and you can say what you want. Nothing is off-limits unless you say it is. Because this is a safe place, we can set boundaries so that you feel comfortable."

"Does he have to be here?" Keith tilted his head toward Marvin.

"What? I know this boy done lost it now." Marvin fumed slapping his hand on the table. "Yes, I have to be here, and I'm going to be here. I'm your father. Where do you get off saying something like that?"

Until Pastor David shouted out his name, Marvin didn't notice he had a handful of Keith's shirt in his hand and was using it to choke Keith.

"Let him go, Marvin. Don't be like Lavell," Pastor David cried, shuffling around the table.

At the mention of his dead father's name, Marvin took stock of the situation. He looked over his shoulder at his young son who stared blankly with tears streaming down his face then at Keith whom he held tightly in his strong grip.

Keith's eyes bulged as he sputtered, "See, see this is why he shouldn't be here."

"Remember what he did to you, Marvin," Pastor David said as he tried to pry Marvin's hand open. "He hurt you. I know he hurt you, Marvin. I saw him hurt you." Pastor David continued to try and peel apart Marvin's fingers.

Marvin wanted to release Keith. Yet as the memory of Marvin's abusive father surfaced and its grasp latched onto Marvin his grip on Keith tightened.

"Marvin, let him go. I'm begging you just as I begged Lavell that night he choked you and everyone else at your mother's house looked on. Let him go, Marvin. Let him go."

Marvin's grip loosened, and he dropped Keith back into his chair.

"Don't ever bring his name up again. I'm not like him. That's my boundary."

"Marvin, you're doing yourself and the boys a disservice if we don't discuss the things Lavell did to you and the scars they left you with."

"The only thing he left me with was some old albums, and that's about as much time as I am going to dedicate to talking about him. I already told you how I felt about not having him around, and I'm not going to discuss what happened when he was around." Marvin arched his neck and stiffened his back and took on his fighting stance until Pastor David retreated to his seat on the other side of the table.

"Okay, Keith. James, the floor is yours." Pastor David looked over at Marvin. "Marvin, just try to control yourself."

Marvin looked at Keith to the right of him. His attack had turned his candor into indignation. He sat there with his lips curled into a furious frown and kicked the leg of the table repeatedly.

"Keith, James, is there anything you would like to say?" Pastor David asked once more.

"No, this is about as much time as I want to dedicate to this discussion," Keith said.

Everyone in the room focused their attention on James. Marvin hoped for a break, for an opening; or was it an open door that Christians prayed for? It didn't matter. He just wanted to hear his son's voice again.

James looked at Marvin with his lip poked out. Disappointment seemed to be tattooed onto the eyes of everyone when they looked at Marvin.

"Pastor David, I'm sorry we wasted your time today." Marvin eased out of his chair. "Let's go."

"Marvin, the Lord allowed some useful things to come up. It's only a waste if we don't find a way to use all of your pain to glorify God. James, I want you to write down whatever you feel and whatever you want to say to your father. Keith, I want you to consider your father's pain, and Marvin, I want you to consider discussing Lavell a little more. We touched on the impact he had on your life in our first session, and it would be really good if you model this process for the boys."

"Yeah, I'll think about it." Marvin snickered, marching out of the room before the boys. He plodded down the narrow wooden steps of the church and out the door, contemplating what would happen if he dug up the bones in his closet. The brisk wind that met him slapped him as hard as the anguish etched on his sons' faces did when they walked out of the church.

What will happen if I don't dig up those bones?

Chapter 36

It seemed as if the earth was spinning rapidly around Cynthia. Finally, everything she worked for was going to become a reality. After spending two and half years in Richmond all the elements were lining up. She'd spent her time training under a master chef and saving every dollar, dime, nickel, and penny to save up for her deposit. It had taken her exactly a year to save up the deposit necessary to secure her loan to open the restaurant of her dreams.

Cynthia adjusted the leather trim on her purple blazer as she gazed in the window of Virginia Credit Union. She wanted to make sure she looked sharp when she signed her loan papers. She could open the restaurant and get the boys down here, she thought while applying lip gloss before stepping through the heavy glass doors. She grinned at the security guard who tipped his hat at her. She saluted the tellers with a pageant wave on her way to the loans department.

"Would you like a cup of coffee, tea, or a glass of sparkling water while you wait for Mr. Fields?" the receptionist asked.

"Water would be fine." Cynthia sat down in the chair across from the receptionist's desk, crossed her legs, and hugged her clutch close to her body, patting her check.

"Good morning, Ms. Hathaway"

"Good morning, Mr. F . . ." Cynthia froze when she looked up into the eyes of Sam Tanner, the bank manager who had attempted to get Cynthia to work evenings helping him make night deposits so he could gain access to the treasures locked up beneath her clothes back when she was a temp at the bank.

"Mr. Fields is not in at the moment." Sam extended his hand to help her get out of the seat. "I'll be seeing you through the rest of this loan process. Follow me." He flicked his head of golden locks in the direction of the cubicles to the far left of the loan department.

Cynthia squeezed into the one seat located in front of the desk in the cubicle. Her knees pressed against the cold metal as she waited for Sam to remove his jacket before taking a seat in the cramped quarters.

"Let's get down to business, Ms. Hathaway." He leaned back in his swivel chair and pulled a folder from the top drawer of his desk with her name etched across the top. He punched in his access code on the computer, popped a mint in his mouth, and sucked on it a bit before addressing Cynthia again.

"Ms. Hathaway, your loan has been denied."

"Denied?" she asked pausing in disbelief.

"I'm sorry to inform you, but you were not approved for a loan here at Virginia Credit Union."

Cynthia squinted at Sam. "I was completely denied? How is that possible? I did everything Mr. Fields said: I'm getting certified in culinary arts, I've held the same job for about two years now, and I have a check here for $75,000, which is the twenty-five percent minimum that he requested." Cynthia pursed her lips together and folded her arms across her chest in her favorite "I ain't buying whatever you're selling" pose. "Get Mr. Fields on the phone this instant."

"Ms. Barclay, Mr. Fields is no longer handling your loan, so that will not be necessary. I am the loan officer who is now overseeing this process."

"Why? So you can finally screw me?" Cynthia shouted across the desk. Her forehead was pulsating. She was contemplating bashing him in the head with his computer, but she recalled the memory verse Cheo had been studying from this week's Bible Study, Ecclesiastes 7:9: "anger rests in the bosom of fools." Sucking in a large chunk of air, she whipped her head around, rolled her eyes, and focused on a small snag in the drab gray material that lined the walls of the cubicle.

Sam placed his palms flat on the desk. "Cynthia . . . I can call you that right?" She nodded without looking at him while humming to herself. "Harboring events that happened in the past is not good for your soul or skin. That probably explains the frown lines and crow's feet I see beginning to form," he said, waving one of his fingers in a circular motion at Cynthia's profile. "I try not to hold on to things like that, and I want to assure you that the bank made that decision, and it is in no way reflective of what we had or did not have. What it does reflect is your lack of a credit history." He ran his hands through his hair and massaged the side of his neck before reclining in his swivel chair. "I'm going to be honest with you: the bank is experiencing some financial setbacks like the rest of America, and it's just too risky for us to dole out a loan for $300,000 to a new restaurant run by a new chef with no credit history. Kudos to you for keeping your slate clean. Frankly, it's a little too clean, which worries us. We don't need any skeletons jumping out of your closet that would negate your payments."

"Is there anyone else who can help me?"

"Cynthia." Sam waved his hand in the air like he was Vanna White. "Look around. Our loan department has been reduced. Fields is gone. I am the loan department," he said, patting his chest, "and it would not be in the bank's best interest to lend you money."

Cynthia leaped from her chair, prepared to make a quick exit before the tears started rolling.

Sam reached out and held her by her wrist. "Unless—"

"Unless what?"

"Unless you can get a guarantor or someone to cosign this loan for you and come up with an additional fifteen percent of the startup costs for a grand total of $120,000. Those are the only conditions under which we will grant you this loan."

Cynthia snatched her hand back and stormed out of the bank, feeling dejected, rejected, and lost. She scrambled to her car and beat up on her steering wheel for a few minutes before verbally assaulting herself.

"This is the dumbest, dumbest thing you have ever done. Dumber than marrying Marvin, dumber than allowing him to put everything in his name, which virtually makes you a nobody. Dumber than abandoning your kids. I don't know why or how you could think this was all going to work out."

Cynthia adjusted her rearview mirror and backed out of the parking lot, well aware of what she had to do.

Cheo knocked on her door right when Cynthia was in the midst of some heavy-duty whirlwind packing. Cynthia tossed the jeans she was folding on the floor near her suitcases and snatched the door open.

"Yes, Cheo," she huffed.

"Doing a little redecorating?" he asked, peering into the apartment over her shoulder.

"No, I'm packing. I don't have too much time to talk. You're more than welcome to come in and help; otherwise, I have to go."

"I don't get it. Why are you packing, *Chula?* Shouldn't you be celebrating?" he asked all smiles. "Today is the day—"

"Hush," she said, waving her hands in a small flurry in Cheo's face. She turned her back and retreated into the apartment. Her clothes were strewn all over the backs of chairs and hanging over her tables. Cynthia resumed her position in front of the pile of jeans on her end table and began folding again.

"Do you have to move as part of the condition of the loan?" Cheo asked, tiptoeing through the obstacle course Cynthia's bags and clothes had turned the living room into.

"I'm going back to New York, Cheo."

"*Que?*"

"I'm going back to New York. Things just aren't working out here for me. I really should have never come here." Cynthia tried to use her eyelids to restrain the well of tears springing up inside of her as she thought of everything she had compromised: the life of her children; her marriage, although it was barely there. As Pastor David always reminded her, while there is life, there is hope, but this little trip most likely dashed all of that away.

"Cynthia," Cheo cooed at her in a whisper.

"I didn't get the loan. I didn't get the loan. I made a bad decision, and I'm paying for it now."

"So, you're just going to run back to New York?" Cheo stepped over a pile of sweats on the floor to get closer to Cynthia.

"I can't do this."

"You can do all things through Christ." Cheo stripped the jeans from her hands and locked his fingers around hers. "Is that what you do in the face of adversity, just give up when you have a chance to test and prove your faith in God?"

"My faith isn't in God right now."

"Well, Christ wants to be in you. Why don't you just get with the program?" He scooted around her and took a seat on the arm of the sofa beside her. "Why was your loan denied? I thought you had the twenty-five percent for the startup costs."

"I did. I mean I do, but because I have bad credit—well, no credit—they won't finance me without a guarantor or someone to cosign."

"You're packing because all you need is someone to cosign the loan for you?"

Cynthia spun around to face Cheo. "Yeah, that and I need another forty-five thousand. You got that, Mr. My Daddy Owns the Cattle Upon a Thousand Hills?" she asked, extending her palm toward him.

"Actually, I have some savings and I'd be more than willing to cosign the loan for you," he said, wrapping his smooth hands around her waist to embrace her.

"No way." Cynthia backed out of his grip and stumbled a little bit on her own clothing. "I owe you more than I can repay already."

"This is not about you repaying me. I want to help you, *mamí. Yo creo en ti,* your vision, *en su restaurante.* What is the name of it?"

"Sabor."

"Sabor. That means flavor in *Español.* You've brought so much flavor into my life. Let me help you bring it into the lives of others."

Cynthia stared at Cheo. His brown eyes were swollen with possibility and pleading for the opportunity to merge their lives in any way possible.

"Cheo, I can't ask you to do this nor can I accept this kind of generosity from you. This is how I wound up in this situation: by accepting things from a man that sounded good."

She rolled her eyes as she recalled all the breathy promises Marvin whispered between the sheets for their bright future that his auto body garage would provide, and she could live her dream once they were established. At one point he too believed in her.

"I'm not him." Cheo rose to his feet and towered over her. He cut his eyes into small sharp slits and glared at her. "I am not him. I don't want to take advantage of you. I want to love you, Cynthia. Please let me do his for you. Let me help you."

"Cheo, I don't know. This would make us partners. Could you handle us being part—"

"I'll be your silent partner. I won't say a word. You can have complete control over managing, hiring, planning menus, and all that jazz. Besides, *mi amor,* I have my own projects to worry about."

"Is the paper letting you do some more articles?" Cynthia asked beaming at the thought that they'd both be accomplishing their goals at the same time.

Cheo rubbed his chin as if he was thinking about keeping the information to himself. "Don't laugh. I'm working on a book proposal for one of the largest publishers in the country. I want to write a poor man's travel guide to Spain beginning in Zaragoza."

Cynthia clapped.

"It gets better," he said holding up one finger. "I want to work with a chef to compile a list of the cheapest eats in the country. So, you have to open your restaurant so you can work with me on this. Now here's the real question, can you handle us being partners?"

Cheo didn't give Cynthia the chance to answer. With a gentle tug, he drew her into his body and sealed the deal with a wet kiss.

Cynthia mulled it over. *Things will get messy.*

She tossed her hands into air and entered into another dangerously provocative kiss with Cheo.

Things are already messy.

Chapter 37

Cynthia lay in bed watching the blades on her ceiling fan spin as her doorbell chimed. She'd finally been able to rest comfortably after nine months of grueling work to get Sabor off the ground.

Really she couldn't complain. The bank had estimated that it would take a year to get the restaurant going between applying for the proper permits and licensing and finding a location. Cheo's connections downtown had made the process of obtaining the proper permits and licensing as easy as applying to Mickey D's. Really she couldn't complain, but it was 6:30 in the morning and someone was ringing doorbell.

Cynthia was exhausted from the festivities of the grand opening of Sabor, Richmond's premier new restaurant; her restaurant. The most difficult part of the whole affair was dealing with worrying about who the food critics were and how many were there. She conducted a brief interview with a food critic Cheo sent over from the *Richmond Sun,* but she was sure there were others present.

She closed her eyes, clicked her heels together under her maroon and sienna Egyptian cotton sheets Cheo actually brought her from his most recent trip to Egypt and chanted, "There's no one at the door. There's no one at the door. There's no one at the door." But the bell continued to chime.

Cynthia climbed out of the bed, pulled on a robe, cinched the belt tightly around her waist, and marched to what seemed to be a crazy person waiting at her door. She did not remove the chain before opening the door in order to create a barrier in the event the person at the door was a little crazy.

Through the crack, she saw Cheo standing in front of her waving a bottle of sparkling apple cider and a copy of the *Richmond Sun* in his other hand. "You're a hit, *mi amor*. You did it. They love you."

Cynthia removed the chain and backed away from the door as he entered. He eased it open with his foot then stepped into the kitchen. Cynthia watched him maneuver around her kitchen as if it were his own. He buried the sparkling cider in the freezer in the middle of the broccoli and mixed vegetables, pulled out some eggs, and rested them on the countertop.

"What would you like for your breakfast celebration? French toast, pancakes with bacon and eggs, or English muffins with butter and jelly? Please say English muffins."

"Cheo, why are we celebrating at six-thirty in the morning?"

"*Tu.* You don't know, do you? Your reviews were marvelous. Listen: 'Most people take a trip to New York to take a bite out of the Big Apple, but Cynthia Ann Hathaway brought a slice of the Big Apple here to Richmond. Hathaway is no stranger to Richmond's culinary scene. Her name may ring a bell and her face may look familiar because she is the very special and talented chef Chef Sullivan introduced to us three years ago at the mayor's twenty-fifth wedding anniversary.'

"'If you've been craving rich, luscious foods, dreaming of Old San Juan, or dying to find out what all the fuss is about crepes, look no further than Sabor. Don't let the name fool you into thinking it is just another poorly lit Spanish restaurant because it is not. Sabor means flavor, and this restaurant is full of it. The foyer resembles an airport terminal. Guests receive their boarding tickets (the menu) stamped with their destination and are then escorted by the hostess to one of the restaurant's culinary destinations. The restaurant is divided into four dining areas, each representing a distinct part of the world: Spain where you can eat tapas, drink beer, and watch soccer. Italy where the pasta is made fresh daily, New Delhi offers patrons a plethora of vegan or curried dishes, and of course there's Midtown. A small section in the center of the restaurant for those patrons who can't decide what it is exactly they want to eat, which Hathaway says was actually inspired by her Harlem upbringing. "You hop on the train and you could have virtually anything you wanted in midtown from Moroccan food to an all-American cheeseburger deluxe." Hathaway also credits her mother's keen sense for interior decorating as a source of inspiration for Sabor's quirky and fun décor. "Every room in my mother's apartment has a different feeling and puts you in a different mood. Food has the power to do that, thus I decided the décor should do the same thing. It should transport you to a different place and complement how you feel.'"

"'After eating a platter of *arroz con pollo* and some flan, you may want nothing more than to take a siesta, so why not relax surrounded by palm trees and the ocean's breeze?'

"'Now if last night's opening is an indication of what the future holds, I recommend you book your tickets in advance for a trip to Sabor. There was not an empty seat in the place, not even in Midtown where I sampled everything from Hathaway's take on fried rice, which included juicy bits of smoked salmon and Brussels sprouts. For dessert, I had pecan custard drizzled in caramel whose origin is unknown, but it made itself right at home in my belly. Sabor is big on personality and offers everything that the name suggests.'"

"You did it." Cheo scooped Cynthia up, squeezed her, and kissed her all over her face. "This is *maravilloso*."

Cheo returned Cynthia to her feet. She looked up at him, frozen in the moment with her hands glued to her cheeks. "Cheo, oh my God. Cheo, we did it."

"No, you did this, *mi amor*."

"Cheo, I couldn't have done this without you. You were so instrumental in me being successful. This is just as much my success as it is yours, partner." Cynthia went through the checklist of things Cheo had done to orchestrate her success: he had introduced her to Chef Sullivan, got her some catering gigs with his journalist friends, fronted a significant portion of the startup costs, and cosigned for her loan. "I don't know how to thank you for this, Cheo."

"I think you do." He playfully tugged at the waist of her robe and used it to pull her close to him. He pecked at her lips.

"Cheo, you're not making celibacy easy. What does the Bible tell you about this?"

They'd both taken a vow of celibacy in front of the entire congregation of Dayspring Church of Divine Healing and Prophecy, but this sister still had urges and the Jesus routine wasn't working for her.

"The Bible says we should get married," he replied. Cynthia gave him a side-eye glare.

"Trust me, I've studied that scripture, 1 Corinthians 7:9. It says, 'But if they cannot contain, let them marry for it is better to marry than to burn.' So, we're going to have to figure out what it is we're doing."

Since Cheo had become a member of the church, he was all about them settling down and getting married. For some odd reason, Cheo had really taken to believing he was Jacob, she was Rachel, and they were destined and ordained by God to marry. Cynthia didn't do much to convince him otherwise except avoid the issue. She still couldn't figure out the right way to say, "I can't marry you, Cheo because I am already married and have two kids."

"Please, let's not turn this into one of those discussions," Cynthia said, clapping her hands to her sides.

"What? The kind where you go all psycho and throw me out for wanting to commit to you after three and half years of dating or whatever this is? No, I won't make this about us right now when it's all about you.

Recognizing his frustration, Cynthia arched her body against his and twirled one of his curly locks around her finger. "Cheo, I . . . I love you, but there are things in my past that I haven't let go of."

"Then let them go."

"I can't." She clutched her chest, recognizing she was lying. She'd let Keith and James go a long time ago. "I'm trying to bury my past and build a better life. I'm sorry I just have not arrived there yet."

"Do you want me to read the other ones?" Cheo asked softly, changing the subject.

Cynthia gasped. "There's more?"

"*Si, si. Hay más, mucho más*. You're big time now, kid," he said lightly checking her chin with his fist. "So you better snap out of it and get ready for the lunch crowd. With these kinds of reviews, you're bound to have a line every day this week. You are aware that you did just launch the opening of one of the most captivating culinary finds in all of Virginia, according to the food critic at the *Richmond Times*."

"Seriously?"

"Seriously," Cheo said, handing her the newspaper. "See for yourself. Now back to breakfast. What do you want?"

"Coffee, just coffee; and some scrambled eggs. I don't think my stomach can handle much more of this."

Cheo retreated into the kitchen and started cracking eggs, leaving Cynthia alone with the newspapers. She fell into the sofa and just looked at the words in front of her. She'd catered every event imaginable, from baby showers to album release parties, in order to generate the funds necessary to open Sabor.

It would've taken her longer if it had not been for Cheo's generous donation of forty-five grand. Renovating and decorating the space at the Halifax Loft complex—the newest and most premier piece of property on the real estate scene in Richmond—had taken seven months and finally she'd done it. Cynthia held the papers to her chest. Now she was, as the *Richmond Times* put it, stepping out of the shadows of her mentor Chef Sullivan to demonstrate she was a pro with a reservoir of talent that would be feeding Richmond for years to come.

Carrying Cynthia's food on a bamboo stick tray, Cheo entered the living room. He placed the tray on the coffee table in front of her and kissed the crown of her head. Cynthia looked up at him, and their eyes locked, causing her to smile from the inside out, momentarily blocking the thoughts of her past that were bubbling up inside of her.

"I am proud of you."

"Cheo, what do I do now?"

Her words hung in the air. She wasn't really asking him about the restaurant. She was asking him about her—about her sons, about a life he knew nothing about.

Despite the chaos of preparing to open Sabor, Cynthia still sent her obligatory monthly stipend to Barbara for the boys, even though her calls home were nonexistent. Sabor had become her new child, and like a good mother she petted it, fawned over it, and nursed it until it was able to stand on its own two feet.

"Cynthia, you work. You work harder than you did before, harder than you have in your whole life. Yesterday no one knew who you were, and now all of Virginia knows you and your restaurant. *Ahora,* you have a reputation to uphold."

Cynthia pursed her lips together to form a pout and rested her chin in the palms of her hands. Cheo paced across the living room floor, rattling off all the things she would have to do now to maintain her status as Richmond's premier chef. All Cynthia could do was list the things she shouldn't be doing as grief besieged her.

As she coasted into the life she'd always wanted, she wondered about the life she'd left behind.

"*Hola, mi amor.* Did you hear anything I just said?" Cheo asked, waving his hand in front of her face.

"No, Cheo," she said shaking her head, "I'm sorry. I was somewhere else."

The doorbell rang, saving Cynthia from having to explain where it was that her mind had taken her. She peered through the peephole and saw that it was Mrs. Richardson who lived with her husband in the apartment directly across the hall from Cynthia.

Mrs. Richardson was the standard nosy old lady. She didn't actually knock on Cynthia's door that often, and when she did, typically it was for some milk when she couldn't make the drive down to the grocer.

Cynthia greeted Mrs. Richardson with a smile. "Good morning, Mrs. Richardson. It's awfully early. Is everything okay?"

"Oh, everything is fine, dear. I stopped by to congratulate you. Could you imagine my surprise? Here I am reading the morning papers, and lo and behold whose beautiful smiling face do I see?" Mrs. Richardson asked, pinching Cynthia's cheeks. "Congratulations! I mean my mouth was always watering when I stepped out into the hallway and smelled the aroma coming from your apartment, and you certainly did a wonderful job on Tiffany's reception, but I never knew you were a world-class chef."

"Thank you, Mrs. Richardson," Cynthia said graciously smiling.

"Cynthia, umm . . ." Mrs. Richardson played coy as her eyes darted side to side. Cynthia braced herself for the request she knew Mrs. Richardson was about to make. That type of hesitation only preceded a favor of some kind.

"I was wondering if I could make a reservation for this afternoon. I'd like a table in Spain."

"Sure, Mrs. Richardson, but you have to do me a favor."

"What is it?"

"Please don't tell anyone I did this for you."

Mrs. Richardson zippered her mouth shut, locked it, then tossed her imaginary key on the floor, and grumbled a thank you through her sealed lips. Cynthia chuckled during Mrs. Richardson's mime act. She'd done the same childish lock-and-key bit when Cynthia gave her a discount on the catering bill for her daughter Tiffany's wedding reception.

Cynthia shut the door behind Mrs. Richardson and calmly walked into the middle of the living room and screamed. Cheo jumped up from his seat at the dining room table, grabbed Cynthia, and pinned her to his chest.

"Are you okay?"

"Cheo, I just booked my first reservation, our first reservation. Can you believe this? Oh my God. Cheo, you've got to get out of here. I have to get dressed. Meet me at the restaurant later if you can." She gave him a peck on the cheek and darted to the bathroom.

After a quick shower Cynthia was out the door. Heels in hand, Cynthia ran through the parking lot and jumped in her car. It was a delightful spring day; the sun was bright and hung tenderly in the Virginia sky. Cynthia cracked the windows as she cruised to Sabor. Upon seeing it, Cynthia thought it was very Tribecaesque. The building had a very industrial feel like many of the buildings in Tribeca where anyone who was someone went when in New York, which was why she selected that property.

Thinking of New York made her think of home. Paused at a stop light Cynthia dialed home after blocking her number first. It was well after eight o'clock. She hoped Keith still rose early in the morning to watch *SpongeBob*. The phone rang several times. She was on the cusp of hanging up the phone when someone answered. "Hello," said a woman in a tangy voice. "Hello," she repeated.

Cynthia prayed she had the wrong the number while she parked her car at a gas station en route to the restaurant.

"Hello. Hello. Hello," the woman shouted through the popping of her gum.

"I . . . I'm sorry." Cynthia's voice cracked as the words came out. Cynthia cleared her throat and continued. "I'm sorry, ma'am. It seems as if I've dialed the wrong number." Cynthia tapped the end button and threw her phone into the passenger's seat.

"Marvin, how could you?" She banged on the steering wheel, and a few tears snuck out of her eyes. "How could he?"

She rested her head on the steering wheel and continued to cry, knowing she did not dial the wrong number. She looked at herself in the rearview mirror.

"Why are you surprised? Did you think he was going to wait for you? When you were there he had other women. He's probably got all kind of freaks running in and out of there teaching the boys to engage in all kinds of lewd and perverse acts." Cynthia pulled a tissue out of the compartment beneath the armrest and wiped the snot from her nose. "What are you going to do about it?"

Before she could answer, the melody to "Independent Women" by Destiny's Child interrupted her.

"Hello," she croaked, answering her ringing phone.

"Cynthia, when are you coming in?"

"Well, hello to you too." Cynthia shook her head at the telephone. "Susan, I know Chef Sullivan taught you better than that."

"I'm sorry. I'm just a little stressed out over here." Susan had grown out of her awkward stage and into a ravishing red-haired delight. As a favor to Cynthia, she was serving as the hostess until Cynthia hired a full-time one. "Everyone in Richmond is trying to get a reservation here. Lunch is booked solid, and I've got like one or two tables left for dinner. Of course, everyone who I deny desperately needs to speak to the manager. I know you're paying me as opposed to working for my dad for free, but this is a lot."

"I'm sorry. I never expected this in a million years. I still need to take care of some business, but I'll be in there in a few minutes. I want you to try this: instead of just saying we're booked, take the customer's number and offer to call them if there is a cancelation, and we'll take it from there. All right?"

"All right, boss."

Cynthia smiled while pressing the red phone icon on the screen of her phone. *Boss. I think I like the sound of that.*

Chapter 38

"Who was that on the phone, Bridge?" Keith asked after Bridget hung up the phone and shook her head at the receiver.

Wiping her hands on her apron, she returned to the pancake batter for that morning's breakfast. Bridget scraped the last bit of batter into the frying pan. Keith observed her movements, trying to figure out who was on the other end of that call.

It was Saturday, so at least he didn't have to worry about the school calling to recommend he and James see a different counselor because they had not shown significant progress. The truth was they'd stopped attending the sessions as soon as the school got off Marvin's back. Since the school didn't see the results they wanted they'd started what Bridget had dubbed as a "witch hunt" all over again.

Bridget pointed her spatula at Keith and Marvin, raising her eyebrows as though she was daring one of them to answer. "I don't know which one of you is out here driving these women crazy, but it's got to stop. In all my forty years on earth, there is one thing I know for sure, when a woman answers a man's phone and the person on the other end doesn't say anything, it's the other woman." She flipped the last two pancakes, put them on the platter, and carried them out to Keith and Marvin.

"Just answer the boy." Marvin slid behind her and wrapped her up in his thick arms. He dropped his voice an octave and whispered in her ear, "Who was it? You know you're my girl."

"I don't know. She didn't say anything for a while, then she said 'I've got the wrong number.'"

Keith's mouth hung open at the thought that Cynthia had wasted her breath on speaking to someone who believed she was dead.

"So, you're the culprit," she said, pointing at Keith.

"I don't know what you're talking about. Pops, can I eat my food in the room?"

"Go 'head. Just don't make a mess," Marvin replied without looking up from his food.

Keith walked into his room. Photos of bikini-clad women had replaced his Spider-Man photos, and simple wooden framed twin beds now occupied each wall of the room. He put his plate on top of his dresser and crept to his window. He prayed for her to call back. He was tired of the phone game, the waiting game, the praying game, and every other remedy that had been recommended to him to deal with this emptiness.

James entered the room, pulled out Keith's choir robe from the closet, and tossed it to him, signaling it was time for him to get ready for choir rehearsal. James may not have been speaking, but he and Keith had adopted signals in order to communicate with each other.

"Thanks, James, but no thanks. I'm not going to rehearsal today."

James put on a scowl that said, "this isn't something you should miss."

"One day you'll understand, man," said Keith trying to impart some of his fifteen-year-old wisdom on his twelve-year-old brother. "Sometimes you got to strike out on your own to find out where you belong." Keith had decided to skip out on men's choir rehearsal because he had something more important on his agenda: waiting for his mother and Rock to call him back.

Solitude hurt Keith. He was used to being cared about, talked to, and loved. He'd spent the past three and a half years trying to get over all of the attention and affection his mother had poured into him and he couldn't. That's why he jumped at the chance to be affiliated with Black Ice, a local gang intent on terrorizing the people in their neighborhood.

Rock, the leader of Black Ice, had presented Keith with the opportunity to get down with them Friday afternoon. Keith wasn't expecting his life to be changed that afternoon.

As usual he waited a few feet from the doors of Leadership Middle School on 133rd and Amsterdam to pick up James when he got out of school. Even though James was now twelve years old and could be trusted to walk home alone, Keith kept a close eye on James since he couldn't or wouldn't speak. And even as three boys poked and prodded James like a young cattle prepared for the slaughter, he didn't utter one word. Keith seized two of the boys and smashed their heads together and went into karate mode on the third member of Black Ice who'd taken a step back to gather himself when Keith arrived on the scene.

The rage that had built up inside of him had finally found an outlet. He beat the boys because his mother left them alone. He beat them because his father beat his mother. He beat them because no one was there. He beat them because his brother couldn't talk. Keith didn't stop punching and kicking, even when the sirens could be heard in the distance.

It was Rock who intervened. He grabbed Keith and threw him to the ground.

"That's enough. We hear you loud and clear. You and your brother are not to be messed with," Rock announced. He pulled out a card and threw it on Keith's chest. "I like how you get down. You're like black ice: can't be seen but can be deadly." Rock stroked his shiny bald head and focused his beady eyes on Keith. "Black Ice is tryin'a expand throughout Harlem, but we need dudes of a certain caliber; you know, the type who's willing to kill their mama if they had to. Holla at me if you think you can roll with us. Now beat it before the cops come and we have to press charges," Rock said, laughing.

James helped Keith to his feet, and they scrambled home. As soon as he got home, he called Rock's cell and said he was down. Now he sat by the phone waiting for Rock to name the time and the place.

While he was waiting for Rock to call him back, he acknowledged that it might not be the right thing to do. Then again Black Ice didn't offer fake promises or tell stories about a great big God who could do all things yet this God couldn't bring his mother back.

The way Keith saw it, there were two kinds of people in this world: the ones who talked about what they were going to do and the ones who didn't wait for anything to happen. They made it happen. If Keith had to choose, Rock and his gang in their True Religion jeans and white tees were looking better than Pastor David and his choir robe crew.

Waiting caused his appetite to dissipate. Keith departed from his thoughts of world domination to handle his domestic duties. He scraped his food into the garbage and proceeded to wash the dishes from that morning's breakfast. The water was pumping at full blast to get rid of the miscellaneous food particles still stuck to a plate. He scrubbed with a passion and only paused when the phone rang.

"Hello. Hello. You could speak to me. I know you spoke to her. You could speak to me. I've never told anyone that you call. It would be nice to hear your voice again. I keep trying to remember it. I keep trying to remember the last thing you said, but I can't, and I don't want to remember anymore. Why don't you stop this? Stop calling until you're able to say, 'Keith, I'm on my way.' I promise no one will take your place, but this I can't do."

He hung up the phone and returned to his dishes satisfied. He'd said most of what he wanted to say and what he imagined his mother would have said. He had to believe she was coming to keep going, and she needed to be released in order to return home, however long that would take.

Chapter 39

It had been awhile since Cynthia had to spend the night stalking the sandman, begging him to stop by her pad. At this point she couldn't care less whether he brought her a dream so long as she could close her eyes and rest her head.

Her second day in business had left her reeling. The restaurant was booked solid for lunch and dinner. It was a night of nonstop schmoozing and boozing with her guests. Cynthia tried to hide in the kitchen and remain low-key. At one point, she even hid in the meat freezer when Breezy, the hottest new rapper on the scene, requested her presence at his table. Everyone wanted her to come out for a photo op or to pay compliments to the chef.

After thirteen hours on her feet, chopping vegetables and performing salt rubs on chickens, quails, and the finch that someone actually ordered, she was lethargic and nearly motionless. Cheo escorted her to her car and drove her home.

"*Tú eres el jefe.* You are the boss. Do you understand that? You're not supposed to be running around like that now. You make a couple of key signature dishes for the prestigious guests and tell your kitchen staff to do the rest," Cheo explained like he owned a restaurant.

Cynthia lurched up from the reclined passenger seat and stared at Cheo like he had two heads. "Wasn't it you who said I need to work hard, and now you're telling me to take it easy?"

"I meant do some interviews, a segment on *Good Morning, Virginia,* go online, set up a Facebook page; you know, try to promote the restaurant in a positive way. I didn't mean run around like a chicken *sin un cabeza.*" Cheo drew his arms up and in close to his sides then began bouncing around wildly like a chicken whose head had just been chopped off. "That's how you look," he said, laughing between arm flaps.

"Next time you need to be clear. Besides, Sabor is my baby. I can't have just any ol' body working on the meals. I just have to be hands on."

"Then you're going to have to get used to being tired," he said, resting one hand on her thigh, "and I'm going to have to get used to picking you up."

They pulled into Riverside's parking lot. Cheo got out and opened the door for her. Cynthia's legs shook like a boxer who'd just been caught with a left hook. Cheo scooped her up in his arms and carried her to the elevator.

Cynthia flung her arms around him and embraced the moment with her head nuzzled against his strong neck. She took in deep swallows of his rustic cologne and tried to forget about the pressures of the day on the ride to the sixth floor.

"Cheo, how on earth can I repay you for your kindness and generosity?" she whispered into his ear as they approached her door. Cynthia let her bottom lip hit his earlobe after every word. She wasn't trying to incite a riot. She was trying to get at least a midnight kissing session to cap off the sheer romanticism and excitement that being carried to her door caused.

Cheo lowered her to the ground, looked into her eyes, and very solemnly said, "You can be ready for church on time tomorrow. I'm tired of sitting in the back row."

Cynthia rolled her eyes and shook her head at Cheo. "Does it matter where we're seated? Church is not like my restaurant; you're not going to get a different meal prepared based on where you're seated. Whether you're in the back row or in the first pew, the pastor has the same Word for us all."

"Sitting in the front is way different from sitting in the back. It's like . . ." Cheo paused then waved both of his hands at her. "Awww, forget it. You wouldn't understand. You don't even care about the Lord one way or the other."

Cynthia folded her arms across her chest, shifted her weight onto one foot, and cocked her head to the side. "Isn't my relationship with Jesus supposed to be personal?"

Cheo nodded.

"Then why are you all up in it?"

Cheo smacked himself on the forehead. "I walked right into that one, didn't I? I'm only concerned because I love you, Cynthia, and to be honest, it really drives me crazy to see how ungrateful you are considering all the Lord has done for you."

"Done for me? What did he do for me, Cheo?" she asked angered by his assumption that God had done something for her. "Where was He when I was struggling and really needed Him? I mean needed Him so desperately; I could have been dead. You tell me where He was then, and I'll tell you how grateful I should be."

"It looks like you're still alive to me. How did you make it out if it weren't for the Lord who I know is on your side? He was always there."

"You don't know anything, I mean anything, about my life," she said emphatically.

"Cause me to know. I want to know," he pleaded.

Rolling her eyes to avoid direct eye contact, Cynthia blurted, "He used to beat me. Cheo, I was black and blue and all bruised up."

Cheo grabbed Cynthia in an embrace. "How long did you suffer through that?"

"Too long." She looked into Cheo's eyes and could feel the judgments forming in his head. "It's not as easy as people think to get out of an abusive relationship, especially when you love the person."

"Love?"

"At one point I did love him." Cynthia paused, contemplating confessing it all. The weary look in Cheo's eyes declared tonight would not be a good one to reveal that she was married with children.

"I tried to work things out. I tried to wait on God, but in the end He didn't deliver me. I just had to run away."

"There's one thing I do know." He held her by the shoulders, creating a little bit of space between them. "Even if He didn't work out the situation according to your desire or show up at the time you appointed to Him, He died for you. Don't you think you ought to give Him credit for that?"

"What do you want me to do, stand on a crate on Hull Street and start preaching? Or maybe you'd rather see me in a knee-length satin suit and one of those ridiculous hats prancing around." Cynthia began hopping back and forth on each foot, mimicking the praise and worship stomp she'd seen the women do at church every Sunday.

Cheo rested his hand on her shoulder putting an end to her mockery. "Cynthia, I can't pretend to know what happened to you, especially when you won't share it, but if you ask God to soften your heart and help you to forgive whoever it was who did you wrong, if you ask Him to forgive you of all your sins, and ask Him to have mercy on you for doubting Him, I'm sure you'll be able to find peace again."

"The only peace I want right now is a piece of cake. You want some?"

"I'll pass."

"Fine. More for me. Listen, why don't you let me work on my issues with Jesus on my own, and you deal with whatever you have to?" Cynthia turned her back on Cheo and unlocked her apartment door.

Behind the veil of the door, she did something she had not done in a long time.

"Lord, Cheo said if I ask you'd forgive me of my sins, but there isn't forgiveness for what I've done is there?"

Although she'd fought Cheo tooth, nail, and little bit of elbow after lying awake all night waiting for God to answer her, she hungered for his knock on the door, a welcomed reprieve from these walls and her demons the church could not provide for her. Like clockwork, Cheo showed up knocking on her door at seven o'clock with the high hopes of making it to the nine o'clock service. Much to his surprise, Cynthia was already dressed in a paisley-print suit with a plain white blouse. Her hair was slicked back in a traditional ponytail. She'd forfeited her makeup on account of the sweat-inducing service that Healing and Prophecy held.

Cheo had become the most dependable thing in her life. Cynthia still longed for the companionship of a girlfriend, one she could shop with, get pedicures with, and share the burden of her secret with. In her three and a half years in Richmond, Cynthia had failed miserably at launching any new friendships.

Recently, Cheo had been prompting her to join the singles' ministry or the women's ministry so she could have some contact with actual people rather than spending her evenings talking to flambéed ducks. He told her that might prevent her from spiraling into the funnel of depression that sucked her in whenever he went on a business trip. Cynthia shied away from those events because they were held in the confines of the church's basement. Those quarters were way too close for her to hide from the Holy Ghost.

They entered the church at 8:55 and were able to attain the last two coveted seats in the front row. Cynthia rubbed her hand along the plush purple upholstery that now lined the seats of the pew. Cynthia was glad to see that the church had been using her tithe money properly.

Usually the service opened with what they called devotion and what Cynthia considered fanfare. Instead this Sunday's pastor, Pastor Wyatt, walked straight up to podium and dived into his sermon. "Good morning, saints. We have got to be careful. The Word says, 'woe unto them who think they are something when really they are nothing,'" Pastor Wyatt shouted into the microphone, interrupting the mental inventory Cynthia was taking of all the upgrades they'd made to the church since she started attending it. "The Lord doesn't need you to do anything. He is the beginning and the end. His Word is already settled in heaven. Whatever minor task He used you to do was already established long before you considered doing it, and had you not done it as Mordecai told Esther, he would have raised up another. Amen?"

"Amen," the congregation responded.

Crossing her legs and folding her arms across her chest, Cynthia tuned into Pastor Wyatt's sermon.

He casually took a sip from the glass of water the first lady had just placed beside him and dabbed his mouth dry with a white handkerchief. Cynthia's eyes fastened on his diamond-studded pinky ring. She could not believe he was preaching humility with an iced-out pinky ring.

"Some of you sheep have gone astray. I mean you have forgotten who the good Shepherd is and have turned to your own way seeking pasture."

Cynthia let out a loud yawn to let everyone know she was bored. Cheo glanced at her with that "what is wrong with you, girl" look in his eyes and scooted over a bit closer to Mother Goodard to create a little distance between them.

Feigning innocence, Cynthia shrugged and whispered, "Sorry." And truly she was sorry she'd let Cheo drag her down here once again, and all Pastor Wyatt was doing was taking that "reduce, reuse, recycle" mantra to heart, rehashing the same old topic, the will of God. Here and there, he switched out a word or two or started off with a different scriptural reference, but he was always on the same topic. Cynthia had gotten weary of waiting for a miraculously divine healing to take place or for Pastor Wyatt to issue a divinely prophetic word to the congregation beyond the textbook "Jesus is going to turn this whole situation around in your favor."

"You know a wicked and perverse generation seeketh a sign. Why are you looking for miracles when you just being alive is miraculous? Jesus could have let Satan have you a long time ago, yet you still doubt God's plan and the Word coming from God's man. You better shake yo'self," Pastor Wyatt said, shaking his thick, manicured hands.

Cynthia looked up to the ceiling, raising one eyebrow to form an arch as if to say, "I see what you're doing, Jesus."

Many of the members jumped out of the pews, shaking their arms, legs, and toddlers. Cynthia peeked at Cheo who sat perfectly still convinced that the spirit of God was in this place. "Goody two-shoes," Cynthia murmured, sucking her teeth. Halfheartedly Cynthia rolled her shoulders and tried to make room in her weather-beaten heart for the Word that was coming forth.

"He wants to lead you to still waters, but you'd rather dig in the sand to find your own because it's taking too long to walk to the path that the Lord says leads to green pastures. You're not God. You don't set the time for deliverance. He frees you."

"Hallelujah!" the first lady shouted, stomping her silver pumps on the floor.

"Some of you in here are just 'churching,' looking good, trying to sound good. You shake my hand after the service and kiss my wife on the cheek knowing you're living a lie. This is not the life God intended for you, and if you don't turn back to Him, you're going to remember." Pastor Wyatt stepped away from the pulpit, walked down from the altar, and into the aisles. He stomped his shoes into the ground. "I said, you are going to remember where you came from. God is going to cause you to recall why you called upon Him in the first place."

Pastor Wyatt paraded up and down the floor. He dragged his hand across his brow and flung the sweat off it. "It's getting hot in here. Can you feel that Holy Ghost fire burning?" he asked. The congregation clapped in agreement.

Cynthia looked at her watch, wondering when the theatrics would stop. Pastor Wyatt picked up the pace again after stripping out of his heather gray double-breasted blazer and got back into his Holy Ghost processional.

"He's going to cause you to know that you don't rule over anything," he said, stopping directly in front of Cynthia. "My Lord," "Have mercy, Lord," and "Bless her, Lord," rang throughout the congregation. The longtime members of Divine Healing and Prophecy knew when the Holy Spirit was on Pastor Wyatt like that, and he stopped in front of you if that Word was for your life.

The pastor extended his hand for Cynthia to hold. He got down on one knee. "The road you're on will lead you to destruction if you don't turn around now."

Cynthia contorted her mouth to the side, a gesture that said, "I don't believe you."

"He that hardens his heart shall be broken without remedy. Are you sure you can stand that pain, sister?"

Cynthia rose to her feet. The congregation held its breath, awaiting her response. She looked down at Pastor

Wyatt still on bent knee. "If you're really a prophet, then you should already know I have boxed with the devil. I lost a few rounds, but not the whole bout. What more could happen to me?" Tears washed her face as she recalled each blow, kick, broken rib, black eye, and bloody nose on top of the profane words Marvin spat at her daily that normally wouldn't even be spoken to a dog.

She looked at Cheo as he sank as low as he could into the pew. She could tell from the frown on his face that he wished they'd sat in the back now.

"*Corre,*" he mouthed to her. Cynthia squinted trying to make out what Cheo was whispering.

"Run," he mouthed to her in English this time. His smoky eyes begged her to run and spare them both of the embarrassment that was to come if she stayed another minute. Gracefully she reached in the pew for her purse, slowly draped it over her shoulder, sauntering up the aisle and out the doors of Dayspring Church of Divine Healing and Prophecy.

Chapter 40

Cynthia only looked back once. She wanted Cheo to run after her. Hold her and caress her. The bluntness of Pastor Wyatt's revelation even though it was coated in courtesy and the glare of the onlookers had crushed her heart. She was bold yet fragile. She presented the grit and grime of the cement-paved sidewalks in New York on the exterior. Inside her heart was just as soft as the dirt of a back country road. Yet Cheo remained glued to the pew.

Marvin would not have just sat there, she thought. His foolish pride would have made him jump to Cynthia's defense, regardless of who he had to confront. Cheo, on the other hand, dared not jeopardize his membership and relationship with God for Cynthia; at least, not today.

"Now how am I going to get to Sabor?" She sighed once she realized she'd left her ride sitting inside the church. The bus wasn't an option since she didn't know the schedule, and unlike the Metropolitan Transit Authority in New York, buses ran on schedule down in Virginia.

Sucking up what was left of her defiance, she began the trek to Sabor. The drive from the church on West Duval to East Main Street on a normal day took seven minutes. The walk would take at least twenty minutes.

When she arrived at Sabor, Cheo was pulling into the lot behind her. She could hear the gravel crunching under his car wheels and see the reflection of Cheo's car in the restaurant windows. Her pride wouldn't allow her to turn around.

"Cynthia," he called out to her.

She froze at the sound of his voice. "This is all your fault."

"This is not my fault," he shouted from the parking lot. Although he was trying to speak to her in tough tone, his reflection betrayed him. Cynthia could see the hurt and confusion in his eyes.

"It is not my fault that you're a fugitive on the run from God. You can hide from me as long as you want. You can't hide from God, Cynthia. You just can't. It's impossible."

"It's so easy for the righteous to judge what they only see."

"*Mi amor,* I'm not trying to judge you."

"Then why did you take me to that church for all of that foolery? A, to show me off; B, to mock me; C, to save me; or D, all of the above?"

"How about none of the above," he said, walking toward her. With each step he took toward her, she moved forward. "I took you there because I didn't want to do a single thing without you. I want to share my whole life with you, Cynthia, including my God."

Cynthia backed up as far she could until the closed doors of Sabor stopped her. His breath massaged her skin. Toe to toe they stood staring in each other's eyes. "Cynthia, I want to marry you. I love you. Why can't you believe that?"

Tears began to stream down her cheeks. "My heart has been trampled on too many times for it to be of good use to me or anybody else," she explained through tears.

"Whatever happened to you, I promise I won't do that to you, but you've got to trust me and the God that lives in me." Cheo stooped down and planted a kiss on Cynthia's lips.

"Cheo." Cynthia wiped the corners of her mouth and looked into those sultry eyes. "I can't marry you. I'm not fit. Didn't you hear Pastor Wyatt? The road I'm on leads to destruction."

Scratching the back of his neck, Cheo asked, "Then why don't you get off? Ring the bell. Request the next stop and walk with me."

Cynthia reached up and traced the hard angles of his jaw with her fingertips. Her hands shook in fear this would be the last time she'd ever get that close to him again. "It's just not that easy. It's almost time for the lunch crowd, and I've got another day completely booked. Cheo, I have to go." Her hand grazed his chest before walking away. "I've done things that there is no excuse for."

"Cynthia, why don't you ask for forgiveness and be free?"

"Abuse creates a cycle, and I don't know how to break free. When I came here, I thought that was what I was doing, but . . . but . . . I don't even know who I am anymore. I know who I used to be."

I used to be a mother. I used to be a wife. The truth was perched on the tip of her tongue prepared to dive out.

"Stop living in the past; stop living in what he's done to you and just come to me." Cheo scooped her up in a tight embrace. He began pecking her lips slowly over and over. "I don't care about who you were. I am in love with who you are now," he declared.

His eyes matched the sincerity of his voice, leaving her with no choice but to fold into him and inspired her to consider something that never crossed her mind: divorce.

"If you go this route things could get ugly. For everyone involved," Barbara stated very simply to Cynthia.

"Say that again, Barbara. There's too much noise in the background," Cynthia said, holding one hand over her free ear.

"I'm sorry. I'm working on a big case so this place is abuzz. Are you sure this is something you want to pursue?" Barbara asked.

Inhaling and exhaling, Cynthia questioned the conclusion she thought she'd arrived at the day before. It was time to divorce Marvin. "Is there any reason why I shouldn't?"

"No, but he could wind up with everything. I talked to a friend of mine who does divorce law. He could get the restaurant, your future earnings, and the kids."

"I really screwed this thing up," Cynthia said, stating the obvious.

"Cynthia, that's only if he fights this thing. With as many connections as your boy down there has, I'm sure he can hook you up with a good lawyer."

"My boy doesn't know I'm not divorced. Actually, he doesn't even know I was married." Cynthia craned her neck in the opposite direction of the phone to guard herself from the verbal assault that was sure to follow this announcement.

"Don't take my word for it, Cynthia. It could go the other way. You never know; Marvin may have changed. He might be willing to settle this amicably, and you won't have to go through too much trouble bringing Cheo up to speed. Listen, I have to run. One of the partners is looking for me. Let's talk about your options and what this would mean for the boys later." Leaving Cynthia with only the dial tone to talk to, Barbara ended the conversation.

Marvin. Change. The two words could not be spoken in the same sentence. Yet the idea of him changing made her wonder what that would look like.

Chapter 41

Marvin paced next to the apartment door.

"Where is this dang boy at, Bridge? Did he tell you where he was going when he left?" Marvin asked Bridget who was seated at the dining room table blowing rings of smoke into the air.

"Marvin, why don't you just come to bed?" she purred, crossing her legs revealing her thighs.

"Bridget, it's one o'clock in the morning. Anything could happen to him in these streets. What am I going to tell—"

"Tell who?"

"No one. Disregard I even said that." Marvin shook his hand in the air. He'd almost asked what he was going to tell Cynthia. It was odd to him that after six years, he still thought of her like she was a part of the family. He'd never shared those thoughts of her with anyone and now was definitely not the time to share them with Bridget. Marvin shrugged and attributed her being on his mind to how close in proximity it was to the sixth anniversary of her disappearance.

"Marvin, is that school still harassing you? Let me go down there and give them a piece of my mind. They ain't got no business messing with a strong black man like you, baby." Bridget capped her compliment off with a sweet smile.

Marvin strutted over to Bridget. He stroked her hair, which was wound up in a fluffy ponytail on the top of her head, and then he caressed her heart-shaped face. Slowly his hands careened down her body and rested on her thighs.

"What, you waiting on an invitation?" she moaned in his ear.

"You know I'm trying to focus on that wild boy."

"Just come to bed, daddy. I promise if he's not in by the morning, I'll help you canvas every inch of Harlem to find our boy."

Her words were simple yet powerful. "Did you say our boy?" he asked perking up a bit.

Bridget stroked Marvin's goatee then kissed him ferociously. "Yes, I said our boy. He is ours." Bridget grabbed his earlobes and kissed him again.

Shaking his head, Marvin pleaded, "Don't do that, girl. You're making me weak. I have to wait up for him."

"I promise we'll settle this by morning. Just come to bed, Marv." Bridget rose from the chair and grabbed Marvin by his belt, dragging him to the room.

"Thank you, Bridge."

"For what?" she asked, looking at Marvin over her shoulder.

"For being here through it all. I know I'm not the best man, but I'm doing the best I can."

Marvin had gotten much better at controlling his temper and he'd cut back on the booze. He knew he was in no position to brag. He was making strides toward progress.

"Come and show me how grateful you are," Bridget said seductively.

Marvin followed her into the bedroom and gave everything he had left in him. The heat of her body and the beat of her heart were the perfect combination to lull Marvin to sleep. He was almost into his third dream when James banged on the bedroom using the telephone.

Marvin kissed Bridget's shoulder blade then pulled the floral-print sheets over Bridget's naked body before telling James to come in. She wasn't who he wanted, yet she always found a way to give him what he needed. Along the way he learned to value that.

James hovered in the doorway and tossed the ringing phone to his father from there.

"Hello."

"Mr. Barclay."

Marvin peeked at the caller ID embedded in the phone. He recognized the number from the local precinct. Marvin shifted the phone to his right hand and used his left hand to rouse Bridget. She looked at him out of one cracked eye. "Police," he whispered to her.

"Yes, this is Mr. Barclay," he said into the receiver. "Who is this?"

"This is Detective Smalls of the 30th Precinct. Usually, I don't do this, but another detective in the station recognized your boy when we brought him and said to call you before we grill him. He's a suspect in an armed robbery. We also believe he is affiliated with the gang Black Ice. We busted him with another little thug—Arnold Johnson, goes by the name AJ—on 155th and Broadway. I don't know if your son is the perpetrator or the accomplice."

"What?" Marvin was stunned by the revelation the detective had made. The charges the detective was laying on him made it sound like Keith should be featured on season five of A&E's *Beyond Scared Straight*. Marvin knew Keith wasn't straight-laced, and since he started hanging out with AJ a few years ago, Marvin knew nothing good would come from that pair.

"Mr. Barclay, you need to get down here now. Do you understand that?"

"Yes, Detective Smalls."

After hanging up with Detective Smalls, Marvin jumped out of the bed and began piling on layers of clothes.

"What's going on?" Bridget asked.

"What's going on? What's going on? I wish I knew what's going on," Marvin said frantically with one arm through his sweater looking at Bridget then at James. "James, get out my doorway, boy. Shouldn't you be getting ready for school?"

James screwed up his face, clutched his stomach, and shook his head no.

"Then get in your room and stay out of trouble," Marvin barked at his now-fifteen-year-old son. Even though they were the same height Marvin did not treat him like the young man he was.

"What do you want me to do, Marv?" Bridget's voice sounded as sweet as honey.

"Get dressed," Marvin commanded, tossing some clothes at her. "Our boy is at the precinct."

When Marvin and Bridget walked through the doors of the 30th Precinct, he noticed nothing had changed since his initial visit six years ago. He could feel all of his strength draining from him as he approached the desk sergeant until Keith came into view from around a wall behind the desk. Even in cuffs he strutted like a panther on the prowl.

"That's my pops over there. You better release me. He don't play," Keith said loudly to the officer escorting him.

"Keith, are you good, son?" Marvin called out across the precinct.

"Hey, buddy, I'm going to need you to not scream across my precinct like that," the desk sergeant said, pointing at Marvin.

"That's my son over there. I will not stop screaming until I talk to him," Marvin said to the desk sergeant. "I'm going to get you out of here, okay, Keith? Relax and don't say nothing about anything. Don't worry, I'm going to take care of you. Bridget's here too. Bridget, say hi to Keith."

Bridget stood and waved at Keith.

"This is all very touching, sir, but I want you to be quiet or we'll lock you up for disorderly conduct. They're about to release him," the desk sergeant said as Keith and the officer escorting him approached the desk.

"Release him?" Marvin's jaw dropped.

"Yeah, release me, Pops," Keith said, cockily slapping Marvin on the shoulder once the officer took the cuffs off.

Reunited with his son, Marvin scooped him up into a tight hug and lifted him off the ground.

"Put me down, Pops," Keith insisted.

Marvin returned his eldest son to the ground, then slapped him upside the head. "What the hell is wrong with you, boy?" he asked, slapping him upside the head again. "Answer me when I'm talking to you." He slapped him again.

"Yo, Pops, chill." He looked over to Bridgette. "Bridge, can I get some help here?"

"Marvin, stop that," Bridget said, sprinting over to them. Bridget lodged herself between Marvin and Keith.

"She can't help you." Marvin laughed. Reaching over Bridget, he popped Keith upside the head again. "Nobody can help you."

Bridget grabbed Marvin's arm before he could strike Keith again. "You better get your hands off of me, woman," Marvin snarled. He could feel his anger rising to the top of him like oil in water.

"Or what?" she countered.

"Yeah, what?" Keith chanted along with Bridget.

"If I were you, I would not play with me right now, boy," Marvin said, pointing at Keith. "Let's go." Marvin snatched his arm out of Bridget's tight grasp and marched out of the precinct.

He walked ahead of them the whole way home. The sun had risen on Harlem. Marvin weaved around mothers with their babies wrapped like burritos to fight the winter chill, businessmen in their wool coats headed downtown, and bunches of schoolchildren all fighting to get to the C train. He wished his life were that simple; he wished he was headed to work and not home with his delinquent son. They were going to have serious powwow when they got home, even though the magnitude of this event seemed to be lost on Keith and Bridget.

Every time he looked back, Bridget was petting Keith and hugging and kissing him. She was probably reassuring him everything would okay. He'd just turned eighteen and she was coddling him like he was eighteen months old. She was probably doing what Cynthia would have done, Marvin thought. *No, if Cynthia were here, this would have never happened,* he said to himself, correcting his own stray thoughts.

"Wait up, Pops," Keith shouted across the street.

"Nah, you better catch up to me 'cause you're too far behind."

Keith jogged to catch up to Marvin dragging Bridget along with him.

"Why you tripping, Pops? They released me. They were going to release AJ, too, but he had a warrant for something else."

"Bridget, do you think I'm tripping?" Marvin asked her looking for some backup.

Bridget wiggled her hand. "You did slap him a couple of times," Bridget said.

"What should I do now? Call him a man 'cause he got locked up for robbery? Robbery! Like we don't feed you and clothe you." Marvin raised his hand to strike Keith. As it came down, he locked eyes with Keith. He paused midair. The despondent look in Keith's eyes sent chills through Marvin's body. He'd seen that look before—on himself.

Marvin dropped his hand to his side, inhaled deeply, and took off running. They were only two blocks away from home and four blocks from Mount Carmel. He didn't stop nor decrease speed when he hit the hill on 145th Street. Marvin looked at the steep incline as one more obstacle in the way of him saving his family.

By the time Marvin reached the locked doors of Mount Carmel, he was too out of breath to holler open the door, so he kicked and pounded on the door until Pastor David opened it himself.

"We open the doors of the church at nine o'clock . . . Marvin."

"David . . . I mean Pastor David, I need to talk to you. I don't want to talk to the holy man of God. I just want to talk to you man to man," Marvin said between breaths.

Pastor David opened the door wide. "Come in, Marvin. Come in."

Marvin walked in and followed Pastor David into the sanctuary. "Stop walking, man. I'm about to have a heart attack. I ran all the way here." Marvin flopped down onto one of the pews in the middle of the aisle and Pastor David sat down in the row in front of him.

"What's up, Marvin?"

"I just picked Keith up from the precinct," Marvin said.

"Lord, have mercy. Is he all right?"

"Nah, he's not all right. I mean he's acting like he's all right. You know he's got his chest all poked out and Bridget stroking him, but I saw something else in his eyes."

"What did you see?" Pastor David turned around to face Marvin. He didn't even wait a beat before repeating his question.

Marvin pulled his shirt over his head. He didn't want to acknowledge what he saw. Keith like his father at eighteen concentrated on picking wallets, playing cards, and playing girls, but he was worse than his father. Marvin couldn't see any evidence of remorse on Keith's face.

"I saw me."

"Marvin. What did he get picked up for?"

"Armed robbery. You got any words of wisdom for me?"

"You remember the first time we got picked up for armed robbery?" Pastor David asked smiling.

"No, but I remember the last time we got picked up." Marvin sat up in the pew and put his hands on Pastor David's shoulders. "They took you to central booking that night, and my mom sent Lavell to pick me up that night 'cause she said she'd had enough."

"Yeah, I remember. Lavell almost got arrested for endangering the welfare of a child. It took about three officers to get him off you." Pastor David laughed.

"I told you I didn't want to talk about Lavell before," Marvin snapped.

"It's been a minute. Forgive my memory lapse, man. So, what did you do when you picked him up?"

Marvin sat back and rubbed his hands together. "I did a Lavell on him. I slapped him upside the head until Bridget intervened," Marvin said chuckling a bit.

"Marvin, how long are we going to dance around the dead before you admit that it's affecting you, and when are you going to acknowledge that Cynthia not being around is affecting Keith? How do you think he feels seeing you running around with another woman?"

"What was I supposed to do, become a hermit? Was I supposed to wait for her?"

"What would you have wanted Cynthia to do?"

"Let's not even go there. It's been six years tomorrow, David. Isn't six like some special number for God?"

"God made man on the sixth day. Maybe through these trials He's making a man out of you." Pastor David stood. "Now, in order for God to make you into something you're going to have to submit yourself. Ask Him to show you how to be more loving and compassionate toward your son."

"Keith isn't twelve years old anymore. What do you want me to do, hug him and kiss him?"

"No, lead him. Lead your family back to the Lord, and He will heal your scars and Keith's."

Marvin waved his hand at Pastor David. "I didn't come here for that. I told you I just wanted to speak to you, man to man."

"That's how I am speaking to you, as a man—a man of God—and I will not come down for you. I hope one day that you will come up for me and for your family. Now if you can't accept that, then there isn't much else for us to talk about," Pastor David said, patting Marvin on the shoulder and walking away.

Chapter 42

Keith sat on the edge of his bed using his video game controller to shoot at the terrorist on his television screen. He had one round of ammo left that was being wasted because he kept missing shots due to his lack of focus on his targets. He was more focused on trying to figure out when Bridget was going to tell him to beat it.

All week long he'd overheard all the pillow talk Bridget had with Marvin about making this weekend special. It was the anniversary of something or other: the first time they met, their first date, or their first phone call. Bridget celebrated every trivial event that happened in their relationship.

Keith did not sulk like James did when he was informed no one would be traveling with him and his team this weekend to the Super Six high school basketball tournament at Rutgers University. Instead Keith tried to map out his evening, which he wouldn't be able to pull off without a financial backer.

Keith didn't plan on budging until he got Bridget or Marvin to invest in his night on the town if they wanted him out. In no way was he trying to hinder the progress of Marvin and Bridget's relationship; unlike his little brother he wasn't angry with Bridget. James and Bridget clashed with each other very often.

The shroud of silence that James draped himself in was often mistaken for rudeness or contempt. Daily, they battled each other. Bridget shot underhanded words of fury at James, and James threw daggers back at her with his cold stare. Despite her smart mouth and sarcasm, of all the girlfriends Marvin had after Cynthia took off, Bridget was Keith's favorite.

She didn't try to become their mother. She just blended into the family like butter melting into a frying pan. Keith favored her because she didn't comment on his rambunctious nature nor try to curb his wily ways. Bridget didn't waste her breath chastising him about roaming the streets for hours and only coming home for a bite to eat and to use the bathroom.

Bridget just took Keith as he was. She helped to guide him through adolescence, which might have proven to be awkward for other boys with the same gangling frame as Keith. Bridget fawned over him, telling him he was handsome every day, and he was, with Marvin's pointed nose, full bottom lip, and indolent gait. She constantly reminded him to moisturize his skin. Bridget's compliments bolstered his confidence and encouraged his strange curiosity for the opposite sex that Cynthia's absence had spawned.

Often in the hallways of Freedom Academy High School, he found himself surrounded by a gaggle of girls lathered in honey blossom body sprays and strawberry-flavored lip gloss vying for the opportunity to allow Keith to sample their wares. Despite having been left back, his stature and street cred made him every girl's fantasy.

Keith found himself almost always caught up in those moments. He was intrigued by their soft skin and the scent that their bodies emitted when he got close to them. Hypnotized by the fluidity of the waves of their hair and the bounce of their flesh, Keith prodded them like cattle and changed them like underwear. Bridget refrained from doing the afterschool special thing about diseases and bashing him over the head with speeches about respecting women.

Bridget never harassed him. Instead of speeches on respect, Bridget offered Keith advice on how to make his exploration of the female terrain a more pleasurable experience for both parties involved, and she slipped condoms into his sock drawer. With that in mind, Keith just sat patiently waiting for the moment when she would ask him to leave and he could ask for the cash. With James away for the weekend at a basketball tournament Keith figured he might get more than the usual seventy-five dollars. He didn't have to wait long either. Before he completed his first mission on the game, Bridget was rapping on his door with her French-manicured nails.

"Enter," Keith said.

Bridget twisted the knob and pushed the door open gingerly before walking into the room. She had a flare for dramatics. Keith glanced up and stared at her meaty thigh, which hung out of her black satin robe.

"Here." She extended her arm toward him holding up a roll of money. His game controller fell to the ground as he snatched the cash.

"Thanks, Bridge." He licked his thumb and peeled back the bills, snap counting each one. He slid off the bed, grabbed his fleece-lined navy blue Pelle Pelle leather jacket, and slapped on a navy blue Yankee fitted cap.

"Where are you going, Key?"

"Probably over to Rock's girlfriend Nikki's house to meet the fellas. First, I'm going to look for AJ and then hit up Nikki's."

"Fine. I'll tell your father."

"All right," he said, stepping around her and exiting the room. Bridget followed him to the door.

"Come here, Key." He stood in front of her. She straightened the collar of his jacket. "Now you look a'ight."

"Bridge, no matter what people say about you, you're good in my book." He flashed her a smile before jetting out the door.

Keith went down the stairs two at a time. With his pockets lined with $150, he was going to have a good time tonight despite the chill in the air as March made way for spring.

He scanned the block with his eyes for his friend AJ. He and Keith had joined Black Ice on the same day and had become like brothers. AJ didn't move without Keith, and Keith didn't move without AJ. Keith planted himself on the corner of St. Nicholas Avenue, asking each person that passed him by if they knew where AJ was.

One of the older dudes said to him, "I saw him in the back of Lucky's shooting pool."

Lucky's was a hole-in-the-wall bar on Eighth Avenue that had been raided by the cops so many times the whole neighborhood was shocked the doors were still open. Every law that could be broken was broken in there, from operating an illegal gambling enterprise to selling liquor to minors.

"Thanks, big man." He gave the guy a pound then galloped to his right toward Eighth Avenue before the money burned a hole in his pocket. He reduced speed when he spotted Tricia who looked like venison, and Keith wanted to be the hunter who caught her. Her hair was cut in a short bob tapered in the back. Generally Keith wasn't into girls with short hair, but her long, smooth neck and amber-infused eyes popped because of the way her hair framed her face making her simply irresistible to Keith. The fact that she had a boyfriend, Dutch, who was reportedly insanely jealous, also made Keith want her more.

"Ay, Trish, where are you going looking so good, girl?"

"To mind my business."

"Can I mind your business too?" Keith asked, standing directly in front of her to block her path.

Smiling and holding on to the belt of her coat, she said, "Keith, you so crazy. I'm going upstairs to get in my bed."

"May I get in your bed too?" he asked, tracing the portion of her collarbone that peeked out of the boat-neck collar of her jacket.

"Dutch wouldn't like that."

"Trish, I don't want to get in there while Dutch is in there. I'm talking about just me and you."

She stepped back. Keith grabbed her. Pressing down on her wrist, he could feel her blood begin to boil. He pulled her back into close proximity of his body. "Think about it, Trish," he said, using his free hand to stroke her high cheekbones. He bent down and whispered in her ear. "I know what you've heard about me, but I promise I'll be gentle."

She grabbed Keith's cell phone from his back pocket and punched in her number. Satisfied with the new acquisition, Keith returned to his rooster's strut.

All of the patrons greeted Keith when he arrived at Lucky's, the men with high fives and the women with tight hugs. No one even thought twice about Keith being underage considering the other violations that took place at Lucky's. Keith slung his jacket around the back of a barstool at the end of the bar and retreated to the rear where the pool table was stationed next to a small door that opened up to one of Harlem's many vast alleyways and served as an escape route for several of Lucky's patrons.

"Yo, Luck, when are you going to get rid of this thing and get with times?" Keith asked pointing at the pool table. "You need some TVs and video games to spice up this place," Keith suggested.

"Naw, I'm good. Business is good, and your mama ain't complaining when I lock up and lay her flat on her back on that table. Can't do that on a television." The whole bar laughed at Lucky's crude comment.

"Ay yo, Key. Come on, man. Get in this game, I'll let you shoot first," AJ barked at him.

Keith dragged his fingers across the hips of a Dominican girl who had volunteered to chalk Keith's stick, slapping her thigh before he squared up at the table to take his shot. He scratched.

"AJ, lemme do that over. My mind was—"

"In the gutter," AJ finished. They fell over each other laughing and slapping five. Keith arched his back over the pool table, pulled back his stick, and someone pushed it.

"Watch where you're going," Keith said, not even glancing up from the green velvet that covered the pool table.

"What?"

"I said watch where you're going. I didn't stutter," Keith said, standing straight up, staring into Dutch's dark eyes. Dutch stepped a tad bit closer to Keith. Dutch's posture wavered.

"What do you want, homie?" Keith asked sarcastically. "I get it. You want me to bless you with another round of drinks," he continued taking a step back after catching a whiff of the scent of alcohol emanating from Dutch's body.

"Naw," Dutch slurred. "What I want is for you to stop smiling all up in my girl's face."

Keith turned his back on Dutch and laughed. He fixed his eyes on the pool table. "Red ball corner pocket," he said, dismissing Dutch's comment. "Do you believe this guy over here stepping to me about some chick?" He directed his comment to AJ.

"He better go and tell his shorty to stop smiling in my face," Keith advised, letting a raucous set of laughter ring from his belly.

On cue AJ began laughing as well. He laughed so hard he doubled over holding his sides and leaned on the pool table for support. The Dominican girl joined in on the laughter.

"You laughing at me, too, baby?" Dutch said, glaring at the girl. "I got something for y'all to laugh about." Dutch drew a .22 from his waist and let off several haphazard shots. He tried to just aim at Keith, but in his drunken stupor he was unable to hold his hand steady. He fired until the chamber of the empty gun clicked; then he bolted out the back door into the alley.

The piercing cry of the Dominican girl ruptured the silence as she tried to push Keith's limp and bloody body off her.

Keith heard his name being called, but he could only respond by grunting. Sirens could be heard in the distance. The bullet burned and burst inside of him. He wanted to cry but all he did was grunt. He called out for the only one who could ever make him feel better when he was hurt. The only sound that came out were unintelligible gargles and grunts as he choked on the blood that filled his mouth, but he did not stop calling his mother's name until he could no longer breathe.

Chapter 43

"Mr. Barclay, open up," a voice boomed between pounds on the door. Instantly Marvin recognized the voice of AJ, Keith's best friend.

"Stop banging on my door, AJ," Marvin yelled. "Keith is at Nikki's. He left here looking for—"

"Open the door, Pops," AJ cried sounding panicked. "Something happened to him."

Shoving Bridget out of his lap, Marvin vaulted over the arm of the couch. Frantically, he tore the door open, practically ripping it off its hinges. He focused sharply on AJ.

"He . . . he's been shot. I don't think he's okay. Some dude just ran up on us and started shooting."

His brown skin turned pallid, his knuckles cracked as he clenched the doorknob. His mouth dried up. Marvin felt like he'd been chewing chalk. The veins in his neck stiffened and bulged. AJ did not say that Keith was dead, but Marvin was smart enough to read that ghastly look in AJ's eyes that said his son wasn't coming home tonight or any other night.

The knot of guilt in his back had to make room for the grief that paralyzed him immediately. Keith was his favorite. Marvin knew the dangers that lay in elevating one child over another. When Cynthia left, all he had was wound up in his sons. At first they were both angry at Marvin. He figured the anger would subside once they realized she betrayed them all and was never coming back. They were young boys, and he expected to become their hero. On the contrary, the gap between Marvin and James became a valley. Keith, on the other hand, clung to him, which helped Marvin get through losing his wife.

Wishing sorrow came in a candy-coated chewable rather than this hard and bitter pill, Marvin screamed through his tears, which curved over his cheeks and fell into his open mouth.

Bridget tiptoed to the door. Placing her hands on Marvin's stiff, broad shoulders, she began to massage him. The coolness of her palms snapped him out of the catatonic state threatening to kidnap him.

"Go put on some clothes," he said to Bridget over his shoulder. She dashed to the bedroom and Marvin remained still.

"Pops, you coming?" AJ asked, tapping him on the shoulder. Marvin bobbed his head. Without so much as saying good-bye to Bridget, he walked out of the apartment.

"Where do you think you're going, buddy?" the officer said with three of his fingers pressed into Marvin's chest in an attempt to keep him back. "This is a closed crime scene, buddy, there's nothing to see here."

With a quick swipe of his hand, Marvin escaped the officer and barreled past him with the crime scene tape wrapped around his waist declaring, "That was my son who got shot."

Marvin made his way through the maze of fire trucks, ambulances, and patrol cars around the detectives on their cell phones calling all their informants, and over to the coroner's van.

He froze and stared at his son's body as the medical examiner zipped the body bag. "The paperwork is going to be simple to complete for this one: DOA."

Those three letters brought Marvin to his knees. Tossing every molecule of pride in him to the side, Marvin collapsed on the concrete and cried. With his head buried between his legs, he wailed and moaned so loudly he didn't notice when Pastor David arrived at the scene.

"Marvin, Marvin." Pastor David squatted to look Marvin in the eye since he wasn't responding. "Marvin, I'm—"

Marvin swatted the pastor out of his way, stood, and reapplied his menacing scowl. "What do you want, man? I didn't call you."

"Marvin, I can't say I understand your pain."

"Then don't say anything at all."

"Marvin, the death of a loved one can be hard, especially when it's unexpected. If you're going to make it through this, you're going to need a comforter."

"What are you going to do, hold me?" Marvin said in high-pitched ladylike voice.

"Jesus is the comforter, and He has promised to heal your dry and broken land, if you would just submit yourself and your family to Him. This isn't some kind of game."

"Awww, get out of here with all of that. I don't want to hear about the power of God and my son is being rolled away in a Ziploc bag," Marvin said.

"Maybe nobody wants to hear it at a time like this, but you should listen with gladness. Do you remember the vision I shared with you? You were walking through the desert."

"Nah, not really," Marvin said rolling his eyes, trying to recall this vision.

"I know it was a long time ago, yet it seems to be coming to pass. You only have one son left."

"What?" Marvin barked, stepping off the curb and right in Pastor David's face.

"You only have one left, brother," Pastor David said, "The doors of Mount Carmel are open to you and your family at any time in this difficult hour." Pastor David patted Marvin on the shoulder once more before walking away.

Marvin returned to his cement seat. The bile that gathered at the bottom of his belly catapulted out of his mouth and onto the sidewalk as his heart convicted him of his role in this tragedy.

He was wrong for beating Cynthia, and she was gone.

He was wrong for leaving the church, and James was swallowed by his silence.

He was wrong for not putting his foot down when Keith joined Black Ice, and now he was dead.

What else could go wrong now?

Chapter 44

Cheo bounced through the door of Cynthia's apartment. Cynthia was in the kitchen removing a round pan with pita bread from the stove.

"Zaragoza," he shouted.

"What?" she queried, resting the pan on the counter in the empty space between her and where Cheo was standing.

"Zaragoza," Cheo repeated, scooping Cynthia up, spinning her around. "I got it. I got Gotham House." He kissed her pouty and confused lips. "The largest book publisher in the country has agreed to publish my next book, *A Poor Man's Guide to Spain,* so we're going to Zaragoza."

"We're going to Zaragoza?"

"Yes, we," he said, pointing at her and then himself. "Remember when I sent in my proposal? Well, they really liked it, especially the part I included about working with a chef to create a list of the greatest eats at the cheapest prices in Spain and a compilation of recipes from each town that travelers can prepare before or after they leave Spain."

Cynthia lined the base of the pita with hummus, staring at Cheo in amazement. "I'm still not sure why I have to go with you."

"First of all, it wasn't even my idea. It was Ron's, my new editor at Gotham House. He wanted to pair me up with a promising world-class chef who wouldn't steal my shine but could add another dimension to the book."

"Then you volunteered me to travel all the way to Spain with you when I could look these recipes up on the Internet from my office. Cheo, why are you always meddling in my life?"

"I didn't volunteer you. He recommended you. He said, 'Hey, you're down in Virginia. I hear there's this great restaurant called Sabor down there and the head chef is a lady. This might be perfect. You're both local. We could play up the male and female thing on the promotional tour.' After I'm done, you'll be global."

Shaking her spoonful of hummus at him, she mocked Cheo. "And I bet you said, 'No problema, *Papi porque, yo conozco ella*. She'll do it."

Cheo's cheekbones rose as he laughed at her. "I can recall the days when you struggled to comprehend my Spanglish, and now here you are mocking me with it. I didn't say it *en Espanõl*. I said it in English." He perused the ingredients on the countertop—lettuce, hummus, and pepper olives. He popped an olive in his mouth, watching Cynthia slice a ham that looked like it had been in a fight with the rotisserie oven and lost.

"I'll admit I did tell them I knew you and that I would speak with you about doing the book. I don't see how that's meddling. Besides, how could I say no when Ron said he was going to make us global?" Cheo said, punctuating his question by waving his hands in the air across his face. "What is this that you're working on?" he asked, pilfering a piece of ham.

"It's a ham gyro salad. I don't know what to call it yet." She plucked his hand as he reached for another piece. "I've been thinking of changing one the sections to the Greek Isles or something with a Mediterranean feel to it. I'm trying to add more local dishes to the menu or find ways to make substitutions with local products so that I can cut costs. Cheo, I don't want to go global. I'm having a hard enough time trying to manage my local affairs. *En serio,* I wish that you would stop trying to force things on me."

"What have I forced on you? Nada. This relationship has been cruising at your speed limit from day one. We can't get married for some reason unbeknownst to me, we barely see each other anymore, and now you're telling me we can't do this one project together," Cheo complained.

"It's not my fault we don't see each other that often. You know we wouldn't have that problem if we were living together, which is a separate issue all together; although I actually might consider that one."

"I will not compromise my values when every decision you make is purely motivated by your emotions. Come here," he said with his arms wide open.

Cynthia stepped into his arms and rested her head on his chest.

"Why do I have to force you to visit the beautiful countryside of Zaragoza, run with the bulls in Barcelona, and lounge on the beach in Cadiz with your boyfriend while being paid to do so? *No entiendo.*"

"How could you not understand, Che? I have my own work to do here. What exactly is it that you suggest I do about the restaurant while I'm off globetrotting with you?"

"Listen, *allí venga un tiempo cuando cada madre tenga que dejar a su nino solo.*"

Cynthia broke away from Cheo's grasp and strutted into the living room. "I don't have time for any Spanish parables today, Cheo," she said, looking at the clock that hung on the wall.

"I said, there comes a time when every mother must leave their child alone."

"Excuse me," she said in an elevated pitch. He'd struck more than a nerve with that statement.

"This is ridiculous. You've been hands on from day one. What do you have a restaurant manager for if you can't leave her there alone to manage the restaurant?"

Cheo was right. Not one day had passed in the three years since the opening of Sabor that Cynthia did not come in. Cynthia had purchased the same loft-style kind of space as her mentor Chef Sullivan had with office space on the second floor. The only difference was she didn't use the whole second floor as an office. She put a partition up in the middle of the floor and turned the excess space into a makeshift bedroom for her late nights and early mornings at the restaurant. Even though she didn't have a breakfast menu, Cynthia still found herself up early doing cooking demos with the women from the Broad Street Domestic Violence shelter and conducting tastings for married couples interested in having their wedding catered by Sabor.

The only reason she was home today was because of Erica, her restaurant manager whom Cynthia trusted to handle the lunch crowd. The reins didn't completely transfer hands. Cynthia still came in for the dinner shift. Erica was punctual, pleasant, and possessed a sensitive palette that assure Cynthia that she would see to it that every meal was prepared as close to perfection as humanly possible.

"Cynthia, every mother has to leave her child alone some time."

Her signature pout began to surface. Her heart felt heavy in her chest, her skin tightened around her bones. Cynthia rolled her eyes searching for the faces of her sons that were once etched into the folds of her eyelids. So many years had passed since she'd last seen them smile. A missing tooth was revealed through the parting of James's thick lips and Keith's strong smile was only a preview of the fine man she knew he'd grown up to be.

That's how they looked when she'd last seen them six years ago hopping off the bus after school, jumping over cracks in the sidewalk, leaping into her arms.

Cynthia tried to imagine them now. In her mind's eye, fifteen-year-old James was thin and knock-kneed with his chest puffed out, and Keith, nearly a man at eighteen, had a sparse goatee, long legs, thick bark-like lips, and sparkling eyes.

A stream of tears fell from her eyes. She sucked back the saliva that filled her mouth. Cheo extended his arm to draw her to him. She shuddered in his hands. It had been so long since she unleashed the memory of the children she left behind to experience the life she wanted. She shrank back until she rested on the door of her deck.

Cheo inched closer to her. He scraped the tears from Cynthia's cheeks with his thumbs and smiled at her. "I feel like we're at the beginning again. Why are you so afraid? I don't want to hurt you. *Mi amor,* I love you. *Vamos,* let's go to Spain."

The more she thought about it, she had to admit that a trip to Spain sounded divine, but she couldn't relinquish any more control of her life to Cheo. He was responsible for finding her first job in Richmond; he was basically the progenitor of Sabor and her entire career in food. Nor could she risk going global and being exposed for who she really was. A few photos in the *Richmond Times* weren't likely to make it up to the small corner in Harlem that her family occupied. Being featured on bookshelves nationwide was way too risky.

"Don't do this to me now," she said, freeing herself from his grip. She walked toward the door. "Cheo, I think you should leave now."

"No, let's talk. I mean this Spain thing isn't that serious. You don't have to do it. I'll call Ron and tell him you respectfully declined. But we still need to talk because

I'm tired of this. You can't keep flaring up every time I propose something."

"Then stop making propositions. Don't give me any more unsolicited suggestions. Don't tell me any more of your ideas. Technically, we're business partners since you won't accept my money, so we are working together."

"I don't want your money," Cheo said lovingly.

"You have the keys to my apartment. What more do you want?"

"*Que desea usted, el silencio? Yo no dire cualquier nada a usted ni le preguntaré nada.* Okay?"

"English," she shouted rapidly clapping her hands. "English. Cheo, speak English, for the love of God. How are we supposed to have a discussion and you keep on flipping back and forth?"

"Suave. You are smooth. Ummm, you're trying to put the responsibility of conducting the discussion on me to make it appear as though I am the source of the problem. How are we supposed to talk when you do this all the time, *todo a la tiempo?* I can't take this, Cynthia. I'm tired of living in dysfunction."

"Then get out. Get out of here." She motioned toward the door.

"Babe, I have a key to this place. I am going to walk out and come right back in again. I hope you'll be prepared to hash this out when I come back."

Cynthia smirked at him. "Since today is Share Ideas Day I have an idea, Cheo. How does this sound? I'll go, you stay here. Make sure you get nice and comfy, and I'll come back when I'm ready." She grabbed her trench coat from the closet near the door and fled the apartment before Cheo could pronounce another syllable. She ran down the stairs, her sweaty palms barely able to grasp the metal handrail. She tripped down the last flight of steps, falling through the door that led to the garage.

Cynthia trotted to her car as quickly as possible. Snapping the door open, she climbed in and adjusted the mirrors after sticking the key in the ignition. The engine stalled on her. Her hands shook with each hard turn of the key. It felt like now was the time for truth. She looked at herself through the rearview mirror. She could see his eyes as she practiced the words, "I'm already married. I'm already married. That's why I can't give you the things you want."

Chapter 45

Cynthia could hear Cheo's voice calling out to her. Then she spotted him in her rearview mirror. Opting out of confessing her sin, she gave the key another twist, pressed down on the accelerator, and sped past him.

Even the afternoon in Richmond was too quiet for Cynthia. The population growth she'd seen in the six years she'd been there had not created the level of noise necessary for her to escape the sounds going on in her head. Right now she needed a New York–style distraction: someone using a jackhammer to rip the sidewalk open, two fire trucks passing in the lane beside her, one ambulance and a police car behind her that suddenly turned on the siren when the light turned green.

Accepting the fact that she wasn't going to get one, she settled for a substitute that served her just as well: Starbucks. Cynthia drove to the Starbucks on North Eighth Street.

"I need a venti house blend, and I'll take these as well." She flashed a copy of the *Richmond Sun* and a package of French coffee pastries at the girl behind the counter.

She took a seat near the back of the store where the lights were dim and the choice of seats limited, reducing the possibility of her having to share her space with anyone else or converse with them like a polite Virginian would do. She hugged the paper to her chest. Reading the daily news always served as a wonderful intermission from her life and left Cynthia grateful when she saw the devastation and tragedy that wreaked havoc on the lives of others. She was then able to look at her simple problems from a fresh perspective.

Scanning the headlines for the most interesting place to start, her eyes locked on a headline about New York, SHOOTING DEATH OF HARLEM TEEN LEADS TO MARTIAL LAW IN THE CITY, SEE PAGE A10 FOR THE FULL STORY. *That poor mother,* Cynthia thought, scrambling to get to page that contained the full story. A disheartening photo of Lucky's bar with a teens out front lighting candles and crying on one another's shoulders was above the headline.

> ON FRIDAY A BARRAGE OF BULLETS ENDED THE LIFE OF EIGHTEEN-YEAR-OLD KEITH BARCLAY INSIDE OF LUCKY'S, A BAR KNOWN FOR HOSTING CRIMINAL ACTIVITY.

Cynthia's mouth hung agape. *There must be another eighteen-year-old Keith Barclay in Harlem.* She continued reading.

> WITH NO EYEWITNESSES STEPPING FORWARD TO HELP DETECTIVES CRACK THE CASE, THE NYPD HAS RESPONDED BY ENFORCING A CURFEW FOR TEENS BETWEEN THE AGES OF TWELVE AND NINETEEN AND LOCKING DOWN THE PORTION OF THE NEIGHBORHOOD WHERE THIS HEINOUS CRIME OCCURRED FROM 145TH STREET AND ST. NICHOLAS AVENUE TO 135TH STREET AND EIGHTH AVENUE. OFFICERS ARE STATIONED ON EVERY CORNER CHECKING ID, AND VISITORS MUST BE ESCORTED TO THEIR DESTINATION. "THIS MEASURE OF SECURITY WAS TAKEN TO PREVENT ANY OTHER SHOOTINGS THAT MAY OCCUR AS RETALIATION SINCE THIS YOUNG MAN IS AFFILIATED WITH THE GANG BLACK ICE," DONOVAN MCNEIL, THE POLICE COMMISSIONER, STATED.
>
> COMMUNITY WORKERS AND ACTIVISTS FROM CONNECTICUT TO CALIFORNIA ARE UP IN ARMS AND STAGING PROTESTS ABOUT

WHAT IS BEING PERCEIVED BY SOME AS THE DEATH OF THE
CONSTITUTION AND A WALK DOWN EASY STREET FOR THE POLICE.
MARVIN BARCLAY, FORTY-TWO, FATHER OF THE DECEASED . . .

Cynthia read Marvin's name five times before she
could continue reading.

WHEN ASKED HOW HE FELT ABOUT THE INSTITUTION OF
MARTIAL LAW IN HIS COMMUNITY HE SAID, "MY SON WAS A
GOOD SON. IF IT TAKES LOCKING DOWN THIS NEIGHBORHOOD
TO CATCH A KILLER AND SPARE OTHER FATHERS FROM KNOW-
ING WHAT IT FEELS LIKE TO LOSE A SON, I AM FOR IT."

Fat tears drenched the copy of the *Richmond Sun* that
Cynthia held in her hand as she recalled the details of her
elder son's birth.

*He was complicated; he went in the breach position
three times, flipping upside down immediately after
being turned each time. It took thirty-two hours of labor
to get him out. He was certainly his father's son. He
was in no hurry to do what you wanted him to do. The
doctors demanded to take him out, but I refused, saying,
"He'll make it out all right."*

"He'll make it out all right" was the same thought that
had enabled her to leave him alone for so long.

The drive to Richmond International Airport wasn't as
quiet as her drive to Starbucks. Cheo called her at least
twenty times. With each ring, she pressed the decline
button on the screen, deferring him to her voicemail. She
wasn't quite sure how to explain to him that her eighteen-
year-old son was dead.

The twenty-first time the phone rang, she answered it.
"Where are you?" Cheo asked. "Erica has been calling me
trying to reach you, and I've been trying to reach you for
her. Is everything all right?"

"I'm at the airport."

"What are you doing at the airport?"

A heavy silence filled the air until the words filled her mouth.

"I'm going to New York. I just found out there's been a death in the family and I have to go," Cynthia explained, her voice cracking as she tried not to break down.

"Oh my God, babe. Are you okay? What time is your flight? I feel so bad now giving you such a hard time and then this. I'm on my way to the airport now. What terminal are you at?"

"No," she screamed into the phone. She cleared her throat. "I mean no, thank you, Cheo. It would really be best if I do this on my own. It's been a long time since I've been home, and this is a real tragedy." The waterworks started again and she couldn't pull the plug.

"I've never heard you sound like this before. Are you sure you can make it alone?"

"Oh, Cheo, I'm so sorry." Cynthia continued to cry. "I'm sorry about everything."

"Calm down, my love. Don't worry about it. Call me as soon as you get to New York. I love you."

"I love you too, bye."

Cynthia wanted to lie down on the ground of the airport to be trampled on by the travelers. Her son, her firstborn, was dead. Cheo was right again. She could not handle this alone. Cynthia choked on her tears and made her way to the check-in area.

"I need a flight to New York," Cynthia demanded from the woman behind the checkout counter at American Airlines.

"What day would like to leave? What time would like to depart? Which airport would you like to land at? Would you—"

"My son has been shot, lady. I don't care where the flight lands as long as it's taking off now. I don't care what you have to do, just get me on a flight," she shouted, slapping the counter. "Now."

While the customer service agent began searching for flight information, Cynthia withdrew her cell phone and called up Chef Sullivan for some assistance.

"Chef Sullivan, I need your help," Cynthia said as soon as he answered the phone.

"Well, hello to you too, Cynthia. I haven't heard from you in so long and that's how you greet me, your mentor."

Cynthia could imagine the bewildered look on Chef Sullivan's face as he quipped with his hand pressed against his chest. She missed his flair for dramatics.

"Chef, I'm sorry. I promise you I'll make it up to you. I really need your help on this one."

"How serious it on a scale of bad review to health department shutdown?" he joked.

"Chef Sullivan, there's been a death in my family back in New York and I have to go right now. Can you oversee Sabor this weekend? I mean I love Erica, but she's never been alone for a whole day let alone the weekend"

"This weekend? I'm hosting a party at the restaurant today, a wedding tomorrow, and a business brunch on Sunday. I would really love to help you, Cynthia." He snapped his fingers. "Susan. She's supposed to help me, but I'll send her to Sabor. She knows her way around the place."

"Yes, I know Susan would do just fine. Oh thank you, Chef Sullivan. We'll get together as soon as this is all over."

"Listen, Cynthia, death can be scary and it can be sobering. Here's something I learned after my wife passed: death isn't just a time to mourn a loss. It's a time to gather all the leftovers and fragments of your life together. It's a time for you to recognize what you've done wrong all this time, face it head-on, and get it right before you're gone."

"Chef Sullivan, I will try to do just that."

Cynthia thanked Chef Sullivan then put in a call to Sabor to let Erica know Susan would be there in her stead overseeing things that weekend. With Sabor safe and secure she directed her attention to procuring a ticket to New York to see about the sons she'd left unguarded.

Chapter 46

Marvin turned off all the lights and blasted "It's a Man's Man's Man's World" at full volume. On the days that Keith and Marvin found that life was winning the wrestling match and their backs were on the canvas, they dimmed the lights and listened to James Brown. There was something about the character of his voice that assured them he had been where they were, and it was possible to get up from the lowly state they'd fallen to.

With his hands folded in his lap, he thought about his boy. *I used to hold him with these hands, slap box with these hands.* Marvin couldn't resist taking a drink any longer. He took a sip of Johnnie Walker Black, which numbed the pang of grief tied up in his chest like Novocain did for a toothache. His head was full of questions and the police didn't have a single answer for any of his questions.

He still had a few hours to spare before James got home from his game. *He won't take this well. How can I even explain this? I can't explain this.* He placed a wet rag on his forehead, hoping it would alleviate the throbbing. Marvin was so glad that the basketball tournament James was participating in was out of the city. He was also grateful for the coach who'd worked with Marvin to keep the bad news at bay by seizing the team's electronic devices, so they could focus on the game.

Marvin pulled himself up from the chair and went into cleaning mode, collecting the empty beer and liquor bottles from the floor. Even he was astonished at the amount of beers he'd put back since in the last two days since Keith's murder.

A light rap on the door interrupted Marvin as he took stock of the room, searching for anything else that was out of place.

"I'm not doing interviews for the forty-fifth time, and if you have a care package, please just leave it at the door. I appreciate your generosity, but I just can't deal with anyone right now."

"Marvin, it's me."

Oh dear God, now I'm losing it. Please, Lord, I can't go crazy now. I know I should have looked after them boys better. Forgive me, he begged God at the sound of that soft purr he hadn't heard in years, thinking he was hallucinating.

She pounded on the door again.

"Who is it?"

"Cynthia."

Marvin did not believe it could be her after all of this time. He figured it was the Johnnie Walker Black trying to have a conversation with him. Just to be sure he wasn't losing it or drunk beyond belief, he opened the door.

It was her. Even with two bulbs out in the hallway, he recognized her in all her splendor. She looked exactly as she did when she left, gorgeous. He loved that messy ponytail look and the side-swept bang added an air of mystery to her face. Her sultry lips were covered in bright red gloss that caused his mouth to water. He wanted to kiss her. He wanted to reach out to grab the belt of her trench coat, draw her into him, and swallow her. Her skin glowed, and she had the whole hallway smelling like wildflowers.

"Marvin, are you all right?" The question reverberated in his brain as he checked her out. *Down, boy,* he spoke to the beast inside of him that wanted to shake her.

"Marvin, are you all right?" she repeated. "Aren't you going to let me in?"

Marvin let go of the doorknob. The door slammed in Cynthia's face. In the past, he would have dragged her in the apartment by that wispy ponytail and pounded on her until she begged him for forgiveness or until she cried for him to stop hurting her and love her. A part of him did want to do that, but he was too full of sorrow to even acknowledge his anger.

Feverishly, Cynthia pounded on the door.

"Marvin, you are not the only one who has changed," she hollered through the door, acknowledging the fact he had dismissed her so peacefully. "I am not moving until you let me in."

"I'm not going to. Why don't you crawl back under the rock you came from?"

"I'll stand here until you let me in or come out. And when you do come out, because you have to, I'm going to follow you everywhere you go. Have your pick. As a matter of fact, I'm going to camp out right in front of the door."

"Why are you here anyhow?" he growled through the door.

"Our son is—"

"Our son? Our son?" Marvin huffed as he swung the door open. "He ain't your son anymore. You've been gone what eight, nine years?"

"Six years."

"I know how to count. I know one thing: only one of us has lost a son. Only one of us has been here. I lost a son." He beat on his chest. "We lost you a long time ago." He walked back into the apartment.

He flicked the light on in the foyer and left the door open, hoping she would follow him in. He couldn't bring himself to invite her in, but he didn't want her to go either. Cynthia crossed the threshold, scrunching up her nose. Marvin knew she was taken aback by what she saw. One, her beautiful apartment was a mess; two, he hadn't changed a thing. Her cranberry curtains still hung from their rods. They were a tad bit faded from sunlight.

Her cherry wood armoire was in the living room and now served as a resting place for his ashtray and a display table for a series of trophies. She ran her fingers along each one, reading the placards: honor roll, basketball, science. A few of them bore Keith's name but the lion's share of them were James'.

Marvin positioned himself near the dining room table, far enough away from her that if the urge to slap her rose up again she could get away. He didn't want to hurt her anymore. Marvin studied his wife as she surveyed the apartment. Her skin glowed because of the glare the moonlight cast into the apartment. Her white button-down shirt hugged the curves of her torso. It was unbuttoned enough for him to get a glimpse of what he had been missing. Her waistline was still small in comparison to his. God, he used to love those hips, those dancing hips. They had their own rhythm and attracted every man in her vicinity to her, but she always walked away with him.

"Why are you staring at me like that?" She looked into his eyes. They had not lost their depth nor hypnotic power, she thought. The somber look that covered his face drew her in. *Man, he plays the wounded cub routine well.* She wanted to hold him. She counted down from five and counted up, trying to count out the old feelings, longing, and magnetism that were surging through her body. Yes, he was her husband, but if this were a Lifetime movie, the info box would describe Marvin as her estranged husband.

Cynthia swallowed him with her eyes. In the dim light of the hallway she could not see just how much he had changed. The hairs around his temple had grayed and so did his goatee. The richness of his brick-colored skin was reduced to the color of the red dust on the side of the road.

"Please close the door."

Cynthia closed the door, stripped out of her trench coat, and stood behind a chair at the dining room table across from Marvin.

Under Marvin's constant scrutiny, Cynthia began to feel uncomfortable. She excused herself to get a drink of water.

"Make yourself at home," Marvin said. The sarcasm in his voice was strong enough to cut glass. The mess that greeted her there scared her. The sink was filled to capacity and grease lined the stovetop. In order to obtain a cup she was going to have to fight through the piles of pots, pans, and plates.

She scrubbed a plate diligently and methodically in a counterclockwise motion to create enough friction to motivate day-old food to go down the drain the way the busboys taught her when she worked at Sullivan's Eatery. The reason for her impromptu visit had almost gotten lost in the soapsuds until she came across a mug with a picture of some girl kissing Keith on the cheek. Her arms were wrapped around his neck with her lips pressed against his chocolate cheek.

"What happened to him?"

She walked into the dining room and found Marvin's sinewy frame standing at the window.

"I don't know, Cyn."

"What do you mean, you don't know?" she asked grilling him. "It isn't like he scraped his knee or bumped his head. He's dead."

"I know. Do you think it's been easy for me raising two kids—two teenage boys at that—all by myself? I have to work night and day just to keep food in their mouth and shoes on their feet." He turned to face her. "I don't know why you care anyway. He stopped caring about you a long time ago. That's probably what got him killed. They say it's gang related, but I know it's chick related. That boy has a bad habit of chasing broads looking for you."

Marvin returned to his post at the window as if keeping watch was going to bring back the dead.

Before she could stop herself, she was standing behind the man she once loved stroking his sinewy arms. "And what about you, Marv? Did you stop caring about me or have you been looking for me?" Her voice was heavy with seduction as her fingers massaged his skin.

"I don't know, Cyn." He shook his head. "I just don't know how I feel. I mean my son is dead and now you're here."

"Our son is dead."

"That he is, and what did you expect to get by coming here? Did you think you could get your conscience cleansed and your back blown out in one weekend?"

"I don't know what I expected, Marvin. All I do know is our son is dead and something inside of me said that we should be together, that I should be here now. You can pretend all you want that I'm not welcomed here, but you didn't change anything in the apartment. You kept all of my stuff, including the armoire, and I know how much you hate that thing."

Marvin glanced over his shoulder at the armoire and broke into a fit of laughter. It was a wedding present from Mildred. It was bulky and ugly. Mildred said it was an heirloom passed down from generation to generation in her family. Often Marvin had joked that the truth was Mildred only used the wedding as an excuse to finally get rid of that old, ugly thing.

"Marvin, what's so funny?"

"You know, I tried to get rid of it. Even Bridget hates that thing. By the time I dragged it out the room, I was in so much pain that I was crying real tears, so I just left it out here."

Cynthia cleared her throat, swallowed hard, and rolled up her sleeves. Her stomach tightened. Her throat felt as if it were closing. She tried to clear it again. She knew Marvin had other women. This was the first time she'd ever heard him say one of their names.

"Are you okay?" Marvin asked.

"Is Bridget your girlfriend?"

Marvin whipped around to face Cynthia. "You ain't been here in a long time. I don't think you have the right to start asking a whole lot of personal questions."

His omission was an admission in Cynthia's book and more than enough for her to figure out where she stood. Silently, she walked to the couch and pushed one arm through the sleeve of her coat and then the other. Hearing Marvin say Bridget's name was a startling reminder of why she'd left: because Marvin had abused their relationship in any way that he could. Bridget's name also reminded her of why she had returned, and it was not to rekindle an old flame. She fished through her purse, looking for a card.

Placing it in front of Keith's honor roll trophy, she said, "I'm not sure as of yet where I'm going to be staying, but the number to my cell phone is on that card. Call me once you finalize the funeral plans. Let me know how much money you need me to contribute."

"You're not going to stick around to see James? He should be home real soon."

"And what time will Bridget be home?" she asked folding her arms.

"I don't know, an hour or two. But this is not about her. It's about you and your son."

"When I get settled in somewhere, I'll call him. He can even come and stay with me if he'd like. Good-bye, Marvin."

"Why do you always do this?"

"Do what?"

"Run away."

"You want me to stay here to meet your girlfriend? What do you want, to see us fight for you? Are you kidding me? Have you lost your cotton-picking mind?" Cynthia said, storming toward the door.

Marvin lunged at her and held her by the arms. "Yes, I expect you to stay. Our son died. I was sitting here in the dark thinking I killed him, going over the list of things I should have done differently and maybe he'd still be alive. I worked too much, I drank too much, I went out too much, and I just could not see that the boy was headed down the wrong path. You should be the one sitting here crying and feeling guilty." He began to shake her. "I'm trying to take the high ground. I'm really trying to take the high ground. This has got to be hard for you too, but not as hard as all of these years have been for me without you."

"Let go of me, Marvin."

"You did this to us. You killed our son."

Cynthia freed herself and took a step back. "You can't lay all of the blame on me. He's gone, and I'm sorry. Do you think if I knew this was going to happen I would have left for even one second? The truth is you did this to us. I left to get away from you."

Cynthia ran out of the apartment, fleeing the scene like she'd just robbed a bank. She had spent the entire plane ride blaming herself for Keith's death. She cried for most of the flight, and she certainly wasn't about to let Marvin beat her down a second time.

Chapter 47

Finding himself alone again, Marvin returned to his seat in the dining room. The chair curved underneath him to form a body cast. He sank into the chair and did not fight against the warm tears that streamed down his face, gladly returning to the near-comatose state that had possessed him since he came home.

The sound of someone banging on the door drew him out of it. Taking no thought for who was at the door, he just opened it, willing to share his pain without anyone open to receiving it. There was Bridget, her hands full of bags. Although her hands were too full to take her key out, she was ready and willing to carry his load.

Bridget squinted, relying on the moonlight to lead her safely into the apartment. She made it into the kitchen, placed the grocery bags on the counter then proceeded to turn on every light, trying to conjure up some artificial sunshine to drive the black away. Marvin observed as she unpacked the grocery bags. It had not occurred to him until that moment that Bridget was pretty in her own right; not like Cynthia, but she did possess something that was near beauty.

With a grand and effervescent smile, she put her arms around him and rubbed his chest as if that would heal the hurt in his heart. "Thank you for trying to clean up."

He brushed her hands off his chest.

Her touch felt wrong, but her words were usually right and comforting. Throughout the years, Bridget had become Marvin's biggest cheerleader, and he was anticipating some comforting words, not any of this touchy-feely stuff. After what seemed like eternity, Marvin decided to initiate the conversation.

"What took you so long to get home, Bridge?"

"Ummm, I went to the funeral home on Lenox and to the grocery store." She dried her hands on the dish towel hanging on the refrigerator door handle and stepped into the dining room. She stood near the end of the table, leaning on the back of the head chair.

"For what?"

"To get dinner."

"Don't play with me, woman," Marvin said pointing at her. "What did you go to the funeral home for?"

"Marvin, Keith can't stay in the morgue forever."

"I know that, but you shouldn't be going around picking out funeral homes either. That's something for his mother to do."

"Marv, I didn't make any arrangements without you. I just picked up some brochures. I figured with this being the second funeral you'd have to plan, it might be a little overwhelming. I . . . I just wanted to help," Bridget explained nervously.

"Bridget, I need to tell you something."

"What is it, Marvin? You can tell me anything," she said, inching closer.

"She's not dead. My wife isn't dead."

She stood straight, staring at Marvin so hard it transcended the darkness.

"I can't do this now," he said, trying to silence her before she even spoke. He already knew what that piercing look in her eyes and her hands on her hips meant: she wanted answers and she wanted them now. Marvin got up from his station for the last two days and walked into the bedroom with his shoulders hunched and his head hung low. He was trying to play on her sympathy. He wanted Bridget to believe he was defeated, not hiding something.

The sound of the bathroom door banging against the wall brought him out of the bedroom.

"Where are you going, girl?" he asked, noticing she had taken down her matronly bun.

"I ain't got no kids here, so I think I'm going to enjoy what's left of this wonderful night."

"Bridge, come on now. Don't do this. I didn't mean it like that," Marvin pleaded.

"Don't matter how you meant it, Marvin. You're right. This is not my responsibility. I heard they had live music tonight at Londel's. I'm going to have a nice meal, a stiff drink, and dance to some good jazz. You and your dead wife can figure this out."

Chapter 48

Cynthia played like she didn't know where she was going to stay to keep Marvin off her back but she knew she could always go home. She sat on the stoop for several minutes contemplating ringing the doorbell.

The thought of having to give her mother an account of how she had spent the last six years living a lavish life in Richmond as an entrepreneur while her son was here in Harlem being shot down kept her from ringing the bell.

"It sure is nice to see you again. Praise the Lord for your safe return," Ms. Marcus, one of Mildred's neighbors, said, welcoming Cynthia with a warm hug. Ms. Marcus held the door open for Cynthia smiling. Cynthia was hesitant to follow her into the building.

She plodded up the steps, praying Mildred wasn't home. Cynthia wasn't ready for the confrontation. Her thinking was that her presence would somehow expiate Keith's murder; instead Marvin greeted her with sorrow and bitterness. There was no telling what kind of greeting she would receive when she knocked on her mother's door.

Mildred opened the door on the first knock. She was still a plump, round beauty. Her honey-colored skin glowed against the fuchsia boat-neck shirt she was wearing. Some strands of her hair fell loosely around her face. She'd cut it in layers to defer some of the attention from the spider web color her hair had morphed into. Mildred smiled at her only child, opened the door wider, ushering her in with her free hand.

In the foyer, Cynthia found everything else to look at except Mildred's eyes. Cynthia studied the wall adjacent to the dining room. It looked like the view from the cliff side of a Mediterranean island. Next she took note that the tiles needed the grout cleaned.

"What did you come here for, girl, to smile at me? Aren't you going to say hello or something to your mother?"

"Of course, Ma." She reached out to embrace her. Mildred squeezed her so tightly Cynthia couldn't tell whether it was an angry hug or an affectionate one. Mildred released Cynthia and went right into praising the Lord.

"Thank you, Jesus. Thank you, Jesus," she shouted at the top of her lungs between jumps. "You brought her back safely. Oh, bless the good Lord.

"Excuse me," Mildred said, smoothing out her blouse. "It's just so hard for me to contain myself right now. Are you okay? Where are your bags? Where are you staying? How long are you staying?"

"One thing at a time. I don't have anywhere to stay, Ma. Can I stay here?"

Mildred raised her eyebrow and looked around the room. "I suppose I have enough room for you, but let's be clear, the last time you stayed with me, that crazy man you have for a husband came pounding on my door. You're not hiding out from him again, are you?"

Mildred's response perplexed Cynthia. Did she not know that her grandson was dead?

"No, ma'am. I don't think he'll be looking for me."

"All right then. It's settled, you can stay here. Are you hungry or something? I don't have much, but I'll fix something up for you."

"No, thank you, ma'am."

"Suit yourself. Are you on a diet or something? Because you look good already, girl. The South has been good to you. Take your coat off, girl. Go wash your hands and sit down and relax."

"Ma," Cynthia said unbuttoning her coat, "how did you know I was in the South?"

"Only the Southern sun can get you that golden brown, you keep calling me ma'am—they only do that in the South—and your cousin Rita saw you in Virginia at your restaurant, Sa . . . Sa. Something foreign. I want to say Saki but I know that's not the name of it." Cynthia was floored by her mother's revelation.

Cynthia tried to speculate how long her mother had known where she was and who else knew. She shrieked at the thought that Mildred might have shared this info with Marvin. Cynthia quickly calmed herself down. Marvin didn't know or he would have dragged her back to New York by her ponytail. *I was there all this time and she never reached out to me.* Covering her mouth with her hand Cynthia wondered what else Mildred knew about. *Does she know about Cheo?*

Her mind had put Cheo in the bottom drawer of a file cabinet. She had not thought about him or called him since arriving in New York. The room seemed to shrink. Cynthia excused herself and went into the bathroom. Cynthia took a few sips of water from the tap to rid her mouth of the taste of rosebuds, pulled her hair back into a tighter ponytail, ran her wet hands along the nape of her neck, and washed her hands and face.

Following her little pick-me-up in the bathroom, she found Mildred seated at the table praying over a bowl of rice and baked chicken. Mildred patted the seat closest to her, inviting Cynthia to participate in the dining experience.

"Like I was saying, your cousin Rita saw you down there. You know, she's a big executive at Bank of America. Don't tell nobody though. With that whole recession thing working at a bank isn't such an honorable thing anymore. Anyhoo, I think she got promoted maybe two or three years ago. They wanted to relocate her. She said she had to check it out first, which is understandable. Now while she was out there, she calls me up all out of breath screaming, 'Aunt Millie, Aunt Millie, you're not going to believe this, but I just saw Cynthia in the newspaper.' I laughed and told her she had to be mistaken. It was probably someone who looked like you. You sure you're not hungry, not even just a little bit, baby?"

"Maybe, just a little bit, Ma."

Mildred disappeared into the kitchen and returned with a bowl of corn, the pan of baked chicken, rice, and a Styrofoam plate for Cynthia. Mildred set each dish down on the table and placed the plate in front of Cynthia.

"This is self-service, girlfriend," Mildred said, snapping her fingers and laughing.

Cynthia's heart was warmed by her mother's rawness. She wasn't rude. She was kind of cute and funny. Cynthia appreciated the honesty, which was in high demand in Richmond. One drawback to running a successful business was finding people who were willing to be honest with you. No one wanted to be on her bad side because they were afraid of what the consequences would be. It felt good to be home and scoop up her own rice.

"Now where was I? Oh yeah. So after Rita saw you in the paper, she decided to do some digging around, either to prove me wrong or just satisfy her own curiosity. She should have been a cop. She stayed behind to check it out. She mailed a copy of the ad for your restaurant to me. She even took photos of you greeting customers and taking pictures with them."

This little anecdote temporarily released Cynthia from having to deal with Keith's death before she was ready to and gave her something else to be concerned about. It troubled her to know that her mother knew where she was and left her. "If you knew where I was, Ma, why didn't you contact me?"

"Cynthia, you know something I learned about people: when they want to be found, they let someone know where to find them. It seemed to me you didn't want to be found, so I put you in God's hands because I knew He knew what to do with you because I didn't," Mildred expounded while stuffing huge spoonful of rice and corn into her mouth.

"Who's watching the restaurant for you now?" Mildred asked.

"Susan, my mentor's daughter. I've got an excellent manager, and my sous-chef is always on point. He works well with the apprentice chef I'm training, and Cheo has the keys if anything goes wrong, but I really hadn't given it too much thought before I left."

"That's a bad habit you've got." Mildred shook her spoon at Cynthia. "Leaving without thinking things through."

Cynthia gnawed on her bottom lip, trying to curb her tears. She could see where this conversation was going. She hoped her mother would take it easy on her, but she was pushing her right into the pit. Cynthia struggled to breathe as she choked on the resentment she could hear in Mildred's assertion.

"Just say it. Say what you really want to say, that I'm a bad mother, that my kids should have come first." The tears sprung from her eyes as she screamed, "I shouldn't have left them. Go on and say that this is my fault. Go ahead, Ma, say it. It's my fault that Keith is dead."

On cue Mildred rose from her seat, grabbing Cynthia. She tried to use her arms to keep Cynthia from falling apart. "I wasn't going to say that. I mean was I disappointed? No, I was devastated when you left. I had the police looking for you and the whole nine yards, but this is not your fault. None of this. It is promised to man once to die and then the judgment. The boy wasn't going to live forever. He was a hooligan if ever I saw one, just like his father. Maybe if you had stayed, he would have lived a little longer, but sooner or later he would have wound up dead. Look at me."

Cynthia spun around in her seat to face her mother as she stood over her.

"All he did was run the street. I can only imagine your pain. I was scared to death something terrible happened to you. Since there was no body I was able to hope that you were alive."

Mildred released her grip on Cynthia and cradled her face. "What you need to do now is sit down for a while, have a little talk with Jesus then with Marvin and figure out what you're going to do for your other son. Burying Keith and building James up should be your main concern." The intercom sounded, preventing Cynthia from answering the call her mother had just issued on her life.

"I'll be down in a sec," Mildred said into the intercom. She returned to the table and kissed Cynthia on top of her head. "Don't wait up for me. That's Pastor David. We're having all-night prayer at the church for the young people in Harlem."

Cynthia just nodded, baffled that in the middle of a crisis her mother was running off. Then she remembered this was her crisis, so she would now have to do what she had forced everyone else to do: cope with it on her own.

It seemed like Mildred floated out of the door. Cynthia envied that light and airy way her mom was able to conduct herself, even at the worst of times. Cynthia used a napkin to wipe away her tears and what felt like some of the shame that came with the death of her firstborn son.

She searched through her purse for her cell phone. The first call she made was to Sabor. Susan had everything under control. Next she sifted through her voicemail. Cynthia tapped her foot on the table leg, impatiently waiting for Cheo's voice to improve her current state of mind.

"*Mi amor,* the end is only the beginning. Call me when you can."

She exhaled when she heard that rich voice full of optimism and love.

Her heart sped up as the reality of the situation set in. *I can never call you, Cheo.* In one day the past and present had collided and blown up in her face. Cynthia folded her arms and used them as a pillow. Her tears ran out of her eyes forming a small pool in the crease of her bent arms. She wished she had a lasso to wrangle her thoughts together as they bounced from man to man in her life. She tried to figure out how she would handle James, manage Marvin, and face Cheo.

First she would have to deal with herself. *Why are you here?* Cynthia asked herself.

Grabbing a napkin from the table she scribbled her objective. Healing. Could everyone be healed without anyone else getting hurt?

Chapter 49

James's hard pound on his father's bedroom door announced his arrival to Marvin. The team bus had just arrived this morning. The blinds were drawn despite the brightness of the Monday morning. Flecks of dust floated in the beams of sunlight that snuck in through the blinds.

"Come in," Marvin croaked.

The hinges on the door squeaked as James opened the door. Marvin stared at James hovering in the doorway. James stared back at his father. Marvin hoped the dry patches that covered his face would not reveal he'd been crying. Marvin scratched his throat contemplating how he was supposed to begin this conversation; announcing Keith's death would be a break from their scripted one-way conversation they shared every morning.

Marvin coughed then got out of the bed and stood in the doorway with his son. "There are some things that we need to talk about, Jimmy."

James laughed a curt, dry laugh, indicating he recognized Marvin's little ploy. Jimmy was his childhood nickname, and Marvin only used it when he wanted no resistance from James or needed to smooth things over.

"I wish I was a bit more eloquent, I wish I knew how to say things in a gentle way, but I only know how to be raw. This is going to cut you to the bone when you hear it." Marvin locked eyes with his younger son. He could see impatience brooding in his eyes. Marvin put both of his hands on James's shoulders before the words maneuvered themselves out of his mouth.

"Keith is dead."

James flinched a little then raised his eyebrows to form a question.

"He is, James. I'm sorry but he was shot on Fri—"

James bolted out the door before Marvin could deliver all the details of Keith's death.

Pulling on a pair of gray sweatpants that were lying in the middle of the floor, Marvin tried to craft a list of all the places James would go seeking comfort, but he didn't know where James would go. He hoped someone on the block had seen him and could tell him where he went. Luckily, Marvin didn't have to go far. As soon as he stepped outside, he found James on his knees weeping in front of Keith's memorial. He knelt down as if he was at the altar. His teardrops fell into the melting candles. He rocked back and forth with his hands folded in front of him. James's lips moved rapidly, yet Marvin could not make out one syllable.

Marvin bent down and put his hand on James's shoulder. "Get off the ground," he whispered in his ear.

"Wh . . . wh . . . where were you?" James rolled his shoulder, shaking Marvin's hand off him. He let go of the silence and hollered, "Were you with that whore? Were you in bed with her when this happened to him?"

Marvin looked James up and down. The sound of his son's voice jolted him; not even the accusation, just the sound. Marvin had never seen James so sad. Tears streaked his brown face. His whole body rocked with sadness. Marvin extended his arm to help his son off the ground. Marvin's hand quivered while reaching out to him. James used the building for support as he hoisted himself up off the ground. He swatted away Marvin's hand that still hung in the air so hard Marvin lost his balance and fell trying not to step on the shrine erected in honor of his son.

With his eyes closed Marvin tried to summon the strength to stand. "When will this get better?"

Cynthia stood over Marvin as he lay on the glittery concrete. Marvin opened his eyes and smiled at the sight of the burnished glow of her skin. What he had to smile about was a mystery to her after watching James knock him to the ground and walk away from the corner. Nevertheless, Cynthia smiled back, extending her hand to help him up. Marvin brushed her off with a wave, stood on his own, and dusted off his clothes. Cynthia shook her head at him. He cut his eyes at her, clearly designating the blame for what seemed to be a never-ending train wreck.

She made up in her mind then what she would do after the funeral. *We're burying Keith, and I'm on a plane back to Richmond.*

"Can a mother forget a child?" she heard in her head. She rolled her eyes, questioning where that voice came from. "Can a mother forget her child?" The second time she heard the voice, she recognized it as one she hadn't heard in a long time. *What do you want me to do, Lord? What can I do, Lord? James is lost already. If I stay here, I'll disrupt the flow of his life, and I can't just uproot him from here just to satisfy some maternal urge,* she reasoned.

The sound of Marvin clearing his throat disrupted Cynthia's internal dialogue. She stared at Marvin. His stomach hung slightly over his pants, his white T-shirt was yellowing, and his lips were dry and cracked. She searched his eyes for the man she once loved. All that met her was the bleak emptiness that filled him. An emptiness that she'd created. She walked to the door and leaned on it while Marvin searched his pocket for keys.

When they entered the apartment, James was sitting on the couch. He didn't speak to either one of them.

Cynthia immediately tore into Marvin and asked, "Why didn't you tell him right away?"

"I couldn't, Cynthia. It was the weekend of the Super Six high school tournament. College scouts come. It's televised. His team needed him focused on the game."

"What about what he needed, Marvin? Did you have money riding on that game or something?"

"You ain't got no right to waltz in here questioning my decisions. It doesn't matter whether I had money riding on the game. I did what I did because he's got something special. You've never seen him on the court, so you wouldn't understand, but it's the only moment of clarity in his life. It's the only time when I can understand what he's trying to say. Do you think it would have made a difference whether I told him on Friday night or he found out today that his brother was shot to death and that's the only reason his mother came home?"

Cynthia waved her arms and pointed her finger at Marvin. "That's really low, Marvin." She was so involved in quarreling with Marvin she'd forgotten James was sitting in the living room shrouded in the darkness threatening to consume the entire family until he began laughing. He was hysterical. His loud, strident laugh filled the apartment. Cynthia and Marvin stared at him quizzically. Marvin's mouth flapped open in astonishment. Cynthia searched for words to console her son. She had none.

"That little bum," James said, smiling. "Too bad he can't see this." He slapped his knee. "He always said you'd come back, and now here you are." He continued laughing. "Someone Greek should have written this story."

Cynthia shrank. His voice had changed from the soft and timid one she'd once heard. Now it was barren and rough, and the tears he was holding back caused his voice to crack like a match being lit.

"I didn't think you were coming back, but he believed in you for some reason." He stood up and stared into

her eyes. Until now, she hadn't realized he had her eyes.
Cynthia could feel the hurt radiating out of his eyes. It
pushed her into the ottoman.

She watched him as he paced. She'd murdered him,
both of them. Cynthia thought she had dealt with the
guilt of Keith's death last night and was ready to work on
healing, and then the guilt came back, barreling through
her like hot lava out of a volcano. She abandoned them
to pursue the life she felt she deserved. *I was selfish.
Look at what I've done to two innocent boys.* Cynthia
grabbed James's hand as he walked past her. He stopped
his pacing, one of his long fingers rested in her palm. His
eyes wandered past her. Cynthia kissed his hand. A wave
of deep and heavy tears took over. The shoulder-shaking,
lip-cringing tears rocked her. She dropped her head in
her hands.

In the past, she had tried to excuse herself. There
were evenings when she rested her head against Cheo's
hard chest, wrapped in his arms, and pardoned herself.
She deserved to be loved; she deserved to have some
semblance of happiness in her life.

When Sabor hosted birthdays, she watched the mothers clapping, singing, and celebrating the milestones in
their children's lives. Cynthia would pinch herself and say
she should be there for Keith and James, but whenever
she walked to her Camry in the parking lot and found
a couple hollering at each other, she eased away and
smiled, glad to have found her way out of that. Now as she
stood there looking at her glassy-eyed son, she realized he
had paid the price for her freedom.

James withdrew his hand from his mother's grasp and
fell back down on the sofa. "Don't cry, Mom. He may have
missed you, yet he hated you for leaving us here. He hated
you; he hated God because of you." James began to laugh
again. "Now he's gone and you're here."

Cynthia didn't know how to respond to that. She wondered if James carried that same hatred for her and God, but she dared not ask. She'd come here seeking atonement, and only James could help her out with that. If he hated her, then this trip was null and void. James walked to the bedroom, slamming the door shut behind him.

Cynthia waited for a couple of minutes before she rose to her feet.

"Where do you think you're going, Cynthia Ann Barclay? Since you're some big-shot caterer, why don't you fix us something to eat?" Marvin asked holding up her business card.

"Caterer, ha," she scoffed. "I'm no caterer. I'm a restaurateur."

"What does that mean?"

"I own a restaurant, Marvin."

"Humph, same difference," he said, folding his arms. "I'm hungry, so why don't you cook something? It's the least you can do."

Cynthia took off her trench coat. Smiling, she stood in front of him with her hands on her hips. All she could do was smile to mask the confusion she felt when it came to Marvin.

Throughout their relationship he had caused her nothing but pain, both physically and mentally. The pain was linked to the joy in their relationship—her struggle to tame him. He was like a lion going through every lioness in the pride. She worked hard to be the one to calm him. As he barked at her to feed him, she remembered how much she delighted in satisfying him. She stepped closer to him, offering herself to him. He put his hand on her shoulder and rubbed her arm. "Are you going to cook or what?" he inquired again with a sly and subtly sexy look in his eyes.

It was the look she couldn't say no to. It was the look he had in his eyes during their first dance, on their first date, and when he proposed. It was the look that sent chills throughout her body.

Beguiled by his eyes and a small ounce of pride that told her to show him who she'd become, she entered the kitchen and looked in the refrigerator, then the cabinets. "What do you want me to make, dirt? There's nothing in here," she said, dismissing the instant macaroni and cheese, chicken wings, and broccoli florets. "Are you sure Keith was shot and didn't die from starvation?" She laughed.

Marvin came near her and laughed beside her. It felt strange to be laughing, and it felt so good. He put his arm around Cynthia and massaged her shoulders. She grabbed the magnetic notepad from the refrigerator and scribbled wildly on it before passing it to Marvin.

"Whole wheat tortillas, tomato, basil, eggs, salmon, feta cheese, asparagus, wild rice, and olive oil. This stuff is going to be expensive, Cyn."

"What happened, Big Marv? You ain't got it?" she asked, sliding her hands into her pockets.

"Oh, I got it all right." Marvin threw on a black hooded sweatshirt and left. Cynthia seized the moment she had alone to talk to James. Several minutes passed before he responded to her continuous knocking on his door.

"What is it?" he asked.

"Would you like to talk, Jimmy?" she offered.

"No."

"Well, I certainly would like to talk to you."

The room went cold and James retreated into his shell of silence. This would be more of a monologue than a dialogue she realized once he pursed his lips together tightly. "Never mind, Jimmy. We'll have this discussion some other time," Cynthia said, backing away from his bedroom door.

Cynthia walked through the apartment raising the venetian blinds in the dining room, parting the curtains in the living room, and opening the window to welcome the light back into the Barclay residence. Without hesitation, she returned to what seemed like a never-ending mess. She dumped ashtrays, scrubbed the toilet, and mopped the floor. Then she dusted the armoire, the trophies, and Marvin's most prized possession, his record player, while James slipped out the door.

She felt confident in her ability to get rid of the physical mess and hoped that somehow her efforts would translate into the emotional mess only she'd made.

Marvin walked in on Cynthia doing her best Aretha impression over the running water as she filled a pot with water and placed it on the burner to boil. The scent of pine wiggled its way up his nose. He looked around at his home. He barely recognized it. The coating of dust and mire that loomed had been removed like a sweeping wind had blown in the apartment through the dining room window. Cynthia didn't hear Marvin come in. She continued scrubbing and shaking as he stood in the dining room watching her slight hips shimmy from left to right.

He thought about getting behind her and squeezing her in his arms. He wanted to lean over, kiss her neck, and whisper in her ear, "My God, how I have missed you, woman. Don't you ever go anywhere. Don't you do that to me again," and cradle her in his arms before pulling her so tight into him they could have a third baby. He crept toward her with his arms open, hoping she would be willing to fill them.

"Did you get everything I asked for?"

"Yeah." He sighed pleased she had stopped him. He set the bags at her feet, withdrawing a Heineken from one and making his way into the dining room. Cynthia busied herself lining the counter with the things she needed to make salmon basil burritos.

"So, you ran off to Virginia to become a cook," Marvin said, putting his feet on the table. "You could've stayed here for all of that."

Cynthia shot him a look that stung like a dart. "I'm not a cook. I have my own restaurant. People do not tell me what to do. I tell them what to do. I couldn't do that here."

"Why not?"

"Your garage, the boys, and . . ." Cynthia paused. "And the beatings, Marvin. I was too wounded to work toward making a dream come true. All I wanted to do was live to see the next morning." Cynthia returned to her salmon.

He kept his head bent. He did not want her to see how much he needed her. There had been difficult times like parent-teacher conferences, first dates, and even a pregnancy scare in which he would have appreciated some backup. In order to survive burying his son, he needed her now he thought as he recalled their vows, for better or worse, in sickness and in health. Right now, he needed the woman who carried his name and bore his seed.

Chapter 50

Crumbs of feta cheese danced in a circle around Marvin's salmon burrito. The scent of the basil traveled deep within his nostrils, causing his chest to expand. The dry rub Cynthia whipped up for the salmon exploded in Marvin's mouth as he bit into the burrito.

"Dang, girl, you learned how to do this in VA? James, you better come out here and get yours before I eat it all," Marvin shouted.

"I'll go tell him the food is ready."

Cynthia wiped her hands on the napkin she'd placed beside Marvin's plate and walked to the boys' room, her hips bouncing from side to side; silently she bewitched Marvin with her new confidence and stride. The girl he'd fallen for at a college party had grown into a marvelous woman. *Why did it take me so long to notice?*

"Jimmy, the food is ready," she announced to an empty room. "Marvin, he's gone," Cynthia said clutching her face.

"Gone? What do you mean gone?" Marvin asked between bites.

"Gone as in not present, was here but is no longer. Where would he go, Marvin? I don't like this, especially with the circumstances surrounding Keith's death."

"He's not going to get shot in broad daylight. This isn't the wild, Wild West, you know, and he's not that type of boy. Pour me something to drink."

"Something to drink?" Cynthia marched right up to the side of the table, folded her arms across her chest, and began tapping her foot. "Something to drink? Marvin, you're not even going to bother looking for him?"

"Cynthia, if I ran out each and every time one of these boys stormed out of here, I wouldn't have this," he said, patting his paunch.

"Marv, I would really feel a lot more comfortable if you looked for him."

"There are officers on every corner of the neighborhood. May I have something to drink please?"

"Marvin," she bellowed.

"Let me finish eating first." Marvin inhaled what remained of his burrito then washed it down with a glass of homemade iced tea.

Marvin took off, kissing Cynthia on the cheek like it was old times.

His first stop was the officer at the corner who was so engrossed in counting the cars that whizzed by him Marvin could have blown his head off.

"Officer."

"Huh?" the officer said, startled by Marvin's voice.

"Officer, have you seen my son, James? He's the brother of the boy who got shot. He's about six three, chocolate, kind of skinny." Marvin noticed the blank stare he was receiving and took out his cell phone to show him a picture of James.

"Oh yeah, I saw him, but I have no idea where he went," the officer said, scratching behind his ear.

"What good are you doing the community if you're standing here not even paying attention?" Marvin preached, regretting having backed the police commissioner's decision to lock down the block. Marvin pushed his way up the hill toward Amsterdam Avenue. A few of James's teammates lived on Amsterdam, so Marvin figured he would begin his search there.

Crossing the light at Amsterdam, the lights shining from within the doors of Mount Carmel caught his eye. *Church lights on in the middle of the day? Maybe he is in there,* Marvin thought.

Marvin opened the doors to Mount Carmel. The sanctuary doors were wide open. Pastor David stood in the middle of the floor speaking to some gentlemen seated in the first three rows. Marvin took a seat in the shadow of the seventh row and struggled to hear what was being said.

"Pastor, I hear you with all this 'love of the Father' stuff, but my son is about fifteen, and I'm sure that he's losing his mind," said a burly, dark-skinned guy. "He's got to be losing his mind the way he talks back to me, defies what I say, and he tried to flex his bird chest at me." All the other men laughed. Even Pastor David chuckled a little bit.

"Be careful, Sean, not to condemn," Pastor David warned the man. "You have to love him back to health and to a right mind to obey. You can't do that without Jesus in your life."

"Amen," a few of the men seated said following Pastor David's remarks.

"You can't do it unless you do it God's way. God doesn't beat us or threaten us into being obedient to Him; 'with loving kindness have I drawn thee,' says the Lord, which is why the Word tells us to raise our children in the nurture and admonition of the Lord. Not with all our fury and big, bad, 'do you know who I am' attitude when we have treated God the same way our children treat us. He said go right, you went left. He gave you a job, and instead of thanking Him, you complained about the location. He picked you up, and you are not willing to do His will."

"All right, all right, Pastor," Sean said, waving his hands over his head as if he was shielding himself. "You beat me up enough. Don't stone me with the Word. I'm going to give the little punk a break." The other men laughed, including Marvin. "I'm going to try this loving kindness thing out."

"You've done it your way already, and it's not working, so you might as well give God's way a try." Pastor David looked down at his plastic wristwatch and back up at the men seated before him. "We have a few more minutes before we dismiss. I just want to extend a Mount Carmel welcome to you. The Holy Ghost bids you welcome in this place. Would you like to introduce yourself and tell us what brings you here, brother?"

Marvin stepped out of the shadows, his jaw tight, his fists balled and stood in the middle of the aisle face to face with Pastor David who outstretched his long arm toward Marvin inviting him to speak.

Marvin's Adam's apple jerked up and down as he took a hard swallow before addressing the men seated before him. "My name is Marvin, Marvin Barclay, and until last week I was the father of two boys; two beautiful boys. I know I shouldn't be calling boys beautiful, but they were, and now I am the father of one, and I can't seem to find that one. I don't want to lose any more than I already have. Whatever God wants me to do I will do to save my family." Marvin fell to his knees and sobbed into his hands.

"Come on, brothers. Let's pray for him." Pastor David went to the altar and got some oil. He poured it directly onto Marvin's head and allowed it to drip down the sides of his face. He placed his hand on the center of Marvin's head and squeezed it tightly as he prayed. "Dear Heavenly Father, you know this man, you know this family, and you know their struggles. I pray that you would break the yoke that the enemy has around his neck and the shackles that he has around their ankles so they would and could willingly serve you. Lord, I pray you would

cleanse Marvin Barclay of his sins and cause him to stand
uprightly before his family to lead them back to you in
this troublesome time. Marvin, stand up."

Marvin used his knuckles to push up off the ground.
The layer of tears covering his eyes made it hard to see all
the faces eagerly staring at him.

"The Lord is willing to perform a new thing in you, but
you must be willing too; willing to accept him as your
Savior and Lord over and above all that you do. Are you
willing?"

"Yes, David . . . I mean, Pastor David," Marvin said
earnestly.

"Then repeat after me: 'Lord, I accept you as my Savior.
Jesus, I believe you are the Christ, Son of God, sent to die
for my sins, and resurrected on the third day that I might
live again. Please, forgive my every sin, and give me your
Holy Spirit, Lord, so that I will not dwell in sin again. In
Jesus' name. Amen.'"

After Marvin had repeated the prayer, Pastor David
grabbed him and hugged him tightly.

"Thank you, Lord, for saving my friend."

The clapping, shouting, and stomping that erupted
from the men was loud enough to make someone passing
by believe there was a full service going on.

"Somebody get this brother a tissue. I think he's having
a breakthrough," Sean shouted.

The men laughed and corralled around Marvin, greeting him and welcoming him to their church. They praised
Pastor David for his down-to-earth and realistic approach
to their lives and the Word of God.

"You and your family are going to love it here," Sean
said, slapping Marvin on the shoulder. "Yo, Pastor, are
you going to dismiss us or what? A brother like me has to
get back to work."

"You work next door, Sean," someone said.

"That's beside the point. The foreman on job isn't Christian. He would love to have a reason to write me up, and I would love not to give him one." Everyone laughed.

Pastor David raised his hand straight into the air for silence. "Brother Sean, since you're in a hurry, please close us out in prayer."

After prayer and a few more handshakes and intense hugs, the crowd dispersed leaving Pastor David and Marvin alone in the sanctuary. Pastor David walked in circles around Marvin checking him out.

"How's Cynthia holding up?"

"How did you know she was here?"

"Sister Mildred told me the other night at the prayer vigil. James stopped in here earlier. I don't know where he went after that. This is hard on him. Marvin, I know you're new to this whole sanctified living thing, but your family has been in the war for a long time. You are seriously going to have to do some praying and fasting to get out from under this."

"Fasting? As in not eating? Isn't that for professional Christians?" Marvin said jokingly.

"No, it's for all Christians. I'll walk you through it. I'll even fast with you. Maybe we can include the other brothers in the Love of the Father ministry. I teach that class four times a week. On Mondays and Wednesdays, we have a class in the morning for the brothers who work at night and a class at night for the brothers who work in the morning, so no one gets left out of the gospel."

"Now that sounds more like it, but I don't see why you can't fast for me. While we're on the subject, I need you to do me a couple of favors."

"Favors? You want me to do you a couple of favors, brother?" Pastor David asked, shoving his hands in his pockets.

"Number one, if James comes back this way, please redirect him to the house. Two, since you're the closest thing we have to a family pastor, I was wondering if you would do Keith's funeral. Three, I'm not sure what Cynthia is going to do, but could you find some time to talk to her and get her focus back on being a wife."

"Anything else, brother Marvin?"

"Yeah, one more thing. I'm sorry for talking crazy to you all those times. You forgive me?" Marvin asked, extending his arm like an olive branch.

"Already done," Pastor David said, pulling Marvin in for a hug. "Are you focused on being a husband?"

"Yes, Pastor."

"I'll come by tonight after my Love of the Father ministry meeting."

"See you then, Pastor David."

Marvin walked out of the doors of Mount Carmel feeling full of something he never had in his life: hope. He couldn't figure out why, but this whole Jesus thing had him feeling like jelly on the inside. He resumed his search for his only living son, singing the one church song he knew: "Jesus, I'll Never Forget." He was full of assurance that if God was able to find him in all of his mess, He could find James on the streets of Harlem.

Chapter 51

The sun was setting and not one Barclay man had walked in yet. Cynthia contemplated starting dinner. She didn't want it to get cold, so she decided to wait. She'd taken Marvin's post at the dining room window, trying to probe the crowd for Marvin's perfectly rounded head or the deep waves of James's Caesar. The vibration of her phone on the table disrupted the quiet of the apartment and her concentration. A number with an 804 area code flashed across the screen. Since she recognized it was someone from Richmond calling Cynthia gave up screening her calls and answered the phone.

"Hello."

"*Mi amor*, I was wondering what I had to do to get in touch with you. You haven't returned anyone's calls."

"Cheo, where are you calling me from?"

"From the *Sun* offices. Since you weren't answering my calls, I thought I might get you that way."

Cynthia rubbed her hand against her chest, trying to relax into the conversation. "Cheo, you know this incident has really brought a lot of things to the surface for me, and when I get back we really need to sit down and have a conversation about . . . about . . . me."

"What about you?"

"You wouldn't understand."

"But I would be there. No matter what it is, whether you have a mother with a habit, a life-threatening disease, or six toes," he said, laughing into the phone.

"Cheo, this is serious," she said flatly.

"Then just tell me what it is. I can't take this back and forth, and maybe this is what we need to take our relationship to the next level."

Cynthia twisted her head from side to side crossing and uncrossing her legs considering what Cheo had just said. They would need to discuss this. She would be going through a divorce soon and possibly bringing a teenage son home with her or he'd be coming to visit at the minimum.

"Cheo, you know the reason I had to run off so abruptly was not just because someone in my family died, but my relationship to the person who died was extremely important. Cheo, I don't know how to say this. I'm not who you think I am, or what you think I am. Keith, my eighteen-year-old son, was murdered on Friday, and that's why I took off like that."

Cynthia took a deep breath, waiting for the explosion to come after she uttered those words. Cheo's end of the line fell silent. All that she could hear was furious typing and the excessive amounts of screaming that went on at the *Sun*'s offices. There was no way for her to know how Cheo took the news. She hoped she had not broken anything else with her confession.

"Come again, Cynthia? What happened to your who?" Cheo asked slowly.

"Cheo, this isn't something we should discuss on the telephone," Cynthia whispered into the phone trying to calm Cheo down.

"Yeah, it probably isn't," Marvin shouted from the foyer.

Cynthia cringed at the sound of Marvin's voice booming behind her.

"Cynthia? Cynthia, who is that?" Cheo shouted into the phone.

"Cheo, you know I love you, and your friendship means a lot to me, so I'm asking that you just bear with me through this. I didn't plan for any of this to happen, and now that it has I have to work it out. Do you think you can bear with me, Cheo?"

"No problem, Cynthia. I love you."

"Thank you." Cynthia pressed the red telephone icon to end the call on her cell phone and turned around to greet Marvin and James who stood beside him. Her hands shook as she tried to estimate how much of that conversation Marvin overheard.

"You found him," she said, clapping. "I'm going to get dinner started. It will be done in a few minutes, okay, guys?"

Marvin and James both walked away from her without a word. Their posture and muted expressions reflected their disappointment. Cynthia knew they both had heard more than she wanted them to. Marvin retreated to the bathroom and James to the comforts of his bedroom.

Cynthia quickly made a plate for James and for Marvin hoping the delectable scent of the salmon she recycled from breakfast and sautéed asparagus would cause their disappointment to disappear. She carried them to the table resting the plates on her arm and their glasses of soda in her other hand. Marvin was the first to come out of the room. He ambled toward the dining room, peering ever so slightly into the kitchen before taking seat at the table with his hands folded in front of him.

"Bon appétit," Cynthia said, curtsying as she placed Marvin's plate in front of him.

"Did you learn that in Virginia, too?" Marvin poked at her as she set James's plate down directly across from where Marvin was seated.

"No. I picked that up here watching *Barney* with the boys." Cynthia snickered. "Close the window so the food doesn't get cold."

"I don't know why you wasted your time setting him a plate. He isn't going to come out here and eat it."

Shoving aside the fear of James not accepting her, Cynthia pushed open James's cracked bedroom door and stepped into his den. They'd changed the color of the walls. In all actuality, only one wall had been painted over; the one on Keith's side of the room was still painted powder blue. James had painted his side of the room ox-blood red.

The contrast shocked her but gave her the context for the life her boys had lived without her. Keith's *Jet* Beauties of the Week and *Sports Illustrated* swimsuit models smiled at Cynthia confirming what everyone had told her about her deceased son. He was obsessed with women and yes, it was her fault. The only thing that hung on James's side of the room was a photo of him and Cynthia taken when he was two years old.

Cynthia searched high and low in pursuit of at least one piece of the boys she'd left behind so she could put all the parts back together again. Cynthia felt James's eyes fastened on her, but whenever she looked down at him he looked away.

"The food is ready," she announced before exiting the room.

At the table Cynthia took a seat beside Marvin and began eating as he sifted through the wild rice and rolled the asparagus around on the plate with his top lip turned up.

"Have you thought about what we are going to do about the funeral yet, Marv?"

"Well," Marvin said, finally taking a bite out of one of the asparagus spears, "Bridget mentioned a—"

"Bridget?" Cynthia interrupted cocking her head to the side. "I'm not paying for a funeral that Bridget wants." She rolled her neck and threw him a look that said, "Negro, are you crazy?"

Marvin put down his fork. He appeared to be readying himself to tackle this argument head-on. "Nobody asked you to pay for anything," he barked at Cynthia. "You came in here dropping your card and your financial stats like someone was supposed to be impressed, Ms. Hathaway. I didn't say we were going to do what she wanted. If you had given me the chance to finish my sentence, all I was going to say is that she mentioned stopping by a funeral home on Lenox Avenue."

"Well, then you should have just said that." Cynthia rolled her eyes and folded her hands against her chest waiting for the old Marvin to spring into action.

"You know you have an awful lot of attitude when you should be gracious. Bridget was here when Keith died, and she was going around touring funeral homes when I didn't have the strength to or know where to find you," he said, pointing in her face. "She's been more of a mother to Keith than you have."

"I brought that boy into this world. I spent thirty-two hours in labor trying to get him here. You can't be more of a mother than that," she said, throwing her napkin in Marvin's face.

Marvin balled the napkin up and clenched his hand into a fist tightly. "You know my first instinct would be to bust you in the head just like old times, but . . ." His hand shook. "But I am not the same Marvin you left here. The years have done something to me, Keith's murder has done something, too, and God has done something to me. I pray He gives me the strength and the opportunity to show you the change in me."

Just then James crept into the dining room. From the corner of her eye Cynthia watched James. He stood behind the empty chair in front of his plate and looked down at his father then glanced at Cynthia before cautiously scooping up his plate.

"You are not eating in your room. Dinner is to be eaten at a table. Have a seat," Cynthia said firmly, reminding James that despite the fact that she had been gone for six years she was still his mother.

"I'm just changing my seat, Ma."

"You sit right there where I put you," Cynthia commanded, her eyebrows and blood pressure raised.

"Yes, ma'am," he said through clenched teeth.

Based on the way that James' hand shook as he raised his fork Cynthia could tell having to stare at Marvin made him nervous. It also made her aware she wasn't the only parent present who needed to be forgiven. Cynthia's seating arrangement was divinely inspired to strengthen the stitch of thread that held them together.

"Jimmy, your father tells me you've become quite a basketball player."

"I have," he said, smiling like the six-year-old she left behind. "I've been in the newspaper and everything. I was even on *SportsCenter*."

"*SportsCenter?*"

"Yeah. What have you been up to?" he asked causally as if he was talking to an old friend.

"Well, I opened a restaurant."

Marvin interrupted Cynthia's monologue before it got underway with laughter. "She's a 'restaurateur,'" he said, making air quotations. "She's some kind of big shot in Virginia. That's what she left us for, you know." Marvin leaned to the side to withdraw Cynthia's business card from his back pocket. "Take a look at this," he said, flinging the card across the table to James.

James took stock of the little black card and embellished gold letters. He flipped the card over and over, glancing at her.

"You see that? Cynthia Ann Hathaway. She isn't even your mother. She isn't even my wife," Marvin exploded.

"That's not true, James. My decision is not a reflection of how I feel about you or your brother. It was about how I felt about me and your father and this marriage." Cynthia shifted her gaze in Marvin's direction. "Marvin, I see you were able to resist the temptation to slap me, but you're not saved enough to let a verbal butt whooping pass by." She turned back to her son locking eyes with. "James, I am so very sorry—"

A knock on the door interrupted their family dinner. Marvin nodded, directing James to go get it. "Who is it?" Marvin asked, chowing down.

"The devil in a blue dress," James said as he opened the door for Bridget.

Cynthia brought her fork to her mouth and rested it on her lip. "I wonder how this is going to play out," she whispered.

Chapter 52

It was clear to Cynthia that Marvin's penchant for burly street girls had not changed. Bridget walked in wearing a knee-length blue dress with a single line of faux buttons going down the middle.

"When did you start talking? I left my keys here last—" She glanced at Cynthia. "What in the world is going on here?" She flailed her arms in the air.

Immediately Cynthia began having a tantrum in her mind. *He cannot be serious. She is not going to plan the funeral arrangements. Uh-uh, no way. I'm not paying for anything this tacky chick picks out. I don't care if she did help raise Keith.* The amount of foundation she was wearing and the heap of vanilla fragrance that caused Cynthia to choke each time she inhaled was a definite deal breaker for Cynthia.

"We're eating dinner. Would you like to join us?" Marvin offered. Cynthia hoped that was an effort to eliminate Bridget's drama and not a heartfelt invitation.

Bridget came closer to the table, taking a gander at everyone's plate. "Salmon and asparagus. I don't ever get that. To tell the truth, you never cook for me, Marvin," Bridget said, placing one hand on her hip, arching her eyebrow, and sucking her teeth.

"Bridget, this is my mother, Cynthia. She made this food for us," James said, smiling at Marvin.

"Your mother," Bridget repeated.

She appeared to be in complete shock. Cynthia felt inclined to stake her claim.

"That's right, my mother, his wife," James responded, sparing Cynthia the trouble and aggravation that clearly came with a woman like Bridget.

"Marvin," Bridget said, her tone begging for none of this to be true. "Marvin, you told me your wife was dead."

Very calmly Marvin responded, "No, I did not. I told you that she was gone."

"Marvin, you told me she was dead," Bridget said, shaking her head at Cynthia who sat there quietly with her hands folded and a smirk painted across her lips.

"No, Bridget, I told you she was gone, and I tried to explain to you earlier that I was misleading you."

"Dead, gone. What's the difference? No one was allowed to talk about her. You took her pictures off the wall. I thought she was dead, but you've been talking to her all this time, Marvin. Have y'all been sleeping together too? Huh? Miss, you been sleeping with my boyfriend?" Bridget hissed.

Marvin jumped up and got in Bridget's face. "Have you lost your mind, woman? Our son just died. Could you please show some respect?"

"Respect, psst. I don't respect no woman who don't look after her own kids." Bridget flicked her wrist as if Cynthia's presence meant nothing. "You're so busy smiling in her face and eating dinner like y'all a real family you ain't find out where she been and when she going back, but I'll ask her." Bridget dipped around Marvin and picked up where she left off with Cynthia. "Where have you been, lady, while we was raising these two boys, huh?" Bridget asked, pointing her long red acrylic fingernails at Cynthia. "And when are you going back? We don't need your sympathy around here," she barked.

Dismissing Bridget's anger and accusations with a roll of the eye and a fierce tiger stare, Cynthia held her ground and remained quiet. She was never one to engage in squabbles with any of the riffraff Marvin was a magnet for and let him deal with the trash.

"Bridget, you know what? I think you better go now," Marvin commanded, assisting her to the door.

"Marvin, I think I better go now too."

"No, Cynthia," Marvin said. Releasing Bridget he rushed to her side. "Please don't go." He pleaded not just with his words but kisses as well. He put the palms of his hands around her face and kissed her, soaking up as much of her as he could. The kiss came from left field but made Cynthia feel right at home. She twisted and turned to position her body close enough to feel the heat generated by Marvin's body. She closed her eyes and stuffed every good memory she had of being with Marvin into that kiss.

"Is this what you want, Marvin? Is this what you want?" Bridget repeated her question until Cynthia pulled out of Marvin's embrace.

It would have lasted all night if it wasn't for James hacking at the table. The unexpected public display of affection must have caused his juice to go down the wrong tube.

"I'm sorry, Bridget." Marvin spoke softly to his mistress.

"You're foul for this, Marvin. I've been here all this time and this is what you want."

"Bridget, you're right. I am foul. You can call me every name in the book if you want, but she is who I have longed for. Cynthia is who I want if she'll have me."

"Lady," she said, sucking her teeth and stepping a few inches closer to Cynthia, "you made this mess and you're more than welcome to clean it up 'cause I'm done here." Bridget stormed out of the apartment, letting the door slam behind her.

Chapter 53

Instinctively, Cynthia began clearing the plates from the table. James disappeared into his room after the fireworks ended. Marvin met her halfway to the kitchen and snatched the dishes from her.

"I'll take care of those. You should take a moment to relax." Cynthia arched her eyebrows in a furtive glance and questioned his motivation for being so caring and affectionate. He seemed different. Cynthia could not place her finger directly on it, but something had snapped in him, and she was glad. Seeing him in this light mood made her believe there was some hope for Marvin. For the first time in a long time she felt comfortable with him. Cynthia crooked her neck to get a peek at Marvin's broad shoulders and strong back as he applied some elbow grease to the frying pan she used for the salmon.

"So, do you think we should discuss the funeral arrangements before I go?" Cynthia asked.

"Yeah. Just give me a minute to finish this last dish," Marvin said, rinsing the soap suds off the pan.

He towel dried his hands and strutted in the living room like a rooster checking on his hen. He took a seat beside her and allowed her to study him and absorb the change that had come over him. Cynthia couldn't figure out if it was just the effect of one day of sobriety or the lack of sleep, but Marvin seemed to sit taller, look cleaner, and sound sweeter.

"Cyn, I'm sorry about that whole Bridget thing. I guess I can't get too worked up about the mystery man on the other end of the phone now considering this. I'm really sorry."

"It's all right, Marvin. Let's just deal with the issue at hand."

"No, it's not all right, and that's why we have all these issues, Cyn. I'm sorry for everything—for the women, for the alcohol, for the beatings. I should have said it sooner. I should have gotten help sooner." Cynthia lowered her head and opened her ears to what Marvin had to say.

"I promise things will be different this go-round."

"This go-round? Marvin, I—"

"Shhh," he said, squeezing her hand before putting on a record.

Marvin bowed in front of her and offered her his hand. Immediately, Cynthia went into protest mode at the sound of the piano intro to "If You Don't Know Me By Now" by Harold Melvin and the Blue Notes.

Cynthia stiffened and sat on her hands. "Marvin, I'm not here for any of these games."

"And I'm not playing any games." Marvin shook his hand in front of her, insisting she join him in a dance. "Just listen to me because I'm serious. Things will be different."

Cynthia placed her hand in his. Marvin lifted her to her feet, pulling her in close.

"I didn't plan on staying after the funeral," Cynthia said nonchalantly, trying to avoid making eye contact with Marvin. He still oozed that alpha male magnetism that pulled her in, and the whole slow dancing thing was a convenient reminder of the first day they'd met. Even then he felt wrong, but his words and his hands on her body felt so right.

"Why not?"

"Marv, I have an apartment, a restaurant—"

"And you have Cheo?" he asked with his eyes fixed on Cynthia's.

"And you have Bridget," Cynthia countered shifting the blame for their problems back onto Marvin's shoulder.

"But I don't want Bridget. I want you, Cynthia. I'm telling you, if you give me another chance, it will be different. You can keep your restaurant. I'll go back to Virginia with you." Marvin kissed the top of her head as it rested on his chest.

"Why should I give you another chance, Marvin?"

He put his hand on her chin and lifted her face from his chest. "Because we're family here. I know it hasn't been good all the time, but can't you give me another chance? Just trust me." Marvin stopped speaking in time for Harold Melvin to finish his sentence.

"I just don't—" Before Cynthia could protest Marvin's advances, the doorbell interrupted her. "Marvin, if that's another woman here claiming her right to plan Keith's funeral, I am so gone."

"No, that ought to be Pastor David."

Cynthia scrunched up her face. "Who?"

"You heard me, woman. I invited Pastor David over."

"If this is some kind of ambush—"

"Ambush?" Marvin shook his head repeating his wife's pretentious statement. "I asked him to give the eulogy," Marvin said, walking toward the door and opening it.

"Hey, David . . . I mean Pastor David. You know you're going to have to give me a minute to get used to saying that," Marvin said, grinning.

"You think he would be used to it by now," Cynthia said from the couch. "Let the man in, Marv."

Marvin backed out of the doorway and let Pastor David in.

"I'm sorry I'm so late. The Love of the Father meeting went overtime. This shooting really shook some parents up, and we had a few new participants present tonight. I hope I'm not interrupting," Pastor David said, taking note of the slow music and dim lighting.

"No, we were just talking," Cynthia said, taking the needle off the record. "Please have a seat. Would you like something to drink? Eat?"

"No, thank you, sister. I'll just have a seat, if you don't mind."

"Not at all, Pastor. Have a seat," Cynthia said pointing at the couch.

"I'm sorry that my first trip here in so long is because of a tragedy like this, but let's discuss this funeral. Where do you plan on having it?"

"Every time I discuss this funeral I wind up in trouble. She's in charge." Marvin pointed at Cynthia deflecting the question to her.

"Before we get into all of that, Pastor David, I know you don't want anything to eat or drink, but would you like me to take your coat at least?" Cynthia offered.

Pastor David removed his jacket and handed it to Cynthia. Walking and talking, she began to discuss her ideas for the funeral. "I was thinking we could do something simple and traditional. I understand that he was in a gang, so I think we've got to streamline this event in order to prevent the opportunity for them to act ignorant. I think the Berlin Funeral Home down the street would be perfect. It's close by and it's small so we can limit the number of people in attendance. Pastor, is there someone in your choir who could sing a song or two?"

"Sister Cynthia, please don't take this the wrong way . . ." Pastor David started his reply.

"Then don't say it the wrong way," Cynthia said, sitting on the ottoman across from the couch. She crossed her legs, determined to make it both verbally and visually clear if this wasn't going to be made easy for her she wasn't going to make it easy for anyone else.

"The blood of Jesus," Pastor David said, scratching his eyebrow. "Cynthia, we're not planning a wedding ceremony, so we don't need to focus on it being small and intimate. We're not planning a peace summit, so worrying about retaliation shouldn't be what you're concentrating on, nor are you planning a talent show, so I cannot just summon my choir members to sing a couple of songs. Maybe you need a moment or two to process what it is we're doing and the chance to ask God to cultivate a tender heart in you."

"I know exactly what I'm doing. I'm planning a funeral for a known gang member who . . . who happens to be my son," she said through tears.

Marvin placed one hand on her shoulder, handed her a napkin, and whispered in her ear, "Why don't you just go ahead and take a moment? Go sit down in the bedroom or freshen up in the bathroom. It's been a long day for us all."

After Cynthia's migration to the bedroom, Marvin sat down on the couch beside Pastor David and heaved a sigh. "I'm sorry about all this. The funeral was the only thing she talked about, and I really wanted to get this thing over and done. I don't know if I can do this."

"I know it all seems like it's coming apart at the seams, but it will get better. Don't get discouraged. Commit Philippians 4:13 to your memory: "I can do all things through Christ which strengtheth me." Since we have this time now, Marvin, let's talk about your new faith," Pastor David suggested eagerly.

"Thank you, Pastor. I feel different, if that makes any sense. I know it's been only a day, but I feel better than I have in as long as I can remember." Marvin combed through his memory in search of a day when he felt this light and airy. "Yet there are still things that I need to work out."

"Like what, brother?" Pastor David patted Marvin on the back.

Marvin dropped his head into his hands and mumbled, "I don't want to trouble you with my issues right now."

"It's no trouble. It's my job to tend to the sheep. I'm already here, and you're going to need a partner if you're going to pull off a job this big. It's going to take a serious move of God to get her to submit to you, and I'll stay all night if I have to."

Marvin leaned back into the sofa and let the cushions swallow him. He smiled at the thought of having his wife back. He didn't see it as reality and knew he couldn't beat his competition, Cheo.

"All night? You mean all morning. It's almost midnight. I couldn't ask you to do that, especially when I have no chance with Cynthia. Did you know she's not even using my last name? We're only married on paper, Keith is dead, and James is almost grown. He's still got some growing up to do, but if she was concerned about that she would have never left." Marvin sighed.

"Marvin, are you really about to get jacked by the devil?" Pastor David asked with his lips curved into a scowl. "You're going to let him rip off all of your stuff, and he doesn't even have a weapon. I don't care what anyone else calls her or what she calls herself, she is your wife, and that's why I'm willing to stay all night with you and fight for her life. I've stayed in hospitals all night long praying with families when their children are sick. Your wife is sick, sin sick, and you think I'm going to run off now." Pastor David planted his hands in his hips and stood with his legs apart like he was Superman.

Marvin doubled over with laughter. "That's it. We're just going to pray this situation away? Pastor, she doesn't want to give me another chance."

"Would you give you another chance after everything you've put her through, Marvin?"

Marvin let Pastor David's words linger in the air before he answered. "No, I wouldn't."

"So then you need to pray, for only God can change the heart, only God can heal the heart. Tonight is a night for you to learn a lesson that many Christians struggle with no matter how long they've been in the faith. Tonight, you're going to learn to trust God. If she wants to go, then know this, 'Can a woman forget her sucking child, that she should not have compassion on the son of her womb, yea, they may forget, yet, will I not forget thee.' The Bible says that a woman can forget about her own little baby but God will not. You stand in the place you are supposed to, man, and the Lord will take care of James. But if she wants to stay . . ." Pastor David jubilantly slapped Marvin on the back. "If she wants to stay, you have to trust that God will reconcile you and cause you to love each other again in a real special way, my friend. Are you ready to trust God and see Him move in your life?"

"Yeah, I'm ready."

"Then rise up out of that chair and rise up in your spirit," Pastor David commanded motioning for Marvin to get up.

Marvin stood in front of Pastor David prepared to follow his lead.

"Come on. Join hands."

Marvin placed his hands in Pastor David's. "Once again, my life is in your hands. You got me?"

"No, Jesus has got you. Bow your head." Both Marvin and Pastor David bowed the heads and closed their eyes. Pastor David inhaled and proceeded to dive into his petition to the Lord on Marvin's behalf. "Father God, in the precious name of Jesus, I present this life to you, Lord. He said it's in my hands, and only you are the sustainer of life, so Lord, I give it to you. Look upon the Barclay household and bind the hand of the enemy. In Jesus' name. Lord, rebuild this family brick by brick until they are standing strong. Look upon my sister, your daughter, and cause her heart to become tender again. Remind her of your mercy, remind her of your love, and call her back to you Lord. In Jesus' name. Amen."

"Now what?"

"Now you let go of my hands, and we wait on God to show Himself," Pastor David said snatching his hands out of Marvin's.

Not sleeping wasn't new to Cynthia. For the first two hours of Pastor David's home visit, she'd sat up on the edge of the bed listening to Pastor David minister to Marvin, instructing him in righteousness, sharing scriptures, and going back and forth to God in prayer for her. She had a mind to go out there and tell him to stop calling her name, but finally, after six years, she recognized the voice of the enemy telling her it was okay to berate a man of God. Instead of accepting his outlandish ideas, she sat tight. Biting her fingernails helped her to remain quiet and absorb all that was going on around her, and when she couldn't take anymore of being painted as the antagonist in this prayer story, she cried out to God for herself.

Lord, I'm probably the last person you want to hear from right now, but I'm calling on you for some guidance. I never meant for any of this to happen. Everything is broken, and I don't know how to fix it. Just tell me, Lord, how do I fix this? How do I get things back to the way they used to be?

Massaging her temples, Cynthia perched herself on the edge of the bed and looked out the window, noting the subtle change in the color of the night sky and waited for some sign—a word, a voice in her head other than her own—to direct her, yet all she could hear was Pastor David teaching Marvin Psalm 51: "Have Mercy upon me, O God, according to thy loving kindness."

"Yes, mercy is what I need," she said in agreement with Pastor David as she opened the bedroom door to join the fellas in an early morning prayer session. A hush fell over the living room as she stepped out of the room. Pastor David and Marvin rose from their seats to acknowledge her presence.

"I just want to make it right. I've been wrong, I've done wrong, and I just want to make it right. I didn't come here to cause trouble. I came here to fix this mess that I've made," Cynthia said, biting her bottom lip to keep it from quivering.

"Cynthia, it is God who fixes broken things." Pastor David took a step toward and continued his mini-sermon. "He makes the crooked straight. You have got to turn it over to Him. He is the restorer. He will cleanse you and restore you to your position as the wife of this household."

Cynthia looked at Pastor David and then at Marvin. She doubted that it was just that simple. "Marvin, I can't be your wife. I've betrayed—"

Marvin reached out and took hold of her hand. "No, I betrayed you, your trust, our love and our vows," he said, clutching her hand. "If you want to go on without me, that's something I can understand, and through the help of God get past. What I'd rather do is to give this thing another try."

"But . . . but I—" Cynthia fumbled searching for an answer to Marvin's questions.

"Forget about you and listen to Him. Listen to the voice of the Lord God, your Creator, the small voice inside of you saying you can't but I will. You can't fix this and neither can I, Cynthia, but His blood can cleanse you and heal you if you want Him to," Marvin instructed.

"Yes, I do. I don't want to live like this anymore, Marvin. I don't want to hurt anyone else." She clutched her heart as she thought of Cheo waiting for her to call with his cell phone glued to his palm.

"Then join us in the reading of the fifty-first Psalm," Pastor David urged Cynthia.

Cynthia licked her dry lips and wiped the corners of her mouth. "Yes, Pastor," she said holding on to Marvin's hand tightly.

Pastor David began reciting the psalm from memory. Marvin and Cynthia followed along from a pocket-size copy of the New Testament and Psalms Pastor David carried with him. As those words filled the air and the darkened sky went from navy to varying hues of orange, a new era in the Barclay family was born at dawn.

Chapter 54

From the sixth row in the center of Rawlings Funeral Home, Cheo watched as Marvin hoisted Cynthia's curved body from off Keith's. The echo of her cries rang in the ears of every mourner.

"Sorry, sorry. I am so sorry. Please forgive me," she pleaded over the body with one hand clutching the stomach that once carried him and the other holding her veiled top hat to her head. But her cries were not loud enough to stop the whispers.

"I wonder where she was all this time. You know what I mean?" a woman asked, elbowing Cheo. Cheo leaned back and questioned her with his eyes.

"That's the mom. She's been gone for like six years and now that the boy is dead and the other one is almost grown."

"The other one?" Cheo asked.

She sat on the edge of the bench and pointed toward the front row. "Yeah, the other one is right over there seated with his hands folded."

Cheo studied the lines of the boy's profile that the woman had pointed to. He could see Cynthia's face in the sharp, clean line of his nose and curve of the corner of his eye. Cheo shook his head as he tried to absorb everything that was coming at him.

"It's a shame what she done to those boys," the woman continued. "Keith done gone out and got himself killed, and James stopped talking when she left. The two of them were awfully close. Someone ought to be tending to him, not worrying about her sorry behind."

"You seem to know a lot about the family. Are you close to them?"

"My name is Bridget. I used to be, but I couldn't let that stop me from paying my respects to the dead." She crossed her legs, sat back in the pew, and kept her commentary to herself for the rest of the funeral.

A dark cloud encompassed Lenox Avenue, and the howl of the wind sent dead leaves and debris running up the block. Cynthia didn't want to watch the pallbearers carry her son out in a box, so she ran out of the room when the pallbearers assembled around Keith's casket.

Cynthia's eyes widened at the sight of the crowd of mourners who waited outside of the funeral. As she shielded her eyes from the flash of the news reporters' cameras, she felt a strong arm curve around her waist and whisk her back into the pavilion of the funeral home.

"Thank you," Cynthia said, straightening the wrinkles out of her dress without looking up. "What a circus. You never realize how crazy the press can be when they're after a story."

"Yeah." The man chuckled. "They'll stop at nothing."

The rich sound of Cheo's accent resonated in Cynthia's ear. She adjusted her dress once more and straightened out her mind as best she could before looking up into his smoldering brown eyes.

"Cheo, what are you doing here?"

"I'm glad to see you too, Cynthia. No, I didn't go through any trouble getting here to support you in your time of loss," Cheo said, reprimanding her.

"I'm sorry, Cheo. It's not that I don't appreciate your presence, but it's kind of strange seeing you here considering I didn't give you the funeral information."

"Oh give it a rest. I'm not out to get you or spying on you. I had to come to New York to finalize my travel plans and renegotiate my contract because my agent noticed something that was a little off, and I decided to tap into my few journalism skills to find you. Since the funeral information was in the *New York Times* along with a picture of a boy who bore an undeniable resemblance to you, I made it here. Sue me for caring about you." Cheo stepped closer to Cynthia with every word until they were standing chest to chest.

"Cheo, there is so much I have to tell you." She placed her left hand delicately on his chest. She could feel his heart beat beneath her hand. "I pray you can forgive me."

Cheo covered her small hand with his. "No matter what it is, I've forgiven you already in my heart."

"The boy who died—"

"Keith?"

"Yes, Keith. He's my son. I mean he was my son."

"I know. You told me that already, Cynthia." Cheo placed his hand on top of her trembling hands.

"That's not all. I have another son as well. I don't know how to explain this so you'll understand." Beholding the pain and anger brewing in Cheo's eyes Cynthia shrank back.

"Well, you've had some time to figure it out. I think you should have more to say to me than that. I deserve more from you than that. I deserve an apology. I deserve an explanation and I want it now," Cheo demanded through his lips that were drawn tightly together to form a grimace.

"Is everything okay over here, Cyn?" Marvin shouted as he approached the pair parked in the pavilion.

"We're good over here, bro. Sorry for your loss, man. I'm Cheo." He extended his palm to shake Marvin's hand.

Marvin froze behind Cynthia. "I didn't tell you because I didn't know how to explain that I was still married to his father," Cynthia revealed. "Cheo, this is my husband, Marvin. Marvin, this is Cheo."

"I'm her boyfriend, Cheo."

Marvin stepped out of Cynthia's shadow and stood next to her. He clenched his jaw and balled his hand into a fist.

"Like she said, I'm her husband." Marvin's voice was brittle and rough. Cynthia had heard that sound before. It was almost always followed by a punch.

"And I'm the man she ran to when she got tired of you," Cheo retorted.

"What?" Marvin inched closer. Cheo didn't flinch.

"What was unclear about that? She is the woman that she is because of me. The devil used you to break her down, and the Lord used me to build her up." Cheo looked down at Cynthia. Possibly for some sign of confirmation, and Cynthia looked around for some divine intervention.

She now realized the truth to the scripture what is done in the dark shall come to light. Cynthia hoped the Lord wouldn't allow her mistakes to continue to wreak havoc.

"Is that right?" Marvin snickered, flexing his fist, prepared to lay a left hook followed by a right cross on Cheo's pretty jaw.

"Brothers, brothers, this looks like a heated discussion, and while there is an appointed time for everything under the sun, according to Ecclesiastes, I don't believe this is the time nor the place for this." Pastor David slapped Marvin on his back.

The thud that Pastor David's palm made when it connected with Marvin's skin reminded him they were at his son's funeral.

"This is your first test," Pastor David whispered in Marvin's ear. "The devil only comes to steal, kill, and destroy. He knows you only just laid the foundation to your new life, and he's calling for the old you to come out. Hold on, brother."

Marvin locked arms with Cynthia to resist the urge of hitting Cheo smack dab on the jaw for messing around with his wife. He gave Cheo the once-over: clean-shaven face, squared shoulders, and a puffed-up chest. He looked down at his paunch of a belly. *She upgraded. I'm going to have to hit the gym.*

"Calm down," Pastor David whispered to Marvin. "Remember, against you and you alone have I sinned," Pastor David said.

Marvin cut his eyes in Pastor David's direction and relaxed.

Marvin and Cheo stared at Cynthia begging her to put an end to the confusion and anger that filled their hearts while Pastor David called on the Lord for an intervention. Finally, her past and present had intersected, and they were both demanding she make her calling and election sure in order to secure her future.

Cynthia turned around to face her husband. Her fingertips traced his jaw and traveled up to his cheekbone. "Marvin, I made a mistake walking out on you like that. Regardless of your behavior, I certainly should have been more responsible and considerate. I should have been more of a wife and a mother," she said, biting down on her quivering bottom lip. Marvin leaned in to comfort her with an embrace. She backed out of it, turning to face Cheo.

"Cheo, *mi amor.*" Cynthia slid her tongue across the top row of her teeth and swallowed the saliva gathering in her mouth. "Cheo, I tried to tell you, I tried to resist you, but you seemed like everything I had ever wanted when the truth is what I wanted was for my marriage to work out. I wanted to be a part of a happy family, and I hid the truth from everyone just so I could have a fantasy rather than waiting on God to repair my reality."

"Cynthia, it's not too late to have what you want. I meant what I said. I'm willing to forgive you and work it out," Cheo said, clutching her hands.

"Cheo, I'm tired of working. I'm ready for restoration."

"*Que?*"

Cynthia placed her folded palms in front of her mouth. "Cheo, I can't run from my problems any longer. Look at what all this running has done. I'm ready to face them head-on with my husband and the arm of Christ carrying me through. I am not the same woman I was; a new me has been born."

Marvin smiled at the ceiling and whispered, "Thank you, Jesus. I'm going to do this right this time."

"I am so terribly sorry." Cynthia wiped a stray tear from her eye and clamped her hands together in front of her chest. "I pray that you can forgive me, let me go, and let God heal you."

"What about everything we've built? What about the restaurant? What about our future?" With his shoulders hunched and his eyes cut into narrow slits filled with frustration Cheo rattled off questions that should have swayed Cynthia.

"This is my past, this is my present, and"—she clutched Marvin's strong arm—"this is my future. Don't worry about Sabor. I'm going to take care of it with my husband by my side. This is the end of us and the beginning of my life as a servant of Christ, a mother to my son who was spared, and a wife to my husband who I pledged my allegiance to."

Before walking away, she planted an endearing kiss on Cheo's cheek to seal that chapter of wandering in the wilderness in her life. Even though she was in pumps, she still had to tiptoe to reach Cheo's cheek.

"Let's go," she said to Marvin over her shoulder midstride.

Marvin sidestepped to catch up with Cynthia. He spotted James standing in a corner near the door and signaled for him to join them. Hand in hand Marvin, Cynthia, and James walked through the doors of the funeral home behind the pallbearers with brave faces on prepared to bury the dead and nurture the new life that had been born at dawn.

Discussion Questions

1. At the start of chapter one, Cynthia had been waiting for Marvin to come home in order to question where he had been. Was she being reasonable? Why or why not?
2. Barbara insisted that Cynthia needed to discuss the issues she'd been having with Marvin with her pastor. Do you discuss your personal issues with your pastor? Why or why not?
3. Was Barbara's attempt to minister to Cynthia too straightforward or just right? How would you minister to a woman who you know is being abused, but you do not have a close relationship with?
4. When Cynthia attempted to explain her feelings to Mildred, do you think that there was anything Mildred could have said to prevent Cynthia from running away?
5. Have you ever felt like abandoning your responsibilities as a wife or parent? What is it that keeps you in check?
6. In chapter fifteen Marvin accused Pastor David of spending more time with Cynthia than he had. Do you think there should be a limitation on the amount of time a married person devotes to the ministry?
7. When Marvin grabbed Pastor David, the pastor used the Word to defend himself. What would you have done if you were in his position?
8. Why do you think both Marvin and Cynthia were able to find substitutions for each other so quickly?

9. Cynthia questioned whether she was crazy for leaving Marvin and the kids, or crazy for staying with him for so long. Which decision do you think was crazier?

10. When Cynthia returned home Mildred did not hold her accountable for Keith's death. Mildred believed that he would have died that way regardless of Cynthia's presence. Do you agree or disagree? Why?

11. Marvin and Cynthia were both willing to work things out together despite them both being in committed relationships with other people all during their time apart. What do you think of their decision? What do you think Marvin should have done? What do you think Cynthia should have done?

About The Author

Nigeria Lockley possesses two master's degrees, one in English secondary education, which she utilizes as an educator with the New York City Department of Education. Her second master's degree is in creative writing. *Born at Dawn* is Nigeria's first published novel. Nigeria serves as the Vice President of Bridges Family Services, a not-for-profit organization that assists student parents interested in pursuing a degree in higher education. She is also the deaconess and clerk for her spiritual home, King of Kings and Lord of Lords, Church of God. Nigeria is a New York native who resides in Harlem with her husband and two daughters. Join her online at www.NigeriaLockley.com.